CW01498601

Montana Sunset

By
Michael Kennard

iUniverse, Inc.
Bloomington

Montana Sunset

iUniverse books may be ordered through booksellers or by contacting:

iUniverse
1663 Liberty Drive
Bloomington, IN 47403
www.iuniverse.com
1-800-Authors (1-800-288-4677)

ISBN: 978-1-4620-2405-6 (sc)
ISBN: 978-1-4620-2406-3 (ebk)

Printed in the United States of America

iUniverse rev. date: 05/25/2011

Montana Sunset

Dedication

On the subject of grandchildren, Geoff Smith once said to me, "There's plenty of time. Grandchildren are like buses, when one eventually arrives another is not far behind." I said, "It's easy for you to say, you've five."

How true his words were, I've now got six! Evie, Harry, Sophia, Violet, Sienna and Lenny. Who better to dedicate this, my latest novel too, than this new generation already setting forth on the great adventure.

Acknowledgements

Strange as it might seem, I'd like to thank, Wade and Alex, Jack and Tara, Merri, Fletcher, Debbie, Charlotte, Bob and Sheila and others that have climbed off the pages of Montana Skies and forced me to write this sequel. For more than fifteen years, these characters have been a comfort to me and somehow or other have found a place in my heart.

A special mention to Paul Brodie and Greg Holmes for the campfire compositions of *Oh, oh the mountains* and *T'was late in September.* Yolanda Smith for her superb painting that fronts this book. I'd also like to thank Geoff Smith, Diane Boud and John Burwell for their encouragement whilst writing this sequel.

Lastly to Elaine for being there.

Montana Sunset

The pain came on slowly at first, and then gradually increased in intensity. Wade gripped the saddle horn like a vice and urged the Buckskin homeward. His left arm and chest felt like they were about to explode. Instinctively he knew that he was in the throes of a heart attack, and that the best chance of survival was to get back to the ranch as quickly as he could. Silently he cursed himself for being a damn fool, venturing so high into the Bitterroots on a whim, was just plain nonsensical. 'You're a damn blasted fool Wade Reynolds, and then some.' At nigh on eighty years old it was just plain foolhardy to ride up into the mountains alone. Then the world turned black.

Wade awoke to find himself on the cold hard ground. His horse was nowhere to be seen and night was falling. He felt weak as a kitten and twice as vulnerable. That he'd suffered a heart attack was obvious, that he was still alive was something less than. He knew that if he was to survive he needed shelter and fast. That damn fool horse would arrive back at the ranch and come first light they'd send out a search party to find him.

Realising he was close to the old cabin at Cougar Pass, Wade began to crawl along the horse track the short distance to the run down shack. With renewed pain in his upper arm and chest, weak and suffering from exhaustion, the desire to rest and let nature take its course almost seemed the best option. But he had always been a fighter, he'd be damned if he'd let a fool heart attack beat him; it was that or die trying.

Wade somehow or other pulled himself to his feet, then with a combination of staggering and crawling, got to within fifty yards of the old cabin before falling; his goal tantalizingly close. Sweat beads formed upon his brow and quickly cooled as the evening temperatures began to drop rapidly. So near, yet so far, thought Wade as he lay on the path and rested as best he could. He knew he'd need one almighty effort to reach the cabin and that if he didn't make it this time, then it was all over. Never in his life had he felt so weak, even being mauled by a cougar some twenty years earlier hadn't drained him as much as he felt right that minute. It was important that he stay focused, that he stop himself from passing out. Steeling himself, he slowly rose onto his unsteady feet, took a few gulps of fresh mountain air and lunged towards the cabin door.

As the door gave way to his weight, he crashed though it and landed in a heap upon the cabin floor. When he awoke this time, the stars were high in the sky and the temperature had dropped below freezing. Realizing he was still alive Wade searched the room with his eyes for any old blankets, anything. He was in luck, his eyes fixed on a couple of worn horse blankets. Fortunately it had been a dry old summer and the snows were still to arrive, so the musty old blankets that were strewn around the cabin floor though cold were not susceptible to the damp. Wrapping himself in them he lay his head down and tried to sleep.

The pain had subsided in his chest and he was feeling strangely relaxed, but sleep wouldn't come. 'Why?' thought Wade, sleep should have been the most natural thing for his body to do under the circumstances, unless it was the memories that this cabin evoked. The shack, because it was little more than that, had known great sadness. Poor Merri had died here and Wade could feel her presence everywhere. Somehow the thought that she was close gave Wade a comforting feeling. If he was to die, then at least he wouldn't die alone, Merri's spirit would see to that.

As his body heat warmed the blankets, Wade couldn't help but reflect on all that had happened since Merri's passing. It was only natural considering where he was that he'd think firstly of that damned cougar attack, son of a bitch nearly took his life that day, largest cat ever found in these parts, then he recalled the subsequent finding of the chilling remains of that Delacroix woman, even now the thought of what might have been, sent an icy shiver up and down his spin. And then of course there was his son-in-law Jack, finally facing up to his demons and returning home to England. 'Hell' he thought, 'a lot of water had ran under the bridge since that day.'

Chapter I

Marlow. 1996

In the early hours of a hot June night in the riverside town of Marlow, Bob Claymore poured himself a large scotch and sat down on one of the chairs on his patio. With his left hand he grabbed a handful of ice from the ice bucket and unceremoniously dumped it into his glass. It crackled and fizzed as it made contact with the spirit. Bob stared blindly into the darkness, his mind in turmoil. His wife, despite the hot and muggy night, was sleeping soundly in their bed at the front of the house. Sheila could sleep on a clothes line, add a family wedding and more glasses of champagne than she could remember and nothing could keep her awake, not even the appearance of Bob's long lost brother, Jack. It was a fact that Bob had kept back from the wedding party. But was it his right? Should he have insisted that Jack join in with the celebrations? Or had it been best to leave sleeping dogs lie? It was that above all else that had kept Bob awake. The events of the day had sunk into insignificance compared to the return of the prodigal son: sleep for Bob Claymore was almost impossible.

'It should have been the wedding of the year,' thought Bob reproachfully, then he corrected himself, 'It was the wedding of the year.'

To everyone, from the bride and groom down, it was a day to remember. From the first sight of the bride, to the horse-drawn carriage, and finally to the ceremony at All Saints, it was to all intent and purpose a fairy-tale come true. Everything about the day had been magical, from the clip-clopping of the horses as they bore the newlyweds across the suspension bridge that spanned the Thames, to the magnificent setting of the reception at the Compleat Angler, nestling close to the river's edge, to the happy couple themselves. Charlotte was that fairy-tale princess and Matthew her Prince Charming. Even the weather had smiled down upon them. The sun glistened across the waters of the Thames and added a jewel-like backdrop to their wedding photos. The day was picture perfect; everything had been done to make Charlotte and Matthew's day as memorable as possible.

'Memorable, that was an understatement,' thought Bob. It wasn't everyday that a brother returned from the dead. He'd often wondered, hoped, even feared that possibility one day, Jack would return. What he hadn't counted on was, that one day, would be Charlotte's wedding day. His world was thrown into a controlled chaos at the sight of his brother Jack.

It was Sheila who'd spotted him first. She was standing on the neatly manicured lawn overlooking the river when she happened to glance up towards the suspension bridge. With a glass of champagne in her right hand she shielded her eyes with her left. Unable to believe her eyes she nudged Bob and discreetly asked him to take a look at the stranger standing on the bridge. He was staring across at the wedding party, and there was something strangely familiar about the man.

"It's Jack, I tell you," whispered Sheila.

As Bob gazed up at the shadowy figure he knew that Sheila's eyes had not deceived her. It was Jack alright, albeit he was leaner, fitter and despite the nearly shoulder length hair, so unmistakably Jack. Notwithstanding the fact there had been no news of him in almost ten years, and his begrudging acceptance that he had to be dead, Bob found he was un-surprised.

Discreetly Bob walked across the lawn, sidestepping guests and waitresses alike as he negotiated his way to the front of the hotel. From there it was a short distance to the suspension bridge and his brother.

He was elated but disturbed by the appearance of Jack. That his brother seemed like a stranger bothered him more than his reluctance to step out of the shadows. There meeting was both emotional and awkward. Jack asking how come Debbie was alive, then Bob explaining as best he could what had happened. It was all rushed, the timing was lousy, the explanations from both of them confused and garbled. He even shared Jack's reluctance to gate crash the wedding, it was understandable, considering the circumstances, but deciding to take off back to where he came without at least talking to Debbie, that just didn't make any sense.

Sipping his scotch slowly, Bob stared into the unusually starry night and began recalling that fateful day in late November and the events that unfolded over the next few months. By morning he'd made a decision.

* * *

Jack stared down at the gravestone of his oldest friend Dave Bryant one last time then slowly made his way out of the graveyard of All Saint's church Marlow. At the gate he reached deep into the pocket of his Carhartt coat and retrieved the card his brother Bob had given him the day before.

"I'll give you a call in the morning," Jack had said before parting from his brother. He'd watched sadly as Bob returned to the wedding party, wanting, yet not daring to follow. He booked a room in a nearby hotel, ordered a bottle of scotch and an evening meal brought up to his room. He picked at the food, drank nearly half the bottle before sleep overtook him. He awoke in the early hours of the morning. His head throbbed and he felt like shit, then it all flooded back to him. For the next few hours Jack went over his options. He glanced at the card in his hand and sadly shook his head. It had been good to see Bob, to chat to catch up to understand just why Debbie was still alive. Yet despite everything he knew he couldn't make that call; too much water had flown under the bridge for that to happen. His plans such as they were had evaporated when he saw Debbie. Finding a litter bin close to hand he dropped Bob's card in and walked back towards his waiting car.

His flight wasn't until the afternoon but he thought the sooner he left Marlow the better. He'd phoned the airport and reconfirmed his return flight, it had caused quite a fuss until he said, how much is this god-damn ticket gonna cost me, after that it was plain sailing. He knew Tara would be surprised; she'd expected him to be gone for at least a week, maybe two. What he was going to tell her would be tricky, to say the least, but what choice did he have? As his hand closed around the car door handle a familiar voice invaded his peace.

"Running away ain't the answer."

Jack looked up to see his brother grinning at him.

"Did you really think I was going to let you leave without a fight," cried Bob leaning against a red telephone box close to Jack's rental car.

"Bob! I was goi . . . ." Realising his excuse wouldn't wash with his brother he changed track. "It's for the best. They've got their lives and I've got mine."

"You owe Debbie."

"Yeah, you're right, but what good would it do. It would complicate things."

"Maybe, but at the very least you should see Debbie, talk to her at least. Explain. Tell her what you told me."

"I can't. I've a new life; a wife and kids that I love very much."

"So you're saying you don't have feelings for Debbie anymore?"

"That ain't fair and you know it," said Jack slightly agitated.

"Then what are you saying?"

Jack's silence confirmed what Bob suspected. His brother still loved Debbie. That she loved her new husband James, he was equally sure, that Debbie still loved Jack, he knew beyond a shadow of a doubt.

"Change your flight, at least stay a couple of days," cried Bob in desperation.

Jack smiled, "Do you know how much its cost me to change my flight already?"

"No and I don't much care. Change it, stay with me and Sheila. Let us know what you've been doing the past ten years. You owe me that, at least."

"Have you thought it through? A couple of days will only make matters worse."

How do you figure that out?" questioned Bob.

"If I stay and Debbie finds out, it's gonna make life mighty uncomfortable for you and Sheila."

"I'll take the risk."

Jack gave it some thought, it was a tempting offer, but he felt his brother was forcing his hand. "Well it's a risk I'm not prepared to take. I can't, I need time to think. I've Tara and the kids to think about. She above all needs to be told. She deserves that at the very least."

Bob resisted the urge to beg and bit his tongue; begging was not his style. He realised he was trying to back Jack into a corner, but knowing Jack of old, he knew that wouldn't work. "Okay, I understand."

Jack's defences lowered slightly.

What time's your flight?"

"Around three o'clock."

"Good, then you've time for a pint and a chat. Yesterday was a bit tense You owe me that at least."

So wrapped up with the shock of seeing Debbie alive, Jack had hardly given his brother a second thought. The sudden realisation that he'd missed him so much over the years hit him like a ton of bricks. The thought of a sit down with Bob was very welcoming in this most confusing time of his life.

"I'd like that."

"We'll get a drink at the airport," replied Bob

Jack looked puzzled.

"Sunday hours, you ain't in America now."

Jack gave a half hearted grin, "Okay, follow me. I'll check in, then we'll have plenty of time to catch up."

Catching up was something he'd expected to do before he found out Debbie was alive, now he was filled with mixed emotions.

*   *   *

Bob brought the pints over to where Jack was sitting and began bombarding him with questions. "Yesterday was a shock; half of what you told me went in one ear then out the other. Now tell me about my nieces."

Two hours later and the loud speaker announced the final call for Jack's flight.

"Promise me one thing," said Bob desperately.

"What's that?" said Jack, already knowing what his brother had to say.

"I'll respect your wish and neither Sheila nor I will breathe a word to anyone, but just think on it. Give it some real serious thought."

I'll do that bruv."

Knowing he still had to pass through passport control and security he made his parting short before running towards airside.

Montana

Throughout his flight Jack went over what had happened over the past twenty four hours. He tried to sleep away the hours but everything kept running around inside his head. Debbie was alive, more than that, she had been faithful. How did that make him feel? For ten years he'd believed that Debbie had been having an affair with his best friend. And Dave, Dave Bryant, how badly he'd judged him. What did it say about Jack himself?

Arriving at Denver airport Jack booked into an airport hotel. His flight back to Billings wasn't until the following morning. Jack sought the comfort of the mini bar. It was the only way to combat another night of torturous sleep, another night of ghosts. Foremost in his thoughts, was how was he going to break the news to Tara. That he had too there was no dispute. Since learning of Pam's child, the son he would never see grow up, and the awkwardness he felt keeping it from Tara, he knew he had no choice but to tell her everything.

*   *   *

Jack phoned Tara from Denver airport just before he boarded the plane. She was surprised that he was coming home so soon, happy, but concerned. She thought she detected something in his voice.

"Is everything okay? I wasn't expecting you until next week."

"Yeah I'm fine, it's just that . . . . Oh I'll explain when I see you."

Before Tara could say another word Jack put down the receiver. Alex who was visiting with her granddaughters looked up at the concerned look on her daughter's face.

"What's up?"

"I don't know," said Tara absentmindedly. "It's probably nothing. I guess he's tired." Even before the words had formed she knew that was not the case.

Alex, knowing her daughter like a book replied, "You're probably right. I'll stay here with the kids, give you time to get reacquainted."

"Mom! Jack ain't been gone more'n a few days."

"Just go," said Alex, "me and Kaycee are going to change little Merri's diaper."

"Are we," replied Kaycee, with an air of sardonic humour that befit a teenager rather than a five year old.

*   *   *

Jack spotted Tara the moment he walked into the arrivals hall. He dropped his duffel as she rushed towards him and leapt into his arms like a wild thing. A surge of warmth coursed through his veins and he kissed her passionately. Gone was any reserve of the Englishman that he used to be. He was a Montana horse rancher, coming home to the lovin arms of a hot woman; his hot woman. That's all that mattered. For a time all thoughts of Debbie were long gone, she belonged to another world, a world he no longer felt a part of.

As they walked across the parking lot to the pick up Tara asked question after question. What was her dress like? What was Charlotte's reaction? How did you announce yourself?

"I ain't one to repeat myself, so if you've a mind I'd rather tell everyone when I get home."

"That ain't fair and you know it," said Tara reproachfully.

"Okay, you win," said Jack as he climbed behind the wheel and stuck the pickup into drive. "The sun shone, the Thames glittered like diamonds and Charlotte looked as pretty as a picture, like all my girls."

Tara clung to him as he drove along the highway, kissing his neck and rubbing his thigh.

"Can't you wait until tonight," he joked. Something magical was happening. Gone were the agonizes of the past few days.

"No I can't, now pull off at the next junction."

Jack did as he was told, the hardness in his jeans dictating his every move. Frantically he surveyed the surrounding area searching for a suitable spot to park. Spotting it he screeched to a halt beneath a grove of aspen sheltered partly from the road. Before the dust had settled, both of them were tearing at each others clothes.

*   *   *

Twenty hot and torrid minutes later their ardour spent, they lay comfortably in each others arms. The passion he felt for her since that first time hadn't dimmed in the slightest. Reinforced by his feelings for her Jack knew he had to tell Tara everything.

"You asked if everything was all right. The answer is yes and no."

"No!" interjected Tara.

"I didn't get to meet Charlotte. I arrived at the church before anyone else, I waited at the back not wanting to attract any attention and then I watched her walk down the aisle, but I never spoke to her."

"Why? Was it all too much?" Tara gave him an affectionate squeeze.

"I didn't speak to her because Debbie was there." It had come out clumsily, but he'd said it.

"Debbie! But Debbie's dead!" Tara's face drained of all colour.

"That's what I thought, until I saw her in the church. She's alive! Tara, my Debbie is alive." He knew before the words had disappeared into the ether that one little word had grown to monstrous proportions.

"My Debbie!"

"I don't mean it as it sounds. You've got to believe me." He tried putting his arms around her but she shrugged him off. Then she climbed out of the pickup truck and walked several paces, before taking a few deep breaths, and then she reeled around and faced him.

"My Debbie, that's what you said."

"It's just how it came out." Jack was getting shit. Shit he believed he didn't deserve. "Tara, what can I say to make you understand?"

"You can start by telling me what happened," she retorted, having somehow brought her nerves under control.

For the next hour Jack relayed all that had taken place. The immediate shock at discovering Debbie was still alive, the meeting with his brother on the bridge at Marlow, how the explanation from Bob of what had truly happened, had all been too much for him to take in. How after a sleepless night he'd visited Dave Bryant's grave and how looking at all that had happened since, influenced his decision to return to Montana without any more contact, then the sudden arrival of his brother at the graveside and his persuasive argument about staying.

"I'd made up my mind; I wasn't changing it for him or anyone. I told him about you and the girls. Now can we go home?"

Tara searched his face for any sign of regret, hoping against hope that she'd see none, but it was there, hidden, disguised and buried deep, but it was there all the same. His sun burnished face didn't give anything away, but his eyes, *someone once said they were the windows to the soul,* his eyes couldn't conceal what Tara knew deep down. In his place would she have felt any different? Tara smiled up at Jack, pushing the unanswered questions to the back of her mind. There would be time a plenty to broach the subject in the days and weeks ahead of them.

"Yeah let's go home. The girls will be dying to see you."

*   *   *

Later that night after Alex had driven back to the Crazy AW ranch and the kids were safely asleep Tara asked the question that had been burning itself into her brain since Jack's revelations.

"Are we legally married? Or are you still married to her?"

Jack having already anticipated Tara's fears reached out for her and held her firmly by her shoulders.

"Yes sweetheart, we're legally married. Debbie obtained a divorce on the grounds of desertion or something like that. She's married to a doctor and from what Bob told me, she's happy. Now can we drop the subject?"

Tara soothed by Jack's words, 'married to a doctor and she's happy,' looked up at him and smiled, "It's been a long day, we'd better get some rest, else we'll be up until morning." 'Rest,' she thought, 'fat chance.' Under the circumstances all she could do was put a brave face on it.

Jack understanding his wife's inner turmoil prayed for sleep. He knew only too well that there would be more questions to be answered before the situation ran its course. He only hoped they'd both come through it. On a whim he leaned over and kissed her gently upon the lips.

*   *   *

Wade could tell something was up by the troubled look upon Alex's face.

"What's wrong?"

Alex looked a little shocked and then a wry smile overtook her worried frown. She laughed, "You know me too well. I guess that's to be expected seeing as we've been together for nigh on forty years."

"Forty years! It can't be that long. It seems like yesterday that I seen you walk into the Metlen in that red blouse." A lot of water had run under the bridge since that day, most of it good but some of it had tasted mighty bitter. Forty years was a long time, thought Wade wistfully.

"You remembered what I was wearing. You're a darling, Wade Reynolds. I'd have bet money that you wouldn't have had a clue."

"Don't underestimate me Alex. My long term memory is as sharp as a razor and my short term memory is almost as good. So no getting away from my question, what's with the worried look?"

"Oh, it's nothing, well nothing I can put my finger on. It's Tara and Jack, something ain't right. I know our daughter probably better than she knows herself. Something's niggling at her craw."

"Jack's just seen his family for the first time in ten years; it's bound to have some fall out."

"Yeah, I know. It's just me I guess," replied Alex as she snuggled up to Wade on the cowhide sofa.

"I'll call in on Jack come morning. See if he'll open up. It's most likely somethin' an nothin'."

Alex smiled up at her man and looked past the weather beaten granite features and saw only the young handsome man that had asked her to dance so many years before. "Let's go to bed. I've a heavy day tomorrow."

*   *   *

Wade didn't get Jack to open up for two weeks, by then it was apparent that something was troubling the couple. It was Alex who brought it to a head over Sunday lunch at the Crazy AW ranch-house, Sunday being the only time when both families managed a meal together.

"Tell me it's none of my damn business if you like, but I'll still keep on until I know what's bugging you both."

For the briefest of seconds you could have heard a pin drop, as Alex's words stunned the dinner table into silence, then Jack put down his knife and fork.

"You're right Alex, it's none of your damn business," his eyes glaring across at his mother-in-law, then his expression softened, "but I guess you both have a right to know."

Alex took Jack's words with a pinch of salt. He was cutting at times, but then he was a damn Englishman, so what did she expect. He was as honest as the day was long and he loved her daughter more than life itself. But what he said next turned her views upside down.

"When I went home, I was met with a surprise that beat all. My wife, my ex wife Debbie is still alive."

Tara looked apprehensively at both her parents, hugged her two daughters and looked up at her man.

"It seems she didn't die in the accident, just lost her memory and didn't get it back until I'd left. By then it was too late to find me. You know the rest."

Alex instinctively glanced at Tara, then across to the table to her husband. Wade sat transfixed, like he'd turned to stone. It was Alex who broke the impasse, "Are you still legally married?" Without taking a breath, she added, "Does she know about Tara, Kaycee and little Merri?" A symbolic line was drawn in the sand.

Wade held out a restraining hand, "Easy Alex, let the boy talk."

Jack gave Wade an appreciative nod and then continued. "The answer to your question is she divorced me on the grounds of desertion and married a doctor. And no she doesn't know about

Tara and the kids because I never spoke to her. I only spoke to my brother; I didn't even speak to Charlotte. I thought it wise to leave well enough alone."

Alex's stern face relaxed a little, "Yes I think that's wise."

Jack glanced at Tara, seeking her approval for what he was about to say. She nodded nervously.

"Yeah, that's what I thought, but now I'm not so sure. I've talked it over with Tara and she thinks I should go back. Get it all out in the open. See my daughter, let her vent her spleen. I owe her at least that much."

"And what if Debbie still has feeling for you, what then?" Alex knew that Jack had already been asked that question. She knew her daughter only to well.

"From what my brother Bob told me, she loves her new husband very much."

"But how do you feel towards her Jack?"

Jack looked troubled, he knew this family so well and he knew he couldn't lie to them. "That I don't know." The room remained silent until Jack cleared his throat. "What I can tell you is that I love Tara with all my heart and I couldn't bear to lose her." He paused for a few seconds to let his words sink in. "It was Tara's idea for me to go back."

"That's right," cried Tara. "All I know is that if Jack doesn't go back and face his ghosts then he'll always regret it and our marriage will suffer in the long run. I trust Jack to do the right thing."

Little more was said that day, but the seed was sown. The only thing that wasn't settled was when.

*   *   *

With it all out in the open Jack was able to break himself back into the daily chores that a horse-rancher encountered. He was reluctant to leave the ranch, summer was upon them and business was brisk. There were foals to look after, fences to mend, the barn needed repairing and a couple of sales coming up and he'd also promised Wade a hand up at the Crazy AW. Putting it to the back of his mind seemed the easiest thing to do. He'd put it off for more than ten years, what difference did another month or two make.

Tara saw it otherwise, she knew Jack well enough to know that he'd find one excuse after another and before too long a year would have passed and then another and another. Maybe Jack could live like that but Tara couldn't, that man of hers needed a prod, she mused.

Jack was just coming in from working the south pasture when Tara rode out to meet him. "Howdy cowboy," she cried in greeted. "Got something for you," she added and handed him an envelope. Jack draped his reins across his horse's neck, gave Tara a quizzical look and tore open the envelope. Inside was an airline ticket to London. Jack looked dumbfounded. "Like I said, I trust you. It's something that needs doing, so go get it done. Just remember you've a wife and kids in this here back water that love you very much."

*   *   *

Tara drove Jack to Billings that Friday where she kissed him hard and passionately at the gate, "Don't phone until it's done," she said as their lips parted. She waited with him at the departure gate until he was called and then kissed him one last time. Her hand slowly slipped between his legs and gave him a gentle squeeze. "Just so you know what's waiting for you when you get home," she added mischievously. "Now go get," she said dry eyed as he reluctantly turned towards the departure gate. Brave faced she watched until he disappeared, only then did she show her true feelings.

Though teary eyes she watched as his plane rose slowly into the cloudless sky. It was the second time in just a few weeks that she'd watched him leave, only this time she felt so vastly different; her very future rode alongside him. Her heart knotted into a ball so tight she struggled for breathe until the inevitable sobs burst forth and slowly calmed her emotions. She stayed there looking up at the silver bird until it turned into a tiny dot before disappearing into the skies.

*   *   *

Alex, concerned for her daughter's welfare, drove over to the Claymore Ranch the following morning. Even though she knew Tara wanted to be left alone she couldn't help herself; she was a mother, hell she was a woman, she knew only too well what her daughter was going through.

"Hi ma, what gives?" cried Tara, putting on a brave face, "I thought you was off to Bozeman this morning for a bit of retail therapy," she added merrily.

"I am, just thought you might like to tag along," Alex said.

"Hell ma, with Jack away, I ain't got a minute to myself."

"Make time," persisted Alex. "I know what's eating you. It'll take your mind of things, at least for a while anyway."

"Shopping ain't gonna help. It's just something I've got to work through myself." She smiled at her mother but Alex could see that her daughter was fretting about Jack meeting up with his former wife.

"Tara, go take a long look at your self in the mirror," cried Alex.

Puzzled by her mother's sudden outburst Tara did as she was told.

Alex appeared behind her daughter and spoke to her through the reflection. "There ain't a man this side of the Bitterroots that wouldn't give his eye teeth to have you decorating his arm."

Tara looked at herself in the full length mirror. Tight fitting Wranglers, a faded denim shirt and a battered straw hat stared back at her. She dismissed the dark flowing locks and the mischievous brown eyes that suggested everything a man desired. She looked beyond the fit body and legs that adorned those Wranglers and replied, "It's the man on the other side of the ocean that I'm worried about."

"I know honey, I know," said Alex sympathetically.

Tara smiled back at Alex and found herself recalling how she'd felt when she'd met her best friend Merri off the plane when she'd returned to Montana. Merri had had an air of sophistication which had unsettled Tara at first, causing her to panic for a little while. Her friend was a sure-fire heart-breaker and unfounded though it was, she feared that somehow her best friend would turn Jack's head. It was an irrational fear as Merri wasn't into stealing other people's husbands and it wasn't long before Tara realised Merri's new found confidence was only a façade and that her friend was still a country girl at heart. But this time it was different, from what Jack had told her about Debbie; she was the real McCoy.

Instinctively Alex reacted to Tara's worried frown. "I know Jack, and I can tell you he ain't the type to go a wanderin'."

"Yeah, but she's his wife."

"She was his wife," replied Alex sharply, "and don't you go forgetting who his wife is now!" Alex above anyone else knew what her daughter was going through. It wasn't so many years before that she'd been through similar heartache, though differing circumstances.

"Yeah Ma, I know, but I feel so damn helpless. I know Jack needs to sort this out on his own, but somehow I think maybe I should have gone with him. Yet I know that was impossible."

"He's your man, and I guess you've got to do things the way you see fit," replied Alex. It would have been so easy to tell Tara to go pack and get herself booked on the first available plane to London, but somehow or other she managed to keep her thoughts to herself.

"I've Charlie Bowden coming from Bozeman this morning. He's here to look at a couple of bay geldings," said Tara changing the subject, the signal that the matter was now closed.

Alex let it ride, she knew her daughter well enough to let the matter rest. Though a gentle soul most of the time, when riled she could be as fiery as all hell. Alex consoled herself that when the time came for action Tara would be ready.

Chapter 2

Kentucky

Pam Lassiter picked up the wedding invitation and looked at it thoughtfully. She wondered how it had all gone, how pretty Charlotte had looked and whether she'd ever see any of the wedding photographs. Of course the wedding invitation had been nothing more than a formality. Her cousin Debbie had only sent it as protocol, she neither wished for Pam and Phil to come nor did she expect them. A Christmas card once a year, a solitary piece of family news once in a while, that was about all Pam could expect. Understandably relations had cooled somewhat since Debbie and James's visit some eight years earlier; learning that Pam had a son by Jack had stretched their relationship almost to breaking point.

She was still looking at the invitation when Phil walked in.

"We could have gone you know," said Phil as he shuffled through some papers on his desk, 'Dumb statement or what!' he thought regretfully. "In life you have to let things go," he added not unkindly, as he retrieved the paperwork he was looking for.

"I know Phil. It's . . . ."

"It's what?"

"It's nothing; I feel I have to pinch myself sometimes. I can't believe we've been given a second chance."

Phil gave her a gently hug, which seemed unnatural for such a big man.

"Well, we have honey, best believe it."

Neither of them talked directly about what happened down in Mexico, it was dead and buried. They'd risen from the ashes of that particular funeral pyre and together they'd rebuilt their marriage and their business. It was more than a second chance; it was as if they'd both been reborn. With a new baby and a new belief that anything was possible Pam and Phil turned around the stud farm and at the same time turned around their own lives.

Pam smiled up at her great hunk of a man, reassured.

"I've got to show this invoice to Gary, it should have been paid a week ago," exclaimed Phil in mock annoyance.

"Well, if you leave it hidden amongst all this paperwork what can you expect," she replied as Phil, invoice in hand headed out the door.

Life at the Lassiter Stud had gone from strength to strength since their return from Nogales all those years ago. A few worthy winners at racing events around the country had pushed Lassiter Stud into the foreground of the racing fraternity. Business was booming.

Pam looked thoughtfully at the invitation, 'We could have gone,' she mused. How far from the truth could that have been. Since they'd got back together the thought of visiting England had been the farthest thing from her mind. She had been painstakingly honest with Phil about everything. She'd had to be, it was the foundation of their very existence, except Pam had held one thing back; the visit of Jack when Jared was three years old. At the time she'd been terrified that Phil would find out and it could open old wounds and that he'd start drinking again. Looking back now, she could see that she'd been wrong; Phil was much stronger than that. He would have believed, he'd have understood the situation.

The phone call had come out of the blue. How Jack had found out about her son Jared she could only hazard a guess, but the immediate problem was what to tell him and how much. It was so like Jack, he'd only just learned about fathering a child and wanted to face up to his responsibilities. It couldn't have come at a worse possible moment, Pam and Phil had just about re-built their marriage, life for them had finally taken an upturn, there was no way that she needed Jack rocking the boat.

Their meeting was brief, no longer than twenty minutes. Pam was slightly brusque as she told him her situation, making it quite clear that Jared had a mother and father and that his help was not wanted. She suspected that he must have known something about her terrible ordeal for when he asked if she was happy there was a searching look. She softened her approach and replied that she'd never been happier. He'd smiled that warm smile of his and said he understood, and that he was pleased everything was working out.

Within minutes she was back in her car and driving home. She'd confessed that her happiness was fragile, but that she and Phil were working on it. Then she extracted a promise from him that he would stay out of there lives forever. On the journey home she kept reliving the look of disappointment on Jack's face at not being able to see her son. She'd been sharp and to the point, maybe a little to sharp, but she had to think about her family's future and Jack wasn't a part of it. She suspected it was hard for him but she knew he'd respect her wishes and to date he'd kept his promise, which made the wedding invitation more poignant.

In their brief meeting he'd told her he'd settled in Montana, but little else only that he was happy. For the briefest of moments she'd thought to tell him Debbie was alive, but self interest and fear had suppressed the news within herself, it was something she'd regretted ever since. She saw Charlotte's wedding invitation as a way to repay Jack for keeping his promise. Not knowing where in Montana, or even if he was still living there, she paid for an article to be written about Charlotte's wedding and for it to be placed in all the main city newspapers in Montana. It was a long shot, and Pam didn't really expect Jack to read the article. Either way it helped to relieve her troubled conscience.

Unbeknown to her that newspaper article was like a small pebble being dropped into a mill pond; the ripples had been far reaching.

Chapter 3

Marlow

It was just an ordinary Sunday morning in the Claymore household; Bob had settled himself down in his comfy chair and was reading his newspaper, while Sheila was busying herself with preparing breakfast. Already the sun had enticed several of their neighbours to clean their cars or trim their already immaculate lawns. It wasn't something Bob prescribed to on a weekly basis but it was part of the ritual of their particular community. He'd begrudgingly set aside an hour before lunch to enter into the spirit of things, mainly on Sheila's insistence. Life had begun to settle down and get back to normal after the excitement of Charlotte's wedding and the unsettling appearance of Bob's long lost brother. It had been three weeks since Bob had said goodbye to Jack, three weeks in which he'd agonised over whether to tell Debbie that her first husband was still alive.

"Leave well alone," had been Sheila's advice, "Let sleeping dogs lie."

It had been good advice and although Bob missed his brother he could see that his wife was right. There was no point in raking over the past. If Jack wanted to stay gone, that was his choice, there was nothing he or Sheila could do about it. Then just when he didn't expect it, the routine of their Sunday morning came to an abrupt end; the phone rang.

"Hello Bob."

"Jack! Is that you?"

"Well who else would call you at nine on a Sunday morning? Of course it's me. Any chance you can pick me up at Heathrow. I've just this minute disembarked, and I'm entering the baggage claim area as we speak."

"What! Yo . . . you you're here?"

"Yeah, I'm here. I thought over what you said, thought about nothing else to be honest. I've talked it though with Tara and we both decided you were right. I need to clear things up once and for all."

"Where exactly are you?" questioned Bob as the adrenaline kicked in.

"At this precise moment I'm waiting for my bag to come off the carousel. Then I guess I'll grab a coffee and meet you in an hour or so at the meeting point in Terminal Four. Okay!"

"Yeah . . . . sure Jack. Just give me a little longer. I'll be with you soon as. I ain't got my pants on yet."

"Nothin's changed there then," quipped Jack.

"Nope"

"Not a word to Debbie! You understand?" cautioned Jack.

"I understand, though it's been hard, even more so since Charlotte and Matt got back from their honeymoon."

Jack chose to ignore Bob's last remark, "Okay, see you in an hour or so."

Bob put the phone down and quickly raced upstairs for his trousers, on his return to earth Sheila pushed a full English at him and said, "I didn't cook this just to throw it in the bin. You've waited ten years, another few minutes isn't going to hurt." Sheila's withering look said it all. He sat down and began to eat.

"I tell you Bob, no good will come of this."

Bob looked up from his bacon, egg, tomatoes, fried bread, and mushrooms, "You might be right, but what choice do we have."

"None," replied Sheila reluctantly.

*   *   *

Contrary to her misgivings Sheila also found herself becoming a little excited that Jack was coming home, in part for Bob but mostly for Charlotte. She'd turned into a level headed young lady and although James had been more of a father than anyone could have hoped for, he wasn't the man that had loved and reared her up until her adolescent years. That was being a little unfair, she reflected. James had stepped in at the right time and had done a remarkable job, that he doted on the girl and her mother spoke volumes. But nonetheless Sheila wouldn't have been Sheila if she didn't have reservations. She'd known Debbie most all their lives; she wondered how she'd cope. What would happen when Debbie learned of Jack's return? How would she react? There were so many imponderables that Sheila was forced to put them to the back of her mind.

All thoughts of problems and upheavals were put to the back of Sheila's mind when two hours later Bob's car pulled onto their driveway. She was there at the front door to greet them when Bob climbed out of the car, his face a picture. Jack emerged from the passenger side a grin stretching from one side of his face to the other.

"Come here you," greeted Sheila.

"Yeah go in, I'll get your bag," stated Bob.

Sheila held Jack tightly and then pushed him back at arms length to take a long hard look.

"You've lost some weight, and your hair it's . . . ."

"Longer than what it was," finished Jack with a smile.

"Considerably," laughed Sheila. Forgotten were her reservations, they could wait for another day. Like Bob she was excited and over awed by the occasion.

"This means the world to Bob. He's been going on about you every day since the wedding." As the words flowed tears of joy rolled down Sheila's cheeks.

They sat for an hour *punctuated by steaming hot cups of tea* while Sheila quizzed Jack over the past ten years. Bob sensing his brother was growing inpatient to know all that had happened to Debbie, intervened. "Sheila, give him a break. There's plenty of time to find out what Jack's been up to later. Right now I think he needs filling in on a thing or two."

Jack was grateful for his brother's intrusion. He'd the gist of what had happened, but the past few weeks had blurred the edges.

"Well Jack, I'll tell it as I recall, I dare say Sheila will correct me if I'm wrong."

"You bet I will," retorted Sheila.

Bob took a last sip of tea, ran his tongue across his lips and began to recall that fateful morning.

It had begun much like any other Sunday morning in the Claymore household, Bob was upstairs shaving, Sheila was busy catching up on a week's ironing, and Charlotte was watching cartoons, when the doorbell rang.

"Charlotte, be a dear and answer that for me," cried Sheila from beneath a pile of freshly ironed shirts.

Charlotte, like most eleven year olds muttered something unintelligible under her breath and lazily dragged herself from the sofa. She shuffled into the hallway, and opened the front door.

"Mum! You, you're alive," exclaimed Charlotte.

Sheila, hearing but not understanding edged her way around the ironing board and walked into the hall. "Who's that at the door Charlotte?"

"It's, it's my mum. She's alive!"

"Sheila, it's me Debbie!"

Sheila gave a start of surprise. For a moment the power of speech left her, then recovering from the awful joke that was being played, she called out to her husband.

"Bob, come quickly!"

Bob, wiping away the residue of shaving cream, raced down the stairs and reeled back in astonishment, "Debbie, you're alive."

Debbie managed a nervous smile, "So people keep telling me. Where's Jack?"

"You, you'd better come in," he'd said shakily. It was then that he noticed for the first time the tall man standing sheepishly in the doorway.

"Oh sorry, this is James, he's a friend," said Debbie.

Bob still reeling from the shock he'd been given managed a smile and invited James inside.

In awkward silence, Sheila ushered them into the lounge and switched off the television. There were questions still forming inside her head, but her most paramount thought was for the poor bemused little girl, that only a few moments earlier she'd thought of as her child. She knew she should have felt euphoric but instead she found herself engulfed in a state of panic and jealousy as Charlotte clung to her mother. Sheila looked towards Bob for support, she was dying inside. Her world was being torn apart, but he didn't seem to notice. At that moment she hated her husband for his insensitivity, far more than the redhead with the shaggy bob. 'It's a mistake, Debbie's dead,' her mind cried out. 'The stranger in my front room's an impostor, why can't Bob see it.' Yet the more she tried blotting out the truth, the more she understood what was happening. Debbie was alive. Somehow she'd returned from the dead. She'd come to take back what was rightfully hers, 'it wasn't fair.' Forcing a smile she sat down opposite her sister-in-law and waited to hear her account of what had happened.

"Until this morning, I couldn't remember a thing. James has been so kind, so patient with me, I don't think I'd have made it without his support," said Debbie in that old familiar husky voice of hers.

Sheila exchanged glances with Bob, but he seemed too engrossed to catch on to what Sheila's look, implied.

"I was making myself a pot of tea, when Marlow suddenly popped into my head. I phoned James at once. Like a dear, he dropped what he was doing and came straight over."

Bob looked towards James for some kind of explanation.

"I've been treating Debbie since she was admitted to the Radcliffe some six months ago. I'm her neurologist."

"And friend," added Debbie. "The moment we drove into Marlow it was like a giant jigsaw, everything began fitting into place," she said excitedly. "Suddenly I realised where I lived. Without questioning me, James followed my directions and drove me to our house . . . . Except it isn't our house any longer." She looked bemused, frightened even.

"Don't worry, I'll explain later. Go on," said Bob gently.

"As I got back in the car, I remembered, I was married to Jack and I had, have a beautiful daughter called Charlotte," she glanced down and smiled. Charlotte beamed up at her.

"For a second I panicked and then everything seemed to come in a rush. I remembered everything, including the terrible crash." Debbie's eyes grew wide with horror and alarm. "Dave! Oh God, tell me he's alive!"

No one spoke, they didn't need to, and their faces said it all.

Realisation began to hit Debbie. "Where's Jack? Where is he?"

"He thought you were dead, he thought the body in the car was you," said Sheila acidly.

Debbie didn't notice her sister-in-law's bitter tongue, but Bob did, as he stared hard at his wife.

"Jack's in Kentucky, he's been there since the beginning of the year. He'll be over the moon when I tell him," said Bob excitedly. His excitement only marred by the niggling doubt he kept locked inside his head, a doubt that had grown to such monstrous proportions inside his brother Jack's head.

"I must phone him," cried Debbie.

"Sure," said Bob hesitantly, "but it's too early." He noted the look of disappointment on her face. "They found a body of a woman, your size and build; we all thought it was you." He wanted to come right out and ask her, but something inside stopped him.

"Oh, that poor young woman!" Debbie raised a hand to her face; it was all coming back in a rush. She was sitting in that old pub in Wycombe with Dave. He was so nervous and fidgety; the poor man was in such torment. The person they'd come to meet was late. She remembered Dave nervously twisting a couple of beer mats into oblivion as they waited for the young private investigator.

"Yes; that poor woman! What my husband is trying to say in that delicate way of his, is who she was and what was she doing in your car. Come to think of it, what was Dave Bryant doing there?"

Debbie was startled by Sheila's outcry. She couldn't understand why her sister-in-law was being so hostile towards her. Charlotte threw her arms tightly around her, and one glance at Sheila was enough. The truth of the situation slowly began to dawn.

"Let me get things straight. You all thought that young woman was me, am I right?"

Bob and Sheila nodded their heads slightly.

"You thought I'd been killed along with Dave." Her hackles were rising as she slowly put two and two together. "Your question suggested more than you've just said. I've known you a long time Sheila; now tell me what you meant by it." Both women's eyes locked on each other.

"Okay. Dave Bryant! What the hell was Dave doing in your car?"

"Sheila, you don't think . . . ."

Bob looked nervously at his wife. "She's upset, you being here, the shock, it's . . . ."

Red faced with embarrassment Sheila interrupted her husband. "He means well. And no, I don't know, I don't know what to think." And then Sheila knew, her face softened, "I'm sorry I ever doubted you."

Debbie's eyes still remained defiant, locked in a nether world of disbelief.

Sheila seeking to repair the damage her words had done continued. "Bob's right about one thing, I am in a state of shock, more than that, seeing you alive has thrown me into a blind panic. Jack thought; we all thought you were dead. You see before Jack left, he made Bob and me Charlotte's guardians. We love her so much, it seemed the best solution."

Debbie saw the love in Sheila's eyes as she stared at little Charlotte and her own anger subsided. She remembered how her sister-in-law couldn't have children of her own, and her heart went out to her. "Come here," she said and held her arms open.

Sheila embraced her, and held her tightly. "Oh Deb, I'm so sorry. I've been mean. You've been through so much and all I can do is to think of myself."

Charlotte looked on in confusion as both women hugged each other and cried.

"I think this calls for a drink," cried Bob, relieved that the tension had eased. "What'll you have James?"

James who until that moment had been entranced with the scene being played out before his eyes snapped to attention. "A small scotch would be fine, thanks."

"Ladies?"

"I'll have a vodka and slimline," said Debbie.

"Same," cried Sheila.

"Wow! That must have been quite a sight, you and Debbie squaring up to each other," laughed Jack.

"It wasn't funny," snapped Sheila.

"Sorry," he replied.

"You should be," said Sheila in return.

Jack sought to change the subject. "How did Debbie react to the news of Tony and Julie?" he exclaimed.

"We'll get to that in a minute," cried Sheila, the hostility in her voice clearly still recognisable.

It was then that Debbie turned bitter; her memory had brought back revelations she'd rather not have to recall. "How did Julie take the news of Dave's death?" she asked.

"Badly I'm afraid, though she seems to be getting it together of late," said Sheila.

"I bet she has," said Debbie bitterly. "Private investigator," she added suddenly. "The woman in my car, she's . . . She was a private investigator."

"Sorry," said Bob as he handed her, her drink.

"Is Julie seeing anyone?"

"Not that we know of . . . . Although Tony's been a dear. He's really tried to help her come to terms with Dave's death. Between you and me, I think he's a little soft on her," said Sheila.

Debbie felt her hackles rising as she remembered the look of despair on Dave's face as Donna Albright the private investigator reached across the table and squeezed his hand. There was no other way of breaking it to him gently

"He's more than a little soft," Debbie said angrily.

"What!" cried the Claymores' in unison?

"Can someone get me a glass of water please?" As the events tumbled into her head Debbie realised she needed to gather her thoughts.

Bob came racing back into the room, glass of water in one hand, a couple of paracetamols in the other."

"Thanks," cried Debbie as she took both the water and the two painkillers.

The room remained silent until Debbie had composed herself.

"I think I'd better start from the beginning. A week, no less than a week before the accident, Dave phoned in a distressed state. I thought at first something bad had happened to Julie. How wrong I was!" Debbie paused and took a sip of her drink.

"That's funny, until just now, I didn't realise this was my favourite tipple."

Bob laughed; Sheila gave a half hearted grin, both anxious for Debbie to continue.

"Dave came round to see me on the weekend before the accident. He looked pale and drawn. I thought he was ill or something. He looked at me and I could see tears forming in his eyes. 'I think Julie's having an affair,' he blurted out. I felt a lump forming in my throat, I thought my world was about to fall apart, 'with Tony,' added Dave. A feeling of overwhelming relief wafted over me. As Dave's words began to sink in, a feeling of guilt quickly replaced it."

"You what!" exclaimed Bob.

"Hush, let Debbie talk," came the reply from Sheila.

"He said he'd suspected for a month or so, and in frustration at not knowing, had hired a female private investigator. He'd arranged a meeting with her for the following Tuesday, and asked me if I'd come along to lend him moral support. What could I say, I had to go, the poor man was on the verge of a breakdown. That's when he begged me not to say anything to Jack."

Debbie looked down at her daughter and smiled. "In all our years together, this was the only time I kept anything from him."

Charlotte grinned back at her mother.

"While we waited in the Nag's Head, Dave told me he was going to confront Julie with whatever proof the investigator had dug up. Just before Donna came rushing through the doors of the pub, he told me he was prepared to give Julie a second chance. He said he'd thought about nothing else for the last couple of days, and decided that however bad the report turned out to be, he wasn't giving Julie up. 'Of course, we'll have to move away, but that's no

real problem, my firm's got a position in their branch in Lincoln.'
He had it all figured out."

"I'll kill him, when I get my hands on him," cried Bob. "That *bastard came in this house and told me that Jack needed to pull* *himself together, and all the time he could have ended his misery.* *I'll fucking kill him!"*

"Bob," cried Sheila.

Debbie put down her glass, "What do you mean misery?"

It was Bob's turn to look embarrassed, he'd said far more than *he'd wanted.*

"Oh shit."

"Go on," cried Debbie agitatedly. The penny had finally dropped *as to why Sheila had thought the worst.*

"It was Tony's fault, he sowed the seed. Jack thought, in fact *we all thought there was something going on between you and* *Dave."*

"What!" It was all making sense, she thought.

Bob fumbled, and began moving about, luckily Sheila came to *his rescue. "That was only after Julie collaborated what Tony had* *said. Before that, it was just a mystery. Jack wouldn't have thought* *it if Julie hadn't said she suspected you and Dave were having an* *affair."*

"I still can't believe it!" exclaimed Jack at hearing Debbie's story. "Bob told me, but I still find it hard to take in."

Sheila could see Jack getting hot around the collar. "Easy," she cried as she squeezed his arm affectionately.

"Yeah I'm sorry. Go on with the story," cried Jack.

It was Debbie's turn to get mad, "The scheming little bitch, *wait until I get my hands on her."*

"Yeah, I'll kill Callahan, you kill that skinny bitch Julie," growled *Bob in the worst Godfather impression Debbie had heard in* *years.*

The tension eased as she cracked up laughing, "Bob, that's *terrible, that's more like Marlon from the Perishers than Brando."*

Bob grinned, Sheila shrieked, Charlotte giggled and even poor James who had been sitting in stunned silence joined in the revelry. The ice was well and truly broken.

"All right, all right, I get the message, don't quit my day job," said Bob now full of good humour. "I'll give Jack a ring."

Debbie felt a pang of nervousness as Bob indicated the phone was ringing. She waited expectantly as Bob held the receiver to his ear. "That's funny; I'd have thought someone would have been at the house. I guess running a stud farm's busier than we thought."

"Give it an hour, and then try again," said Debbie, her disappointment clearly showing.

They rang several times during the evening and even left a message on the answering machine of Pam and Phil's business line.

Jack felt a little uncomfortable at the mention of Pam and Phil. Kentucky he hoped, wasn't general knowledge.

By nine o'clock Charlotte was exhausted and Sheila said," Right young lady, that's enough excitement for one day, bed."

"Oh mum do I have too," said Charlotte as she looked imploringly up at Debbie. Sheila flushed with embarrassment, "Oh, I'm so sorry Deb!"

"That's all right, I fully understand," replied Debbie. "Auntie Sheila says it's time for bed, so hop to it. I'll be up to tuck you in, in a few minutes." Charlotte stifled a yawn, as finally the excitement of the day caught up with her.

"Good night trouble," said Bob as he playfully tousled her hair.

"Trouble yourself," replied Charlotte.

"Night little un," said Sheila cheerily as she bent down and kissed Charlotte's little button of a nose

Charlotte playfully blew her a kiss, "Night, Auntie Sheila."

Sheila turned away and walked into the kitchen before her watery eyes turned to tears.

"Goodnight Mr Henderson," said Charlotte as she began climbing the stairs.

"Good night Charlie," he responded.

"*Charlie, I like that, Charlie.*" *then she hopped quickly out of sight.*

Debbie followed Sheila into the kitchen. "She, are you all right?"

"*Yeah, I'll be find, I'm just being silly, that's all*"

"*No you're not; you're just being a woman. I'm back, that doesn't mean you can't see Charlotte as much as before.*"

"*I know,*" *said Sheila, "I know," though deep inside, her heart was breaking.*

"I'm not saying it was easy Jack," cried Sheila breaking away from her narrative. "You put us in an impossible position." Jack detected a little reprimand in Sheila's voice. Then satisfied she'd got her point over Sheila continued with the story.

As Bob turned off the bedside light, Sheila reached across and hugged him. "Hold me Bob, please hold me."

Bob put his arms around her and lay there looking up at the ceiling. "I'm sorry too. But you'll see Charlotte almost as much as before."

I know, it's . . . . I don't know. I feel terrible. I hated her today, I wanted her to disappear, be gone, like she'd never existed.

"*You can't mean that! I thought you'd be glad that she's alive.*"

"*Of course I'm pleased that Debbie's alive, who wouldn't be. Did you see the look on Charlotte's face, I've never seen her look happier. It's just the shock. I guess it's worth all the heartache.*"

"*She'll be a whole lot happier when Jack comes home. First thing in the morning, I'm ringing Kentucky. I don't care if it's the middle of the night there.*"

"*Good, you do that, get him home as soon as possible. Meantime I'll set the clock good and early, I want Debbie and Charlotte to wake up to a fresh start.*"

Sheila looked across at Jack, then glanced towards Bob, "I know it's a little early, but in these circumstances I think a little drinky wouldn't go a miss, wouldn't it Bob."

"She hasn't changed, any excuse," he joked as he moved towards the kitchen and the refrigerator. Minutes later, with glass in hand Sheila continued with her narrative.

"That's funny, I just got Phil on the line, he sounded drunk," said Bob.

"That's probably because he is, it's still night time there," replied Sheila.

"Yeah, I told him Debbie was alive. 'That's great news,' he said, 'let me call Pam,' then the phone went dead."

"He'll probably call back. If he doesn't, we'll call later this afternoon. Now go wake Debbie and Charlotte, breakfast is about ready!"

Debbie picked at her breakfast in silence, her mind preoccupied with the sudden return of her memory. Even Charlotte's constant calls for attention fell by the wayside. "I'm sorry darling; I've things on my mind." Charlotte frowned and threatened to go into a sulk, until Sheila reprimanded her with a withering look.

"Right, one of us has to keep the wolf from the door," said Bob, as he rose from the table and grabbed his sandwiches.

"Just make sure you're not knocking on Red Riding Hood's door," joked Sheila.

"See you tonight," he said as he lent down and kissed her playfully on the cheek.

"See you later Uncle Bob."

"See you too Princess," said Bob, blowing her a kiss as he reached the door.

Sheila followed him out to the front and watched as he climbed in his light blue transit van. Turning back to the house, she realised it was a school day and if Charlotte didn't move herself, she'd be late. She stopped herself from calling out Charlotte's name, just in time. It wasn't her job anymore; her days of playing mother were at an end. For a brief moment she thought she'd breakdown, then stifling a sob, she re-entered the house.

Charlotte beamed at her as she walked back into the kitchen, "Mum said, as it's a special day, I don't have to go to school."

Debbie gestured with her hand, "That's not what I said. If it's all right with Sheila, you can take the day off," she emphasised.

"You don't have to ask, she's your daughter."

"I know, but."

They fumbled around in embarrassment until Sheila said, "Okay, let's start over. You've been away, I've helped out. Now you're back. Why the hell are we treating each other as strangers?"

"I don't know," said Debbie as the beginnings of a smile appeared at the corners of her mouth.

Later when Charlotte had tired of hanging around and had taken herself off to her bedroom, Debbie turned towards Sheila and mouthed a silent thank you."

"What's that for," enquired Sheila.

"For being you, even though I didn't remember a thing, it's good to know, my little girl was being taken care of." Debbie looked across at Sheila, her eyes haunted by an inner pain. "I remember it so clearly."

Sheila looked on sympathetically.

"I was such an asshole, I should have stuck it out," said Jack guiltily.

"Yeah maybe you should have, but you weren't to know. We were all taken in by those lowlifes. After a while even Bob and I began to think Debbie was having an affair. We should have trusted her a little more than we did. We should have realised that she was the sort to help anyone in a fix. But we didn't."

Jack could sense Sheila's recollection was raking over old wounds, but he urged her to go on. He had to know what to expect when he came face to face with Debbie. "Go on Sheila, tell me everything."

"Debbie stood in my kitchen and it was like a revelation as it all came flooding back. She surprised me with her clear and precise recall."

"The accident, I remember it as if it was yesterday. Poor Dave, that poor, poor sweet man. When Donna handed him her report, I think he was expecting, hoping even that she'd prove him wrong. He went white when he read it. I thought he was going to collapse in-front of me. The confirmation of Julie's betrayal was devastating, to say the least."

"Oh poor Dave," cried Sheila as she let out an involuntary sob. "I'm sorry Deb, go on."

"Oh Sheila I've never felt so sorry for anyone in my life. He cried in my arms. I tried comforting him as best I could, but it was no use, he was beyond consoling. All he wanted to do was go home."

"Oh Debbie."

"And to make matters worse Donna looked at me in embarrassment and asked if I could give her a lift to Stokenchurch."

Sheila looked puzzled.

"You see, the reason she was late was because her car had broken down. It was pouring with rain when we left the pub. So I didn't really have much of a choice."

"I see," said Sheila. "It all fits."

"Visibility was poor as the rain and spray from the many cars and trucks lashed across my windscreen. No one spoke as I concentrated on my driving, I remember Dave was slumped in the front seat, and Donna was sitting bolt upright in the back. And then it happened. One minute we were heading towards Stokenchurch and then from out of nowhere a black saloon, I think it was a Nissan, side swiped me and sent my car out of control."

"Oh Jesus," interrupted Sheila.

Debbie stared up at the far corner of the room, her mind a torment as the scenes of carnage that followed formed in her memory. She shuddered, but then forced herself to go on.

"I think I must have blacked out. It could only have been seconds, but when I woke up, my world was in chaos. I'll never forget the uncontrollable screeching of car horns, the smoke, the stench of petrol fumes, and the rain, the merciless driving rain, it just kept beating down. I remember looking up at the darkening November skies and thinking I'd be late home and that I hadn't got the dinner on. It was such a strange thought. Then somehow I guess the instinct for survival kicked in. I found the strength to force open my door and I staggered onto the tarmac. Twisted wreckage, smashed windscreens, a body in a grotesque pose of death greeted my eyes. It was like a scene from hell. Petrol gushed from an upturned tanker and washed over the road like a raging tide."

She paused and took a breath, it was clearly painful for her, but somehow she managed to go on.

"*I was dazed and confused, yet I still had the presence of mind to realise death was but seconds away. Spurred on by the screams of pain and anguish, the roar of an engine racing, a clap of distant thunder, I finally pushed my way through the tangled walls of metal. The pungent smell of petrol was everywhere.*" *Her eyes grew wide with terror as she remembered those last moments,* "*I'd reached the hard shoulder, when I remembered Dave, I looked back and screamed his name, his name, his name . . . .*"

"*Easy Deb, don't torture your self!*" *Sheila held her sister-in-law as Debbie broke into a fit of uncontrollable sobbing.* "*It's over Deb, nothing can hurt you now.*"

"*I know, I know. I want Jack, why isn't he here. I need him. I want to hear his voice.*"

"*You will, we'll give it a little longer, then we'll phone again.*"

Debbie wiped her eyes and blew her nose. "*I'm sorry. I shouldn't . . .*"

"*Nonsense. You let it all out. It'll be better, you'll see.*"

"*You're right. I need to purge myself of it.*" *She remained silent for all of a minute.* "*The explosion, I guess that's what must have happen, it . . . it must have blown me off my feet. When I woke up, it was pitch black and apart from the drone of traffic high above me, there was nothing. I was in the centre of a small copse or wood, soaked to the skin and feeling bitter cold. My body ached as I scrambled to my feet, my head felt like it didn't belong to me. It was then I realised I didn't know who I was, yet I knew enough to know I had to get out of there before hypothermia set in. I found myself walking into the darkness of an open field. I don't know why I walked in that direction, only that the further I got away from the sound of traffic, the better I felt. My progress was slow, my body had taken a battering and every movement of my limbs was torture. I walked for hours before finally collapsing close to a country road. I was found the following day and rushed to Wantage hospital.*

"*But that's only half an hour away,*" *exclaimed Sheila.*

Debbie ignored Sheila's outburst. She had to go on. It was all coming back.

"At first, they thought I'd been attacked, and left for dead. Apart from the injuries sustained in the crash, my body was covered with minor lacerations from the many hedgerows I'd scrambled through. They were so kind to me, treating my injuries and offering words of comfort. Even when they discovered I hadn't been sexual assaulted they still didn't connect me with the horrific crash that had taken place on the motorway, five miles from where I was found. They did all they could for me physically but they could do nothing to get my memory back. That's when they transferred me to the John Radcliffe General, and that's where I first met James."

"He's a nice man," said Sheila, giving her sister-in-law a long searching look.

"He is, and no, we're not seeing each. He's been very sweet and attentive to me over the few months I've known him, but that's all it is," said Debbie defensively.

"Yeah sure, and you don't find him in the slightest bit attractive," added Sheila teasingly.

"Well . . . . He is a handsome man, I'll grant you that."

"Is he married?"

"No," said Debbie.

"Why not, is there something wrong, is he gay?"

"Of course he's not," Debbie said all too quickly.

"Thank God for that! It'd be such a waste," said Sheila, noting the quickness of Debbie's reply.

A fact that didn't go undetected by Debbie, "All right, I'll tell you. I've been to dinner with James a few times. He's charming, sweet and gentle, and has always treated me with the utmost respect. He's told me he'd like more from our relationship, but I've said that until I know who I am, I can't make any commitments."

"And now?"

"And now, nothing," replied Debbie. "James knows the score, we've spoken about this very situation many times during the last three months. He's been there for me, and he's promised that whatever happens I can rely on him for anything. He's become a good friend."

Jack felt a lump form in his throat and not for the first time felt a little guilty of his thoughts for his former wife. Had Debbie been seeing James before her memory came back? Quickly erasing the thoughts from his mind he asked about Tony Callahan.

Sheila gave Bob a wry smile. "I think I'll leave that to Bob to tell you about."

Chapter 4

Montana

Tara woke early and after looking in at her two babies asleep in their beds, left a note for Martha Redbird, the Indian housekeeper/nanny, saying she was going for a ride and would be back before the kids awoke. For years she'd been in the habit of taking an early ride up into the foothills, but of late she'd forgone her regular sojourn into the mountains. Jack's revelations had turned her world upside down. She knew from the moment he'd told her about his wife that he would have to go back. He'd been gone two nights and she was going crazy with worry. She needed to clear her head. Saddling up Bucky her favourite bay quarter horse she clipped out of the yard at a fair gait.

Once clear of the outhouses and corrals she nudged Bucky into a fast lope. Although feeling his age the bay responded to Tara's touch with an almost humanlike enthusiasm. As the early morning air blasted her face she urged him into a gallop. Tara loved the exhilaration of speed, the sure footed pounding of hooves and the comforting warmth of Bucky, it was what made Tara what she was; it was something she'd inherited from her ma. Whenever Alex had felt troubled she'd race up into the foothills in the early mornings, surrounding herself with the voices of the land and sky. Often she'd gaze down on her home and somehow her problems fell into perspective. It was her way of clearing her mind of everything and a place where she could concentrate on what needed doing. It worked for her ma, why wouldn't it work for her?

Tara pulled up breathlessly amongst the Ponderosa pine and pointed Bucky back towards the ranch house. The bay's body heat warmed Tara as she leaned forward and wrapped her arms around the horse's neck. Bucky whinnied nervously and fidgeted amongst the pine needles that adorned the ground like a tan carpet. Involuntarily Tara began to cry and once she'd started there was no stopping. Pent up emotions, suppressed almost to breaking point erupted like a volcano. Bucky fidgeted and turned several times, mystified at his mistresses' distress. Ever the horsewoman she stifled her tears and patted the horse's neck and spoke to him with words of reassuring comfort. Bucky settled.

She loved her man and felt powerless to fight against the situation. Jack was everything, apart from her kids he meant more to her than life itself. Before Jack there'd been her pa Wade, the man she'd most depended upon and looked up to. But Jack had appeared at a timely stage in her life and swept her off her feet. She couldn't bear the thought of losing him. And in that time and moment high up in the foothills she began to see the impossibility of Jack's task. That he loved her she had no doubt, that he still felt something for his former wife, she would be foolish to discount, yet what of Jack's family, would they welcome him back with open arms or would they be downright hostile to him? Would Debbie still have feelings or would she have changed? These and more questions had been floating around inside her head and now finally she knew what she had to do. She sat upright on Bucky and wiped away the tears from her eyes and smiled. The land, the mountains and the sky had worked there magic as they had for Alex before her. Tara made her decision.

*   *   *

"I'm worried about her, Wade," said Alex as she laid the table for breakfast. "She acts like she hasn't a care in the world, but I can see it."

Wade took his time before answering, "Truth be told, I don't know what I'd do if I was caught up in a situation like Jack's got himself into. What I do know is he'll play fair by Tara."

"I don't doubt that, but in the meantime it's tearing our little girl apart," added Alex, "I should know, I'm her mother and besides, I've been there."

Wade flinched a little at the barb in Alex's voice, "That was altogether different," he protested. "Kate was dying; I did what I had to do."

"I know, I'm sorry, I didn't mean for it to come out that way," replied Alex softly. "It's just the helplessness that she must be feeling right at this moment."

"I know honey, I know," cried Wade as he looked down at the plate of pancakes that Alex had just taken of the griddle. "What I will say is Tara ain't the sort to lie down and take any crap."

Then the phone rang, "You're what!" cried Alex. Wade looked up, a smidgen of maple syrup clinging to his salt and pepper moustache.

"It's Tara," mouthed Alex.

"I'm going over there. I've booked my flight, I'm leaving Saturday lunchtime."

"Does Jack know you're coming?"

"No. And I don't want him to. It'll be a surprise."

"It will at that," responded Alex, "Have you thought this thing through." She steeled herself from adding that Tara might get more than she'd bargained for, but then she knew her daughter and in her place she'd have done the same.

"Yes ma. You see, me and Jack, well we've been though a hell of a lot together, things that his first wife couldn't even contemplate. Seeing us together should sure as hell make up his mind."

"Oh, so now you're saying that Jack's gone over there to check out what breeding stock he should leave his brand on!"

"No ma! I ain't saying that at all. I trust him, it's just I'm saying what all you here about are thinking."

"We're not thinking that," replied Alex, "Oh I guess you gotta go and do what you've a mind."

"It'll be fine, just you see."

Alex put down the receiver and slumped down into a chair opposite Wade, "Well that's that, I guess we'll just have to await the outcome."

"We will at that," agreed Wade. A few minutes later he was out the door and heading for the feed barn.

Tara's phone call had set Alex to thinking about the last few years. Life had settled down since the shooting at Cougar Pass and apart from the mountain lion attack, which nearly took Wade, peace had returned to the valley. But now with news of Jack's first wife still being alive her whole world seemed like it was about to be turned on its rear. She feared for Tara, venturing into a foreign land alone and in truth she'd half a mind to go with her. Yet this was only wishful thinking, Tara was her own woman and would have refused her company.

*   *   *

Once out of the house Wade's concerns switched to the job at hand. His life was as busy as ever, the winter months had been especially cruel, cow and calf deaths had been unusually high and the snows seemed to take forever to leave. Fortunately spring roundup went without a hitch, but the day to day activities still kept him and the boys busy for nigh on twelve hours a day. Hay and salt distribution alone took up more days than you could shake a stick at, fence mending was a never ending job, artificial insemination, moving cows from one pasture to another, branding, calving, checking the drop, you could go on and on, not that this fazed Wade any, hard work was something he thrived on

Wade had other worries to contend with, not the least the return of the Timber Wolf. He'd seen it coming since 1994 when the reintroduction of wolves into Yellowstone Park and

Northern Idaho reached fruition. The Endangered Species Act of 1973 and subsequent amendments had paved the way for such madness. The reintroduction of Wolves into Wyoming, and Idaho and the fact that Canadian wolves were now establishing themselves in North Western Montana had at first appeared to be a nightmare from the ranchers' point of view, but as yet their worries had been unfounded. To the relief of conservationists and environmentalists alike the perceived threat to livestock had been minimal, the wolf was alive and well and living in perfect harmony with nature. Ranchers, farmers and hunters were not so sure, and resentment towards the federal government was given another lift. Over time who knows what damage this legislation would cause. It was yet another encroachment on the rights of the indigenous population, thought Wade and others bitterly.

Now less than two years since their re-introduction a pack had been sighted in the Western reaches of the Bitterroots. Though the government had given re-assurances to the ranching communities of full compensation for any cow or calf took down, everyone knew that in the long run it would be the farmer and rancher that would end up the loser. Wade didn't intend for that to happen, not if he could help. He instructed Larry to send out a rider twice weekly to check for sign. So far he'd been lucky, but taking a man away from his work just in case, didn't sit too well with him.

Although Alex shared Wade's fears about wolves in the area, it had given her an idea. The dude side of the ranch was doing well, but over the years the overnight pack trip had become stale and routine, now with Wade's paranoia towards the wolf and her insight into what people wanted she saw the perfect opportunity to revive the pack trips by labelling them 'wolf sighting trips'. It would save Wade man-power for the coming months and add zest to the overnight stays.

She suggested rerouting one of her weekly dude ranch pack trips to cover the Western end. It meant a night camping in the open but it added a sense of adventure to the normal weekly routine. So far the break from the usual dude ranch activities had been welcomed by the guests although no wolf sighting had been reported.

Wade, from the vantage point of a small hill surveyed his kingdom. The ranch though now known far and wide as the Crazy AW would always be referred to as the old Pendleton spread by the local old timers. Wade and Alex had bought a half share from her uncle some thirty five years earlier and worked alongside Bill Pendleton for nigh on ten years before buying Bill out. It had been, including Alex and Wade's tenancy, in the family for close on one hundred and thirty years. And now thought Wade sadly it would terminate when he drew his last breath, unless . . . .

Chapter 5

Marlow

"Right now I want you to tell me what happened with that son-of-a-bitch Tony Callahan," cried Jack eagerly.

"Well you know how it is bruv. A man's got to do what a man's got to do," replied Bob with a twinkle in his eye.

Bob dropped Alan, his young apprentice at the site and drove off. 'Tsssrrruth, e's in a bad mood,' thought the youngster, as he watched the blue van roar off. Bob gripped the steering wheel hard as he fought for control. He'd contained himself whilst in Sheila and Debbie's presence and to a lesser degree with Alan, but now he was alone he was able to vent to his feelings.

"Bastard!" he shouted into the windscreen. He'd listened to Debbie's explanation of things and knew what she was telling him was the truth. Looking back, hadn't he also seen a car like Tony Callahan's parked around the corner from Dave Bryant's house one Friday night a few weeks before the accident? He'd meant to bring it up to Jack, but with one thing and another he'd put it out of his mind. The more he thought about it, the madder he got, "I'll do the bastard," he cried at the top of his lungs.

He'd voiced his feelings to Sheila as they lay in bed that night. "Having an affair with Dave's wife's none of my business, but Callahan watched the disintegration of my brother and did nothing to ease his pain. More than that, he'd actually encouraged the rumour. He even came to my house and complained about Jack's unreasonable behaviour."

"Easy, easy. Don't get worked up about it. It won't do any good," chastised Sheila.

"That's easy for you to say, that bastard even cheated Jack out of his half of the business. The fucker's gonna pay when I get my hands on him!"

"Don't do anything silly! Go and see Waterstone, get some advice. Whatever you do don't go off half-cocked."

It was sound advice and Bob had begrudgingly conceded that Sheila was right. It was a job for a solicitor. Young Alan hadn't helped his mood any, he was late and as far as Bob could tell, was losing interest in the job. This in itself made Bob mad as he'd given the boy more than one chance. As he waited he began to stew. Sheila was right about Callahan, she usually is, he thought, 'But that was then, this is now,' he thought angrily.

Bob was a little over six foot and his outward appearance suggested he was a little too gaunt to be able to punch his own weight, which was a mistake which a few hard men had made over the years. Gaunt he might have been, but it belied the fact that his body was made up of solid muscle and was as hard as granite. Though not as handsome as his younger brother, his face did possess a rugged charm, partly because of his permanent five o'clock shadow and those laughing blue eyes of his, except at that very moment as he drove into Callahan's yard, they'd turned murderously dark.

"How you doing Bob," said George the labourer, as Bob climbed down from the transit. The van's door slammed noisily as Bob walked passed him without giving him a second look.

"What's got into him," exclaimed George.

"I don't know, and as far as I can see, you don't want to know either," said Patrick O'Reilly another of Callahan's labourers. Both men stood silently as Bob kicked open the door of the porta-cabin that Callahan used as a site office.

Callahan looked up in surprise at the sudden entrance of his ex partner's brother. "What the fuck!"

"How long have you been fucking Julie Bryant?" screamed Bob.

"What," cried Callahan, as he rose to his feet? "What are you talking about?"

"I asked you a question; I don't really need an answer. You just need to know why you're gonna get the beating of your life."

Tony Callahan, a big man, and not a stranger to a fight, lunged forward instantly. Bob side stepped and caught him with a right hook, just behind the ear. The momentum of Callahan's lunge and the blow from Bob's right sent him spiralling out of the portacabin.

George and Paddy stood back and watched from a safe vantage point. Since Jack's departure from the firm, things had gone from bad to worse. Callahan wasn't the easiest man to work for, and both George and Paddy had faced a barrage of abuse in the months since Jack's exit from the firm.

Tony was on his feet and looked like a crazed bull as Bob stepped out of the office, both fists clenched. Callahan threw a left, then a right, the left missing while the right was just a glancing blow. Bob countered with a short left to the nose, followed by a right to the cheekbone.

"You're losing your touch," cried Bob. "Fucking another man's wife and cheating your partner has softened you up."

The abuse rallied Tony, who landed a right to Bob's jaw, and followed with a wind stealing blow to the lower stomach. The triumph of the contact, spurred the bigger man forward. "I'll teach you to come into my fucking yard," he screamed as he kicked Bob in the testicles. Claymore doubled up in pain, but saw Callahan reach for a short piece of two by two. Dodging the piece of timber that Callahan wielded, Bob threw a straight left at Callahan's face, and then followed with a right to the nose. The big man dropped the piece of wood and began trading blows with Bob.

"Should we stop it," cried George.

"I don't think either of them would thank us, if we did," said Paddy excitedly, "and besides how often to we get to have a ringside seat."

Both men crouched like wounded bulls fighting to get their breath back. Out of the corner of his eye, Callahan spied a shovel *propped up against a pile of concrete blocks. In an instant, he lunged for it and swung it high above his head. Bob grabbed a sand faced brick from a stack and dived under the murderous weapon and at the same time smashed the brick as hard as he could into the face of Tony Callahan. The shovel dropped from Callahan's hands and landed harmlessly on the ground a split second before his hulking frame crashed down beside it.*

Though battered and bloodied Bob looked down at Callahan, "This is only a taste of what you've got coming, unless you pay my brother what you owe!" Turning his back he walked unsteadily towards his van. "Morning lads," he said breathlessly as he passed the two employees of Callahan.

"Morning Bob," they cried in unison.

Jack grinned in satisfaction. Sheila feigned a frown and Bob preened himself. Then Sheila poured herself another wine and began refilling Jack's. He allowed her to refill to half full before calling a halt.

"I'm going to see Debbie in a few days, so I really need to be brought up to speed." He feared Sheila was getting a little sidetracked by the wine.

He needn't have worried, Sheila knew wine and knew just when to stop. "Right, where were we? Oh yes Pam and Phil."

By mid afternoon of Debbie's second day back in Marlow she was becoming increasingly worried. She'd phoned the stud farm and tried talking with Phil. He was rambling and incoherent and kept babbling on about a fight he'd had with Pam and that she'd left him.

"She'll be back," said Debbie. "You two are the perfect couple, just give her time."

Jack felt decidedly uncomfortable at the mention of Pam and Phil. About now he was thankful for the half a glass that Sheila had poured. He hoped it masked his guilt as he studied his brother's face for any sign that he knew what had gone on. Thankfully there was none.

"*Yeah, that's it, she'll be back,*" he slurred.

"*Phil, I'm trying to locate Jack, is he there?*"

"*Nope, he done left here about a month ago. Out of the blue, he up and went.*"

"*Did he say where he was heading?*"

"*I love her, you know . . . . She's gone and left me . . . .*"

It was useless to continue, the phone call was too one sided. It was clear to Debbie that Phil had been drinking. Debbie had known from past phone-calls with Pam, about Phil's drinking bouts, his drug addiction, and his depressions. It was obvious to her, Pam had had enough and taken off.

"*Phil, give Pam a few days. I'm sure she'll be back then. Just tell her to give me a call.*"

"*Don't worry Deb, soon as the news reaches Jack that you're alive, he'll be on the next plane home, mark my words, you'll see.*"

"*I hope so,*" *said Debbie dejectedly. The euphoria of the morning had turned into disappointment.* "*I guess I was expecting too much too soon.*"

"Well that about sums me up too," said Sheila unexpectedly. I thought we could fill you in, but there's so much more to tell. If I carry on drinking this wine, I'll be too tiddley to cook dinner."

"Oh that won't do," cried Bob. "We'll tell you more later this afternoon. First of all I'll show you to your room. Let you rest a while then call you for dinner.

Jack started to protest, but Bob and Sheila were having none of it. About then, the wine coupled with jet lag started to kick in. They were right of course. If he allowed them to continue, they'd just have to repeat it all over again the following morning.

* * *

Jack woke with a start and stared at unfamiliar walls and décor. It took him almost a minute before he recalled that he was in the back bedroom at his brother's house. He glanced at the neon lit alarm clock on the bedside cabinet and calculated he'd been asleep for four hours or so. The emotion of his reunion with his brother and sister-in-law coupled with the wine and their explanation of Debbie's re-appearance had been a little too much for him. He'd crashed upon the bed and fallen almost immediately to sleep.

As he grabbed a towel and made his way to the bathroom he could hear activity downstairs and the aroma of a roast invaded his nostrils. Quickly washing, he changed his clothes, slipping into a pair of worn Wranglers and a tee shirt. Then with a cursory glance at his features, he swept his hair back from his forehead and descended the stairs.

"Hey guys, you should have woken me up."

"You needed your sleep, and besides it gave us a chance to tidy up and prepare dinner," cried Sheila.

"Sit there Jack," said Bob as Sheila put a plate of roast beef, Yorkshire pudding, roast potatoes, cabbage and runner beans in front of him.

"Wow, that looks good," cried Jack as he settled himself onto the chair. "I'd forgotten what a Sunday roast looked like."

For a minute or two Jack was transported back to a time long ago, before his life changed so dramatically. Thoughts of Debbie invaded the dining table as Bob and Sheila politely passed the condiments around and made small talk. He'd had three weeks to contemplate what he would do about meeting her again. Somehow it had seemed much easier when he'd thought about it on the grassy plains of Montana. Now, faced with the familiar, yet somehow alien lifestyle, he was beginning to feel out of his depth.

"I don't know how I'm gonna face her!" he blurted out after they'd finished their meal.

"We'll do all we can to help," reassured Bob.

"Thanks. I just didn't figure on it being so difficult."

"Is it because you still have feeling for Debbie?" Chipped in Sheila.

"Yeah, you could say that, but don't get me wrong, I love Tara with all my heart. She's everything to me and more." His eyes lit up at the mention of her name. "She's sexy, she's sassy, she's fun lovin, oh and she's tough but above all she's the kindest sweetest woman I've ever known."

"Then you've nothing to worry about then," said Sheila, though her eyes told a different story.

"She sounds fantastic, can't wait to meet her," cried Bob.

"And my kids, they . . . they're something else. K.C's the oldest, she's going on six while Merri's not quite two yet."

"K.C?" asked Sheila.

"Oh yeah. Sorry. Kaycee is short for Katherine Claymore," said Jack apologetically.

"Katherine?" exclaimed Sheila.

"It's a long story. I'll tell you about it sometime."

So with the dishes in the dishwasher and the kitchen tidied up Sheila wiped her hands, told Bob to get his brother a beer and sat down opposite Jack.

"Okay. Are you ready for another instalment?"

"I sure am. Knowing Tony the way I do, or thought I knew, I'm intrigued as to what fallout came after Bob gave him that beating."

Sheila gave Bob a withering look as he handed Jack a beer and sat down beside him.

"Oh shit Jack. Why'd you have to bring that up," he said mockingly.

It had been a little over two weeks since Debbie had arrived on the Claymore's doorstep. During that time a lot happened, not the least when the police took Bob to the station. Sheila learnt of Bob's arrest when he phoned and told her of the fight with Callahan.

"Oh Bob, how could you be so stupid!"

"It's in the blood," he said, in that matter of fact way of his, that she'd come to know and love. "All I know is, I couldn't function properly until I'd done for the bastard. Phone Waterstone's and ask Henry if he can come to the station to represent me."

"Right, I'll do that, then I'm coming up there myself," she said in a mock menacing tone.

*   *   *

Henry Waterstone sat with his client and listened patiently while Bob relayed his version of the fight.

"I didn't go around to Callahan's to do him any harm, all I wanted was to give him a piece of my mind," said Bob cagily. Henry wasn't fooled, and secretly he was pleased that Bob had the presence of mind to try to lie his way out of the assault charge. At the very least it made his work just that little bit easier. If he couldn't talk Callahan into dropping the charges, then he would get Bob to cross summons him. No one had witnessed who'd thrown the first punch, so it was Bob's word against Callahan's.

Waterstone was somewhat taken aback by the extent of Callahan's injuries and for a brief moment of time doubted whether the battered and bandaged man would withdraw his complaint. Within minutes the quiet and subdued Callahan was flaying his arms about demanding that Bob be punished to the fullest extent of the law. The heated argument ensued for almost ten minutes until finally Callahan, his solicitor and Henry Waterstone accepted they'd come to an impasse. Tony Callahan was a lot of things, but he wasn't a fool. He'd called the police in a state of haste, now it was being spelt out to him how costly that incident could become. Reluctantly he agreed to withdraw the assault charges

*   *   *

Back at the site, Callahan called George Norris and Paddy O'Reilly into his office. 'What's the point in employing people who won't back you up,' he thought bitterly, referring to their reluctance to follow him to the police station.

"Your cards," he snapped. "Now sling you're fucking hook."

Both men looked at him dumbfounded. It was Paddy O'Reilly who recovered first. Checking his pay, he looked across the desk at Tony Callahan. "You're a fucking arse hole Callahan. You always were. Bob Claymore should have hit you just that little bit harder. Come on George; let's get the fuck out of here."

"You was always a prick," added George as a parting shot.

"Good old George!" exclaimed Jack. He was beginning to feel comfortable. Then his thoughts turned to Dave's wife. "What about Julie?"

"Well, let's say she didn't get away with it scot free."

For a week she'd managed to elude Debbie, but she knew a confrontation was imminent. Over the years they'd become good friends, sharing everything from confidences to cosmetics. She tried reasoning it out, after all, what did she have to fear, it wasn't as if she'd been screwing Jack. Yet she knew Debbie well enough to know trouble was coming. She only hoped it would be in the privacy of her own home.

Unfortunately for Julie hope didn't come into it. Her jaw dropped just as she was just about to take a bite of her meal. Debbie, along with her sister-in-law Sheila and her husband Bob, had just entered 'Roberto's' the most exclusive Italian restaurant in the area. 'No, not here, and not while I'm with Colin,' she thought, as she tried concentrating on her date.

"What's up Julie?" Colin was attentive to her every whim.

"Oh, nothing, it's just somebody I didn't want to see," she said, without a trace of the panic that was building inside her. "Oh shit," she exclaimed as she saw Debbie making straight for her table.

"Julie darling, how are you," greeted Debbie as she came abreast of the table.

"I'm fine. But you, you're looking so well considering the terrible time you must have had," said Julie.

"I'm doing okay. And you, I can see life's been good to you since poor Dave's death."

Julie feigned a look of abject grief, but too late realised her mistake.

"I'm sorry, we haven't been introduced, I'm Debbie one of Julie's closest friends," she said, addressing Colin, the MD. "I was with him, you know, just before the accident. He was a funny man, always cheery, always laughing, but then who wouldn't married to someone as lovely as Julie."

The sarcasm was almost lost on Colin, until . . . .

"But not on that day. He was crying like a baby, in a crowded pub. He didn't care about his dignity; he didn't care about his pride. No, all he cared about was Julie."

Debbie switched her attention to Julie.

"He was prepared to give you a second chance. Nine years you were married to him, nine years. But you had to throw it in his face. Screwing someone's bad enough, but you went one better, you had to belittle him, you had to screw that worthless piece of shit in your own bed."

Debbie's mind clouded over as a series of flashbacks bombarded her mind, as if searching for a single truth, a segment of time. Her eyes became watery as that segment fell into place. "I remember, as I climbed from the wreck looking back at Dave. He wasn't injured; he was just sitting there, staring through the frosted windscreen. He could have got out, but he chose to remain. Death must have seemed infinitely preferable than a life of living hell, in the knowledge that you'd betrayed him."

Julie lowered her head in shame, while Colin looked on in utter disbelief. On the table in front of her, a full glass of Cabernet Sauvignon seemed to will Debbie to pick it up and throw it in Julie's face. The temptation was almost too great, but somehow she resisted.

Without another word Debbie turned and walked quietly back to an anxious Bob and a seething Sheila.

"You should have thrown it in her face," cried Sheila as she glared menacingly across the room.

"No," said Debbie firmly. "Dave wouldn't have wanted that."

Bob put his arms around both women and guided them towards the exit. The altercation had caused a mass lost of appetite. "Let's get a drink," said Bob as he pointed to a pub across the street.

"Debbie always had class," volunteered Jack. I'd have been like you Sheila, but Debbie always had a subtle knack at delivering the killer blow."

"You're right, you're dead right there."

"I think I should let Debbie know I'm alive. Don't you think?"

Sheila instinctively glanced across at Bob and in an instant Jack knew he had a mountain to climb.

"I think you'd better let me feel her out first," said Sheila seriously. "Let me break it to her as gently as I can. She's a brand new life now, it won't be easy."

Jack felt a stab of emotional pain, this was his life they were talking about, yet somehow he was being excluded, sidelined. Quickly he pulled himself together, what was he thinking, he had a life, his life was in Montana with Tara and his kids. Debbie was the past; she'd moved on, could he?

He wanted to speak out, but the words wouldn't come. He knew it wasn't going to be easy and in truth he welcomed Sheila's intervention. "I guess you're right. If I'm honest with myself I haven't given others a thought. I'm forgetting how Debbie's husband will take it and more to the point how Charlotte will react. I reckon I've been a coward all these years. I should have let her know I was alive at the very least."

"We can all be wise after the fact Jack," added Bob. "But I reckon Sheila's right. Leave her to break the news."

"And I think it's up to Debbie to tell you the rest. So I'll wait until Monday then I'll give her a call and arrange to meet up," said Sheila. "But in the meantime you can fill us in on that family of yours".

Jack smiled, grateful for the stay of execution. He was back in familiar mode; he was a horse breeder and a good one at that; it was the skin he felt most comfortable in. "Well what I'm going to tell you, I'm sure you won't believe. No shit."

Chapter 6

Montana

Tara drove into Dillon and picked up her tickets. Excitement coupled with anxiety coursed through her veins at the thought of the adventure ahead. She was thirty four years old and hadn't ventured out of the continental United States. Fortunately for her Jack had insisted she get herself a passport.

"Oh hell! There's so much of this darn country to see, why would I ever need a passport?"

"Because, my dear sweet country girl, one day you might want to venture a little farther afield."

"Won't!" taunted Tara.

"You will," came Jack's reply.

"Okay, give me one good reason why I need one?"

"For when we go visit my folks in England," replied Jack.

Argument over.

And so Tara was now in possession of a brand new passport. Which when she received it she threw to the back of a drawer. It was an act of playful defiance. It was speculative at best; as Jack had seemed to have turned his back on his past life. 'Thank God, he insisted,' thought Tara as she walked out of the travel services office.

Minutes later panic seemed to overtake her as she looked in the store windows, 'Perhaps I should have gone to Bozeman,' she thought. None of the clothes seemed suitable.

"Hell," she muttered under her breath, "I ain't got a clue as to what to wear." It was then that she really began to question her decision to go. Fighting back the panic Tara climbed into her car and drove to the one place where she knew she'd get the best advice.

*   *   *

"Be your self!" cried Alex when Tara paid her mother a visit right after her shopping trip. "Jack loves you the way you are. I ain't saying you have to turn up dressed in work duds, but a couple of pairs of designer jeans, a few coordinated tops, a light jacket, maybe a pair of heels."

Tara looked lost.

"What the hell, I'll take time off tomorrow; we'll make a day off it. Drive through to Bozeman. When he see's you, he'll be only to willing to hot-foot it back to Big Hole Pass."

"But I've too much on; I can't take another day off!"

Alex was having none of it. "Nonsense, I'll get Bud up there to mind the store, just don't you go telling your pa."

There was no way she was going to allow her daughter to go ill equipped for the trip she was making, even if it meant two shopping trips to Bozeman in under a week, rather than her twice yearly visits. What Wade would make of it she could only hazard a guess, but then she had no intention of telling him.

She reflected upon how she'd felt when she'd toured Europe with Patrick. She'd felt so out of her depth, it was like living another person's life. She'd travelled to London, Rome and finally to Paris. It had been both wonderful and terrifying at the same time. That Tara was about to embark on her first trip to Europe filled her with all sorts of emotions. When Alex had gone she'd been wined and dined in the best of places, but the people she met were anonymous players in her fantasy visit. She guessed Tara's ordeal might just be that little bit harder.

Jack's brother and his wife might be okay, the husband of Jack's former wife, would, Alex suspected, be an ally, the daughter, the half sister to her own two off spring might be a little difficult, but her main adversary would be the wife, Debbie.

Deep down Alex knew that Tara was right to go over there, fight for her man if need be. Not that she thought it necessary, there marriage was strong, of that Alex had no doubt, but who knows what deep seated emotions long buried would surface.

*   *   *

Alex and Tara shopped with a vengeance. Alex was determined her daughter would be able to compete in a totally foreign world, but without giving up her own personality. Bozeman, though a backwater to the likes of Los Angeles, New York, Paris or Milan had enough designer shops to satisfy the most earnest shopaholic. Alex knew that picking the right clothes to match the personality of the wearer was the secret, simple but classy.

Alex gave her daughter one piece of advice, "Just remember, be yourself. You're as good as any of them, and dare I say it, better than most." If truth be told Alex was proud of what Tara and Jack had achieved. Over the years they had built up the Claymore Horse Ranch selling only top quality stock under the brand name 'Reynolds Horse', they held membership of the AQHA, and various other associations. They were as good as it gets, selling as far a field as New Hampshire and up state New York, and closer to home, Pocatello in nearby Idaho plus several ranches in the Big Hole Valley and a couple in nearby Wisdom. They bred mainly Quarter Horses, but in reverence to Tara's father kept a breeding stock of Morgan and Appaloosa's. Selling and renting out to local ranches was their bread and butter trade, keeping the Claymore's busy through most of the year. Their outfit was smaller by far then the great cattle spreads in the valley, but much easier to manage. Having in excess of four hundred and fifty quality stocked horses, some spread around the ranches' pastures, others stabled at the Crazy AW and a number out on rental at Wisdom. In a way Alex envied them both. In comparison with the Crazy AW, the horse ranch was small potatoes, but it allowed Jack and Tara more free time together.

With Jack gone, free time was at a premium as Tara found to her cost. She'd had to hire a couple of extra wranglers from Wisdom to help out whilst she was away. Hiring transient workers was usual in ranching circles, but at least with these two she'd got lucky. She knew one of them personally, he being a distant cousin to the late Tyler Henry, the best wrangler they'd ever hired. Blaine Henry's judgement and horse sense was second only to Tyler's. If it all worked out, she was thinking about taking Blaine on full time.

Nonetheless Tara knew her trip to England wasn't open ended and both her and Jack would be needed back at the ranch within a week; two at the latest. She knew Alex and Wade would help when wanted, but they had their own hands full. A romantic life it might have seemed to the outsider and moviegoer, but in reality it was damn hard work, freezing conditions in winter, baking hot in summer, heart breaking at times and exhilarating at others. It was the life she'd known since birth. It was the life she loved; it was the life Jack had chosen after the tragedy that cost him the life he'd known.

'Going back!' thought Tara as panic seeped into her thoughts, 'would it change everything?' Tara had tormented herself over Jack choosing his first wife over her, but what if by going back he realised what he'd missed? Another woman would be a big enough battle, but another way of life, that was something Tara wasn't sure she could handle. Going over there seemed all the more important as she thought of the possible consequences.

Tara made arrangements with her mother for Martha Redbird and the children to come live at the Crazy AW whilst she was away. She hated leaving them, but what choice did she have? She knew that whatever else was thrown at her through life, things couldn't get much bigger.

Chapter 7

Marlow

"Hi Debs, its me." said Sheila speaking into the handset of her new mobile phone. "Are you doing anything in particular? Because if you aren't I thought we could meet for coffee in town and catch up on the local gossip, after all we haven't seen each other since the wedding."

"Yeah Sheila, that sounds great, but I've a mile of things to do. Washing, ironing you know." Debbie detected a fractional pause before Sheila replied.

"Oh okay, I understand, how about tomorrow?"

This was so unlike Sheila, thought Debbie, she was eager; too eager. Something was bothering her, her tone was altogether on edge.

"To hell with the washing and ironing, they can wait. A nice gossip seems more appealing. Shall we say 11o'clock at that new coffee house in Marlow?"

"Yeah that's great, if you're sure?"

"Of course I'm sure. See you at eleven."

Sheila pressed the green button on her phone and looked worriedly at Jack. "I think she suspects something's up. God I hope this doesn't blow up in my face."

*   *   *

On the other side of town Debbie stared at the grey phone now seated comfortably on its cradle and thought about Sheila's strange call. She hoped her friend wasn't about to pour her heart out about Bob having an affair. For one reason or another more than a few of her friends had used her as a sounding board, not the least, Dave Byrant.

As she climbed the stairs to get dressed for her meeting she reflected at how lucky she was with James. It could have been so different, she mused. He'd been so patient with her once she'd got her memory back. He could have cut and run, but he didn't. She remembered it as if it was yesterday.

"That does it," said Debbie, "I'm going over there!"

"What," cried Sheila.

"I just called the stud farm again. It seems that husband of Pam's has just booked himself into a rehabilitation unit. Talk about shutting the gate after the horse has bolted," exclaimed Debbie angrily. "There's still no sign of Pam. God knows what's been going on."

"What'll you do, where will you go?"

"Sheila, at this moment, I don't really care. All I know is my husband has vanished and no one seems to know where he's gone. I guess I'll have to start at the farm."

"Kentucky!"

"You've got it."

James had greeted the news of Debbie's decision to fly to Kentucky with trepidation.

"I know I can't stop you, but have you really thought this through?"

"Oh James, you've been so kind, but my mind's made up. I'm going insane, not knowing where Jack is, or what he's up to. I have to find him."

"At least wait another week or so, if there's no news then go."

"I'm going now James," said Debbie in a tone that he recognised to mean the subject was closed.

"Well at least let me come with you," he pleaded.

"I'm going alone. It's going to be hard enough for him accepting I'm alive as it is. What'll he say if I turn up with a complete stranger?"

"Oh, is that all I am, a complete stranger?" cried James, the hurt undisguised.

"I didn't mean it like that, I'm sorry, it's just the way it came out. Look, I'll only be gone a couple of weeks. If I don't find him, at least I'll know I tried."

James took some small comfort from her words.

Her answers to his questions were well rehearsed; she'd said almost identical words to Bob when he questioned her wisdom. What neither of them knew was that Debbie needed to get away from them all.

For six months she'd been plain Jane Doe, though she called herself Holly after the area where she was found, Christmas Common. She'd begun to build herself a new life, a new identity, she knew she was fairly intelligent and from what people had said, very attractive. James had been marvellous, showing as he confessed when they shared a pub lunch in the Royal Oak at Oxford, a more than professional interest in her well being. She'd been flattered by his attention and to some extent shared that mutual attraction, but her rational mind wouldn't allow herself to commit to anything other than a platonic relationship. Out there, a husband, perhaps a child, maybe several, all of them waiting for that knock on the door, that would restore their lives to normality. And then without warning, her memory returned. Gone was the vulnerable Holly, in her place the vivacious, confident, caring Debbie, loving wife and mother.

Debbie reflected on her situation, if only Jack had been there, her transition back to the world that she'd known, would have been complete. But he wasn't, and James was, it was a dilemma that she didn't want to face. She loved Jack with all her heart, nothing could change that, but she couldn't ignore the feelings she had for James. How often she'd lain awake wishing James was there beside her, how many times she'd placed the invisible barrier that she now knew as Jack, between them. As the days turned to weeks without any news of Jack's whereabouts, Debbie grew fearful for her feelings towards James. How much longer would it be before *she finally gave in to her own desires? These were the questions that frightened her. All she knew was, she had to find Jack, she had to distance herself from James, she had too . . .*

James drove Debbie to the airport and insisted on escorting her to the check in desk at Heathrow's Terminal 4. In the inside pocket of his jacket he carried his passport, 'just in case,' he thought hopefully. He'd already provisionally booked the time off; a phone-call and the purchase of a ticket were but formalities. All Debbie had to say was, "I wish you were coming with me." Nearing the entrance to International departures his hopes faded.

"I'll miss you," he said as he kissed her affectionately on the cheek.

"I'll miss you too," she replied, and it was true.

Debbie arrived a few minutes early at the coffee shop and found a suitable table close to the window, but with enough privacy for a heart to heart. The waitress appeared almost instantly, pencil and pad in hand.

"I'm waiting for someone," she said rather too abruptly. "Sorry," she corrected herself. "My friend should be here in a few minutes, so when she does could we both have a cappuccino."

"Certainly madam," said the waitress just about recovering from her rebuke.

As if on cue Sheila bounced through the open glass door of the new and fancy coffee shop, smiled and sat her self down facing Debbie.

"I took the liberty and ordered you a cappuccino."

"Perfect," replied Sheila.

Sheila quietly complimented herself on her casual entrance while steeling herself for the announcement that would throw Debbie's life into turmoil.

"So how did the honeymoon go? Are they both suntanned and relaxed or are they still white and tired looking like all honeymooners," joked Sheila.

"They're fine; they had the time of their lives." Debbie felt herself on edge, why she hadn't a clue. But something was wrong. "Now what gives? You haven't brought me out here just to discuss the love lives of twenty some things."

At that point the waitress re-appeared carrying two cups of cappuccino complete with a side biscuit each.

"Thank you," said Debbie slightly agitated that the waitress had chosen that moment to deliver their drinks.

As the waitress turned her back and receded to the other side of the room Sheila answered her sister-in-law. "You're right. I haven't. But it's not the love lives of twenty something's I'm on about, its forty something's. Jack in particular."

At the mention of his name Debbie's blood ran cold. It wasn't that she was averse to talking about him, because from time to time his name would be brought up, it was only natural. But it was in the context of Sheila's words.

"Jack. What about him? Have you news?"

"He's alive. He was at Charlotte's wedding. Don't ask me why, I couldn't tell you if I knew. Bob saw him. He tried to talk him into seeing you, but the shock at finding out you were still alive threw him, threw him bad. He left the next morning and went back to Montana."

"Montana!"

Debbie was dumbfounded. Sheila waited, allowing her words to sink in.

"All these years and Jack's been living in Montana and not a word!" cried Debbie in disbelief.

"Was in Montana," replied Sheila. "He's here, he wants to meet you."

Debbie shook her head from side to side, "No, no, no. I can't meet him. My life's changed, I'm a different person. No, no, no . . . ."

"He's changed too. He's . . . ." Sheila stopped herself, but she knew it was too late.

"He's what? Sheila he's what?"

"Keep your voice down, people are looking. He's married; he's got a couple of kids."

"More than a couple," said Debbie bitterly. He sired one in Kentucky as well."

"What!" It was Sheila's turn to be taken aback.

"Oh you didn't know about that one." Her voice took on a shrill edge. "You remember Pam, nice sweet Pammy." Debbie was hurting inside and under normal circumstances would have kept that to herself, but it hurt, it hurt like hell.

Still reeling, Sheila pulled herself together. "Kids or not, he's come all this way and he wants to see you."

"I'm going," cried Debbie, "I don't want to see him. Tell him to go back to Montana! You tell him that, he isn't wanted here, tell him to go back to his wife and kids!"

The cups shook as Debbie grabbed her bag and raced out of the coffee shop in a very distressed manner. Sheila was left in a state of shock.

Chapter 8

Marlow

It had been one of those days when everything that could go wrong does go wrong, but at least he had the evening to look forward too, thought James. When he walked through the front door he sensed his day was going to get a whole lot worse. He found Debbie in tears on their bed.

"What's wrong darling. Tell me, it can't be that bad, you know a trouble shared is a trouble halved and all that." It had been one of James saying for more years than he could remember.

"Not this time. It's Jack, he's alive, he's staying at Bob and Sheila's and he wants to see me."

James felt like someone was pounding on his chest with a sled hammer. This was the moment he'd feared, a fear that had stayed with him through their early years together and now finally that fear had started to diminish, only to be resurrected with a vengeance.

"I've told Sheila I don't want to see him. I've told her to tell him to go back to his home in Montana, back to his wife and kids."

James lifted Debbie into his arms, snatching a sprig of hope from her final words, "back to his wife and kids."

"How could he? Why now? Oh why couldn't he have remained dead, well dead to us I mean," she added quickly.

The evening wore on, with nothing resolved until mentally exhausted Debbie retired to her bed. As James lay on his back staring up at the ceiling, Debbie's grief torn body asleep by his side he began to remember the pain he'd felt when she first left him to try to find Jack so many years before.

Sadly he'd watched and waved, as she'd hurried through the entrance to passport control. Even when she'd disappeared from view he remained transfixed, hoping to catch a final glimpse of her, before she rushed for her gate. He couldn't help himself from hoping her trip would be a waste of time. He'd known her but a few brief months, but she'd transformed his life.

A widower for the last nine years, he'd thrown himself into his work. Long hours, the bane of young doctors hadn't fazed him in the slightest. In fact he welcomed the busyness of his life; it helped him to cope with the tragic loss of Jill. Indirectly the death of his wife led to his discovery of Debbie. Jill had died suddenly from a virus that attacked the nervous system. For a time James was overcome with grief, how could someone as lovely and full of life as Jill be taken from him? But as the weeks of mourning became months, he suddenly pulled himself together. The swiftness of the disease focused James's mind and career in the direction of neurology. Throwing himself into years of dedicated study he finally arrived as a leader in his field of medicine. With his success came financial rewards and the inevitable string of glamorous girl friends. Yet none could hold a candle to his dead wife, until Debbie literally stumbled along.

As he drove back from the airport, he passed the very spot where the accident that brought Debbie into his life happened. He couldn't help himself from visualising her terrible ordeal that cold and dark November night, when she staggered across fields, fell panic stricken into ditches, and scrambled frantically though hedges not knowing who she was or what had happened to her. She was some lady, he thought as he recalled their first meeting.

He'd expected a confused, frustrated, perhaps bad tempered patient, which in his experience was quite common. Instead he found a beautiful lively and chatty young woman, though underneath the exterior he sensed a deep vulnerability. She affected him almost from the moment he first saw her. He resisted it at first, telling himself she was a beautiful young lady who would have turned any man's head. But deep down he knew there was more to this sensitive, vulnerable woman than he'd first thought. As the days became weeks, he found his attraction to her growing, so much so that as soon as he was sure he'd done all he could for her, he discharged her into the capable hands of a colleague. Debbie was hurt and a little apprehensive at another doctor taking over her case, that was until James reassured her, she was in safe hands. It was over dinner that night he told her he wanted to take a more positive role in her rehabilitation.

Debbie in that easy going manner that he'd fallen in love with expressed her feelings towards him.

"You've been a good friend to me, more than that, you're everything I could ever want in my life at this precise moment, but it's too early for me. Until I find out who I am, I can't possibly embark on a new relationship. I might be married, I might have children. I know if that's true, that I'd love them very much. Don't ask me how I know, it just feels that way."

"But it could take years before your memory comes back. It may never come back," James said, and regretted it the moment the words trembled from his lips.

"I know, but until I'm entirely comfortable with who I am, then . . . " She left the sentence unfinished.

"That doesn't change a damn thing," he said, pausing while he thought through his next words carefully. "No matter how long it takes, I'll be there for you. At the very least, I couldn't bear it if we weren't friends. I've never wanted anyone since Jill's death, but you've changed all that. For the present, I'll just have to accept being your friend."

And good friend he turned out to be. Using his considerable influence he sorted out her new identity, insurance cards, the tax office, and he even managed to swing Debbie a job at the local newspaper.

"You need somewhere to stay," he said after there second date. "It just so happens, I own a small cottage in Weston on the Green, it's a little run down and could do with a coat of paint, but if it's any good to you, it's yours for a nominal rent."

"No! I can't possibly accept. You've done so much. I need to be able to help myself," she exclaimed.

His face broke into an enormous grin, "Yeah, fine. How are you going to accomplish that without a little help from your friends?"

"I can't keep taking from you," she implored.

"One day little lady, when you're on your feet you can repay me. But until then, let me indulge you."

A mischievous smile appeared on Debbie's face, "Answer me one question, and answer it honestly."

"Okay."

"You've been more than kind, but would you have been so generous if I'd been old and grey."

James was thrown off balance. He was a kind and thoughtful man, but if Debbie hadn't have been so beautiful, would he have left the caring to others? His eyes answered for him.

"I'm sorry James. That was unkind and cruel of me. But you have to understand how I feel. I don't know who I am, I don't know where I come from, but I do know, any feelings I have towards you must come from the heart, not from any misguided feelings of gratitude."

"Good, I'm glad that's settled," he said sardonically. "We'll move you in over the week-end."

*   *   *

He was almost to the hospital gates when he indicated and turned around at a nearby junction. "Sod it, they can do without me today," he said out loud to the dashboard. Within twenty minutes he was in the centre of Weston on the Green. He parked in a designated parking spot and fished in his pocket for the keys Debbie had given him just before she flew out.

"I won't need these anymore," she'd said not unkindly, but her words burned into him like a white hot knife. It was as if she was severing all ties. She'd have laughed if she'd known what he was thinking, even he knew that. But it didn't alter the fact that she was gone. She wasn't even in Marlow, she was at that moment crossing the western coastline of Scotland, winging her way to a *husband that had believed she was dead for the last six months. James looked up and down the small village, it was pretty at any time of year, but his favourite had to be the springtime, when the tree lined thoroughfare was a mass of pink blossom. Now spring was giving way to summer's rush of colour. Hanging baskets of lobelia, fuchsia and petunias decorated cottage, shops and pubs alike. Wispy clouds floated in a sea of blue, while the sun's rays bathed the village in sunlight. 'Debbie would have loved Weston at this time of year,' he thought sadly.*

Since the return of Debbie's memory he hadn't been inside the cottage, so it didn't come as a surprise when he found himself hesitating at the front door. He steeled himself as he put the key in the lock. It was as he'd suspected, her presence was in every room. James looked longingly at the open grate and remembered the fireside chats they'd had during the cold days of winter. He'd always enjoyed the spring, but looking back he wished those long dark nights could have gone on forever. Torturing himself even further, he entered the small bathroom and caught a faint whiff of her perfume.

"God, what's wrong with me," he said as he caught a glimpse of himself in the mirror. He wasn't the type to wallow in self pity, but his frustrations were at last getting to him. He'd known, even before he'd embarked on the crusade that it could all end in tears. He couldn't help that, he was infatuated with her. He'd said as much to his old friend and colleague Don Lawton one night whilst under the influence of too much drink. "I don't care, it might be this year, the next, or maybe even never," he'd said hopefully. "I just love being in her company." Well now it was all over with, and in a couple of weeks Debbie would return with her husband and all he'd have left would be memories.

Sometime during the night James had fallen into a troubled sleep. He awoke to find that Debbie was already up and dressed and making coffee. She too had lain awake for part of the night and she too had remembered their first parting.

Within minutes of collecting her suitcase from Louisville Airport's baggage claim, Debbie emerged into the Kentucky sunshine. Her first impulse was to hire a car and head straight to the stud farm. But then she realised that she was tired, Phil was in rehabilitation, God knows where, and Pam still hadn't surfaced. Deciding to book into a decent motel, get a good night's sleep and be fresh for the following morning, sounded the best option.

It seemed funny phoning the Lassiter Stud Farm and making an appointment. An anonymous voice answered and listened patiently as Debbie explained who she was, and why she'd come.

"I'm not sure I can be of much help, but Gary's the Farm manager, he'll maybe throw some light on the subject," he offered.

"Gary," said Debbie excitedly. At last a familiar name, she thought. She'd known Gary almost as long as she'd known Phil. "Yes, I know Gary."

"Good," said the anonymous voice, "I'll see he's at the house around eleven o'clock, if that's okay."

"Eleven's fine."

It was five past eleven when Debbie arrived at the white entrance gate to the Lassiter's Stud Farm. She climbed out and opened the gate then remembering all she'd been taught closed the gate after she'd driven through. As she approached the house Gary came out to greet her.

"Hi Debbie, it's been a while." He scratched his head and smiled. "Ain't you the prettiest ghost I've seen in a long time?"

Debbie smiled, unsure what to say.

"Come into the house. A cold glass of lemonade will perk you up."

Gary led her into the ante room which doubled as an office. "Take a seat, I'll go fetch that lemonade."

Debbie sat down on the padded green leather backed chair and looked around the oak panelled room. Nothing had changed much.

"Here you go," said Gary as he re-entered the room a minute or two later and handed Debbie her lemonade. He placed a white paper coaster on the green leather top of the desk that Debbie was sitting in front of and then he walked around and sat opposite her.

"Thanks. I'll come straight to the point. I take it from what you said earlier that you're aware of what happened to me over the last six months?"

"Well yeah, but I'm a little puzzled."

"I thought you might. It's a long story. I won't bore you with the details but suffice to say I had an accident, I lost my memory, and everyone thought I was dead." Impulsively she blurted out, "Gary I'm looking for Jack. Do you know where he is?"

"Nope. I'm sorry I can't help you. All I can say is he was here up to a couple of months ago. He seemed to like it here, and that's the funny thing. He just suddenly took off, without a by your leave or nuthin. Of course he said his goodbyes to Mr and Mrs Lassiter. She even took him to the airport, and that's about all I know. I will say one thing though."

"What's that? The hesitancy in Debbie voice rang loud and clear.

"When he arrived I'd never seen a man so cut up as him. I reckon when he finds out you're still alive he'll come racing back faster than any of those horses we got in them stalls."

It was meant in the friendliest of terms and under normal circumstances Debbie would have smiled and took the compliment in her stride, instead she blushed. "Where's Phil staying?" She couldn't bring herself to say more.

"He's at Green Gables. It's close to Louisville; I think it's on the last off ramp before you head into the city."

"Thanks Gary," said Debbie as she stood up and extended her hand across the desk.

* * *

Manicured lawns sweeping up to the walls of Green Gables were like an advancing sea of green The imposing structure of white stucco and green tiled roofs, lent the building an air of Southern grace. Debbie couldn't help thinking that this brief sojourn must be costing Phil a pretty penny. She parked the rental car in the visitors parking bay, looked towards the entrance and within a few seconds she climbed the steps to reception. There she *was escorted to a private day room and offered afternoon tea. She accepted gracefully and waited for Phil to arrive.*

She'd barely sipped her tea when the tall imposing figure of Phil walked in.

"Debbie, I can't begin to tell you how good it is to see you."

"It's good to see you too," said Debbie pleasantly.

Phil could tell by her body language that she wasn't comfortable with the pleasantries. "Right, I'll come straight to the point. I'm sorry I wasn't as communicative as I should have been when I spoke to you on the phone."

"Apology accepted," said Debbie, and a familiar smile erupted across her face. "Phil, I'm sorry you and Pam are having a rough time of it. I expect things will turn out okay in the end."

"Debbie you ain't come all the ways here to wish me well, so spit it out. What is it you're a wanting?"

"I just want to find Jack."

"Okay, let me tell you all I know, then you can tell me how you rose from the dead."

Debbie gave out a nervous laugh. "Begin."

"Jack was distraught when he arrived. His world had fallen apart. I think I know how he feels. His time with us seemed to work wonders. Pam was very patient with him. He was troubled and, well you know Pam, she was trying her best to help him through his problems."

Debbie felt a twinge of jealousy; Pam was an extremely attractive lady. "I think I know what you're alluding to, the problems, I mean." she interjected.

"It's none of my business, but I'm sure you'll tell me," cried Phil, his embarrassment clearly showing.

"I'll explain later," said Debbie.

"He'd been with us a couple of month when he told us both that he wanted to invest in a small stud farm."

"He, what!"

"Yeah. I know it sounds crazy, but he started making all sorts of plans, until . . ."

"Until what?"

"Until he phoned Charlotte and asked her to come over to live. I believe she refused and begged Jack to come home. He's a

stubborn one that husband of yours, seems he couldn't face living back there in Marlow."

"They're both stubborn. Go on."

"Well that's about the long and the short of it. A couple of days later, out of the blue it was, he tells me he's heading west."

"What did Pam make of it?"

"I don't know, she kind of went quiet on me after he'd left."

Debbie's face grew ashen, and the words came out before she could stop herself, "You don't think anything was going on do you?"

"Hell no, Pam and me, well we're both going through a rough time. Ain't nothing to do with Jack. He's like a brother for Christ-sake."

Debbie felt a warm glow of relief, "Out west you say, where?"

"Phoenix as I recall. Going to look up old friends, that's what he said."

"The Chandlers! They live in Phoenix." The excitement grew in Debbie. At last she was getting somewhere. Containing her excitement she turned towards Phil and enquired what had gone so terribly wrong between him and Pam.

"I can't tell it all, but the roots of our problems are back there in Saigon. Things happened there. Bad things! I don't want to dwell on it, but needless to say it's taken a strain on our marriage. I'd get drunk, stoned, well you name it I did it. I never hit her."

Debbie looked at Phil slightly accusingly.

"Believe me Debbie, I wouldn't, I couldn't harm a hair on that girl's head. I love her to bits. Now she's up and went. I reckon I've got to find her and if she's willing, bring her back."

Debbie noticed tears welling up in Phil's eyes.

"I love her. That's why I'm in here. I've got to get my head straight. Then I can go look for her."

"Where will you look?"

"I don't rightly know at the moment. There are ways to find out most everything if you've a mind."

Debbie rose to her feet, the meeting was over. She hugged Phil and wished him well.

"You too Deb, I reckon we'll be laughing about all this come Christmas."

"Before then, I hope," snapped Debbie.

And it was hope that she felt that morning. Perhaps, just perhaps things would work out right. She looked at James sadly, almost apologetically and he knew almost before she spoke what she was about to say.

"I've been thinking. I've changed, you've changed, even he ..." She couldn't bring herself to mention his name, "even he must have changed. Perhaps I should see him, if just to clear the air. But if you don't want me too, I won't. If it's going to distress you I won't go anywhere near," and she meant it too.

Even though James knew she meant it and even though she'd give him her word not to see him, he knew she would regret it for the rest of her life. Choking back his emotions he said, "You have to see him, if you don't it'll come between us."

Debbie said nothing.

Chapter 9

Kentucky

Pam had had difficulty in sleeping. Phil had commented about it but she'd brushed it off as just a slight case of insomnia. "It'll work itself out." she'd said casually that morning. And she was probably right, but the truth of the matter was from the moment she'd place that announcement in those Montana papers she'd begun to worry. She hoped for everyone's sake that she hadn't opened Pandora's Box. Pam remembered oh so clearly that time. A time of rebirth, a time of new beginnings and she remembered clearly the time when Debbie and James paid them a visit.

Pam nursed Jared Barclay and paced up and down the bedroom floor. She'd seen the car pull up suddenly in the long driveway from her window, and then seconds later watched in nervous anticipation as it continued its journey towards the house. It was Debbie, her intuition told her, she'd come seeking answers. Pam had known this moment would arrive, yet despite the dramas she'd been through during the last eighteen months she was surprised that this meeting should feel so daunting.

Her marriage to Phil had for many years been a sham, but now after what happened in Mexico it was at last, she hoped, on firm foundations. She'd often envied Debbie her marriage to Jack. They were contented in everything they did and it was obvious to everyone that they were very much in love. This must have made it more heartbreaking for Jack when he thought he'd lost her, in more ways than one. The torment in his eyes was what drew her to him, she should have seen the dangers, but she was caught up in a maelstrom of emotions that could have only one outcome. She regretted her infidelity, her betrayal of Phil, the man she'd loved for better or for worse for so many years, but looking down at her baby son she realised that she wouldn't change a damn thing.

Pam settled Jared Barclay down in his crib watched and waited until she was sure he'd fallen asleep, then tip-toed across to the dressing table. A quick check on her makeup and hair, a glance across at the sleeping form of her son and she was ready for anything. As she approached the stairs she could hear Phil's deep throaty voice entertaining the new arrivals. Small talk seemed out of place, but circumstances had brought them to this point. She took a deep breath, put on her best smile and descended the stairs.

It was clear from the first moment that this was going to be an awkward situation. Debbie smiled at Pam but the latter could feel no warmth from it. James was introduced as a friend. 'How much of a friend?' thought Pam in a catty sort of way that she instantly regretted. It was abundantly obvious to Pam that Debbie had her suspicions and that she was impatient to get down to the nitty gritty.

"Mind if I join you?" she said as she poured herself a large brandy.

"As you're probably aware I'm still looking for Jack," said Debbie nervously. "He seems to have vanished off the face of the earth."

"And you think we, I can shed some light on his disappearance."

"Yes I do," said Debbie firmly.

Pam looked at Phil for support; he smiled back at her and nodded his encouragement. She'd thought to bluff it out, but she had too much respect for her cousin. If she asked, then she deserved the truth, if nothing else.

"Jack and I thought you were dead," cried Pam.

"Well I'm very much alive!"

'She knew,' Pam could see it in her eyes, in her stance and most prominently in her voice. "I'm so sorry."

Those words confirmed to Debbie what she'd suspected all along, but she hadn't counted on the blow her stomach took. She felt sick enough to throw up over Pam's new carpet. Dignity however prevented her from it.

"You slept with Jack!"

James and Phil exchanged uncomfortable glances.

"It only happened the one time," it was a white lie, but Pam saw no point in rubbing Debbie's nose in it. That particular chore would come after Jared Barclay woke from his slumber.

"One time or not, what gave you the right?"

Debbie was red faced with anger, 'The bitch, she's my cousin for Christ-sake, I looked on her as a friend, some friend she turned out to be,' the rage inside Debbie threatened to explode.

"I'm sorry Deb. It happened, we can't go changing it." Her words were strongly put. "We all thought you were dead, it's Phil that was betrayed, not you!" Now it was Pam's turn to be red faced with anger. "He's the one that suffered, we've both suffered more than you could possible know."

"And what's that supposed to mean?"

Phil looked across at Pam nervously, but it was too late. "Upstairs, there's a baby, my baby, mine and Phil's."

"Bu . . . but I thought!"

"You thought right, but what's important is that Phil has accepted the child as his own."

"It's Jack's baby?"

"No! It's mine. Jack knows nothing about it."

Debbie slumped back in the tanned leather chair, her face white with shock.

Phil looked across to Pam and said quietly, "Pam, she's a right to know the whole story."

"Are you sure? What about . . . ."

"Tell her everything."

"Debbie, I owe you at least that, but first you have to know that it would never have happened if we'd thought you were alive."

Debbie still reeling from the shock news that Pam had Jack's child upstairs glared angrily at Pam but nodded her acceptance.

Pam took a deep breath, "Are you aware of what Jack believed?"

"Yes, but there was no foundation," snapped Debbie.

"I know that now, but Jack was eaten up with the thought. It was destroying him from within. He was a tormented soul, and I did my best to bring him out of himself."

"I bet you did," interrupted Debbie bitterly.

Pam chose to ignore Debbie's outburst, in the circumstances she'd have done the same or even worse.

"During the three months he stayed with us, both Phil and I worked at getting Jack over his loss. We encouraged him in his interest in the stud farm. It seemed to take him out of himself. We saw it as a good sign of a recovery. Believe me Jack was suffering more than you could possibly imagine. We even encouraged him with his harebrained scheme to open a stud of his own. After Charlotte told Jack she wanted nothing to do with his dream, he retreated into the man he was when he first arrived.

"Don't you tell me it's Charlotte's fault!"

I'm not saying Charlotte was wrong, on the contrary she was probably right but it put him back. You see over the months he'd begun to piece his life back together again. The stud farm or the dream of one was his way of starting a new life, and Charlotte had thrown it back in his face. I couldn't bear to see him so down, we'd become very close. I reached out to console him and it happened, you see my marriage to Phil was all but dying," she smiled up at her giant of a husband

He smiled back reassuringly

Pam was almost in tears, but she took a deep breath and continued. "Anyway the day after it happened he told me he was leaving. He said he was ashamed of what he'd done."

"It takes two," spat Debbie.

"Believe me I know that. He left the following weekend, a month later I found out I was pregnant."

Phil put a reassuring arm on Pam's shoulder, he sensed the tension needed easing, and that she needed a break "I'd like to say a few words. Pam's telling the truth, although I didn't realise it at the time. I wasn't fit to live with, drink, drugs, you name it, I took it."

"Hey!" cried James, "this is family stuff; you don't want a stranger listening in to family secrets. I'll go wait in the car."

"No need for that," cried Debbie. "You've been there for me from the start."

Pam involuntarily gave Phil a knowing look, which Debbie couldn't help but notice.

"It's nothing like that, we're just good friends, I'm not like you, I don't have the morals of an alley cat!" She could have bit off her tongue, she hadn't meant to let herself go, but it was done.

Pam felt her hackles rise, she'd been open and above board, yet Debbie wouldn't let it rest.

"There's no call for that! I think you'd better leave!"

"I think you're right," replied Debbie.

Minutes later they were in the car and heading back to the hotel.

Yes it had been a stormy meeting; it couldn't have been anything but, thought Pam. But at least it was out in the open. Why, she kept asking was she tormenting herself with these thoughts? They belonged to a different time, to a different place. She cursed herself for being such a damn fool. The thought that Jack might read that article and fly home seemed almost unbelievable, but the more she thought about it the more she saw the repercussions. What if Jack read the article, what if he actually went to the wedding? The permutations in her head were endless. She needed space to think, to clear her head, to sort out what was bothering her once and for all.

Jared was at school, Phil was in Knoxville, and Pam had an urge to ride. Saddling up an Arabian that was gentle and responsive she rode out to the lower pasture at a fast gait. With the wind in her hair and the sun against her back she gave the Arabian its head. The exhilaration of the first time she'd ridden a fast horse had never left her. By the time she'd brought the horse to a rest she was in the meadow where she and Jack had had many talks during that fateful time.

Pam again thought back to that visit with Debbie and how it had turned out.

The phone rang just as Pam was putting Jared down for his morning nap. She grabbed it quickly so as to not wake him. It was Debbie.

"I think I owe you an apology, I had my suspicions, but I never expected a baby, it threw me. Anyway, I'm sorry, I shouldn't have shouted at you like that. You were right, in your eyes you only betrayed Phil. I guess in time I'll come to accept what happened."

"Debs, you don't have to apologies to me, I understand what you must be going through, I'm so sorry it happened, but then again if it hadn't I wouldn't have Jared Barclay." Pam could feel Debbie cringe at the other end of the phone and wished she'd kept her mouth shut.

"I bet he's a good baby, one day maybe you'll let me see him."

"Debbie I'd love you to see him, he's beautiful. Why don't you and James come back to the farm? Yesterday was a shock to all of us, I don't know where Jack is, but I did go in search of him. I was pregnant with his child, Phil was like a time bomb ready to explode, you were dead, well at least I thought you were. I was going out of my mind and thought that if I could find Jack he'd know what to do. Things happened to me . . ." For a moment the phone went dead.

"Hello," cried Debbie, are you still there. Pam, speak to me."

"Sorry, I'm still here. It's just that it's too painful to talk about on the phone."

Intrigued by Pam's phone conversation Debbie agreed a time with her and arrived back at the farm the following morning.

* * *

Jared Barclay was crawling around the nursery when Debbie and James arrived. Pam picked him up like the proud parent she was and presented him to Debbie, "Not the most tactful thing to do," said Phil later that night. Debbie held Jared Barclay in her arms and looked into his deep blue eyes; the resemblance to Jack was uncanny. She felt a tinge of jealousy but let it waft over her.

James tactfully asked Phil about the workings of the stud farm and Phil was only to willing to give him a guided tour.

"We're best out of it, women's talk," quipped Phil.

James grinned, "Right, show me the winners."

When Pam put Jared to sleep in his crib, a tension crept over her. She knew she was about to revisit the horrors of what happened in Mexico. She didn't know whether Jack was alive or dead, what she did know was that the woman before her deserved to know the truth of that crazy time. Only then could she begin to understand why God had given her and Phil a second chance. She poured Debbie a very large gin and tonic, sat her down and began her narration.

"I knew Jack had booked a flight to Phoenix, so I followed."

Debbie interrupted her just as she'd begun. "I know about Phoenix and the Chandler's. They as I'm sure you're aware were very good friends of mine and Jack's. I paid a visit on Karen Chandler, but she couldn't throw any light on where Jack had gone. Sorry I didn't mean to be a bit previous, go on with your story."

"After visiting with Karen I took a bus down to Tucson."

"Tucson! Why Tucson?"

Pam looked at her questioningly.

"Why Tucson?" repeated Debbie. "Karen never mentioned Tucson."

For a moment Pam was lost for words, then she recalled that it was on the way back to Sky Harbour Airport when Tom Chandler who'd kindly offered to drive her back, realised that he'd driven Jack to the bus depot, not the airport as he'd first thought.

"The bus depot, why the bus depot?" she'd asked.

"As I recall, Jack didn't know where he was heading, but he did mention Tucson."

"Take me to the bus depot, forget the airport."

Debbie excited by the new revelation exclaimed, "Why didn't Karen mention this to me?"

"I'd hazard a guess that Tom never mentioned it to her. As you'll recall they both had more important things on their minds"

"Yes, I suppose they did," replied Debbie.

Pam looked at Debbie's empty glass smiled and offered her another. She was about to take Debbie on a journey, a journey that would need the fortifications of a few very stiff drinks.

"Where in Tucson? I thought. It was turning into my worse nightmare. When I found out I was pregnant I panicked, I hadn't allowed myself time to think. My only plan had been to find Jack, and put as many miles between myself and Phil. I was beside myself with grief and worry, but things were about to change."

"Oh Pam, you must have been in such torment. I never realized," cried Debbie.

Pam smiled back at her cousin and hoped that she'd still feel the same when she knew the rest of the story.

Pam relived the visit to the hospital, where she learned about an Englishman that had been seriously wounded in a knife attack.

"He's not dead, tell me he's not dead," cried Debbie in a blind panic.

"No, Debs, he was very much alive. One minute I'd been lying there, contemplating the journey home, the next I'm showing the hospital staff a photograph of Jack. Even then, if it hadn't been for one young nurse recognizing him, I might not have continued my odyssey."

It was only by luck that I found a small cantina called Kate's Place. I learned that Jack and another man had hung out there, until the shooting."

"The shooting? You can't be serious."

"Something happened across the border and I believe Jack was involved in it somehow."

Debbie broke into Pam's story, "What did the police have to say?"

Pam smiled, "That was my first reaction. But we're talking Mexico." She left the rest unsaid.

"Tell me, tell me before you go on, is Jack dead?" cried Debbie.

"I don't know, I truly don't." said Pam. I'd reached a dead end, the trail ended there, but for me there was the birth of my son Jared Barclay. I was so happy; I was getting my life back on track. I'd decided to face Phil, take what was coming to me and get on with my life, but fate had another turn awaiting me." It was as if a dark cloud had settled over Pam, she appeared weak and exhausted, as if what she was about to reveal to Debbie was so horrible to contemplate. "Do you mind if we wait for Phil, I don't want to go into what happened without him by my side?"

Pam sat there staring into space; she recalled that visit had really reopened the wound. It had caused her more suffering than she could bear leaving a festering silence which lingered between her and Phil.

For two days they'd fought shy of any conversation about their recent visitors, using only polite chi-chat as they moved uneasily around each other. Phil knew that if the silence wasn't broken between them the healing process would soon unravel. Since they'd left Kate's Place neither of them had spoke of those dark days. Somehow or other both of them had believed that blocking it from their memories would make matters right. True the pain and suffering of Pam's ordeal and Phil's intervention had dimmed to a distant memory but what remained was something neither of them had been prepared to contemplate, until now.

Thankfully Phil, unable to continue the pretext, made a decision. With heart in mouth, he knew he had to breach the subject with Pam if there was any chance of the marriage surviving. He caught her standing on the veranda with her back towards him as she gazed aimless towards the fading light of early evening.

"Pammy, we need to talk," he said to her back as he stepped onto the veranda and placed his hands gently upon her shoulders. Pam just stared out towards the far meadows of the farm, tears obliterating the dying rays of the evening sun.

"I know," she sobbed.

"Look Pam, I meant ever word I said to you in Nogales; every word."

"I know you did, but what if Jack came back? What then?"

Hearing Pam utter Jack's name sent a searing white hot flame coursing across his heart. With a conviction he didn't hardly feel, he replied. "That, my dear, would be down to you. If you love me the way you say you do, I've nothing to fear."

"Oh Phil, I love you more than words. Jack shouldn't have happened, but he did and there's nothing I can do about it. If he hadn't happened, well maybe things between us might have worsened."

"You're right Pam and maybe in a strange way it's brought us closer. I hope so." Then Phil spun her round and kissed away

her salty tears. "*That you love me is all the reassurance I need. Everything else can go to hell. It's you and me and Jared Barclay that matters, not outsiders.*"

The wound that had so recently been reopened started to heal.

Even now the thought of what happened sent an icy shiver down her spine. Pam cleared her head, thoughts like those could eat you up inside. She'd been punished in the worst way possible for her misdeeds, dwelling on them served no purpose at all. That in a small and clumsy way she'd tried telling Jack that Debbie was alive was best left to speculation. She had the stud farm, she had a comfortable lifestyle, she had the man of her dreams in Phil and she had a son that she loved beyond anything. Yes, thought Pam as she kicked the Arabian into a gentle lope back towards the farmhouse, she had it all.

Chapter 10

Marlow

Jack stared into Debbie's dark almond shaped eyes and was transported back in time. "You . . . you haven't changed, you're just lovelier than ever," his eyes blurred with watery tears. That she'd agreed to see him came as quite a shock. Sheila had returned to the house and told Jack that Debbie had told her in no uncertain terms that she didn't want to see him ever.

"I'm sorry, I was wrong," said Bob. "I could have sworn . . . ."

"Jack, I reckon it's knocked the stuffing out of Debbie. Maybe in time she'll come around. I just don't know," said Sheila dejectedly.

"Well I guess that's that," replied Jack. "Reckon I'll book my flight home."

"In the circumstances, I think that's wise," said Sheila.

Jack accepted that going home was probably the best option. True it was the coward's way out, but he reasoned it was Debbie's choice. Then on the Thursday the phone had rung and turned all his plans on their head. Debbie had agreed to see him the following morning around ten o'clock on the suspension bridge at Marlow.

Seeing her there brought it all back. Instinctively they fell into each others arms only to recoil moments later, embarrassed and angry at their automatic reactions.

"Let's walk," said Jack.

Debbie nodded in return and fell in maybe a defensive step behind. They crossed the Thames and made their way onto the tow path and started walking up river

It was Debbie who broke the silence. "What a mess, I should have told you about Dave and Julie. He was your best friend."

"Possibly, but I had no right to believe what I believed."

"Yes Jack, you're right about that, but what I find harder to believe is that you'd abandon our daughter. That's what I can't figure out."

"I have no defence. I acted like a child; I let my feelings get the better of me. I should have known you wouldn't cheat on me."

"Yes you should have!" Debbie reproached herself for raising her voice. She looked back the way they'd come and forward to a woman walking her dog. She gave the woman an apologetic look then turned back toward Jack. "But I think you must have been in a terrible emotional state to do what you did."

"It's no apology, but yes I was in such a state. I couldn't help myself, I was wallowing in self pity, all I could think about was getting away from it all." Jack refrained from telling her about his suicidal thoughts that Christmas Eve on the suspension bridge. It would serve no purpose other than to fudge the blame. Debbie didn't deserve that.

"So you took yourself off to my cousin's to be consoled." She hadn't meant for it to come out that way, but it was done.

"You know all about that," replied Jack a little taken aback.

"Oh yes! I know everything, including the little matter of the child that you spawned." Why she'd said it she couldn't rightly say, perhaps to shock, to cause hurt, to create mischief?

"I know about the boy," he said defensively. Their meeting wasn't going to plan, but what did he expect, moonlight and roses.

Debbie looked stunned.

"It's a long story, but someone told me I'd got Pam pregnant. Once I found out I flew back to Kentucky."

"Do you love her?" interrupted Debbie.

"No, I didn't then nor since. We met, she told me about Jared Barclay and she begged me to stay out of her life, which I've done. At the time the only person I loved was you!"

"And now!"

"And now," said Jack, his thoughts returning to Montana, I love my wife, my Tara."

"And how do you feel about me. You loved me once; you loved me enough to move to another country."

Jack stopped in his tracks, turned and faced Debbie. He smiled that broad smile; that smile with that certain sparkle in his eyes and said, "I still love you, I've never stopped loving you."

Any hostility that Debbie still held against him melted like snow on the Sahara.

"Oh Jack," then without warning she threw herself into his arms and found her mouth pressing firmly and passionately to his. They stayed that way as a cyclist manoeuvred around them, another dog walker tut tutted and a couple of school girls giggled. Then the moment was broken as they retreated back within themselves.

Shocked and embarrassed Jack took a step backwards, "Wow! That was something I hadn't expected." He scratched his head and began to unscramble his brain. "If my memory recalls there's a nice little pub up a head. I think we need a drink, don't you?"

Debbie recovering from her actions smiled embarrassedly.

*   *   *

They found a table outside the Flower Pot pub and after Jack had ordered their drinks, sat across from each other.

With a mischievous grin Jack spoke, "Right where do we go from here?"

"I think," said Debbie, now fully recovered from their spontaneous embrace, "we should talk. Fill in the gaps and then we should see how we can tackle the subject of Charlotte."

"Well I think you should start, I gather from Sheila that she's albeit briefly filled you in on my life," said Jack.

"Yes she has, but I'm intrigued to learn more about your extended family."

"Ladies first," he said quickly.

Somewhat taken aback, Debbie searched for a beginning. "James, I have to tell you about James."

"Bob and Sheila told me he was your doctor; they say he was instrumental in getting back your memory. That he fell in love with you, that he even went with you to Kentucky the second time. The man must love you very much."

"Yes he does and it was while we were in Kentucky I realised how much. Without his support I would have found it hard coming to terms with Pam's revelations, what with the baby and all."

"Yo, you, you've seen him," stuttered Jack.

"Seen him, held him in my arms," it was a cruel thing to say, but Debbie couldn't help herself. "It had been a particularly tough time for James, seeing us women sparring around each other. We'd reached a truce of some sort and James had thought it wise to leave us to iron things out by ourselves, so he asked Phil to give him a guided tour of the stud. During the time they were gone, we'd cleared the air, sort of; and had begun having a heart to heart. Pam was about to tell me something terrible when Phil and James walked back in."

Debbie paused for a moment, she knew if she carried on it might be painful for Jack to hear, but she felt she owed it to him to let him know how she felt about James.

"Where was I? Oh yes Phil and James had just walked back in."

"Honey, there's no need to go on, I've filled James in about what happened." said Phil firmly. He smiled at Pam and rested his firm hand upon her shoulder, "You okay?"

"Yes Phil I'm fine." But the drawn look on her face said otherwise.

James looked across at Debbie, "I think that's enough for one day. I don't think Pam needs to relive it."

"But . . . ."

"No buts, I'll fill you in on what happened once we're back at the hotel." said James forcefully. His normal relaxed and casual expression had been exchanged for a look of shock and bewilderment.

"Yes, that would be better," said Phil softly, *"I know how much you want to know, but I think it best coming from James."*

*   *   *

Minutes later they'd said their goodbyes and were driving back to the hotel.

"What is it?" cried Debbie, *"Tell me."*

"Best we wait until we get back to the hotel," James said patiently.

"No! I want to know now," shrieked Debbie. She'd acceded to Phil's suggestion, mainly because of the distressed look upon Pam's face, but she was damned if she was going to sit in the car for the next hour before they got back to the hotel.

"Well Debbie, despite what you want, you'll wait until I'm ready,." replied James, his voice only slightly raised, but enough to shock Debbie into silence. To Debbie that hour felt like an eternity, but eventually they arrived back at their hotel.

James poured him and Debbie a large drink from the mini bar in his hotel room and handed her a gin and tonic. *"Wow! Is Phil on the level? Was he in Special Forces?"*

"I don't know, I'm not sure, maybe, it's possible. Pam met him in Vietnam. He didn't talk much about that time."

"Okay. Oh God I don't know, I guess Phil had no reason to lie. Promise me one thing. What I tell you mustn't go beyond these four walls."

"Steady James, you're frightening me."

"Promise me!"

"Okay, I promise."

"Pam arranged to meet up with this woman called Conchita, who had said she knew the whereabouts of Jack. It turned out that she was a Mexican whore and it was a trick to extort money. It seems Jack had met up with her in the past and she bore him a

grudge. Pam was knocked unconscious and when she woke up she was systematically raped by this foul woman's brothers and held in a filthy room above an old cantina."

"Oh my God!" cried Debbie.

"It gets worse, the long and the short of it, is that Phil tracked Pam to Kate's Place, learned of her disappearance and then called in a few favours at Langley . . ."

"Langley?"

"CIA, or something like them. Phil learned of Pam's plight and took extreme measures to rescue her."

"What about this Conchita person and her brothers?"

"Like I said, Phil took extreme measures."

"And Pam, how . . . .."

"It took months before she was able to come to terms with what happened, but from what Phil told me, she's making good progress. That's why I bundled you out of the house. That and the drive back to the hotel allowed me time to think."

"That sounds ominous."

"Not really. It depends how you look at it." James took a deep breath, thought carefully about his next sentence, and then launched himself. "Jack, whether you like it or not, has disappeared. He might even be dead. Judging by the company he's been keeping, that seems quite likely. Pam hit a dead end and it nearly cost her her life."

Debbie could see what James was alluding too. "But I've got to try . . . ."

"Going to Nogales will get you nowhere; it might get you dead or worse. You've just got to face it Debs, Jack's gone."

Debbie looked at this man, this man that had never raised his voice or spoken out of turn, he was telling her in no uncertain terms that Jack was gone. That there was no point in pursuing the search any further. It was an attractive quality in him that she'd never seen before. All she could do was listen.

"You've done the best you could. Taking it further is both futile and dangerous. If he's alive, he'll surface someday."

Debbie turned white with shock. She knew James was talking sense, that what he said was true, but there was something else in the tone of his voice. There was finality in his words. He was giving up; he'd been patient and caring, going beyond anything Debbie had dreamed possible. He was a good man, better than she deserved, a man that she'd come to rely on, a man that without realising she'd taken for granted, and now she was in danger of letting him go.

"Leave me alone, please leave me alone," she said, "I need time to think."

"If you want me I'll be in my room," replied James.

He gave her one last look before turning towards the door. As he closed it gently behind him, he reflected that he'd done more than most men, given the situation. He likened her to a foreign country, a country without extradition. Minutes later he was repacking his case. He knew Debbie, he knew she would press it to the limits, but this time he was determined she was going it alone. From the phone in his room he called the airport and made a reservation for the following day. He felt numb and a little shell-shocked, but strangely relieved. He'd been living in false hope for over a year now and things hadn't gotten any easier. It was time to quit, He'd given it his best shot, but it hadn't been enough.

As he sat slumped in a chair with a large scotch in his hand he thought about his wife Jill and wondered if his pursuing of Debbie had been his way to deal with the past. He'd loved Jill with all his heart, he still loved her, but she was gone. Was he a fool to think he could find happiness with someone else? Was he that stupid?

"What the hell," he cried as he downed the remaining miniature. "Damn," he cried as he rummaged though the mini-bar, there was no scotch left. Quickly he snatched at the phone and called down to reception. "Could someone bring me up a bottle of Glenfiddich?" He could feel his anger transferred down the phone line and tried to retrieve it, "please."

He replaced the handset and stared at the empty glass, 'I can't get that right either,' he thought, his intentions were to get drunk, to blot out the last few days, but as he waited for his bottle to arrive, he realised he just wasn't in the mood. Almost on cue there was a knocking on his door.

"Shit," he cried at the familiar sound. He reached for his wallet and retrieved a twenty dollar bill and walked to the door.

"Hi. Can I come in?"

Debbie stood framed in the doorway, a look of slight repentance mixed with an air of mischief spread across her face. James stood there for a few brief moments and watched as Debbie clad only in a rather skimpy black negligee placed a do not disturb notice over the door handle.

"You're right; I've taken it as far as I can. Jack's gone, if he's out there, he'll surface one day. But I can't put my life on hold any longer," she purred. Then her arms were around his neck and she was kissing him with an urgency she'd never shown him before.

"Oh Debbie, do you really want this," he managed to say between kisses.

"Oh yes, oh yes," she responded as she felt the edge of his bed brush against the calves of her legs. Gently he arched her back and lay her down softly upon his bed, his lips never far from hers as he began to explore the continent that until that moment he could only dream about.

"From that moment onwards I put you to the back of my mind. I thought of you often, but I had a man that truly loved me, a man that was prepared to take on our child, a man that I grew to love."

Jack sat in silence, taking in all that Debbie was telling him. His life had been turbulent enough during the past ten years. Knowing that his actions had caused such horror and heartache filled him with unresolved remorse.

"I didn't know. Poor Pam, she never told me anything. Oh I'm so sorry so truly sorry," he began to weep.

Debbie reached out for him, "It wasn't your fault. How could you know?" she said softly.

Drying his eyes Jack looked across at Debbie, "What now?"

Through Debbie's narrative he'd been forced to confront events beyond his control, but what worried him the most was when Debbie told him of her love for James. He found himself eaten up with jealousy.

"We say our sad goodbyes, you return to Tara and I to James. Oh I don't know Jack. I thought I'd feel different towards you but I don't. I still want you."

Jack felt a lump form in the back of his throat, this couldn't be happening, but it was, "And I you," he stammered. Seeing Debbie had thrown his life into turmoil. He wanted her, he so desperately wanted her. But it wasn't just them. There was Tara and Kaycee and little Merri. There was his life in Montana, his friendship with Wade and countless other reasons why he couldn't have her.

"I know it's impossible, I love James and I couldn't bear to hurt him." Then she looked into his eyes and added, "I think the pub has rooms." Debbie couldn't believe the words as they flowed from her mouth. It was as if she'd become possessed.

All rational thought went out the window as Jack took a decision that could so easily destroy all he held dear. Fate had torn Debbie from him; fate had somehow conspired to throw them back together. Would it be so wrong to delve back into the past?

"Just once, life owes us at least that," sighed Debbie.

Jack mesmerised by the moment had but one lingering thought. 'How can it be just once?'

Minutes later, key in hand Jack entered the low ceiling room and in one swift motion closed the door and kissing Debbie passionately pushed her gently towards the four-poster.

Chapter II

Marlow

Tara boarded the plane at Billings with trepidation in her heart. At home, back in the mountains the task ahead of her had seemed so easy, yet now that she'd taken her first tentative step she was having her doubts. Her shopping expedition with her ma had helped restore her confidence some what. The outfits Alex had helped her buy reflected her character but equally emphasised a modern American woman. Basically she didn't want any of Jack's family thinking she was just some country hick. That she could out ride, out rope and out shoot everyone she'd meet would in her opinion mean nothing.

The flight out of Billings was uneventful, but it meant an overnight stay in an airport hotel in Minneapolis before her Intercontinental flight to London Gatwick. It was only after she'd purchased the tickets that she discovered she'd been booked on an entirely different flight-path and airline than Jack. It had caused her some concern, but she assumed that as she'd purchased an open ticket Jack would be able to fix things for there return trip. Obsessively she kept thinking it wasn't a good sign. She didn't want to travel back on her own. These and many more thoughts invaded her, whilst she flew ever closer to Minneapolis.

She hardly slept, the Days Inn at the airport was clean and tidy, efficient and convenient, but her troubled mind kept her awake until three in the morning. She questioned her way of life, the open air, the sense of freedom, but was it enough for Jack? There was a life outside of Montana, her brother Taw had witnessed it and had liked what he'd seen. Even Tara had been in awe of her brother and his new life style. But there was ugliness too. An ugliness that had destroyed her brother, an ugliness that had seen her best friend Merri return to her roots. But for others this life, spent with the sun at their back, the icy wind beating at your face and a desolation that had to be experienced to be believed, there was no place like it on earth. She'd seen it in Jack, or at least she believed she'd seen it.

Once onboard the 747 bound for London, Tara's demeanour changed, she became excited, euphoric it fact. Her mother's fighting spirit had kicked in. Jack had been more than honest, he'd told her of his feelings and he'd reassured her that nothing and no one would ever come between them. He was the man she'd pledged to spend her life with, he wasn't just any man, he was her man.

By the time Tara landed at London's Gatwick airport, she'd been well informed of the distance she was from Marlow. Her original plan was to phone one of the numbers Jack had given her. Say "Surprise, surprise!" Then expect Jack when he'd got over the shock to drive to the airport; but she was at Gatwick, not Heathrow, it would take him hours to get there. She decided to alter her plans; she'd show him she was capable of looking after herself. Her only problem was she had a phone number, she knew it was in Marlow but she didn't have an address. Collecting her luggage from the carousel Tara walked towards the exit.

It was a surprisingly hot morning when Tara and her luggage emerged from the terminal building. Hailing a cab, she gave the cab driver the directions. He did a double take.

"Where do you want? Marlow, you say."

"Yeah Marlow. Is there a problem?"

"No luv, it's your money."

Tara gave him a quizzical look and then climbed inside.

* * *

For Jack the weekend had been a troubled blur, tinged with guilt. The excitement of his passionate meeting with Debbie at the Flower Pot had given way to self-reproach. What had happened between him and Debbie shouldn't have happened, but it did. He kept telling himself that it was beyond their control. That it was only natural things like that could happen. Both of them had felt remorse, yet somehow it had seemed right at the time.

But now after a guilt-ridden weekend he was having doubts. His first thoughts were to run, to get as far away from Debbie as possible; to go home to Montana. But there was Charlotte to consider. Meeting Debbie for lunch at the Flower Pot wasn't the smartest of ideas, but they did have to discuss the problem of Charlotte and it gave him the chance to rake over what had happened that Friday afternoon. He had to get it clear in his head.

"Is that wise?" said Bob when Jack told him about meeting up with Debbie at the Flower Pot.

"What do you mean?"

"You know only too well what I mean. I'm your brother, I know these things."

"Nothing's gonna happen. We're going to discuss me seeing Charlotte."

"Okay bruv, whatever you say. I'll see you tonight," replied Bob shaking his head.

Minutes later Jack looked out the window and saw his brother's van pull away from the kerb. Deep in thought he began planning out what he was going to say to Debbie when he saw her at lunchtime.

* * *

Bob wiped his hands down his jeans and climbed back inside his van. He was in the middle of installing a new boiler into Mrs Holdsworth's kitchen when he heard the new ring-tone on his phone. He would have missed it except for having to come back out to the van for another coupling.

"Hello. Claymore Plumbing. Bob speaking."

"Hi! Is Jack around? It's Tara."

Bob's blood ran cold. Minutes later he was driving at more than the legal limit towards Marlow town in a state of shock and inner panic. His first reaction was how she got his number. Tara told him she dialled the number Jack had given her. Bob then recalled how Sheila had set up his new fangled mobile phone to take all diverted calls. Once that was clear, he got the shock of his life when she told him she was standing outside a pub called the George and Dragon by a quaint suspension bridge.

"Stay right where you are. I'll come and get you. Give me ten minutes."

Frantically Bob had rushed back into Mrs Holdsworth's and asked for the phone directory. In a rush he ran his finger down the page until he found the phone number for the Flower Pot. It seemed like hours before the phone answered.

Bob wasted no time in asking if a man answering his brother's description was there. The barman did a cursory look around the half filled lounge bar and told Bob that no one of that description was in the pub. Just as Bob was about to ring off, "Hold it a minute, there's a bloke sitting on one of our tables outside, I served him earlier think he might be a Yank or something."

"Yeah that's him. Could you get him? It's most urgent."

Bob kept looking at his watch as the minutes ticked away. He slammed the van into gear and hurtled off toward town.

"Hello!" crackled the mobile.

"Prepare yourself brother. Tara's in town."

"What!"

"I'm on my way to meet her at this very moment."

* * *

He was already five minutes late when he turned into the high street and slowed to an almost walking pace. Lunchtime always saw congestion on these narrow streets, something his new sister-in-law might find quaint, but he found frustrating. And then he saw her standing outside the phone box.

"Struuuth!" he exclaimed.

Clad in a designer fitted jacket and black jeans stood Shania Twain, or her double at the very least. Miraculously Bob found a place to park outside the George and Dragon, looked at him self in the rear-view mirror, ran his hand through his hair like a makeshift comb, stepped out of the van, hitched his pants up and walked towards her.

With a big cheesy grin he held out his hand to Tara.

"Hello, I'm Bob."

Tara took his hand, stifled a grin at her new brother-in-laws awkwardness and smiled back at him.

"Hi. I'm Tara."

Chapter 12

Marlow

Jack's face said it all when he returned to Debbie at the table. He was in a blind panic. The one thing he'd not expected was for Tara to have followed him over. She'd told him not to phone until he'd settled what ever he had to settle, which was what he was in the process of doing. So why feel guilty?

"What's wrong?" cried Debbie on seeing the look etched across his face.

"That was Bob on the phone, Tara's here."

"What!"

"Bob's bringing Tara to us as we speak."

Debbie's look said it all.

"We've done nothing wrong," said Jack

"I can't meet her, another time perhaps, but not now!"

Jack held Debbie's hands tightly, "Listen to me. It's no secret that I'm over here to see you. It's only natural that we would meet somewhere on neutral territory."

"But I can't!" panicked Debbie.

"You must. What we had is over, you just said that yourself. Now listen, Bob will be here in about five minutes. What's important now is breaking the news to Charlotte."

Debbie looked defeated rather than frightened; their lives such as they were hung in the balance. How they acted, how Tara reacted, both imponderables. They had come to a fork in the road. Sadly Jack looked across the table at Debbie, "What ever happens just remember I loved you, I always will."

"Oh Jack, if only things were different. I never thought it possible to love two people, but I do. I only wish I didn't."

Jack knew the next hour would be the hardest he'd ever have to endure. Loving two women as he did and being faced with the scrutiny of Tara he hoped he'd come through unscathed but he expected different.

Bob took the longest route he could to the Flower Pot pub making small talk as best he could. He'd told Tara what Jack had said. He was meeting his ex wife for the second time and they were discussing how and when to tell Charlotte.

"I actually think you being here will make it just that little bit easier." He'd said after he'd bundled her baggage into the van and placed an old blanket across the seat. Tara had told him not to fuss, she'd seen dirt aplenty.

As they drew closer, Bob couldn't help thinking how his brother could be this lucky. Debbie was a looker, smart, sophisticated and intelligent, but the woman that sat next to him had his heart racing. She was on first impressions, in Bob's simple words 'crumpet.' That she was intelligent, he had no doubt, that she'd hold her own against anyone, he was more than sure. She was, thought Bob, the girl of Jack's dreams. He only hoped he wouldn't blow it when his ex met the present Mrs Claymore.

"It's okay for some," joked Bob as he and Tara emerged from the car park and walked across the patio and lawn, "wish all I had to do was drink away the afternoon."

Jack stared at the woman he'd nearly lost.

"Tara."

"Thought you might need some company," she replied in way of explanation with a smile that melted his heart. That she was putting on a brave front, he didn't doubt, her insecurities hidden from the world. He loved her the more for it.

"Tara, this is Debbie," he said nervously as he introduced the two women in his life. The look on both women's faces said it all. It was obvious from the start that they could never be friends.

They saw a threat in each other, but both women knew that a cordial relationship was needed in the days ahead.

"Tara, what would you like to drink?" said Bob.

"Oh, just a Coke, thanks!"

"Same again for you two," he added. "Would you give me a hand with the drinks Deb?"

"Yeah sure Bob," said Debbie grateful to be out of the spotlight if only for a few brief minutes.

"I reckon you two need a little time on your own."

"Yeah Bob thanks. Take your time with the drinks."

As Bob and Debbie disappeared inside the lounge bar Jack turned towards Tara, "I don't understand," he said feebly.

"I thought you needed company, maybe I was wrong!" she repeated in an icy manner.

"Tara, come here. Don't be like that, it's . . . . it's been difficult. I met Debbie for the first time last Friday. It was an uncomfortable situation. Please understand."

"Do you still love her?"

"It's you I love!"

"You haven't answered my question," said an unrelenting Tara.

"Tara . . . . 'Listen to me."

She pulled away and tears began to trickle slowly down her cheeks. "Oh no, I promised myself I'd act more ladylike, more mature."

"Tara you're as ladylike as I'll ever want." Then he pulled her to him, hugged her gently then looked her straight in the eye. "Okay, you want an answer," He knew that what he said had to be the truth, Tara would have seen through it if it wasn't. "The truth, yeah I love her, but you knew that already. I thought she was dead and yes I loved her, but I love you. Debbie's the past, you . . . you're my present and future. I can't switch off how I feel, but I wouldn't give you up for her." Jack's heart was in his mouth, had he said too much, or too little?

"Oh Jack!" cried Tara and the tears burst forth as she flung her arms around him. "I've been so worried, I thought . . . I tho.."

Jack stopped her in mid sentence, "I know what you thought, I don't blame you. I would feel the same in your shoes. Now dry your eyes Bob and Debbie will be back soon." As she did so Jack stole a look at her, "You look amazing. You look a million dollars!"

"Only a million?" replied Tara, her confidence now slowly returning.

From the window of the lounge Bob and Debbie had witnessed the confrontation and reunion. "I reckon it's safe to go outside now," said Bob

"Give me a minute," said Debbie as she fought back the urge to cry out. "It hurts like hell."

"I know," replied Bob as he gave her a gentle brotherly hug. "I know."

During the next half an hour they talked around in circles about how Debbie would break the news to Charlotte. The conversation slightly stilted and punctuated by eerie moments of silence. In the end Debbie picked up her mobile, dialled Charlotte's number and asked her if she was free that evening.

"James and I have something very important to discuss with you."

"What!" cried Charlotte impatiently?

"I'll tell you tonight."

"You can't just leave me suspended."

"Trust me, all will be revealed this evening. No I haven't got a terminal condition!" She looked at her companions and rolled her eyes. "See you tonight!" Debbie pressed the green off button. "It's done, I'll phone you with her reaction tomorrow." she said abruptly.

Chapter 13

Marlow

Once things were settled Debbie said she had to be making tracks, she held her hand out to Tara, "It was nice meeting you."

Tara accepted her hand and said, "Likewise."

Jack's eyes locked on Debbie's and conveyed a silent farewell, then spontaneously he hugged her to him and said, "Take care."

"I will," she muttered and then Bob came to the rescue, ever the diplomat, offering a lift back to her car. Debbie gratefully accepted. Jack said he and Tara would stroll along the tow-path back to Marlow and would phone later for a lift.

Jack waited until Debbie and Bob disappeared into the car park, then he put his arm around Tara's shoulder and walked her in the direction of the tow-path.

"Any regrets?" asked Tara. She'd tried not to mention the obvious but she couldn't help her insecurities coming back.

"If I'm honest; then yes and no. Debbie is a wonderful woman, and if things had been different, then I guess we'd still be together. But then I'd never have met you." He hugged her to him for reassurance. "She's changed and for the good I think, but I could sense she was not the same Debbie as I once knew. And to be honest I've changed. I'm glad I came back, if only to shut the door on this my other life."

Tara squeezed him tightly in return. "You've a little matter of your daughter, remember."

"I know, but with you by my side I reckon I can weather any storm that's coming my way."

Tara felt her confidence fully restored, Debbie was a threat of that she had no doubt, but a threat of the mind. She hadn't missed the look Jack gave Debbie. It was sad and emotional. A look that said, what we had was special, but now it was time to say farewell.

* * *

Charlotte surprised everyone. She arrived at Debbie's around eight that evening with Matt, punctuality not normally being one of her virtues.

"Okay, whatever it is tell me."

Debbie looked first at James then Matt before turning back toward her daughter.

"It's your father, he's alive and he's staying with Bob and Sheila."

"What! You're kidding me." The look on Debbie's face confirmed she wasn't joking. For the briefest of moments Charlotte was silent, the wind had been knocked out of her sails. As she struggled to regain her composure she gathered her thoughts together.

"I wasn't expecting that," she said in as calm a voice as she could manage. "Why now after all this time?"

Debbie felt truly sorry for her daughter. She was keeping it together but beneath that façade she was hurt and angry inside. The girl had been denied a father through a cruel twist of fate. True James had stepped in and to all intent and purpose had played the surrogate role. He was good and kind, firm but fair, yet Charlotte had never accepted him in the fatherly role. She thought of him as a friend, a very good friend, but nothing more. She'd clung to the belief that one day Jack would return and be the father that she yearned after. For years she never gave up hope that he was alive and that one day he would return. Yet the years had stretched through her adolescence, through puberty and finally adulthood, and as surely as time itself that dream slowly faded.

Charlotte sneaked a fond look at Matt and pushed the hurt to the back of her mind.

"I always wondered if he'd show up. Oh why couldn't he have come sooner? Missing my special day by weeks, it's so unfair."

"He didn't!" cried Debbie.

"What . . . what do you mean?"

"He was here, he was at the church. He'd somehow found out about your wedding and he'd flown over from Montana to see you get married."

Charlotte stunned that he'd actually watched her walk down the aisle, sat in stunned silence.

James had expected anger at the very least. But there was none. He felt sick, drained and helpless. There was not a thought for the man that had actually walked her down the aisle some four weeks ago. No, her first reaction was to be sad that he missed her wedding. He felt like a stranger in his own home. He'd accepted that he couldn't be the father that Charlotte craved. Yet despite everything he'd done his best, bringing stability back into her life, sending her to the best schools and giving her the best upbringing possible.

"Well; why didn't he show himself," cried Charlotte as a single tear trickled from her eye.

"Shock I suppose, at seeing me alive."

It was all too much for James. He turned his back, took a glass from a cabinet and poured himself a large scotch. Then he walked into the kitchen and grabbed some ice from the freezer and unceremoniously threw it into his glass. In less than a week his life had been thrown into turmoil. Debbie had been cool and silent since the weekend. She'd told him it had been a shock and that she needed time to come to terms with everything. He wanted her to talk, to tell him it was okay and to reassure him that he still had a marriage. Oh how he hated this man from Montana, this spectre that had haunted his life for the past ten years.

"My father, he saw me get married."

"Yes sweetheart he did."

"What does he want?"

"He wants to see you; he wants to put it right with you."

"What if I don't want to meet him?"

"That's your prerogative, but I think you should hear him out."

"Oh you do, do you!"

Debbie looked for James for support, but only caught a glimpse of his back as he walked out onto the patio. She'd sensed rather than seen the body language from James and wanted so desperately to follow him out outside. She wanted to tell him, she so desperately wanted to tell him that she loved him, yet Charlotte needed her. Firstly the shock, then the realisation, Debbie knew the recriminations would quickly follow.

An hour later red-eyed and exhausted Charlotte and Matt said goodbye to Debbie and drove off. It had gone as she expected. Her daughter was sensible; a little head strong maybe, but once Charlotte had talked it through with Matt she was sure her daughter would come to the right decision.

"Whatever you decide, call me first thing."

Debbie strolled through the house, poured herself a glass of wine and walked outside. James was slumped in a patio chair doing his best to polish off the remainder of the bottle of single malt.

"James I'm so sorry."

James slowly looked up, "Really, what for," he said cruelly.

Debbie felt the colour rush to her face. "I'm sorry because I've been thinking about myself, my feelings. How this whole mess has left me screwed up inside my head. I should have looked at the whole picture. I thought I did, but I can see it now. I still love him James."

James felt like he'd been hit by an express train. "That's honest, I guess I can't ask for better than that," he said as he rose unsteadily from his chair.

Debbie looked at her man and her heart went out to him. "I told you that because I can't lie to you, but much more importantly, because I love you."

James looked confused, he was clinging on but barely. "How can you love both of us?"

"The same way as you can still love Jill."

"But Jill's dead!"

"She was your past and you loved her. Jack's my past. He's not the same Jack that I knew and loved, he died the moment I lost my memory and first met you."

It was a simple analogy, but effective.

"You mean . . . ."

"I love you, you're my life. You're everything to me."

James, who only seconds before thought he'd lost everything, threw his arms around Debbie and kissed her full on the mouth. She responded to him and her tongue snaked between his lips causing his senses to explode in a firework display of passion.

Morning came too quickly in the Henderson household and by Debbie's reckoning they'd only had a little over four hours sleep between them. 'It had been quite a night,' she thought naughtily.

Over breakfast James had a sudden troubling thought. He was about to keep it to himself when Debbie looked up from pouring her corn flakes and saw that worried frown. "Come on, I've seen that look before, spill."

"It's nothing Debs, just a thought. What if he feels the same way towards you as I do?"

"Hopefully he does, but I couldn't compete with his Montana cowgirl, she's quite something!"

Debbie was having a lazy morning, because of Jack she'd taken a few days off and wasn't due back to work on the Courier until lunchtime. James on the other hand had to be at the hospital by eight thirty sharp. For the first time since the news broke he left with a spring in his step.

"Let me know what Charlotte decides to do," he said as he backed the car out of the drive.

"I'll do that," cried Debbie as she waved him off.

As James's car turned at the corner of the road Debbie smiled to herself as the events of that Friday afternoon at the Flower Pot public house and hotel began to unfold in her head.

Overcome with a burning desire and a passion that had never quite been extinguished she'd fell back upon that four poster bed with Jack's lips pressed firmly to hers. Any guilty thoughts dashed by the fire burning in her loins. She could hear Jack tugging at his belt and jeans as she blindly began to slip her panties off.

And then it happened. Jack stopped struggling with his belt and both arms reach around her and he began to cry. She hugged him in return and found herself crying with him.

"I'm sorry, I'm so sorry," he sobbed, "I can't . . . I just can't."

"I know," replied Debbie, relief creeping into her voice. "I don't know what came over us? It would be sheer madness to continue." The moment they pulled back from the brink was indescribable.

They lay entwined in each others arms for an indeterminable time until Debbie finally untangled herself. "I still love you," she said quietly, "but we were right to stop before we did something we'd both regret."

Jack nodded in agreement. His feelings for Debbie unaltered, but his feeling for Tara had strengthened beyond words. His love for his Montana cowgirl had saved him and he was more grateful to her than she would ever know.

Relaxed and comfortable in each others company they talked for hours about how their lives had changed since that cold and rainy day in November of 85 when fate had intervened. When they parted, Jack and Debbie made a solemn promise to each other. What had so nearly happened would remain with them and them alone.

Debbie was brought back to reality as the phone sprang into life.

"Hi Mum. I want to meet him!"

Chapter 14

Marlow

As the plane started its descent into Billing Airport, Jack couldn't help thinking about how lucky he was. Things could have been so different. If he and Debbie hadn't stopped when they did, who knows what might have happened. One thing was certain; he couldn't have lied to Tara. She didn't deserve that and maybe that's why we stopped; hurting Tara was something he could never do. He loved her far too much.

When Debbie phoned the following day and gave Jack the news that his daughter wanted to see him, he was over the moon. They arranged to meet the following day at a small park on the outskirts of Marlow town centre. Sheila took Tara under her wing and suggested buying her two nieces something special from their auntie Sheila. Though reluctant to leave Jack's side after their very brief reunion Tara smiled and said she'd like nothing better. This was one meeting that Jack had to do on his lonesome.

*   *   *

There was a freshness to the air that morning, due no doubt to the rain that had fallen during the night. The early sun had quickly dried up the rain and now hung majestically in a blue and cloudless sky. It was the perfect morning for new beginnings thought Charlotte excitedly. Like a lot of girls her age she should have been filled with a mixture of anger, resentment and a little self pity at those missing years, but Charlotte wasn't like most girls. Sure her first reaction had been anger, but at the knowledge that her father was here the anger subsided and was replaced by more rational thinking. Her mother had never told her of why Jack had seen fit to leave England and it had always remained a mystery, but when Debbie broke the news of Jack's return she sat Charlotte down and told her everything.

"Your father was by all accounts in a terribly emotional state when he left. I don't think he intended staying away as long as he did. It just happened."

Debbie left nothing out. She knew her daughter. Once the anger had died away she would analyze everything she'd been told and would make her own judgement. When Charlotte had phoned and said she wanted to meet him, deep down Debbie was not surprised.

* * *

Tears blurred his vision as Charlotte walked up to him. The little girl he'd left behind was gone forever and in her place stood a young confident woman, already clear in her head of where she was going. Thanks in part, thought Jack, to James's intervention. She was a younger version of her mother. Jack couldn't help but love this vision of loveliness.

"Hello dad," she said tentatively.

"Charlotte, I'm so so sorry," was all he could say before she ran to him and threw herself into his arms. They talked and talked for what seemed like hours covering everything from Jack's departure, to his time in Kentucky where Jack discretely left out the reason why he'd left. If there ever came a time to know about Jared Barclay then it would come from Debbie's lips. He told her about how he'd met Wade, the shooting in Nogales, the months spent hid out in a cave, the horse drive, and finally Tara and the fire at Yellowstone.

"Wow! You must tell Matt, he won't believe half but you've got to tell him anyway. And I've sisters; I can't wait to meet them."

They had a spot of lunch in a nearby pub, where Charlotte quizzed him more about his life in Montana. Jack in turn asked about her schooling and her future plans.

"I'm doing a law degree, but in a few years, well before my thirtieth birthday we're going to start a family."

"Well I can see you've got it well and truly mapped out."

The next few days flew by so quickly. Before long it was time for goodbyes. Charlotte said she and Matt would fly out later that year when they'd sorted out leave. Bob and Sheila had already booked their holiday for this year but promised Jack and Tara that they'd be over sometime the following year.

"Make it around roundup time. We could do with the labour," joked Jack.

"Just tell me when, we'll be over, guaranteed," cried Bob.

After a tearful farewell to Shelia and Bob they climbed into their taxi. Bob had offered to drive them, but Jack had insisted on getting a cab.

"We've a slight detour to make, before heading for the airport," said Jack. The inference didn't need spelling out.

*   *   *

As the cab pulled up outside Debbie and James's mock Tudor house, Jack turned to Tara and she gave him a reassuring smile before they both climbed out.

"We'll be ten minutes at the most," cried Jack to the black cab driver.

"No worries, you're paying," laughed the cab driver.

Jack had phoned ahead and told Debbie that he and Tara were stopping by on the way to the airport.

Debbie saw them coming through the window and went out to greet them as they walked up her driveway.

"James sends his apologies; he had to be in early this morning. He asked me to wish you both a safe journey home."

"That was nice of him, "said Tara. "Now could I please have a loan of your bathroom? Flying always does this to me."

"Sure!" said Debbie bemused by the request. "Just go in the house, up the stairs and third door on the right."

"Thanks," cried Tara as she rushed into the house.

Jack understood and loved her more for it. His wife had grown some, she'd found a new confidence and maturity. "I guess Tara thought that our goodbyes should be private."

"She's quite a girl. You look after her."

"I will." he said and his eyes misted over. "Debbie I know we've said it all, but I'd just like to say one more time; I'll never stop loving you. When you think of me, just remember the good times."

"I will," replied Debbie, "And I'll never stop loving you either, Jack Claymore, cowboy."

Montana

As the tyres screeched on the runway at Billing, Jack turned towards Tara. At last he'd put his old life to bed. True he hoped that Bob and Sheila would stay in touch. He knew from the time he'd spent with Charlotte that whenever she had the chance she and Matt would be over, but he guessed he'd seen Debbie for the last time. He'd been right to go back, to mend fences. The thought amused him, mend fences, it seems like that's all I've been doing the past ten years. He reached an arm around Tara, smiled into those deep brown eyes and said, "Well Mrs Claymore, welcome home."

Chapter 15

Montana

Since arriving back home Jack and Tara had been working around the clock to keep up. Blaine Henry had been a godsend and the other hired hand Jake Harmon had also proven his worth.

"Like old times," cried Jack as he watched Blaine walk across to the bunkhouse.

Tara nodded in agreement, "Walks like Tyler, talks like him too," she added sadly.

There wasn't a week passed that Jack and Tara didn't think of that day up at Cougar Pass. Tyler Henry had signed on at the Claymore Ranch and walked slap bang into trouble, first being beaten half to death, then being hog-tied with barbed wire, and that wasn't all, a year or so maybe less he was killed up at Cougar Pass. The shooting had caused a stir like the Big Hole Valley hadn't seen since Chief Joseph's surrender. It made the papers too, though to be fair not too many people heard about it outside of Montana, Wyoming and Idaho maybe. I guess the deaths of seven people killed in a shoot out didn't rate too much coverage in cities like Los Angeles and the like. There shootings like that seem to be the norm as far as the good folks of Montana could tell.

It had brought great sadness to the valley and left a terrible wound that was only now beginning to heal. Jack saw the sorrow in Tara's eyes as Blaine disappeared into the bunk-house.

"I can pay Blaine off if you want, he'll understand," cried Jack.

"Oh no, that wouldn't be at all right. Besides, I think ol' Tyler would be pleased that his kin are following in his footsteps."

"It's Merri you're thinking about, ain't it."

"I guess it is, but that ain't a bad thing. Talking about her, kinda keeps her alive, you know," replied Tara.

"I know," said Jack softly. "Talkin about Merri, you know what's around the corner?"

"No! What?"

It's Labor Day Weekend in a couple of weeks."

"You're kidding," said Tara, aghast at forgetting Dillon's premier event of the entire year. The events of the past few weeks had obliterated it completely from her mind. "I'll talk to ma about it this evening."

"See you do," replied Jack as he jumped into the pickup. "Guess I'll head out to Wisdom to fetch those spare parts we ordered," His words drowned out by the pick up as it roared into life.

*   *   *

The Labor Day Rodeo at Dillon held mixed emotions for Alex. She'd met Wade for the first time at the rodeo; she'd seen the friendly rivalry between Tara and Merri develop as they competed against each other in the barrel racing. How she'd sit there high up on the bleachers, heart in her mouth watching as Wade climbed onto the worst bulls this side of hell. The suppressed fear and anticipation mingled with annoyance at Wade as he looked up to her and smiled that smile of his that said, don't worry, I'm fine, this bull's a pussycat, only to find himself eight seconds or less dumped on his ass with only his agility and the rodeo clowns to save him from the attentions of said pussycat. Those were the happy times. But like big gathering where testerone was king, there were the inevitable fights. One such fight resulted in the curtailment of Alex's son Taw's promising career as a world famous concert pianist and the subsequent depression which resulted in his untimely death. It took Alex a few years before she could bring herself to attend another Dillon Rodeo. But those years were in the past and a future generation of barrel riders, bull riders and saddle bronc riders was now being introduced to the wonderful sport of Rodeo. Kaycee was as excited as all get up and her excitement spread too little Merri, who had just mastered the art of walking and was only months away from sitting a saddle.

Wade took an active role in the organising, Jack supplied a number of horses for the saddle bronc event and was even temped to enter but Tara put a stop to it.

"This event has caused more than a few broken bones in this here family. We've lost enough time this year without you being laid up for a couple of months."

Secretly Jack was relieved, not so much because of taking part; it was more on account of the local dignitaries that were going to attend. Up and coming political figure Vince Holbrook and his wife Ruth were reputed to be attending, Jason Connors the star of the new hit TV series 'Rodeo Man' and Country singer Ty Boland were also expected to attend.

Jason Connors had bought himself a ranch up near Ennis and was looking to improve the bloodline of his horses, whilst it was also rumoured that Ruth Holbrook was on the look out for an anniversary gift for her husband. Vince Holbrook was renowned for his love of horses and his policies towards ranching and farming were very favourable to true Montanans. Selling to the wife of the possible future governor of Montana would certainly add to the reputation of 'Reynolds Horses'.

Tara and the kids climbed high on the bleachers that overlooked the chutes. Kaycee giggled with excitement, whilst little Merri looked all around her taking in every movement and noise. That she was going to be a thinker Tara had no doubt. From the moment she was born she'd express an uncanny nosiness to every thing and everyone. She cried out with glee as her daddy mounted on a powerful looking bay circled the arena making sure everything was ready for the day's event.

Alex and Wade were sitting with members of the Beaverhead Chamber of Commerce when news came of the imminent arrival of Vince Holbrook. His helicopter had just landed in the car park of the Paradise Hills Motel and a motorcade was expected to arrive within fifteen minutes. Wade being one of the chief event organisers that year was asked to see to it that the start of the Rodeo was delayed until the Congressman and his entourage had arrived and been seated. Knowing how busy the Holbrook's were, Wade had already put into place contingency plans. As the arena filled up and the crowd became restless Wade made an announcement over the loud speaker.

"Ladies and gentlemen, boys and girls, I know you've been waiting a while for these here festivities to commence but I'd ask you to hold on a little longer. As you're aware Congressman Holbrook, his wife and Jason Connors the star of 'Rodeo Man' were suppose to attend," a groan emanated from the crowd, "well they're on there way as I speak and will be arriving in a little over fifteen minutes," Wade was working the crowd, one second they were down the next up, "so during that time Charlie Sparks and Tim Rogers or as you know them best Old Sparky and Dodger Roger will entertain you."

No sooner had he said the names then Old Sparky and Dodger Roger walked into the empty arena. The kids whooped and hollered. Two of the pro Rodeo circuit's best rodeo clowns were about to unleash themselves on an unsuspecting bull by the name of Bodacious Jim, or was it the other way around.

Merri shrieked with excitement as the Bull was released from the chute. Old Sparky ran straight towards Bodacious, stopped suddenly feigned blind panic and turned tail with the bull right on his heals. Dodger expertly distracted Bodacious, allowing Old Sparky to throw himself into the protection of a rubber barrel. Then it was the turn of Rogers to be chased, all the time Wade and several members of the Chamber of Commerce looked to the horizon for the Congressman's motorcade.

With relief, the motorcade drove into the cark park of the Beaverhead Fairgrounds a few minutes later. Congressman Holbrook and his wife Ruth emerged from their limousine and were promptly ushered towards their reserved seating. Wade and Jack, noted with relief Jason Connors climbing out of the second car a few seconds later. Both knew that it wasn't Holbrook and his wife, *although they were a good looking couple* that the crowd were waiting to see.

Jason Connors was building himself quite a fan club in the Western states. Connors was a onetime pro rodeo circuit saddle bronc rider who'd broken one too many bones. That he'd managed to keep his rugged good looks made him a natural for the new TV series. To his credit Jason Connors looked the real deal, worn Wranglers and faded salmon shirt, designer boots and a straw Stetson completed his outfit. His laconic walk was unmistakeable as he advanced towards the bleachers, to the accompaniment of shrill cries from a number of teenage girls

"Ladies and gentlemen, boys and girls, I give you the future governor of Montana," cried Ralph Hunniford through the loudspeaker.

Congressman Vince Holbrook unfurled his frame from the bleachers and stood up. A look towards Ralph Hunniford, a quick smile at Ruth then he went into his sales pitch.

"Firstly I'd like to say what a great pleasure it is for myself and Ruth to be attending Montana's biggest rodeo here in Dillon." The crowd roared their approval. Vince Holbrook waited until the noise abated, then continued. "Secondly, I think Ralph was being a little presumptuous, the next governor of Montana is still some ways in the future and it's you the voters that will decide. I hope it's me, but we live in a true democracy and I guess it will be the man or woman that's policies ring truest. Now I understand that the rodeo has been delayed some, so without more ado let's 'Cowboy Up.'"

Wade had to stand and admire the man; he had been there no more than five minutes and had the crowd eating from his hand. 'Perhaps later,' thought Wade, 'I'll be able to ask him where he stands on the introduction of Wolves in Idaho and Wyoming. The wolves coming into Northern Montana were a different matter altogether so maybe a more radical solution might be found.'

As the rodeo got underway Wade couldn't help noticing the interest and the eagerness of Jason Connors. He'd climbed down from the bleachers and was watching the action close up Wade had seen him a time or two over the years, a true professional, a man that had mastered his craft, albeit at the expense of being in traction a number of times. Rodeo was in his blood, once a rodeo man always a rodeo man. It never leaves you, thought Wade as he remembered his time so many years before.

First up were the calf ropers, next the steer wrestlers, followed by the fans favourite the saddle bronc riders, then the ladies barrel racing, an event that Tara and Merri felt they owned once upon a time.

Wade looked towards the bleachers where the congressman, his wife and their entourage sat. He noted that the congressman was deep in conversation with his aide, and appeared more distracted with politician talk than the events in the arena, whereas his wife Ruth seemed enthralled. He guessed a politician's life was all consuming.

Next up were the team ropers, another timed event, which the crowd always seemed to appreciate. Then rodeo's classic, the superstars of rodeo, the saddle bronc riders. Jason Connors ex saddle bronc rider, now TV star waited in anticipation as the announcer introduced the first rider.

"Let's hear it for Dale Wendell, all the way from Fresno, California."

Dale and Shadow Dancer flew into the arena to a thunderous applause, only to find the young Californian flying through the air in three seconds flat. Wade glanced across at Jason Connors and felt he could read his mind, 'Oh hell, I could do better than that, broken bones notwithstanding.'

Next out of the chutes was Wayne Garfield on Dangerous to Know. The horse did a series of small kicks then without warning bucked high into the air before it spun into a 360 degree turn. It was enough to have thrown any rider, but Garfield stuck to the saddle. Jason Connors looked at the timer. Six seconds were on the clock; Garfield was heading for maximum points, when suddenly Dangerous jumped suicidal like towards the railings. The timer had just flipped seven seconds as Wayne Garfield was dumped unceremoniously into the dust near the corral fence that Jason Connors was watching from.

"Good ride! You almost had him," encouraged Jason.

Wayne Garfield picked up his hat and glared angrily at Connors. "If I want you're intake I'd have asked. You washed up has been."

Wade saw a flash of anger in Jason Connor's face, before he turned it into a smile and replied, "It weren't me that got dumped on his ass."

Wayne Garfield spun around, his fists ready to do the talking, until he looked into Jason Connor's steely blue eyes. He thought about it, but I guess being dumped in the dirt once was clearly enough. Turning his back he skulked off.

"Buy you a beer!" cried Wade.

Jason smiled and nodded. Tackling the congressman about the wolf problem could wait. Watching rodeo was thirsty work.

*   *   *

Later at a private reception held at the Chamber of Commerce, Wade eventually button-holed the congressman.

"Supposing you were elected governor, where do you stand as far as us ranchers are concerned?" It was a broad and ambiguous statement that was meant to feel Holbrook out.

"Wade, excuse my familiarity but I like to address people by first names, it's less formal and it has a way of getting people to open up. In your case I can see that's not necessary you're a man that comes to the point. So I'll cut the crap. You're a rancher; you've got issues with the federal government, with the environmentalists and just about everyone that doesn't hold to your point of view."

"I reckon," was all Wade could say at that moment.

"I was born on a ranch in the Judith Basin, spent my formative years there. I know what it's like; I know the hardships of a bad winter followed by a poor summer, the restrictions put on you by a government that only knows it's a cow when it's sitting on a plate surrounded by vegetables, I know all the pitfalls and worse those federal taxes that help keep the country afloat. I saw it all first hand, my uncle died of a broken heart trying to hang on to his ranch, he failed." The congressman paused momentarily as his past flashed before him. "My allegiance is to the hard working folks that moulded this state into what it is today. If I'm elected governor, I'll fight for you tooth and nail. I ain't saying we'll win every fight because then you'd know I was lying. But I will give it my best shot."

"That was quite a mouthful," replied Wade. "I guess I got my answer and then some." With that said Wade held out his hand, "It's been a pleasure talking to you."

The congressman took Wade's hand and shook it firmly, "Likewise, and the name's Vince.

*   *   *

Later that night Wade told Alex of his conversation, "First impressions I'd have to say, he's a mite slick, not my kind of man, but probably the kind this state needs right now. He can certainly talk the talk, only time will tell if he can walk the walk."

"You and Jason Connors seemed to get along. I spotted you sneaking off with him for a quick beer."

"Yeah, not a bit like you'd imagine. Nice guy; and from what I can make out, he surely can walk the walk."

"Goodnight Wade."

Chapter 16

Montana

He couldn't help but admire the magnificent physic of the grey wolf as it appeared in the cross hairs of his rifle sights. He likened himself to the wolf, yet in reality he was nothing more than a pack animal. True Karl Bremer's ice cold temperament had turned him from a quiet boy into a ruthless killer; but in reality he was nothing more than one of life's soldiers. A smile so malevolent crossed his lips as the wolf sensing danger began to react. Karl could see the fear in its eyes as he squeezed the trigger. The sound echoed through the canyon and reached as far as Flathead Lake. The alpha male dropped like a stone. A clean shot right between its eyes.

Bremer raced towards his kill knowing he had but little time before the Ranger patrol would start sniffing around. Breathlessly he reached the fallen wolf and quickly hacked at its neck until he'd severed the head. Then quickly dropping the head into a sack he raced off. Minutes later bathed in sweat from his exertions he emerged from the undergrowth at the deserted parking lot. Slinging the sack into the back of his pick-up he threw himself behind the wheel and drove off.

Karl was twenty two years of age, blond haired, tall and powerfully built. He could have been someone, but three years in and out of the correction facilities at Pine Hills and then Riverside only made him an arrogant punk, destined for more time at Montana's State Prison. At twenty one just out of Deer Lodge, jobless and without prospects he was a natural for recruitment by the militia. There he found friendship and camaraderie, things that had been lacking in his short life. Karl was an only child, brought up on a farm by hardworking parents, whose efforts around the farm left them too tired to give their child any real affection. He was poorly educated, due mainly to helping out on the land when he should have been getting on with his schooling. Turned off by farm work he tried his hand at one dead end job after another. Fighting with workmates and employers didn't endure him to the folks of Polson It was around this time that he attempted his first burglary. Success followed success, it was easy money, then he graduated to robbing a liquor store where he badly pistol whipped a young college student working a late shift. A year at Pine Hills followed. During that time he was sexually assaulted by an inmate. Several weeks later that said inmate met with an accident, which left him blind in one eye. After that there were no more assaults on Karl Bremer.

Karl spent less than three months outside of Pine Hills Correctional Facility before he ran across Jeannie Taplow, a girl big for her age but with a mind of a child. Due to lack of evidence it went down as sexual assault but everyone at Rollins knew it was most likely rape. Bremer was sent to Riverside and placed in the Sexual Depredations wing of the facility. Protesting his innocence all the time he was incarcerated only increased the resentment he was feeling towards authority. Gradually the bitterness grew like a cancer inside Karl's head. The final straw was a barroom brawl at Whitefish. An argument ensued over nothing and Bremer beat a man to within an inch of his life. It was eighteen months later when he emerged from Deer Lodge, alone, friendless and with a hatred towards everything federal. Karl had become the perfect candidate for the Militia.

For the first time in his life he wasn't alone, he had friends that shared a common mistrust of anything Federal. Amongst these friends Karl gyrated towards the more extreme and violent men and women that lurked in the darker recesses of the Militia. Their hatred towards the Federal Government knew no bounds.

At last Karl had found his family, a family that he was eager to please, hence his hunting trip into Mission Valley. His prowess with all manner of guns was noted and he was duly nurtured.

Amongst Karl's friends was thirty nine year old Ray Guthrie. Wanted under several aliases in as many states for armed robbery, murder and arson. Dark greasy thinning hairline, face to match, five eight, and wiry, but what he lacked in statue he made up with cunning and guile. He'd drifted into Montana a little over a year ago and almost naturally breezed into the militia. A security truck hijack had gone disastrous wrong, leaving one guard and two armed robbers dead on the sidewalk outside the mercantile bank of Amarillo. It had left Ray with no doubt that if caught he'd booked himself a one-way ticket to the big sleep, courtesy of Governor Bush. On his side the state of Texas had a very poor identi-kit picture, a name that meant nothing and a partial fingerprint. He had no known criminal record and provided he stayed clear of Texas he was home free. The militia and in particular this group of misfits were stockpiling weapons and planning something big. Ray didn't care what that something was, what he did care about was the bundles of cash they would need to steal to finance it.

Another of Karl Bremer's friends *in fact his mentor* was Gulf war veteran Bob Knox. He was a man that loved his country; was prepared to die for it and almost did several times. He'd seen his best buddies blown to smithereens by roadside bombs; his platoon sergeant had his leg severed clean off by flying shrapnel and he could do nothing to help the man as machine gun fire strafed the area. Weeks later as acting sergeant he'd led his men against a machine gun post and wiped it out without loss.

Written up for a decoration, Bob Knox was an all American hero, until a simple twist of fate changed all that. On a routine patrol a month later, an error of judgement resulted in the accidentally death of a young goat herder. It was a mistake like so many others in that so called war, but this was secretly recorded and posted on Al Jazzeria television. The United States Government not wanting a scandal used Bob Knox as their sacrificial lamb. He was subsequently court-marshalled, made an example of, spent three months in custody before the department of war decided to send him home with a dishonourable discharge.

Shunned by his own government Bob Knox got into trouble almost as soon as he'd got back. Treated like a pariah, his fists did the talking until his wife left him. With nothing to live for he drifted from town to town until he arrived at Great Falls where he joined the militia. There he met fellow veterans that had been treated just as poorly. He began to hate the country of his birth but as he listened to the rhetoric of the militia he realised it wasn't the country, but the illegal government that ran it. Over the next five years Knox earned himself a reputation as a leader, proficient with weapons, unarmed combat and an enthusiasm to inflict pain and suffering. By the time he met Adam Coulter he was prepared to do anything for the militia's ideals.

Adam Coulter was a man of vision, a brilliant mind with an ability to see the bigger picture even before the artist had put brush to canvas. The siege at Ruby Ridge and the massacre at Waco had galvanised a certain section of the community. Survivalists, men and women down on their luck, conspiracy theorists, white supremacists and right wing activists turned to the Militia in several states. For the most part these individuals were just a harmless bunch of free thinking Americans, preparing themselves for the day that they all hoped would never come. But amongst these were the Timothy McVeigh's'. Men and women that were prepared to carry out atrocities like the Oklahoma City bombing, men that Adam Coulter could use and manipulate for his own ends.

Adam Coulter wasn't militia, he was anything but. Only Bob Knox knew of his existence and even he didn't know Coulter's real agenda. Because of his army experience and his handling of men Bob Knox was the perfect candidate to lead the mission that Adam Coulter had in mind. But before that he set the group a few initiation tests, low level but enough to cement the men into a group capable of mass destruction.

Coulter had met Knox in a bar up in Kalispell some six months earlier. Both men seemed to hit it off right from the start. Bob Knox was no angel, the Gulf war had honed him into a fighting killing machine, but getting slam dunked because of some rag head goat herder was the pits. "You'd have thought they'd have pinned a damn medal on me for it! What's another gook here or there," he told Adam Coulter over a few beers. "You ask me, we should have nuked the fucking asses of the whole damn bunch of mother fuckers."

Adam Coulter had read Bob Knox's file, he knew he wasn't as lily white as he professed to be. "Yeah, you're right, the whole region ain't worth a bucket of shit," coaxed Coulter. But then Adam Coulter didn't give a damn either way, he was more concerned with Knox's attitude towards the federal government.

"Damn stinking government, cares more about the civilians in Iraq than they do about their own troops," railed Knox.

"Government needs a lesson," said Coulter quietly.

"Yeah, mother fuckers need another Oklahoma!"

Adam Coulter suppressed a smile. Just over a year had passed since the bombing of the Murrah building which left one hundred and sixty eight dead and over five hundred injured. In that time militias in several states lost many of their supporters. Only the hardcore extremists or the criminally insane would even contemplate another atrocity on the scale of Oklahoma.

Adam Coulter had found his leader, it had been easier than he'd thought possible.

"Bob, I've a proposition for you. One that I'll finance and one than will earn you more money than you'll see in a lifetime and you get to kick the government in the ass."

"Who do I have to kill?"

That had been four months ago and Bob Knox had already proved he was worthy of the faith Coulter had in him. Along with Karl Bremer he robbed a sporting goods store on the edge of Polson just as the owner was closing up for the night. At gunpoint they ordered the storekeeper to empty his shelves of ammunition, several hand guns, two pump action shotguns, an M14 snipers rifle complete with a Leopold MK3 scope and all the cash in the register. Both men had entered the store wearing ski masks with robbery on their mind, but robbery was not the motive. They killed the storekeeper execution style on the orders of Coulter. Karl Bremer calmly and casually loaded a Ruger Blackhawk .44 Magnum straight from an unlocked gun cabinet, pointed it at the shopkeeper's head and fired. Then both men picked up the loaded duffels and casually walked out the front door.

Coulter had selected the target, told Knox that the planning and successful execution of the operation was down to him. "Call it a test," he'd said coldly. "If you pass I'll be in touch within a month." No phone conversations, no elaborate plan, just the simple act of pointing a pit bull in the right direction and saying kill. If it all went pear shaped there was no link to Coulter, if it succeeded then the initiation of two trusted men was complete.

The second test was a little more extreme, a bank in Havre. The same orders to Knox, find two other recruits and knock off the Western Savings Bank. It was a little bit more daunting than the cold blooded murder at the sporting goods store but Knox said he was up for it.

"You find your men, you plan the heist. How you go about it I leave to your initiative. When I'm satisfied that you've all passed the test, I'll be in touch with your final test. At that time I'll fill you in on the main target. Believe me; you'll appreciate all the planning. For that mission I shall lead, understand sergeant."

"Yes sir!" cried Knox instinctively as he saluted Coulter.

Adam Coulter acknowledged him with a slight nod of his head. "I'll be in touch." He could hardly stop himself from bursting out with laughter. The poor sap had bought all his rhetoric hook line and sinker.

Six weeks later, with Ray Guthrie and a hard nosed activist called Max Schneider in tow; they knocked over the Western Savings Bank at Havre. Only a couple of busted heads, a vicious pistol whipping from Bremer on the bank manager and Guthrie's expertise in robbing banks proving his worth as they got away with twenty three thousand dollars, more money than Bremer, Schneider and Knox had seen in there entire lives. Knox took charge of the money much to Bremer and Guthrie's displeasure.

"We split everything after the final mission, not before," spat Knox. "If we go on a spending spree we'll blow the whole operation." Both men begrudgingly accepted Bob Knox's last word on the matter. "We've one more mission to take care of, before the big one. I'll tell you when."

Coulter phoned Knox to enquire how the bank raid had gone.

"It went like a dream; the guys I brought in are true professionals, although they're a little anxious about dividing up the money."

"Just keep them in line. The big payoff is just around the corner."

Agitated about being kept in the dark Knox pleaded with Coulter. "I need something, tell me at least."

"You have one final test, a simple matter of political assassination." He could sense Knox's jaw dropping but added quickly, "Not anyone with a high profile, so no cause for concern. I'm working on the small details as we speak. After that, the big one, the one that will gain world attention; Hungry Horse?" Carson let his words hang; he'd given Knox the carrot.

"Hungry Horse!"

"I'll be in touch."

"What the fuck!" exclaimed Knox as the phone line went dead.

At least he knew or believed he knew where this was heading. Appeasing the men would take some doing. Bremer was cool about it, Guthrie wasn't happy he wanted his share, but Knox managed to persuade him that what they'd stolen was just small potatoes.

Schneider was only sore because he hadn't killed anyone. He was a sociopath who'd joined the militia in the hope that one day he'd be able to turn his guns on the National Guard. He'd been at Kent State during the early seventies and had seen at first hand the government at work. Only fourteen at the time, but the sight of innocent unarmed students gunned down had had a lasting affect. Dropping out of college, he spent a few years on the road before joining a biker gang. He rode with them for three years running drugs, guns and women, taking part in robberies and rape and was indicted but got off on a technicality for an affray which decimated a small town. The bikers' hatred of authority matched Schneider's and at times surpassed it, until he took part in a vicious beating of a patrolman where his last kick put the poor unfortunate officer in the paraplegic ward. His arrest a month later saw him facing a life sentence until he named names. His sentence was reduced to fifteen years, which he served under an assumed name before being released into the community. His hatred of the uniform reinforced by the viciousness of the prison guards had not diminished. In Idaho afraid to rejoin a biker gang in case he was recognised he found the perfect organisation; the militia. After the Oklahoma bombing the Idaho militia became too tame so he moved across the state line into Montana. During that year he became even more frustrated by the Montana militia's lack of real action and made it known he was looking for some real work. He was only too willing to answer the call when Bob Knox came knocking and invited him to join his little cell.

For the next six weeks the quartet under the leadership of Bob Knox laid low at the aptly named Warlock Ranch down in Missoula owned by a right wing rancher called Jim Haggerty. To allay suspicion the quartet did the occasional fence riding, helped with the general maintenance around the outbuildings and hauled hay. Jim Haggerty was in his sixties, he'd seen change over the decades, but of late that change had been far to dramatic for his liking. Not one to sit back he'd expressed a desire to call for action. He'd joined the militia, petitioned the governor, he'd spoken out at rallies and actively demonstrated at the state capital as much as his ranching chores allowed. On the whole he wasn't a bad man, just a man down on his luck. He'd seen his state change and he'd been one of its casualties. With debts up to his eyeballs and the bank only a few short steps from foreclosing on the ranch he didn't much like what the future held for him. When asked by Bob Knox to board him and his men in exchange for the occasional chore, he'd had his reservations, but he'd gone along with it for the sake of the cause.

Karl Bremer had driven the eighty odd miles from Flathead Lake to the Warlock ranch in under an hour, which according to Knox was breaking the rules. He'd been told by the ex sergeant to stay under the radar but what the heck, he'd bagged the wolf and he'd taken the precaution of removing its head, eliminating any trace of what weapon had been used. So what, that he'd broken the speed limit. The sniper's rifle with the Leopold sights was really something, but shooting at targets wasn't Karl's style, hence his little hunting trip up at the lake. When he told Knox what he'd accomplished he was sure the ex soldier would approve. Hunting was in Karl's blood and from the little Bob Knox had told him of the next mission familiarity with the weapon was going to be all important.

He was surprised when Knox examined the contents of the bloodied sack. "You done well," he said, "now take that wolf's head and burn it. Then crush up the skull. I'll be along shortly to see you've carried it out."

Karl was confused, he'd expected Knox to chew him out about speeding, but he'd not mentioned it. He seemed more preoccupied with destroying the evidence of his crime.

Inside the barn Knox kicked viciously at the table Guthrie and Schneider were playing cards on.

"What the fuck!" cried both men.

"Damn kid, takes a fool risk. It could cost all of us," Knox said to Guthrie and Schneider in an agitated manner.

"What the fuck's he done, "cried Guthrie.

"He drove back from Flathead Lake like a bat outta hell, that's what! Took that sniper's rifle and that fancy scope, bagged himself a wolf's head. If a State trooper had picked him up we'd all be serving time in Deer Lodge. Fuck, fuck, fuck . . ."

"Damn fool kid, he could get us all killed!" cried Schneider.

"No brains," added Guthrie.

"I'll go see he'd done what I told him," said Knox after he'd cooled down. Then he turned on his heels and walked back towards where he'd left Bremner

Karl Bremer turned sharply as Knox approached the small fire. "What's with you! I could have just buried the damn head!"

"You could at that," replied Knox, now calmer than he'd been since Karl arrived back at the ranch, "but then you and I wouldn't be having this conversation. Yeah, I'm mad as hell at the damn risk you took, but an hour or so before you drove in I received a call that puts your fool ride into perspective. I just got word; the mission is off for the time being. We've an informant in the camp.

"What!"

"You heard. I know it ain't me, and I know it ain't you on account of you killing that gun shop owner, which leaves Schneider, Guthrie or Haggerty."

"Jesus, fuck!"

I'm guessing it ain't Haggerty. He doesn't know shit, but Schneider and Guthrie, well they both come with good credentials, it could be either of them."

"Then we get rid of both of them," said Bremer coldly.

Chapter 17

Montana

Despite it being a bright September morning Tara noticed a chill in the air. It was a reminder, if she needed reminding that winter was fast approaching. Already the leaves had begun to change colour and she could sense the first snowfalls were not far away. It had been an eventful summer, a heart churning, gut wrenching summer, but they'd weathered it together. She thought they were stronger for it and in time she guessed she'd look forward to the visits of her extended family. Life was back to normal, 'normal's good,' she thought as she brought in a pile of pancakes from the kitchen

"Wade seemed mighty impressed with the congressman, even said he might vote for him," said Jack as he reached across the breakfast table and grabbed hold of the maple syrup.

"Yeah well you know pa, anyone that supports his view of things," replied Tara as she put away the cereals. "Times are changing, there's nothing any of us can do about it. Change is inevitable," added Tara, with a philosophical air.

"Those old values shouldn't be ignored. Take the liberals in the state capital; if they have their way there'll be hell to pay. They care more about saving the planet than the people living on it."

"Jack," she said with a smile, "now you're sounding like my father."

"Maybe so, but look at the papers. I ain't saying we're like L.A or New York, but crime is on the increase."

"That's just paper talk, we're no worse than neighbouring states."

"Yeah I know, but we've got our own brand of trouble, the militia for starters, they're always trying to stir things up."

"Yes, but even pa says they aren't doing any harm, in fact he goes along with most of what they're saying, most of its hot air anyway."

"Ah, that's how it starts;" exclaimed Jack, relishing his chance to climb on his soapbox, "I dare say Timothy McVeigh was only spouting hot air at first. You take that murder up in Polson a few months back. Gun shop owner gunned down execution style; weapons stolen, that smacks of militia."

Tara, understanding that Jack was going into one of his rants, normal's good, she reflected decided to change the subject.

"Enough of that talk. Jason Connors was quite something, don't you think," she teased.

"Tara Claymore, don't think you're gonna make me bite. Jason Connors might look the real deal, but I know you're only interested in how many horses he'd of a mind to buy."

"Oh is that so!"

"That's so!" replied Jack playfully.

Tara had flirted with Jason at the barbeque held after the rodeo and had negotiated a tentative deal for a dozen quarter horses, subject to inspection. He'd agreed to visit the Claymore ranch the following weekend. Tara had been pleased with herself ever since. Jason, hunk that he was, wasn't her type, but he'd proven charming and amiable, and said work permitting he'd personally look over the stock with his ranch foreman. "If what I've heard about 'Reynolds Horses' turns out to be true we'll have a deal on the spot."

"He liked me," continued Tara devilishly. "That's why we got the deal."

Jack laughed as he stuffed his face with pancake; he had a trick up his sleeve to counter Tara's impish behaviour.

"You're not the only one that can charm a deal from a member of the opposite sex." Jack let his words hang like a worm on the end of a fishing line.

Tara's face changed slightly, which in turn made Jack smile.

"Yes I know I saw you in deep conversation with the congressman's wife. She's not your type," Tara added cattily.

"Ruth's a nice looking woman, a handsome looking woman as you western types like to say," he mocked.

"Sssh," replied Tara.

"Ruth told me her husband had a fondness for Morgan horses and she'd heard we specialised in Morgans' so I told her about Dark Shadow. She seems genuinely interested."

"Hah, but you ain't got a deal!"

"Not yet, but she's promised to phone in the next few days. She says it has to be kept a close secret, as his birthday is in two weeks."

"We'll see," said Tara.

*　*　*

The following weekend Jason Connors good as his word arrived with his foreman Lucas Jacobson, a gnarled old hand that knew horse-flesh better than most. The older man entered the corral that held a hand picked bunch of Quarter horses and proceeded to inspect each and everyone. On his say so the horses in turn were loaded into the horseboxes that Jason had brought with him.

"Tara was all smiles and teeth," as Jack told it the following day at the Crazy AW ranch-house. "I tell you Wade she was like an overgrown school girl, starry eyed or what."

"I wasn't you dumb ox, I was negotiating a lucrative deal."

"Smiles and teeth," Jack repeated.

"I detect a little of the green eyed monster," interrupted Alex.

"Well I have to admit Lucas was the real deal," continued Jack with his joshing. "He must have been coming up to his seventies."

"Well he was cute," cut in Tara. The good humoured banter continued a little longer until . . . . "Okay Jack, cut to the chase, did I negotiate a sweet deal or what?"

"You did sweetheart, you done good." Jack gave Wade and Alex a mischievous wink.

Just when he thought the bantering had stopped. "Oh tell them about the phone-call that never happened," the bantering was resumed.

"There's still time," replied Jack.

*   *   *

It was a couple of days later; just as Jack had given up on the congressman's wife's promise, he received the phone-call.

"Hello Jack, its Ruth, Ruth Holbrook. I'm sorry for the delay in calling, I've been busy. I've no time to see the animal we discussed, but I'll take your word he's everything you say he is and more. I'd like you to deliver him to the ranch this Saturday at three in the afternoon. I'm throwing a surprise garden party for Vince in the grounds and I'd love for you and your lovely wife to attend."

Jack was thrown by her automatic assumption that he could drop everything and bow to her whim. "It's not that easy, we've commitments," he protested.

"Oh Jack this is so important to me. You can't let me down, I'll owe you."

Jack guessed this was as close to begging as this woman had ever been. He began to reel off a list of excuses which she dismissed just as quickly. His resolve began to crumble, which she seemed to sense immediately.

"Oh thank you Jack, thank you. We'll expect you at three sharp."

Then the phone went dead leaving Jack to pick up the pieces. Rich important people always seemed to get what they wanted, no matter what. It stuck in his craw, but business was business. All he had to do now was sell the idea to Tara.

* * *

"I tell you Tara, she's paying top dollar."

"Top dollar my ass! She's got you running around in circles!"

"That ain't fair, and you know it. What's wrong with us mixing with the congressman and his associates?"

"Hell Jack, we won't be circulating, we'll be classed as the hired help."

"I won't let that happen. We're as good as them, perhaps even better. I say we're going. If you feel uncomfortable we'll make our excuses and get the hell out."

Tara loved it when he was masterful. It was one of the things that had attracted her. Jack was right, she thought, 'it was good for business and who knows we might even make a few sales while we're about it.'

"Okay, you win. Now where is the Holbrook Ranch?"

"It's on the outskirts of Deer Lodge."

"Deer Lodge! That's the state prison!"

"It's closer to the old Grant Kohrs ranch than the prison."

"Oh, that's alright then!" exclaimed Tara with a hint of sarcasm.

* * *

Ruth Holbrook nervously checked her watch, everything had gone off as planned; she only hoped the final part of her surprise was on schedule. In front of a crowd of influential friends and business associates she announced the highlight of the afternoon's festivities.

Ruth glanced once more towards the entrance to the ranch and was relieved to see a pickup with a horse trailer entering under the oak beamed gateway. "Happy Birthday Vince," she cried and gestured with a sweep of the arm to the fast approaching pickup.

A crowd formed as the pickup and horse trailer made a wide circle before coming to a stop in front of Ruth and Vince. Jack climbed out of the pickup tipped his hat to Ruth and said, "Happy birthday Congressman Holbrook."

Tara had taken the distraction of Jack's entrance to slip unnoticed to the rear of the horse trailer and set down the ramp and opened the rear tailgate. A wow went up from the crowd as Tara led the Morgan gently towards Vince Holbrook.

"He's yours darling, happy birthday," cried Ruth.

Vince Holbrook hugged his wife appreciatively, "I don't know just what to say, he's magnificent."

Dark Shadow stood proudly and whinnied his approval as Vince gave him an affectionate rub. "Friends already," cried Vince. The crowd echoed his approval.

"Darling, you remember Jack and Tara from the Dillon Rodeo."

"I surely do. If I remember rightly your pa gave me the third degree," he said looking straight at Tara.

"That's pa alright," she replied, slightly embarrassed.

Ruth sensing the discomfort called a stable hand over, who took Dark Shadow towards the stables. "Hey we've a party to celebrate, you can spend time with Dark Shadow after the guests have all gone. Tara, Jack let me introduce you to some of our friends."

Tara smiled nervously, looked towards Jack for reassurance, caught his grin and began to relax. These were not Tara's kind of people, but they were polite and friendly enough and it wasn't too long before she realised she was enjoying the afternoon. With Jack at her side she could conquer anything.

"Jack, Tara, I'd like to introduce my very good friend and possible running mate next time around, Carson Burroughs," cried the congressman.

Jack stared into the dark brooding eyes of Carson Burroughs and felt an icy sliver run up his spine. His smile fixed on Tara, then switched to Jack almost in an instant. His hand outstretched in greeting, the quintessential politician's politician.

Jack and Tara in turn shook Carson's hand and Jack very clumsily asked if he was a lover of horses. Carson grimaced and said, "To tell you the truth, they frighten the hell out of me." Jack and Tara laughed politely at his confession. "I'm afraid I like to keep my feet firmly on the ground."

"I can understand that," replied Jack. "Before I came to Montana the only horses I ever saw were the ones at the racetrack."

"How long have you lived in Montana?" asked Burroughs.

"Close on ten years I suppose."

"What brought you to Montana in the first place?"

"That's a long story."

"Hold it, now I remember. It was all over the papers. Wasn't you involved in a shooting a few years back?"

Jack's face darkened, the man unsettled him, that Burroughs had done his homework was obvious, even to a Montana horse breeder.

Tara intervened; diplomacy wasn't one of Jack's traits. "No he wasn't. I lost three friends that day and I don't like being reminded of it."

"I'm sorry, forgive my insensitivity."

"It's forgotten," replied Tara.

Just at the right moment Ruth moved in between Jack and Carson. "Carson, darling, I'm afraid I'm going to have to deprive you of Jack and Tara's company for a while."

Glad of the distraction Jack and Tara followed Ruth across the manicured lawns towards the mock Ranch style house. It was a magnificent structure, in fact the whole set up of Vince Holbrook's ranch looked quite wonderful, but its neatness told its own story. Tara didn't doubt Ruth and Vince's sincerity in their choice of house and grounds but it wouldn't fool a real Westerner.

"Sorry to drag you away, but I believe we have some business to attend too."

"Ruth, there's no need to break away from your party, we can bill you in the usual way," said Jack lamely as he ascended the steps to the house.

"Nonsense, I'm sure Dark Shadow is everything you said he was and more. The asking price, four thousand I believe."

Jack nodded and watched as Ruth opened a drawer and began writing a cheque. With a quick flourish she put pen and cheque back in the drawer and handed Tara the cheque.

"There's a mistake!" exclaimed Tara, "this cheque is too much."

"Five hundred dollars, yes I know. But you did deliver the horse and on time I might add."

"Tara's right," added Jack.

"She might be, but I've monopolised your whole day. It's my way of showing you how much I appreciated you taking the time and trouble. I did leave you no choice." Ruth smiled and left them no room to manoeuvre.

"Well thank you," said Jack gracefully, "and I must say it's been a wonderful afternoon."

With business attended too, and the sun slowly sinking in the west Jack and Tara said their goodbyes. It was a pleasant balmy evening and the drive home was relaxed and mellow.

"They're a nice couple, don't you think," said Jack almost to himself.

"Yeah, I suppose you're right. They were not at all what I'd expected. Vince seems to be a nice guy, for a politician, that is! I might even vote for him."

"Yeah, me too. She was nice."

"You would say that. Good looking, sophisticated and charming. I don't buy it."

"What! You'd have liked her better if she'd been plain and down right boring!"

"No! I'm saying I can't make her out. No one could be that good."

Chapter 18

Montana

Karl Bremer was growing twitchy and Bob Knox didn't like it one bit. Bremer's coldly calculated manner in how to deal with the solution was sitting heavily on his shoulders. Shooting both Guthrie and Schneider would eliminate the problem, but finding others out there with the same cause and ruthless streak wouldn't be easy. He guessed that Coulter needed two shooters for the target, catching him whoever he was from two different angles. It made sense to Knox's military background for Bremer and Schneider to be the two shooters, and for him and Guthrie to supply back up. He was reluctant to lose a good soldier. It was then that he hit on a plan. Both men had proven able in the Havre bank robbery, but as Bob Knox recalled, the robbery had gone off without loss of life, mostly down to Guthrie's smooth planning. To smooth, he pondered. Then Knox recalled how Schneider had been frustrated at not killing anybody, but was that just an act?

Acting on instinct Bob Knox pulled Schneider to one side a few days later.

"I've reason to believe Guthrie isn't who he says he is. You've been itching to prove your worth. Deal with it!"

Knox figured that if Schneider was working undercover he'd make some excuse to get out of killing Guthrie, if he didn't then Ray Guthrie bank robber extraordinaire would be dead meat.

On the pretext of testing out their weaponry Knox lured both men into a secluded wooded area of the Warlock Ranch. Karl Bremer had cried off, a stomach complaint being his excuse, but in reality he'd been ordered by Knox to set himself up in the woods to cover the two suspected men. In truth Karl wanted to take them both out but Knox had ordered otherwise.

"If Schneider hesitates for more than a minute, clip Schneider," it was a coldly delivered order and Bremer set himself for the task ahead.

In a clearing a half mile from the ranch house, Knox gave Schneider the nod. Seconds later the truth was exposed. Schneider pointed the Ruger Black Hawk at the back of Guthrie's head and squeezed the trigger. The man flew backwards with half his head blown away.

"Does that satisfy you," said Schneider coldly.

"Damn," muttered Karl Bremer under his breath as he eased off his trigger finger.

*   *   *

It was mid-morning of the following day in a clearing not far from Elmo when a couple of fishermen found the burnt out wreck of a car. Inside was a badly charred body. By lunch-time the Highway Patrol had sealed off the area and forensics had moved in. By evening the FBI were apprised of the situation, and the local TV stations were relaying the news footage hourly.

The old TV gave out a poor reception but it was enough to unnerve Bob Knox, he was clearly shaken, but a call later that evening from Adam Coulter's throwaway cell phone eased him considerably. "Sit tight, you did everything that I told you?"

"We did everything to the letter. Schneider drove in Guthrie's old Ford to the location you said, set the car ablaze, then walked a mile down the road where Karl was waiting to pick him up."

"And no one saw you on the road?"

"It was dark, the road was quiet, ain't no one saw us."

"Then you're home free. I'll call when the time is right. In the meantime, use the time wisely. You'll need another recruit. I'd suggest you look for new blood, but not from the militia."

"Why not?" asked Knox.

"It's infested with informants. Use Jim Haggerty, he'll have an idea of the kind of man you're looking for. Don't tell him any more than you have too. He's with the militia, but there's a line even he won't cross."

"And if he gets wind of what we're doing?"

"Make sure he doesn't."

"In the meantime, what do we do?"

"It's covert operation; you've now become a sleeper cell. As such Sergeant Knox I'd expect you to act accordingly. Take a break, drink beer, buy a couple of women, do what you want, but keep your noses clean and your mouths shut. This is a military style operation and it has to remain so for however long it takes."

"Yes sir!"

Adam Coulter smile to himself, he could almost see Knox standing to attention. He'd chosen wisely, the sergeant would control his men with military precision and whoa betide any one that stepped out of line. Coulter removed the SIM card from the throwaway cell phone and destroyed it. Now there was nothing that could link him to Knox. It had all been going smoothly until he heard an off the cuff remark from a colleague that an unnamed agent had infiltrated an extremist militia cell. On it's own it wouldn't have raise any alarm bells, but when the colleague mentioned the Havre bank robbery Coulter's blood ran cold. He could have dropped the operation like a hot potato, but knowing that the Bureau was on to the cell could and would work to his advantage. The Bureau knew that something big was being planned, what they didn't know was just how big.

Frustrated though he was, Adam realised that everything comes to him that waits. And in a way Adam had almost all he'd every craved. That his relationship with Ruth had to stay under wraps for the foreseeable future wasn't so bad. Playing the waiting game just that bit longer, couldn't hurt none, as Carson Burroughs he'd been playing the waiting game most all his life.

Tall, ambitious, darkly handsome and going places was how you'd describe Carson Burroughs but it wasn't enough. He'd been in Congressman Vince Holbrook's shadow most all their working lives. Best friends at college, they studied law together and then politics, Burroughs more than edging it in all departments, but it was always Holbrook who came out on top. A little matter of Holbrook's family wealth and standing saw to that. But not this time, all that was about to change and it was a woman that was at the heart of it, Holbrook's wife Ruth to be exact.

Carson Burroughs couldn't believe his luck when Ruth Holbrook first came on to him. Congressman Holbrook had been called away unexpectedly and couldn't make a charity dinner, not wanting to disappoint his lovely wife he asked his best friend Carson Burroughs to escort her. Burroughs had just gone through a messy divorce and the last thing he wanted was to escort his friend's wife to yet another social engagement, but as Holbrook's aide he had no choice in the matter. Vince Holbrook was an ambitious man who'd designs on the next governorship and beyond and whatever the next Governor of Montana wanted he got, including his best friend as running mate.

It wasn't the divorce, nor the boring charity dinner that irked him, it was being in the presence of Ruth Holbrook. Ruth had always remained aloof to Carson, which only added to the torment he was feeling. He'd been in love with her from the first moment they met. It had been at a charity dinner some three years earlier. Carson remembered it as if it was yesterday. Vince made a late entrance with Ruth on his arm. He apologised gracefully then with a smile so wide it would shame a Cheshire cat, he introduced Ruth to Carson and his then wife Gloria. Ruth was a knockout and Vince Holbrook knew it. The look on Carson's face as he gazed at her said it all. Vince could see the look of envy etched across Carson's face and inwardly grinned to him self. Despite being friends from college day he secretly revelled in his friend's discomfort, his also ran status and the very fact that Carson though brilliant at his job was only there because Vince Holbrook deemed it so. Holbrook had designs on being the future governor of Montana. He knew it was going to be an up hill struggle; Marc Radicot had been re-elected in 96 and his

Lieutenant Governor was a woman, a woman popular with the electorate. Vince knew if he was to stand an outside chance then he needed the very best. Despite everything, Carson Burroughs was the right man for the job. Yet with all Holbrook's conniving and game playing he'd forgotten just one thing, his wife.

Ruth Holbrook had done everything in her power to make Vince love her. Her wedding day some six months after they'd met was when she finally knew it was just a marriage of convenience. Yet she went through with the wedding hoping he'd change. In public Vince was the most charming, most loving man she'd ever known, but when out of the public eye he was cold and distant. At first Ruth had put it down to his growing career and ambition, but as year followed year she began to realise hers was a loveless marriage.

Since Carson Burroughs' divorce, Ruth found herself steadily growing closer to him. It was little wonder that after a few drinks she'd made a pass. She regretted it almost from the moment it happened. It was wrong, it shouldn't have happened. She knew just how much he felt about her, she'd played to his emotions, and that was unfair. She tried turning the clock back, but it was too late. She'd dropped her guard and was defenceless to resist Burroughs charms.

Carson Burroughs, long-time friend and confidant of Vince Holbrook set in motion a plan that until he slept with Ruth had been little more than wishful thinking. Unbeknown to her she'd become the catalyst in a plan that had been festering in his brain, a plan that would see him with the woman of his dreams, a plan that would eventually see him elected governor of Montana.

Ruth's first reaction was to break off the affair as quickly and quietly as possible, and she did just that. But she'd misjudged one thing; Carson himself. He'd begged her not to end it, and then he declared his undying love for her. It was too much for Ruth to bear, she'd craved love, but been denied. With Carson there was at least a furtive chance at love.

Carson had kept his secret desires to himself, he'd loved Ruth since the very first time he'd set eyes on her. Her generous pink lips that framed her perfect white teeth, the smile that emulated from them lips, the cute button nose and those hazel eyes framed by the silvery blond hair, he could go on and on in his head, he loved every part of her. When she declared her love for him he became putty in her hands.

But it was Vince Holbrook himself that had finally forced Carson's desire to the fore. In an act of petulance over some new legislation that he'd been forced to shelve he vented his anger on Carson. "I asked you to do a simple thing and you failed. Tell me, what good will you be when I'm elected governor?"

Carson was rendered speechless; the legislation that Holbrook alluded to was absolutely nothing to do with him. He just stood there and took it. As Holbrook's temper subsided and his recollection of whom the main culprit was he changed tact and continued talking as if the outburst hadn't happened. No words of apology came forth from the Congressman's mouth. It was then that Carson Burroughs decided to carry out his plan.

It was a simple plan, the best plans are just that; simple. His knowledge of the criminal mind, his case studies of the Montana Militia and the recent tragedies at Waco, Ruby Ridge and finally the bombing in Oklahoma showed him the lengths people would go to in their fight for what they believed in, no matter how misguided.

Trawling through government and police records, he selected then shortlisted suitable candidates before finally settling on ex marine sergeant Bob Knox. It wasn't by accident that Bob Knox met Adam Coulter in a bar in Kalispell. Carson Burroughs heavily disguised, had parked his rental car in a disused parking lot south of town, then he'd taken out a foldaway bike and cycled to the outskirts of town before walking the short distance to Kalispell. He knew Bob Knox's habits better than the man himself, so locating him was easy. Engaging him in conversation wasn't hard. A couple of return visits later he had the man eating out of his hand. His story was that he was a retired Colonel that felt just the same as most other militia types, that he had a plan that would bring down the government, that he needed a leader, someone that would obey orders without question. Bob Knox was sceptical until Adam handed him ten thousand dollars to finance the mission.

Two stages of the mission had been carried out and there was no way that Carson/Adam could be connected to the crimes. That a man, two men in fact had been killed did not faze Burroughs in the least, taking Vince Holbrook out of the equation was priority number one. He had covered his tracks, Knox was the only contact and after the third part of the mission he wouldn't be a problem. Knox believed that stage one, two and three were just the dress rehearsal for the big one. Carson had hinted at the importance and that he would lead the mission, it was just smoke and mirrors.

Chapter 19

Montana. 1997

Wade kicked the snow from his boots and entered the house. He could feel the warmth of the room fit around him like an old glove.

"Damned if it ain't cold as hell!"

"Now that's an oxymoron if ever I heard one," cried Alex from the kitchen.

"An oxy what?"

"Forget it, you wouldn't understand. If it ain't got four legs, bellows from one end and does just about every thing else from the other then it's no use to you," cried Alex in return. Her manner was light and airy. Wade sensed she had things to tell.

"Okay, spill the beans," replied Wade absentmindedly as he took off his coat and pulled at his gloves. Before she could answer he'd discarded the gloves and was rubbing his hands together and holding them over the fire.

"You'll get chilblains," she cried.

"Chilblains my ass," replied Wade good-humouredly. "Now what's gotten into you?"

"Nothing, only do you remember a couple of months back, over Christmas dinner it was. We were all sitting around toasting the season and our good fortune when you up and said it would just be complete if only Fletcher had been there with us." Wade turned from the log fire and Alex had his full attention. "Well guess what! Fletch phoned earlier today."

"What did he say? Is he coming home?"

Just then the phone rang. Wade stood up and walked across the floor cussing, "Now who in the Sam Hill would be calling us at this time?"

Alex smiled to herself, "Answer it and you'll find out."

"Reynolds ranch."

"Hi Wade, its Fletch."

"Fletcher!"

That was all he talked about over dinner, through the evening and finally in the bedroom. "Fletcher's coming home, I cain't hardly believe it. Johnny J's son is finally coming home."

"Just don't be getting your hopes up," cautioned Alex.

* * *

As Fletcher ended his call and put the handset back on its cradle the airport's speaker system announce the last call for his flight to Seattle. Grabbing his grip he headed straight for the departure gate.

Fletcher Coppersmith was coming home, not the home of his childhood, nor the formative years of his youth. No, he was coming home to the land of his ancestors. Home to a place where he belonged, but for how long? The place had special memories for him, but it was also a place of great sadness. It had been four years since Merri's death and he hadn't fully gotten over it, he doubted he ever would. He was coming home to be with Merri, to sit at her graveside up near Cougar Pass and talk. He believed that being close to her he'd find the answers to his questions. He was sure Merri would guide him along the true path.

* * *

"When did he say he was arriving?" said Wade over breakfast the following morning.

"He didn't. He said he was coming but he was kind of vague about when. So I guess we'll have to carry on much as before. He'll come when he's good and ready."

It was a similar reaction when Alex phoned Tara. "Yeah, it was out of the blue. He phoned Wade last night and said he was coming home," Alex detected a pause, "Yes that's right, he said he's coming home."

"To stay?"

"Well your pa seems to think so, but then he would. I don't know. It could be, or then again it might only be a visit. I told Wade not to get his hopes up."

"Well you know pa. When's he arriving?"

"That we don't know, he was a little vague about when, so I guess we'll see him when we see him."

* * *

For the first week Wade was full of optimism, then as week one flowed into two, then three his cheerfulness decreased. Alex told him to forget about the pending visit and get on with running the ranch.

"Soon as you do, Fletch will appear," she kept telling him.

Winter slowly began to release its grip on the valley, green shoots like little islands in a sea of snow slowly formed. As every day dawned those islands became countries then vast swages of greenery forced back the retreating tide of winter and became continents, spring had announced its arrival.

Irritation and impatience gave way to new hope. Spring had arrived and work was a calling. It was Wade's favourite time of year. That was one of the reasons why he was glad that Fletcher was coming home. The man had proven a willing and very capable hand during the few short years he'd been at the ranch and as Wade's natural successor he could take over the reins maybe sooner than later.

Years before when Fletcher was to marry Merri, Wade had signed over a half share of the ranch, the other half would in time go to Tara. Wade had believed he owed a debt to his old partner and best friend Johnny J, a man that had asked for nothing more from their partnership than a paint horse. Wade thought long and hard before he made his decision. He'd consulted with Alex, who'd said it was Tara who he should be talking too, after all it was her inheritance he was messing with.

It caused Wade a sleepless night, but he needn't have worried. Tara thought it was a wonderful gesture.

"From what you've told me, Johnny J was a rightful heir, so why not, besides me and Merri are as good as sisters."

Tara and Jack had their own ranch over at Big Hole Pass and although small in comparison to the Crazy AW, it was all both of them wanted. They had made it quite clear they preferred to run a horse ranch, although both activities took up more hours than daylight allowed, to them horse ranching was more rewarding. Wade had begrudging accepted their decision and vowed to keep going for as long as was humanly possible, but with Merri to marry Fletcher he'd seen a way out without the necessity of selling the Crazy AW.

"Needless to say, you and Jack will be entitled to fifty percent of any profit from the Crazy AW."

"Yeah pa, I get the picture," said Tara.

But with Merri's untimely death Fletcher had been too overcome with grief to take up Wade's offer. Now thought Wade excitedly, after four years in the wilderness he was returning to claim his birthright.

For the next month Wade and the crew had their hands full with every chore imaginable. Wade didn't have time to dwell on when or even if Fletcher would turn up. Then as with everything else the moment you forget about what's on your mind, things happen.

Wade was bringing in a few strays when in the far distance he saw an unfamiliar car drive under the gateway and head towards the ranch-house.

"Larry, if I miss my guess, I'd say that's Fletcher. You okay by yourself? I've a mind to welcome the son of a gun."

"Don't mind me Wade, go too it. Say hello to him from me."

"If it's him, stop by the house tonight. We'll maybe have a beer or two."

"I reckon," replied Larry with a wide grin.

Wade broke away from the bunch and rode at a fast lope towards the house. From his vantage point atop of his favourite Morgan he watched as the car came to a halt outside the ranch-house. As the driver of the unfamiliar car unfurled himself from the driver's side Wade recognised the shock of jet black hair that graced a near bronzed face that on seeing his approach, broke into a wide tombstone white smile. Fletcher had finally come home.

Wade swung out of the saddle in an easy practised way and advanced on the visitor. "I swear, you look more like your father than ever." He extended his hand. And Fletcher gripped it hard and pulled Wade forward and hugged him hard as hell.

"I've missed you Wade, more than you'll ever know. How are things?"

"Fine, fine . . . Beef prices are levelling out, grass is over grazed, the winter took a long time dying, yeah things are about the same as when you up and left."

Wade and Fletcher walked the horse to the corral, where he was unsaddled, rubbed down and brushed. The smell of horses, old leather and liniment invaded Fletcher's senses causing him to smile broadly.

"It's good to be back," he cried as Wade finished off brushing his horse and led her into a stall.

"Come on now; let's be up to the house," replied Wade with a grin to match the return of the prodigal.

Alex came out onto the porch to greet Fletcher a smile as big as Texas spread across her face. There were hugs all round.

* * *

"I took the liberty of inviting Larry and the boys up to the house tonight," said Wade to Alex after she'd shown Fletcher his room. "Did he mention how long he's staying," continued Wade in the same breath.

"No he didn't and don't you be worrying him none about it. He's only just arrived," chastised Alex.

*   *   *

An hour or so later came the knock on the door. Larry's beaming face was the first to enter. His bulk obliterating the others as he walked up to Fletcher one hand outstretched the other swept his hat from his head.

"Great to see you," he said as he shook Fletcher's hand vigorously.

Then Bud Angel appeared from behind Larry, nodded then shook Fletcher's hand before reaching out for the offered cold one which Wade handed him.

"Hey, you old reprobate, you're still in the land of the living, now don't that beat all," joshed Fletcher as Thadeus Barnes stepped into view.

Throughout the evening there was much hand wringing, as others emerged from the bunkhouse. There were old tales told, beers drunk, jokes pulled on the unsuspecting, and a general feeling of companionship, something Fletcher hadn't experienced too much of during his lifetime. But there was one thing missing. He guessed those that had known her would know how he was feeling.

By nine thirty that evening, Larry and the boys had said goodnight and headed back to their respective lodgings, Larry to his wife, Bud to the bunkhouse with the rest of the boys and Thadeus to a little cabin close to the back of the house.

"The boys have grown a mite sensitive since I left," said Fletcher just as Wade was about to excused himself and head for bed.

"How so," Wade replied.

Alex with a knowing look towards Fletcher said. "The boys didn't want to spoil your home coming I reckon. I guess they'll get around to it tomorrow or sometime. She's never far from any of our thoughts."

"Yeah we miss her too," added Wade with a hint of melancholy to his voice.

Fletcher smiled sadly, "In truth, that's why I've come back. I've a lot on my mind right now and I need to get my head clear. If you'll loan me a horse I reckon I'm going up to Cougar Pass first light. I need to sit with her awhile."

Wade looked at Alex but ignored her silent pleas. "Horse and supplies are where they've always been, this is your home remember, so don't you go forgetting you own half this here spread."

Alex could see that Wade was pressing to hard. "Let the boy rest. You two can do all your talking tomorrow evening when the chores are done."

Taking the hint Wade stood up, "See, she doesn't change. Good night Fletch."

*   *   *

At first light Fletcher threw a saddle across an Appaloosa that kinda took his fancy. It looked a sturdy and willing animal, strong of legs and sharp of eye. It whinnied nervously as he pulled on the cinch. It felt good, there in the barn with the smell of horse and leather. He reckoned that if Merri had lived he'd have felt comfortable enough to spend the rest of his life riding these mountains and foothills. But she was gone and without her Fletcher couldn't see himself sticking with the life that Wade wore so well.

Four years in the wilderness, sheep farming in Australia, horse wrangling in New Zealand, then a spell at sea before returning to the States. Maybe if he'd come straight to Montana, things might have been different. But instead he'd disembarked from his ship at New Orleans where he'd fallen foul of the US Immigration Department. He was slightly taken aback when he was stopped. His passport and papers were in order, he was an American citizen born and bred. When asked to accompany an immigration officer and two surly looking security staff he'd gone willingly through a door marked authorised personnel only, along a narrow corridor and finally into a small windowless office. Told to sit down, he protested and demanded to know what was going on. The immigration officer ignored his protests and stated that a man would be along to see him presently and that it would be in Fletcher's interests to sit down and shut up. Then he left, the two surly security staff stood on either side of the door, almost baiting him to make a try for it. Five minutes, where Fletcher found his patience brought to near breaking point, his mind exploring his past for something concrete for him to grasp.

Things changed for him after that meeting, he changed, his whole way of looking at things changed and now he was here, on the land that his father had called home but it wasn't his home. A part of his heart lay buried up in these hills, but beyond that the land meant nothing to him.

*   *   *

As he rode up through the foothills the memories came flooding back. Bitter sweet they were, but nonetheless they brought comfort to him as he climbed higher. He passed through a stand of silver birch, their fresh green leaves shimmering in the mid morning sun, re-awakening the time he's watched as Merri had ridden unsuspectingly through the trees then across a clearing before glancing back towards his hiding place. A lump formed at the back of his throat. It could have been so perfect.

The timber became thicker, darker, the pine fronds blotting out the rays of sunshine, cooling the temperature dramatically. There was a sense of foreboding about the place. The appaloosa whinnied nervously as it trod its path noisily over dried pine needles and cones and then suddenly after twenty minutes of darkness the sun broke through revealing the clearing that preceded the old cabin.

Tears filled Fletcher's eyes as he spied the tiny grass mound that was Merri's grave. He thanked God for the kindness of others as he noted that the grave had been well taken care of in his absence. Slowly he brought his horse to a halt and dismounted. He tied the reins of the appaloosa to a nearby branch. Taking off his hat he walked slowly towards the grave and knelt down.

"Oh Merri, I miss you so much!"

He remained there until the sun went down, before slowly standing up. "It's late my darling. Time for me to see to my horse, water and feed him, then I guess I'll turn in for the night."

Gathering up the reins he led the horse to the old cabin. It was then that he noticed the appaloosa he'd ridden up on that morning. It was Merri's favourite horse. He'd a choice of horses that morning; all as good as one another but subconsciously he'd chosen Merri's. It was a sign, his Crow ancestry rose to the fore. It was a sign from Merri, a sign that she was looking over him. She stayed with him through his late meal, the unfurling of his bedroll and finally as he slowly drifted off.

It was before five o'clock when he arose from a strangely comforting sleep. His mind was clear, clearer than it had been in weeks and the reason for him being there was clearer still.

Chapter 20

Montana

Carson Burroughs hesitated as his thumb hovered over the send button. It had been six months since he'd last spoken with Bob Knox. Was he prepared to open Pandora's Box? It was a question he'd been asking himself through the dark days of winter. His resolve to have both a crack at the governorship and the hand of Ruth Holbrook was still as strong as ever. How long could he bear to put up with a few furtive moments, a touch of hand, a look, it was tearing him apart. He'd agonised over leaving things as they were, telling Vince Holbrook he didn't deserve Ruth and run for office against his friend. It would be the honourable thing to do, but deep down Carson knew he was a coward. He knew Vince with all his wealth would ruin him and Ruth into the bargain. 'Would that be so bad,' he thought. 'At the very least I'd have Ruth.' But in reality he knew that was impossible for him; he wanted it all. The woman, the position, the power, the adulation of others, Carson craved it; he wanted to be Vince Holbrook! 'Yes,' he thought, 'this is the only way.' His thumb hit the send button.

"Is that you Knox?"

"Yes," came the guarded reply. "Coulter? We'd just about given you up."

Burroughs ignored the agitation in Knox's voice, "How are things your end?"

"Okay, Karl's going stir crazy and Schneider's climbing the walls, but we're hanging tough."

"So, no repercussions?"

"None man, that was in a different lifetime. Why's it taken you so long to get in touch?"

It was the inevitable questions, which Carson chose to ignore; he only hoped the long delay hadn't diminished Knox's enthusiasm.

Before he could say anything Knox interrupted. "When are we going to move, this damn government needs another shakeup! I trusted you man, but I'd almost given you up."

"Yeah, I'm sorry about that, but circumstances weren't favourable."

"You said it would be big, but hell man I really thought you'd be in touch before now."

Carson could sense Knox's irritation, "It's big, as I told you, bigger than Oklahoma." The sucking in of breath told Burroughs all he needed to know about the man he'd put in charge. He was dangerous beyond words, capable of causing terrifying death and destruction on many innocent lives. Carson reflected that Knox and his ilk would be no loss to mankind.

"So when?" enquired Knox.

"I'm working on the schedule of the target, once I know, you'll know."

"Okay," said Knox, the irritation clearly heard in his voice, "but you'd better make it soon or we're gone!"

"Three weeks, a month at the latest," replied Burroughs as he pressed the disconnect button. He hoped he'd said enough to keep the man onside. Then he removed the SIM card and threw it down a drain. He smiled to himself, 'no repercussions,' he was home and dry. Experience had shown Carson that the less someone like Knox knew the more eager he would be to carry out the next stage and go on to Hungry Horse, except there was no Hungry Horse. The political assassination of the next governor of Montana was the end of the line for Bob Knox and his bunch of psychopaths.

Carson Burroughs political views matched that of Vince Holbrook's. Defence of their country above all else, which meant fighting unpopular wars, the eradication of terrorism both urban and international, law and order, healthcare for everyone, the stamping out of illiteracy, and full employment. A tall order for any party, but essential if you wanted to ride the gravy train. And he felt he was far more qualified than the flamboyant Holbrook. 'At least with me at the helm the good people of Montana had a chance,' thought Carson as he justified what he was putting into motion.

The political assassination of Holbrook wouldn't be easy unless the persons carrying out the deed had prior knowledge of his whereabouts. One of Carson's responsibilities as Vince Holbrook's running mate was to review all safety procedures. He'd know in advance all the public meetings and social events that Holbrook would be attending. The assassination was liable to cause a shit storm, but the way Carson had planned it, Knox and his obsession with the government would take all the blame, and he and his cohorts weren't coming out of this alive.

Chapter 21

Montana

Fletcher gathered some spring flowers from the copse of woods and lay them on Merri's grave. Stretching himself to his full height he gazed down at the neatly manicured mound and his eyes misted over. He so hated to leave her, it had been hard when he left the last time, but it was tempered by the fact that one day he knew he would return. This time was different, he had things to do, things of major importance, things which could get him killed.

He wiped the tears from his eyes and mouthed a silent goodbye. Within a minute he was saddled up and heading back towards the ranch. He'd just about reached the clearing from where he'd once spied upon Merri when he spotted a familiar rider approaching him. There was no mistaking the man on the big Buckskin.

For a moment Fletcher felt the beginnings of panic. He'd wished to have avoided telling Wade his true intentions until later that evening, but as usual Wade had a way of forcing the issue.

"Howdy Wade, what brings you up here this morning?"

"You, my friend. We've got things to discuss," replied Wade.

Both men stretched themselves in the saddle. Fletcher knew he'd have to take charge before Wade started on about the ranch and such.

"You're right Wade, we have things to discuss, but not the things you're apt to be talking about."

Wade was slightly taken aback, "I thought . . . ."

You thought wrong. I'm sorry, but I ain't here to settle. I know you might feel bound in some way to my father, but you ain't. I don't want this life!"

Fletcher's word bit into Wade like an arctic wind. He struggled for the words. "Well why are you back?"

"I don't mean to be unkind, you and Alex are the nearest I got to kin." He risked a look at Wade, the disappointment still clearly etched upon his face. "What you're offering is far in excess of my needs. It was a generous offer, but that was for me and Merri. If she'd been around things would have been different, but without her this life ain't for me."

Wade wanted to say something, anything, but it wasn't his way. He wasn't in the habit of begging. "Go on," he encouraged.

"I spent the last few years, as you know, on faraway out stations in Australia and New Zealand. I needed time alone. I needed to look back over the mess my life had become. I wanted to find my true self. As you know I've done some bad things in my past. Things I ain't proud off. Loving Monique was probably the biggest mistake of my life."

Wade couldn't help but comment, "You put that right."

Fletcher gave Wade a withering look, "Yeah I did didn't I." He looked back from whence he came and let out an involuntary sigh. "If only things had been different. You know Wade, it took me nigh on four years to straighten myself out. I wanted my life back, I wanted to be the carefree Fletcher Coppersmith that I once was, but you can't go back. I tried it. I got as far as the port of New Orleans and even then I knew it was hopeless. I had no direction, I had no idea of where my life was heading, until I met a man called Sam Kilbane."

As Fletcher let the story unfold he was somehow transported back to that windowless office with the two burly security guards.

New Orleans. Louisiana

Fletcher looked up as the door to the room was flung open and a tall man around fifty wearing a finely cut suit and carrying a manila folder walked in and sat himself down at the table facing towards Fletcher. A quick flick of his arm and the two security men stepped out through the open door and shut it.

The tall man in the finely cut suit stood up and reached out his hand.

"Name's Kilbane, Sam Kilbane. I'm with the FBI!"

Fletcher took the offered hand and shook it, all the time wondering what the hell he'd got himself mixed up in.

"Bear with me a few minutes while I go over what I have in front of me." Without waiting to hear anything that Fletcher had to say he began to read from the folder. "Your name is Fletcher Coppersmith, aka Fletcher Delacroix, aka John Two Horses"

"I was never known as Delacroix. I was brought up by Roland Delacroix, but I was never family." The bitterness in hearing that name rose to the fore. "I was never a Delacroix, in name or in deed. I might have been there, I might have seen things but I was never one of them!"

"Okay, okay. We'll leave that for now. Let's concentrate on your birth parents. You were the only son of Annie Sparkling Waters and Johan Johanson. You lived the first years of your life with your mother in Oklahoma City. Then you moved to Rochefort where your father was reunited with you and your mother. Subsequent events, which we don't have to go into detail, happened and to all intent and purpose you were orphaned." Kilbane paused, his eyes looking straight at Fletcher.

"That about sums it up." In truth Fletcher couldn't recall too much that happened first hand, but after years of digging he'd finally learned the truth.

"From then on you were brought up by Roland Delacroix, given an education and finally became legal advisor to the Delacroix family."

"Okay, you know my life better than I do myself. I left that life behind. I saw what was going on and I finally got out."

Sam Kilbane was an expert at when to push and when not too. He chose his words carefully and got the reaction he expected, "Not before having an on off relationship with Monique Delacroix."

"Get the fuck out of here! I ain't done anything wrong. I know my rights. You can't pin a damn thing on me!"

"That's where you're wrong. I can pin anything I damn well want on you. As for rights, you ain't got any unless I say so!" threatened Kilbane. "But we don't want to go down that road." Years of interrogation had finely tuned his technique. "We," He let the word hang, "I need your help. Just let me finish and then I'll explain."

Fletcher was thrown by the man's words. It was true he could delve into his past and find something. He could make life difficult, but Fletcher sensed the man had other things on his mind.

"Al'right, I'll listen, but if I don't like what you have to say I'm free to go?"

"You're free to go," agreed Kilbane.

Fletcher listened intently as Sam Kilbane outlined how Fletcher had travelled to Montana with the now obviously insane Monique, where he'd falling head over heels in love with Merri and then to the subsequent failure of Monique's plans. There wasn't a thing left out in the folder that Sam Kilbane read from. The shoot out at Cougar Pass was especially detailed, Fletcher suspected most was from the coroner's report and the subsequent case the District Attorney had compiled for the manslaughter charges he'd hoped to bring against Fletcher and Wade. The case never reached court and never really looked like flying. There it all was, his life all wrapped up in an inch thick manila folder.

"Sorry I had to put you through all that, but to tell you the truth it was the first time I've read it. Your name was flagged. I was briefed and rushed down to interview you. We need your help. And after reading your file I can see why."

"You need my help!"

"I wasn't familiar with you, but I am familiar with a case of national importance. You're familiar with the Oklahoma bombing?"

"Yeah, they get papers out there too," replied Fletcher with a sarcastic edge to his voice.

"We're led to believe that an attack bigger than the Oklahoma bombing is in the final stages of its conception. We need a man inside, a man that knows the country, the people, especially the people. We need a man with a past, a man that's been out of circulation for awhile, a man that has a grudge. We're thinking you could be that man."

"Forget it!" replied Fletcher, "I ain't interested in risking my neck."

"That's what I thought you'd say. A man would be dumb to get involved in something that ain't his concern . . . ." Sam Kilbane paused before adding, "but it is the concern of Wade Reynolds, and his entire family."

"What!"

"To tell you more you'd have to sign a D notice."

Fletcher looked puzzled.

"It's an official document, effectively swearing you to secrecy," explained Kilbane.

An hour later Fletcher signed the D notice.

Montana

"So that's it in a nut shell. I'm on secondment to the FBI!"

"Well if that don't beat all," replied Wade aghast at Fletcher's story. "If this affects my family I've a right to know."

"That was a slight exaggeration of Sam Kilbane's. He wanted my full attention. What he meant was that the whole state of Montana and neighbouring states could be affected. Not you personally"

"Well, after whatever it is you've got to do, then maybe you'll return to us," said Wade hopefully.

"Sure, I'll come back, but not to take over the ranch. I know I took to the lifestyle very naturally, but the draw for me was Merri. It was always Merri."

Wade could see he was beaten, his shoulders dropped and he slowly turned his horse.

Fletcher called after him, "Wade, I need your help."

Wade turned back towards Fletcher, "And what do you think I can help you with," his tone carried a bitter resentment. He'd always felt in his heart that Fletcher would return and take over the ranch. Sadly he realised it was his dream, not Fletcher's.

Fletcher knew his next few words would probably hurt Wade even more. "I want you to revoke that agreement."

Wade looked puzzled.

"In fact I want you to tell the world that I'm a no good son of a bitch and that you wouldn't spit on me if I was on fire. I want you to go public; I want everyone to think I bear a grudge against you and your family."

"Why?"

"I think that's obvious. You know folks from here to Canada. I want the word spread that I came back seeking my inheritance. I want you to kick me off the ranch. I want every ranch hand, his wife, his girl friends, the local feed and grain store owner, just about everyone to know that I'm a lying two bit ass hole looking for a hand out."

Wade looked at his best friend's son and shook his head. The man was asking the impossible.

"Believe me Wade; it's vital to my cover. I wouldn't ask you if there was any other way. You've got to do this for me and you've got to tell no one."

"If I do this, I'll have to tell Alex. If I didn't she'd know something was up."

Reluctantly Fletcher agreed.

Both men walked their horses and stretched themselves in the saddle. Wade looked across at Fletcher, "When this, whatever this is, is over, promise me you'll come back and visit." Don't ever be a stranger.

Fletcher smiled, "When this is over, I'd be glad too."

* * *

It left a sour taste in everyone's mouths when news got out that Fletcher was only here for his share of the ranch.

"I'd have given it too, only I found out the son of a bitch had plans to sell it off to a large corporation."

"It just don't make any sense!" exclaimed Larry. "He always seemed such a nice guy."

"Four years can change a man," replied Wade. "I reckon there was more Delacroix in him than we'd thought."

Tara and Jack were equally mystified by the change in Fletcher. "How could we have got it so wrong? Merri would never have fell for a man like that. There's more too it, you hear!"

"Leave it girl! Leave it!" The subterfuge was killing Wade inside, but thankfully he had Alex to confide in.

* * *

It was four hellish long weeks of bar hopping, bad mouthing the Reynolds family, the inevitable fights that ensued because of it, the falling down drunk and the more than inevitable sleeping it off in the local jailhouse before Fletcher finally got the break he was looking for. Jim Haggerty an old rancher posted his bail.

"Why?" said Fletcher, as Jim Haggerty led him across the road and into his pickup.

"Let's just say, I know Wade and I know what a son-of-a-bitch he can be."

"It's more than that, he owes me big-time. Damn fuck swindled me out of my inheritance. Bastard needs to understand what it is to lose everything," mumbled Fletcher. "Now where do we get a drink around here?" he snapped.

"Mister, I can't help you get what's rightfully yours but I got some friends that can help you get even and you'd make a few bucks into the bargain."

Fletcher acted like he hadn't taken in Haggerty's offer. The hairs on his neck stood on end. Call it intuition, but he thought that at long last he was on to something.

Yet again he found his mind wandering back to that windowless office. Sam Kilbane had told him that their agent mentioned the Dam at Hungry Horse. It had sent alarm bells ringing all the way to Washington. When Guthrie was found dead up near Elmo, the FBI had put together a small taskforce.

New Orleans, Louisiana

During the next half-hour Sam Kilbane outlined all they had on the terrorist cell that it was believed were contemplating blowing up the dam at Hungry Horse.

"Millions of tons of water would come cascading down into the valleys and towns, wiping out everything in its wake. The death toll alone would be catastrophic, the damage to the local economy would be immense and the fall out would be felt for decades to come."

In truth the Federal Government had looked at the possible scenarios relating to a terrorist attack on their dams many years before and had put in place ways to protect the country from such an attack. This part Sam omitted.

Fletcher understood only too well what a terrorist attack of this size could do to Wade and his family. From that moment on he belonged to Sam Kilbane. Within a relatively short time Kilbane explained what it was they wanted him to do.

"You won't be going into this without undergoing an intense course in undercover techniques, physical training and the use of firearms, which I understand you have had some experience."

Fletcher was taken back to that fateful day when he'd killed Monique. It still haunted him, but the nightmares of that day were becoming less frequent. If he'd thought he'd have time to dwell on what happened he was mistaken. In the relatively short space of thirty six hours Fletcher was flown to FBI headquarters in Washington and had begun his course of training.

Montana

He'd passed the first test; patience, and was about to embark on the most dangerous part of the mission; acceptance. How he was perceived was crucial. If they smelled a rat he was as good as dead, if they had the slightest doubt, he was as good as dead, if they accepted his story but they didn't like what they saw he was as good as dead. He hoped the survival course that he'd done in Seattle wouldn't be needed.

"There's someone I'd like you to meet," said Haggerty. "Be in that bar across the street tomorrow night around ten. Oh, and stay sober. My friend is a stickler for discipline. You know these ex military types."

Fletcher nodded his understanding. Inside his brain was racing, military type, it fit the bill. This had to be the cell Kilbane had spoken about. Using the cell phone that the agency had provided he called Sam Kilbane and advised him of the meeting. "It may be something, it may be nothing. I've just got a feeling."

Sam Kilbane trusted intuition. On more than one occasion he'd gone with his instincts and it had saved his life. Minutes after Fletcher's call, the agent put in motion a surveillance team to watch the bar and photograph everyone that came into and out of that bar.

Chapter 22

Montana

Tara was worried and a little perplexed about the fall out between Wade and Fletcher. She didn't understand what had gone wrong with their relationship. When she asked what was going on Alex said, "Best leave well enough alone, you pa will tell you when he's good and ready."

There was something in her mother's tone that quelled all resistance, so reluctantly Tara took her advice and let it be. Her intuition told her there was more in it than Alex was letting on. She couldn't believe Fletcher was motivated by greed, but the look on Wade's face spoke volumes. She was almost tempted to say that she'd keep the ranch going when he was gone, but she knew that was impossible. It was a pity she thought, if things hadn't gone so tragically wrong for Fletcher and Merri, her pa's problems would have been solved.

Jack, although he mirrored Tara's concerns had his mind elsewhere. Charlotte had promised to come over before Christmas, but a shake up at work had put all their plans on hold. She'd said that once she'd got things sorted they'd be over. It was fast approaching July and he'd heard nothing for the past eight weeks.

"Do you think, that all said and done she's decided to forget she has a father," said Jack to Tara just as they were getting ready for bed.

"I don't think anything of the sort and nor should you. I expect she has her reasons. People do have lives to live you know. I wouldn't let it trouble you."

"Yeah, I guess you're right, you usually are," he conceded. Jack thought back to his last meeting with Charlotte and mulled it over in his head. He so wanted Charlotte and Matt to visit, there was so much he wanted to show them, not the least, Kaycee and Merri. The business was showing all the omens of a good season. Selling Dark Shadow to the Holbrook's had been a master stroke. Friends and associates of the Congressman had made enquires about livestock and two of them had already purchased a smart little Quarter Horse and an Arabian stallion. It would be great, thought Jack wistfully if one day Charlotte could see what living on a horse ranch was really like.

It was easy to say, thought Tara, "I wouldn't let it trouble you." but she knew the reality. Her niggling doubts about the apparent rift between Wade and Fletcher wouldn't abate. It kept going over and over in her head; it just didn't make sense which ever way she looked at it. Alex and Wade were keeping something back, of that Tara was sure. The family were close, closer than most families; they had no secrets; so Tara consoled herself with the fact that eventually Wade and Alex would explain everything. What worried Tara the most was her pa and how he'd look upon their decision not to continue with the ranch after Wade and Alex were gone. They had made it quite clear that when the time came, they would not take over the ranch at Big Hole.

"It's all consuming!" she told them. "It's your life, not ours."

With the return of Fletcher she'd thought the matter would resolve itself. Now that it looked unlikely that Fletcher would inherit part of the ranch, she thought the onus was back on her shoulders. They'd talked it though, they'd spent many a night agonising on Wade's wishes. But in the end they had come back to the same decision time and time again. When the ranch passed to Tara and Jack, they would have little choice but to put it on the market.

Tara had a different mind set to her parents. Big Hole Pass was her home, as it had been her father's before her. It was where Jack and her had begun there married life, it was where her kids had taken there first steps, it was and always would be the family home. The Crazy AW down in the Big Hole Valley was Wade and Alex's dream, not hers. The ranch was big and spread as far as the eye could see, and Tara had rode over most of it. It held memories of childhood and great joy, yet also great sadness. Taw her talented and gifted brother had died there. And then there was Merri, buried not more than a hundred yards from where she'd been slain. It was a harsh, brutal and beautiful landscape and neither Tara nor Jack was prepared to sacrifice their lives in trying to tame it. She wanted a fuller and more rounded life for her kids.

Marrying Jack had opened up a new world; going to England had reinforced it. Her mother had tried a different life. She'd dipped her toes in the water and found it wet, but Tara wasn't Alex. She could see that Wade and Alex were meant for each other, and the ranch was the cement that bound them. They were old school westerners, prepared to face each challenge on a daily basis. Tara and Jack were very much like them, but they were not prepared to be bound to the land, to the history or the tradition. They thought of themselves as a new breed, westerners yes, prepared to fight tooth and nail for what they believed in, but more than that they wanted an all encompassing world, a world where their kids could make their own way in life. It wasn't a popular ideal as far as Wade was concerned but he'd accepted it, mainly because of the return of Fletcher. Alex on the other hand had known where her daughter was coming from right from the start.

"It's your life and you need to live it as you see fit."

"It's not like we're deserting this life, it's just that the world has so much to offer and we owe it to Kaycee and Merri," said Tara to her mother defensively.

"I know, and you're right."

That had been a few weeks before Fletcher's return and Tara didn't know how her father would react now that he wasn't around. The panic and fear she'd felt at the thought of losing Jack, the trip to England, the history both of them shared had confirmed and reinforced what she'd gradually been thinking. But it wasn't only that, the visit she and Jack had made to the Holbrook home had such a profound effect on her. It wasn't that the Congressman and his wife's lives were grander or more opulent it was just the realisation that life can be as diverse as you want it to be.

*   *   *

No one was more surprised than Tara when she received a call from Ruth Holbrook a few days after they arrived back from their visit. Ruth said how much she enjoyed visiting with them and that if ever Tara was in Deer Lodge she should give her a call and maybe they could do lunch. Tara had said that would be nice and if she was in the area she'd most certainly phone her. Not that Tara expected to be in Deer Lodge any time soon. A day later Ruth phoned again. She invited her to lunch, the following Wednesday. Her persuasive manner left Tara with no choice and she agreed. Surprisingly the lunch date went exceedingly well and Tara found to her amazement that she enjoyed Ruth's company.

"You know Jack, I think she's lonely. I think being a politician's wife isn't all it's cracked up to be."

"Oh, you like her now!" said Jack in a mocking tone that made Tara give him a playful shove.

Since then Tara had been meeting up with Ruth twice a month. They talked about everything from the latest fashions, to music and movies, their favourite recipes, kids, horses, religion and on one occasion Tara brought up politics. Ruth laughed and held her hand up in mock protest, "Don't even go there!"

It surprised Tara that each time they met, they never exhausted their conversations, but she did notice that Ruth never talked about her marriage to Vince. She asked if they were thinking about planning a family and Ruth side stepped the question. Tara sensing things weren't all they appeared to be quickly changed the subject and the moment passed. That had been six month ago and she was beginning to suspect that the Holbrook's marriage had a hairline fracture. And then Ruth dropped a bombshell.

Chapter 23

Montana

A bombshell of a more agreeable source finally hit the Claymore household in late July. Over breakfast on a crisp but bright Sunday morning the phone rang. It was the call Jack had been fretting about for months, he'd even made up his mind to phone Debbie later that day to find out what was up with Charlotte.

"Hi Dad!"

"Charlotte!"

"How do you feel about being a Grandfather?"

"What!" Tears welled up in his eyes.

Tara guessed by the dumbfounded look on Jack's face that he'd been given the best news ever.

"We didn't want to ring until after twelve weeks, hence my delay. If I'd phoned sooner I'd have given it away."

"I understand. It's just fantastic news. But I thought you had it all planned out."

"We did, but I decided law wasn't for me, so I quit around Christmas time, dumb or what? In the New Year I applied for several job opportunities but with little success, then it struck me, I was getting broody. I talked it over with Matthew and we both decided we'd go in for a baby. I can't tell you how thrilled we are."

"About as thrilled as we are I bet," countered Jack.

"Unfortunately we won't be coming over this side of the birth," Charlotte stammered.

Jack paused, momentarily stunned and disappointed.

"I know how you were looking forward to us visiting, and I know I could come now, but I don't want to jeopardize the baby's health in any way. I know it sounds daft, but that's me."

"I understand. In your shoes I'd probably have done the same," said Jack now fully recovered from his disappointment. "A granddad, hey I'm too young," he joked.

Tara waited her opportunity before quickly taking the phone from his grasp and began asking all manner of things relating to the baby.

When Tara finally hung up, Jack began pacing the floor. "A granddad! I'm going to be a granddad."

Yeah, and that makes me an official step-grandma," replied Tara, "and I'm only thirty five," she added.

"You know this means we'll have to fly over there once the baby's born."

Suddenly Tara felt outside her comfort zone. The thought of returning to England so soon after her first encounter with Jack's family, filled her with dread. She questioned the why and found the answer. Jack was hers, he'd always be hers, but deep down she knew that a part of him would always belong to Debbie. And that's as it should be, she reasoned.

"Hold me Jack. Hold me tight," she cried.

"What's all this?" he said as he put his arms around her and gave a gentle hug.

"It's nothing, oh I'm being silly. Your first grand child, it's another claim on your heart."

"Now you are being silly. You're my life, you and K.C. and Merri and Charlotte too. My heart's big enough for at least one more and I'd hazard a guess that in years to come we'll both have our hearts bursting at the seams with off spring."

Tara felt warm inside, her man had a natural way of putting her at ease and she loved him for it. She guessed that her insecurities were triggered by the news she'd received days earlier. It had been playing on her mind.

"If I tell you something, you must promise not to tell a soul," cried Tara.

Jack looked into Tara's dark brown eyes and saw the troubled look return. "Tell me something? What's up?" concern written across his face.

"You must promise me."

"I promise," he said with urgency in his voice

"Ruth's having an affair! She told me yesterday."

"See I told you there was something about her," he said, the urgency in his voice now clearly lacking.

"That's unfair. Being a politician's wife is a lot harder than you'd think."

"Yeah, it looks it," replied Jack, his tone almost mocking.

"You may mock, but I'm telling you she's been unhappy for a very long time."

Jack sensing the irritation in Tara's voice decided to take his wife seriously. "Sorry sweetheart, so tell me what you know."

"Vince Holbrook is a career politician; he's an unfeeling brute of a man."

"Yeah, I always thought he was too good to be true," replied Jack.

"Do you know they haven't slept with each other for months? It's no wonder she's been having an affair."

Tara then outlined to Jack the lead up to Ruth's confession. It seems that Vince Holbrook's whole life was one big lie. He'd bought into the whole political system from an early age. He cared little for the land and even less for its people. He'd met Ruth and using his irrepressible charm swept her off her feet. The honeymoon period had lasted little over six months. Ruth had thought it was the pressure of his work load that had changed him, but after he'd had several affairs not caring whether Ruth knew about them or not, she began to get the message.

"She could always file for divorce," volunteered Jack. "You wouldn't have put up with anything like that."

"It takes all sorts Jack. When they first met, Vince was a Svengali like figure. She was a beautiful but vulnerable young woman from small town America, who thought she'd found her Prince Charming. He brought her into a world that she could only have dreamed about; he'd educated her, taught her how to behave, breaking old ties as he expertly manipulated the poor woman. Yet even now she still believes that deep down he still cares. But from everything she's told me, the bastard cares only about himself."

"If she cares that much, how come she's having an affair?"

"Vulnerability I guess," replied Tara. "Alone in a loveless marriage, a faint smile, a touch of a hand, a look, who knows?"

"Well then, perhaps this new man is the answer to her prayers," said Jack flippantly.

Tara's features took on a troubled look, "That's what bothers me. You know that good looking guy that came up to us at Vince's birthday party."

"Yeah," replied Jack, as he fought to recall the man.

"Carson Burroughs."

"Yeah that's the guy Carson Burroughs, smarmy type. Holbrook's running mate."

"That's him. According to Ruth, he's besotted with her, says his best friend is a damn fool."

"Some best friend!"

"Well best friend is not strictly accurate. It seems they met at college and Vince being the more flamboyant of the two, took Carson under his wing and he's been there ever since."

"So what you're saying is Carson Burroughs has been living in the shadow of Holbrook for years."

"That's just what I'm saying. My only fear is that if Holbrook finds out, according to Ruth he's ruthless enough to destroy them both."

"Does Ruth love this Burroughs bloke?"

"That's just it. She doesn't; she likes him, but not enough."

"Can't say I blame her; thinking back he was a bit of an odd ball, good looking, but there was something missing."

"That's how I see it too," concluded Tara.

"It's there problem, not ours and it's never likely to be," said Jack as he began to understand his wife's small insecurity. He realised how dangerously close he'd come to being in the same boat as Ruth and a small part of him understood her unhappiness. 'There but for the grace of God,' thought Jack, as he counted his blessings. He was over the moon at the pending birth of his first born grandchild and couldn't help thinking back to those long ago days when he thought he'd lost everything.

Later that morning he saddled up a bay gelding, put his foot in the stirrup and swung himself onto his mount. Then as he took in his surrounding he took a steady lope across his land. At a high point he stared across the undulating hills and plains. In the distance he could make out Dillon, just a speck, but a vibrant little community nonetheless. As he turned in the saddle to a chorus of creaking leather he looked in a northerly direction towards Polaris and further north to the small town of Wisdom. The sky above him was a vivid blue without a whisper of cloud, and all below him a harvest of gold. He thought of Tara's fears, he thought of the England he'd left so many years before and he thought of his family here in Montana. He grinned to himself, and mouthed the word Granddad; it had a nice ring to it. Jack felt he was the luckiest man alive.

Chapter 24

Montana

Staying alive was Fletcher's problem. He only hoped that Sam Kilbane was as confident as he'd appeared in that windowless office.

"Any sign that your cover's blown hit the number seven on your cell phone."

Fletcher had looked at Kilbane with an expression that said 'then what?' He could only assume the cavalry would come charging in. "What happens if for any reason I don't have the cell handy?"

Sam opened the back of the throwaway phone and removed the SIM card. "This is your lifeline," said Kilbane seriously, as he replaced the SIM back into the cell phone, "That and a duplicate SIM card, your ace in the hole so to speak. Keep the duplicate safe, you might need it. It will fit most cell phones."

It was later that evening that Fletcher cut a slit in the lining of one of his boots and secreted the SIM card. It was all new technology to him; he only hoped it would be the same with the people he was meeting.

*   *   *

Fletcher sat up at the bar of the Lucky Cuss Saloon sipping on a Coors Lite when Haggerty and another man walked up to him.

"This is the man I was telling you about Bob," said Jim Haggerty.

Bob Knox looked at Fletcher suspiciously. He had learned though military training to trust no one except his proven comrades. This man was a stranger, which meant he couldn't be trusted, at least ways until he'd been interrogated. With suspicion oozing from every pore Bob Knox motioned to an empty booth.

"Move!" exclaimed Knox.

Fletcher reacted and eyed the man up. Instinct told him the man was one dangerous hombre. One wrong move, one sideways look and he could be dead.

"Look man! Your friend here came on to me. I don't need this kind a shit!"

Knox smiled, but it wasn't a nice smile. "Easy boy! I mean no offence. Just being careful is all."

Fletcher slid into the booth. Haggerty sat down next to him and the big fellow with the cropped hair sat opposite. A waitress appeared.

"Three more of the same," cried Knox pointing to Fletcher's bottle.

The waitress took the order then in a disinterested fashion turned and walked away. Bob glared straight into Fletcher's eyes.

"Jim says you've a grudge against a rancher down in the Big Hole Valley. He said you were friends once and that he swindled you out of your half of the ranch."

"It's a long story," replied Fletcher trying not to appear too eager.

"I've got all night."

"Shit! You might have, but I don't take kindly to strangers prying into my affairs." He made to stand up.

"Easy man." The tone in Knox's voice was still threatening. "Fifty grand, fifty big ones. You walk away fifty grand richer and your friend's business is in ruins."

Fletcher sat back down. "Fifty grand! Who do I have to kill?"

Knox ignored the question. "Tell me everything about your past. Miss anything out and you're a dead man."

Fletcher stared defiantly at the big square jawed ex marine. He wanted to tell him to go fuck himself.

"I know you're angry with me, and I dare say you'd like to tear into me, but hear me out. If after hearing your story and after I've had it verified, if it checks out, then you and me are buddies. Then you get to hear who you have to kill."

Fletcher took a swig of beer, and then swallowed hard. "I was brought up in a Louisiana crime family called Delacroix . . . ."

As Fletcher narrated his life story he began to understand why Sam Kilbane had picked him. Every word he was saying was true, although he did downplay his relationship with Merri. Telling Knox that as Monique grew steadily unstable he switched his attentions to Meredith Breakenridge. Worming his way in with the Reynolds family could and should have reaped rewards. But on Merri's death and the killing of Monique he lost his way. Four years in the wilderness had changed all that.

"Coming back to Montana should have seen me a rich man, as it turned out it was a big mistake," said Fletcher regretfully.

"Mistake or not. If you check out, you're in for some big money."

"If I don't, then what?"

"Then you're dead!" The coldly calculating words seemed to hang in the smoke filled bar-room. For a second Fletcher felt the first signs of panic. Beads of sweat appeared upon his brow. This was the moment of truth, after this there was no backing out.

"Check me out; I'll be here tomorrow, same time, same place."

The bravado wasn't lost on Knox. He'd seen the fear in Fletcher's eyes, he was unsure, fearful, perhaps a little scared, but then he had every right to be. If he'd been otherwise, then Knox would have shot him twice in the belly with the silenced Glock he had pointed at Fletcher under the table.

"No you won't, you're coming with us," said the ex marine coldly.

"That wasn't part of the deal," protested Fletcher

"If you've nothing to hide, there's nothing to fear."

"So okay!" exclaimed Fletcher, "I'll go with you, but I'm carrying. I've a nine millimetre Beretta stuck in the waistband in the small of my back. I keep it."

This seemed to throw Bob Knox, his brain in overdrive, his trigger finger tensing. It was risky to kill in the crowded bar-room. Why kill at all? If he was who he said he was, then he was the perfect recruit. If he wasn't, Bremer could take care of him.

"You have to trust me, I have to trust you. What guarantees my safety? The gun stays or you can forget it!" It was a grandstand play and Fletcher knew it could get him killed.

Bob Knox's face twitched, Fletcher stared into the big man's eyes, and relief came as the tension in Knox's face evaporated.

"Keep the damned gun. We're wasting time, make for the back exit."

The three men rose as one. Knox left a twenty on the table and they walked towards the rest rooms along a narrow corridor then out the exit. Once Haggerty and Fletcher were outside Knox pointed his Glock at Fletcher's stomach.

"No offence, but empty your pockets." Fletcher looked a little surprised and nervous. "As I said inside, if you're on the level, you've nothing to fear."

Fletcher reached deep into his pockets, and placed a wallet, a small lock knife and a cell phone on the hood of Haggerty's pickup. The older man searched the wallet, looked at Knox and indicated that it was clean. The lock knife he opened and closed before giving it a cursory glance. Knox indicated to him to hand them back.

"The cell phone . . . . why do you need a cell phone?"

Sweat dripped into Fletcher's eyes. His mind racing . . . .

Chapter 25

Montana

"The signal's gone!"

"What!" cried Sam Kilbane.

"One minute it was there, the next it's gone."

"Jesus H Christ! Be discreet, but check out the bar-room. Check the back, check the parking lot, check everywhere, but be discreet. If our agent's still alive I don't want us tipping those sons of bitches to the contrary. Understand!"

Sam Kilbane waited in his car. He'd never lost a man in the field. But Fletcher was different, he wasn't a trained agent, he was a green recruit. A man that Sam Kilbane had selected, a man that he'd backed into a corner, a man that was prepared to face dangers, take a beating or two, a man that was now despised by all that knew him. A man that if found dead would have no one to mourn for him.

It was an agonising ten minutes before FBI agent Lewis Whittaker walked up to Sam Kilbane's vehicle. "No sign of a struggle. No blood, nothing except this."

Whittaker handed Kilbane the smashed remains of Fletcher's cell phone.

"Oh fuck!"

He'd told Fletcher about the phone being his lifeline but he hadn't told him about the bug he'd planted inside the phone. Had it been discovered? Had Fletcher's cover been blown? Or was it a precaution on behalf of the terrorists? He could only hope the latter.

"The surveillance photos, any luck on identifying the suspect?"

"None as yet," said Whittaker. "But I marked it top urgent. We should get some results come morning."

Sam Kilbane scowled. His thoughts went back to that day in New Orleans when he'd bamboozled a man into putting his life on the line.

Fletcher signed an official national security document, similar to a D-notice, then listened intently as Sam Kilbane explained what would be asked of him, he gave a smile of incredulity.

"Is this some elaborate joke?"

"There's no joke. This is deadly serious." Sam's tone changed emphasising the extreme gravity of the situation.

"Forget it!" exclaimed Fletcher. "You've trained field operatives, why me?"

"Basically because you fit the bill," Sam then read through Fletcher's file, hinting that there was enough to put him away for a very long time.

"Like I just said, forget it! Do your damnedest." Angered by the loosely veiled threat Fletcher stood up as an act of defiance.

"You're free to go," said Sam with a look of stone etched across his face. He watched as a look of puzzlement crossed Fletcher's bronzed features. He calculated the time perfectly before he spoke again. Fletch had his hand on the door handle when Sam Kilbane stopped him in his tracks.

"How much to you value the life of Wade Reynolds."

Fletcher looked alarmed and when Sam motioned for him to sit back down he did so without question.

It had been that easy. Sam Kilbane was paid to make these decisions; it was a matter of homeland security. He'd been taught to see the bigger picture, the sacrifice that others took in creating a safer world, but it still left a bitter taste.

By morning Sam knew the search would be futile. His only hope, the surveillance photos of the two suspects. He'd barely entered the local headquarters of the FBI when an excited Whittaker ran up to him.

"Sam, we've got something! The man that met up with Coppersmith is known to us. He's ex marine sergeant Robert Knox, veteran of the Gulf war and get this, he received a dishonourable discharge for his overzealous behaviour towards the enemy."

Sam read through the file. Robert Knox was a very dangerous man, a man with a grudge against his country, but there was nothing in his records to suggest he could pull off terrorist activities of the magnitude of Hungry Horse. That he was a leader of men Sam didn't doubt, but a planner?

The other man with him had kept mostly in the shadows. If he'd been on the FBI file they'd have a record. Sam could only guess that maybe he was local. Quickly he ran the photograph of the suspect through the local police data base. It came up negative.

*   *   *

A day later and still there was no news. Unshaven and lacking sleep Sam turned to his first smoke in three years. He'd barely lit it when Whitaker came rushing into his office.

"It's just a thought. Assume suspect two is a local man. Fletcher's cover story is or was local knowledge. Now assume suspect two is known to that rancher in the Big Hole Valley."

Sam stubbed out the un-smoked cigarette, grabbed the file that lay open on his desk, "Lewis, you're a fucking genius!"

Within minutes agent Lewis Whittaker and Sam Kilbane were heading south to the Reynolds Ranch.

*   *   *

The events at Whitefish kept being replayed in Fletcher's head days later. His face had almost given him away when Knox asked why he carried a cell-phone.

"Oh for fuck-sake!" exclaimed Fletcher as his brain raced to find an answer. "I've had one since I was herding sheep in Australia. Man you're out there in the outback with snakes and crocs and all manner of things that can kill or maim yah. Carrying a cell-phone can be the only form of communication you've got out there." It was a lame excuse, it leaked like a sieve and Fletcher knew it. He only hoped Knox wasn't up on modern technology.

"Hand it over!" snarled Knox.

Fletcher handed the cell-phone across to the big ex marine. Knox examined the phone carefully. He pressed the memory button and stared at the most recent calls. He recognised them as Montana phone numbers.

"Who did you phone?"

"Reynolds. If you look closer you'll see the last call was made seven weeks ago."

Knox scrolled down, memorising the number that was on screen. Then without another word he dropped the cell-phone on the ground and stamped on it.

"You won't need a phone were we're going," cried Knox. "Now get in the pick-up."

Fletcher sighed with relief; Sam Kilbane had instructed him to only phone with the spare SIM card in place, so far his instructions had kept him alive.

In the dark Fletcher watched as the town of Whitefish disappeared and within minutes Haggerty pulled onto an unpaved road. In the dark confines of the pick-up Knox became more amiable.

"Fletch, I can call you Fletch, can't I?" continued Knox. "We debrief you tomorrow. Don't take anything personal, it's for your security as well as ours. Once we've checked you out you're one of us. It doesn't pay to be too friendly, just in case."

*   *   *

Wade's hackles rose as he stepped onto the porch. A black sedan was coasting its way to his front door.

"If I miss my guess, I'd say the feds are a calling," he said to himself.

He watched unmoved as the black sedan pulled up to the ranch-house. His suspicions were confirmed as two suited men in ties climbed out of the vehicle.

Alex appeared at his side, "What do they want?" she muttered as the elder of the men stepped onto the porch his hand extended.

"Name's Kilbane, Sam Kilbane, I'm with the Bureau."

"I know who you are!" replied Wade.

"I'm here to talk about a mutual friend, Fletcher Coppersmith."

"Last I heard, he weren't no friend of mine," replied Wade.

"Quite," said Kilbane. "Now can we come inside and talk?"

"I guess," said Wade as he stepped aside to let the two federal agents inside his house.

"I won't beat about the bush. Things have moved on a mite. I'd like you to take a look at a couple of pictures."

Whittaker spread four surveillance photos across the table. Kilbane picked up one and showed it to Wade and Alex.

"Any ideas' who this guy in the feed and grain cap might be?" asked Sam Kilbane as he handed the grainy black and white image to Wade.

Wade took a long hard look, "I think that's Jim Haggerty, though I can't be sure"

Sam looked across to his colleague. "I owe you one!"

"Where's Fletcher? Is he all right?" asked Wade.

"As far as we can tell, he's okay," replied Kilbane.

"You son-of-a-bitch! He'd better be okay," cried Wade angrily. "He's putting his life on the line for you!"

"Easy; I understand your concern. Now how much has Fletcher told you?" replied Kilbane, sternly.

"Only that you shanghaied him into working undercover. Said it was a matter of national importance," snapped Wade. "Asked me to pretend that I'd turned against him, other than that he didn't tell me anything."

"Good. Then we'll keep it that way."

"If he'd a asked me before you feds got your claws into him I'd a told him to tell you to shove it where the sun don't shine. You see here, we don't take kindly to feds, especially the FBI!"

Kilbane chose to ignore Wade's outburst, "About this Haggerty feller, tell me everything you know about him."

Wade wasn't on his own as far as the FBI was concerned, a lot of Montana folks loathed the very sight of them, but under these circumstances he felt he had to make an exception. "I'm warning you, Haggerty ain't no friend of mine, but he ain't a criminal either, so you better not be planning another Ruby Ridge!"

At this moment in time all I'm concerned about is Fletcher," offered Sam Kilbane.

"Okay then, he's got a run down ranch north of here, near Whitefish.

"Thank you. Now does anyone else know about Fletcher?"

"Only my wife, but my daughter and her husband didn't buy into the story."

Sam looked imploringly into Alex's eyes, "Begging your pardon ma'am but have you mentioned anything to anyone."

Alex looked him squarely in the eyes, "We've seen our fair share of trouble. We don't look for none, but if it comes our way we deal with it. My husband told me, only because he had no choice. I ain't said a word."

"I believe you ma'am," said Sam Kilbane, "Your husband said he thought your daughter and her husband didn't buy the deception."

"That's right. They ain't nobodies fool, but would they relay there suspicions to anyone else. Not in a million years."

"I just hope you're right."

* * *

Fletcher's interrogation brought back painful memories. Explaining to Bob Knox in the bar had been painful enough, but to have every detail minutely gone over by a young thug like Bremer caused him more grief than he could imagine. Haggerty was just a hanger on; Knox, Bremer and Schneider were the real deal.

That they were being guided by an outside force was becoming increasingly obvious, especially when Knox received a phone call which he took away from everyone. Fletcher guessed the ex marine was relaying everything about there new recruit. He just hoped that Sam Kilbane didn't have a mole in his department. Three hours later Bob Knox's cell-phone rang again. As he walked outside he glanced at Fletcher and an icy shiver ran down Fletcher's spine. That he'd been allowed to keep his nine millimetre Beretta, was no comfort, as each man there was heavily armed and suspicious.

Twenty minutes passed before Knox re-entered the cabin, his face still tense. Fletcher eased himself into a flight or fight position.

"It's on!" exclaimed Knox. I've to meet with the man tonight at Whitefish." Then he smiled directly at Fletcher. "You're coming with me."

Chapter 26

Montana

Ruth Holbrook stared at the ornately framed picture of her wedding day and wept. Back then the future had looked bright, young and full of hope. But as she settled into married life, things changed. At first there were subtle changes. Being wife of the future governor of Montana had its responsibilities, as Vince was forever telling her. A rift with her mother in Indiana, small though it was, was enough for Vince to sever the embarrassment of family. Ruth thought that once she'd settled down as Mrs Vince Holbrook she'd be able to mend old wounds, she was wrong.

Then things took a turn in the right direction. Ruth found herself pregnant. Cold as Vince had become, the news thrilled him and he became his old self. Ruth had put his coldness down to pressure of work, so she was delighted to have the old Vince back, but it wasn't to last. She was nearly three months when she miscarried. It was her worst nightmare, she was beside herself. She looked to her husband for support, but there was none. She'd done everything in her power to carry the baby full term. She'd followed all the advice she'd been given, yet Vince blamed her for the miscarriage.

Not that Holbrook needed an excuse, but Ruth's failure to produce a child, led to his many affairs. As the months rolled into years she began to accept her role in the marriage. Being charming became second nature to her. She was living an idyllic lifestyle, one that some women would give their soul to achieve. As time moved on Ruth found herself adjusting to her loveless marriage, but since she'd embarked on an affair with Carson Burroughs she was questioning her very existence.

Outwardly Ruth portrayed herself as confident, assured, masterful and charming in equal portions, but deep down she was none of them. Finding Tara Reynolds had been a lifeline. She'd sensed that day at Vince's birthday party that Tara was her kind of people. She found to her great delight that Tara was everything she thought she'd be.

During their lunch dates she'd encouraged Tara to talk about her life, her love of horses, her kids, ranch life and her husband. To Ruth, Tara had everything that a woman could ask for and a future that looked very bright indeed. To say that Ruth was jealous would be wrong; that she envied her new friend might be nearer the truth.

For weeks Ruth had been building herself up to tell Tara about the sham she called a marriage, about Vince's affairs and about her own infidelities with Carson.

"Do you love him?" Tara had asked simply, no judgement in her voice.

"I care for him, but I don't love him."

That had been two weeks ago and as a fretful Ruth stared at the clock in the restaurant she thought she'd lost her only friend. Tara was late. Ruth thought back to when she'd confessed all. She been shocked, she'd been amazed at Ruth's revelations but she hadn't seemed the type to run out on her. Ruth's insecurities were getting the better of her. Just at that moment Tara hurried into the restaurant, apologising as she walked towards her friend.

"I'm so sorry. Traffic! What more can I say."

"I thought after what I'd told you last time that you'd had second thoughts about our relationship."

"You're kidding!" said a bemused Tara. "Friends are just that, friends. If I can help in any way I will."

They ordered lunch, sipped on a glass of Chardonnay and chatted much as before. They talked about the usual things, sparred around the unusual and were just about to call for the check when Tara asked her what she was going to do about Vince and Carson.

"That's the point," said a red faced Ruth. "Carson has been coming on a bit heavy. He keeps hinting about us getting together on a permanent basis."

"Is that such a bad thing?"

"It is when your husband is Vince Holbrook," replied Ruth. "Carson seems to have some big idea that his future is about to take off and that Vince won't be able to touch us."

"Well then, maybe he's right."

"Maybe. But you're forgetting one little detail, I don't love Carson!"

"Well do you love Vince?"

"Not anymore." With the realisation that she'd finally admitted what she'd suspected for a long time Ruth burst into tears. It was finally out, she'd spoken the unspoken and the emotional rush was too much. Tara rushed to her side and tried comforting Ruth, but it only made matters worse. Customers and restaurant staff alike all turned their attention on the two women. Tara called for the check, then taking a firm hand told Ruth to pull herself together. The sobbing woman reacted to Tara's command and slowly the tears subsided.

"You're not going home like this." Tara made a decision, "Dry your eyes; go put some makeup on, compose yourself, then phone that husband of yours and tell him you're spending the night at our place."

"I couldn't!" cried Ruth.

"You could, and you will," said Tara firmly. "And besides you'd be doing me a favour, Jack's away overnight delivering some horses to a ranch just outside Miles City. He won't be back until late tomorrow afternoon, so do as I tell you."

Ruth looked at Tara and a great weight was suddenly lifted from her shoulders. The outburst had released all her pent up emotions and frustrations. It was the first step, and then an immensely mischievous grin spread across her face.

*   *   *

Bob Knox swung the pickup into the parking lot at the back of the Lucky Cuss saloon. Coolly he switched off the engine and turned in his seat to face Fletcher.

"We're a mite early, but that's all right. I wanted to talk to you before I go see the man."

Fletcher felt the hairs on the back of his neck bristle. He'd been prepared for the worst when Knox said they were taking a ride. But here he was in the rear parking lot of the Lucky Cuss being told that Knox was seeing the man. It was more, much more than he'd hoped for.

"Firstly, you checked out, I'm satisfied who you are, that out of the way, I need someone to watch my back. Bremer is young, ruthless and highly strung. Schneider is a sociopath, Haggerty's too old. And none of them have the brains they were born with. But you on the other hand are brighter than you make out."

"Whoa! That's a bit of a speech. Only the other day you were set to kill me without a second thought." Fletcher's instincts began to kick in.

"This man, this man I'm about to meet with, Adam Coulter. There's something about him I don't trust. There's something about his story that doesn't sit well with me." Knox stared vacantly at the windshield. "He could be a fed!"

"Then I'm out!" replied Fletcher feigning panic.

"I said he could be a fed, not that he was a fed. He wants something and he wants it bad, which means he'll be prepared to pay for it. How much? Well that my friend is where I do the negotiating. There's big money, I'm sure of it, but I need someone else to help pull it off."

"Okay, I'm listening,"

"Let me start at the beginning. I met this Adam Coulter in a bar in Kalispell. We kinda got to talking. Both of us it seems had a grudge against the government. I suppose I bought it at first, mainly because I wanted to hit back at the government for the way I'd been treated. But as time went on I got the feeling this guy knew more about me than he was letting on." Knox grinned, "This guy misjudged me big time."

"Go on."

"Well Coulter reckoned he had a plan to create maximum damage to a specific target, but first I was to recruit a bunch of same minded people, which I did. Now the strange part, he sets up a series of initiation tests."

"What!"

"Yeah, my first thoughts, but he was financing the operation. Now just shut up and be quiet!"

"Karl and me knocked over a gun store in Poulson. Coulter gave me a shopping list of weapons he wanted. But that wasn't all. We had to kill the owner."

"Why?" It was involuntary but Fletcher needed to know, if not for himself but for a future court date.

"It was Coulter's insurance that we were who we said we were. It wasn't long after that I received a phone call; we're to hit a bank in Havre, which we did. No one got killed that day thanks to the efficiency of Ray Guthrie, the man you replaced. Now this is where it gets interesting. Not long after the bank job I receive another phone call from Coulter to say there's an informant in our ranks."

Fletcher couldn't believe his ears; Knox was giving him chapter and verse.

"I know it ain't me," continued Knox, "Karl Bremer killed the gun shop owner, so it ain't him. I set Schneider and Guthrie up to kill each other." He laughed at his own ingenuity. "Guthrie hesitated Schneider didn't."

"Jesus H Christ!" exclaimed Fletcher. "This is getting real heavy man!"

My sentiments entirely," said Knox in a matter of fact way, "That's why it's just you and me."

What time did you say you were meeting this Coulter feller?"

"We've plenty of time. I drove us here early so I could lay it all out for you. You ain't been involved until now. In theory you could walk away, but I'm thinking you're not the kind to walk away when the going gets tough."

"You got that right. If there's a big score to be had I want in! Go on."

"Coulter knew we had an informant in our midst, which led me to thinking he could be a fed. That and the fact he broke contact with me for more than six months. What ever it is he wants doing, I think he got cold feet."

"But now it's back on?"

"Seems like it. He kept hinting about Hungry Horse. I acted like I was up for it, I figured he meant an assault on the dam, which believe me would be plain suicide. Those dams are so heavily guarded it would have been a squirrel shoot. Which leads me to believe the next mission is the real deal."

"What is the next mission?"

"That my friend is what you and I are about to find out."

"Okay Bob, you've brought me up to speed, that I appreciate, but you've known me days, whereas you've known the others months, possibly years. Why me?"

"For that very reason," replied Knox. "Coulter wants something from us. He's a slippery customer, so we have to stay one jump ahead. Nothing's changed, only he pays up front. We'll say half before; half after the job's done, except we won't be completing the transaction."

"We're gonna stiff the son of a bitch!" cried Fletcher with as much enthusiasm as he could muster.

"Exactly!" grinned Knox, "Which only leaves us to sever the ties."

"The ties being Coulter?" questioned Fletcher.

"The ties being Coulter, Bremer, Schneider and Haggerty," said Knox coldly, "They all know too much."

"What makes you think I'll help you dispose of them?"

"You've killed before; I guess you'll kill again if the price is right."

"That only leaves me and you," said Fletcher cautiously. "What makes you think I'd trust you to keep your side of the bargain?"

Knox laughed, "Being too greedy can get a man killed. Double crosses can get a man killed. I expect you'll be watching my every move, likewise me watching you. We split the money down the middle, and go our separate ways. Have we a deal?"

"Let's find your man," replied Fletcher.

* * *

Carson Burroughs sat in the last booth towards the back of the dimly lit barroom nursing a drink that he didn't care for. Everything was going to plan and after tonight his troubles would be over. Yet Knox was late, something that had never happened before. It irritated the hell out of him, but he tried not to let it show. After all, what were a few minutes when he had the rest of his life to look forward too? He despised Vince Holbrook; no that was a lie; he hated the man. Only earlier that day Carson had seen how he'd displayed his ingratitude towards Ruth. He sipped on his beer and replayed the last few hours in his head.

Vince Holbrook put the phone back on its cradle, his mind deep in thought.

"Anything wrong?" enquired Carson.

"No, just that fool wife of mine. I tell you Carson, she's becoming a bit too independent for my liking. She's staying the night with that hick rancher's wife at Big Hole Pass."

Carson feigned disinterest, "Who did you say?"

"You met her at my party last year."

"Oh yeah, now I remember. Not bad looking, if I recall, married to that Englishman."

"You got it. If the elections weren't next year I'd soon put a stop to her nonsense."

Carson stole a secret glance at his supposed friend and for the briefest of seconds felt sorry for him.

"Yeah, right!"

Carson was awakened from his daydreams as Bob Knox slipped into the booth opposite.

"You're late!" he exclaimed.

Knox smiled, ignoring the impatience in Coulter's voice. "I'm here now," he replied as he began his journey to gain ground. "And things have changed some what!

The colour drained from Adam/Carson's face.

"What to you mean!" he spat.

"You've played me for a fool long enough. Hungry Horse ain't gonna happen. You know it, and so do I. I'm guessing the real deal is this low key political assassination."

"What are you talkin' . . . ."

Knox cut him off, "I ain't got time for this. You want someone killed that's all right by me. Only I want paying half up front, the rest after the job's done. Two hundred thousand dollars; take it or leave it."

'This wasn't how it was supposed to pan out,' thought Carson as he struggled to come to terms with the new situation, "Jesus, I ain't got that kind of money."

"But you can get it! Rich fucks like you can always get it."

Burroughs tried to protest, but Knox cut him off dead. "Do you want it done or not, just say the word."

Knox rose to his feet as if to go. Carson implored him to sit back down, "It'll take a couple of days," he replied.

"Tomorrow night! Same time, same place."

Carson thought about Ruth and his political ambitions. He had no choice, he just nodded.

"Now, who's the mark?" Knox was quite enjoying the reversal of roles.

Still shaken by this new turn of events Carson reached into his inside jacket pocket and pulled out a publicity shot of Vince Holbrook. Pulling himself together he looked Knox in the eye. His foolproof plan had been kicked into touch, but Knox was going to carry through on Holbrook; for a price.

"You get half tomorrow, the rest when the job's done."

With a renewed confidence, Carson still careful not to implicate himself relayed Holbrook's movements over the following weekend. "I don't care when or how you do it; just make sure he's dead before Monday."

"You just bought yourself a political assassination," replied Knox. "I'll see you tomorrow night."

In the dimly lit barroom Fletcher only managed a brief sighting of the man that called himself Adam Coulter. Knox's huge frame had obscured his view during much of their conversation. Hoping for a better look he stepped forward just as Knox rose from the booth and made for the back exit. Coulter stood up almost at the same time and turned his back and walked through the crowded barroom, head down and baseball cap firmly pulled over his face.

"Fuck!" cried Fletcher in frustration as he too made his way to the back exit and the parking lot.

"Its set," cried Knox excitedly, "one hundred thousand tomorrow night. The rest on completion of the deal"

"When's that?"

"Monday night!"

"We got four days! Who's the mark?"

"Vince Holbrook, future governor of Montana."

"Jesus H Christ!" exclaimed Fletcher.

"He might just as well be," replied Knox. "The man's untouchable, one hundred thousand big ones for doing absolutely nothing. I might even vote for him myself. We collect from Coulter tomorrow night, kill him, then we take care of Bremer, Schneider and Haggerty. Then it's adios amigo."

Fletcher smiled, "That'll do it!"

Chapter 27

Montana

Tara woke at her usual time of 6' o'clock and smelled the aroma of freshly brewed coffee. Going down stairs to investigate she was greeted by a rejuvenated Ruth Holbrook.

"I hope you don't mind," she said as she indicated to the coffee pot, "Only it was such a beautiful morning and I couldn't do it justice without my first injection of caffeine."

"Be my guest. No one stands on ceremony at 'Chez Claymore.'"

"You know what!" exclaimed Ruth, "I really like it here. Thanks Tara. I'm so glad you invited me. I think if I hadn't I've have gone out of my mind."

"I don't think you would have," said Tara in a comforting tone. "You're a more together type of person than you give yourself credit."

"Yeah, you might be right. But it's unbelievable how a day away from that house has made me see things so much clearer."

"Well, phone Vince, tell him that you'll see him early evening or whenever," suggested Tara flippantly. Both women broke into fits of giggles. Late the previous evening, the two had talked themselves out, and Ruth had resolved to end her relationship with Carson. More importantly, she intended telling Vince that if their marriage was to continue he had better stop screwing around and become more of a husband.

"I can see him now," laughed Ruth, "he'll shout and rant, but I intend to stand firm. He's hoping for the governorship next year, which means a messy divorce would be out of the question. Who knows, maybe I'll get the old Vince Holbrook back." Even before she'd said it she knew deep down that was a forlorn hope.

"Phone him, Martha's taking the kids over to her folks for a visit, and Blaine says he'll double up on my chores, so my day's free. I'll just saddle a couple of horses." Tara paused for a second, "You do ride I take it?"

Yes, of course I ride. I'm from a small town, remember."

"I know, just checking."

*   *   *

It was 6.11 in the morning when the first shots rang out. Harley Truelove thought he was dreaming. The night's observation had taken its toll; he was slumped down in the seat of his car. 'I must have nodded off,' he thought as he peered through the misted up window of his car. From his position high up on a hill overlooking the Warlock ranch he gazed out and couldn't believe his eyes.

"What the fuck's going on?" he said as he reached for his field glasses. "How the fuck did that happen?" he gasped as he spied what looked like a Sheriff's department vehicle, being riddled with automatic gunfire from the ranch house. More importantly Harley spotted that two men were down, both police officers. One was not moving, while the other was crouched behind the squad car and firing his service revolver at the occupants of the house. At that moment a sheriff's department vehicle shot past him, and turned into the driveway of the Warlock ranch. Seconds later, another squad car screeched into the driveway.

"Oh fuck, fuck, fuck, fuck," screamed Harley, "Kilbane will have my head!" as he punched the speed dial number that connected him to his superior Sam Kilbane.

"Sam, I don't know how it happened, but all hells broken loose. The Sheriff's department is laying siege to the Warlock ranch."

"How the .... Never mind just get down there, tell that Sheriff to hold off until I get there."

"Will do!" replied Harley as he gunned his car into action. Now fully awake, the agent brought his entire vehicle training to bear. Gravel and dust flew up as he barely made the turn into the driveway of the Warlock Ranch. Ahead of him he spotted the three squad cars. One up close to the house, riddled with bullets, the other two further back in what Harley could only describe as a makeshift barricade. Three Sheriff's deputies were engaging fire with the house, while another was speaking frantically on the radio. A wounded officer stood up from his cover behind the third car and stepped towards Harley's oncoming vehicle. Truelove slammed on the brakes and came to a screeching halt next to a sheriff's department squad car, barely missing the officer, who looked badly shaken and in need of medical attention.

Ignoring the wounded officer Harley raced towards the Deputy in charge of the radio. Raising his badge high in the air he shouted, "Who's in charge? The deputy flushed with anger, pointed to the dead body of Joshua Crawford.

"I guess I am. Mother fuckers gunned down the Sheriff. He didn't have a chance. Now what the fuck's the FBI doing here?" Emmett Larson didn't know nor care why the agent happened to be there. He was in charge and no fed was going to interfere with his operation.

Ignoring the question Harley proceeded to order the Sheriff's Deputy to cease firing. "My boss will be here within the hour. You've got to hold off until then."

"The hell we will, they killed Josh. The bastards didn't give him a chance. We ain't giving them one either!"

"You can't," replied Harley. "One of ou . . . ." Agent Truelove fell back against his own squad car, a sickening feeling welled up from his stomach as a stray bullet thudded into his right shoulder.

"Get him outta here!" cried Deputy Emmett Larson. His blood was up and he didn't need anymore distractions. A paramedic crew who'd just arrived took charge and after hurrying the wounded deputy into their vehicle attended to the now unconscious Harley Truelove.

* * *

It had been a little after 6.00 am on a normal late July morning, the sun was up and Jim Haggerty was going about his chores as usual, when Sheriff Josh Crawford and his Deputy Lane Bradley drove onto the dirt forecourt of the Warlock Ranch.

"Now what in the blue blazes . . . ." muttered Jim Haggerty under his breath. "Howdy Sheriff," he said nervously, "What brings you out this early?"

Josh Crawford, unfurled his somewhat overweight frame from the squad car, reached back inside and retrieved his hat. False alarms were something he could do without, but when the call came he knew he'd have to answer it. Still there might be a pot of coffee boiling away on the stove. He'd barely raised his hand in greeting when Karl Bremer stepped outside. Sheriff Josh Crawford stretched himself to his full height, still relaxed but a little nervy. Shocked by the sight of the two men in uniform, Bremer began walking backwards to the house.

"Hold it son!" cried Josh Crawford, as his hand closing around the walnut butt of his holstered revolver.

Karl Bremer froze, and then he smiled as his hand instinctively reached behind his back and he pulled and fired on Sheriff Crawford, hitting him twice in the chest before turning his gun on Lane Bradley. The deputy shocked by the sudden violence took a flesh wound to the left arm before ducking behind his squad car. He blew off three rounds from his revolver before reaching inside the car and grabbing the radio mike.

"Officer down! Officer down! We're at the Warlock Ranch, just off highway 93."

Karl Bremer retreated inside the house, his eyes wild with excitement. "You wanted a war, well now you've got one!" he screamed at Knox and the others. Knox being the first to grasp what had happened looked across to Fletcher. Both men thought the same, Adam Coulter.

Haggerty, fear and anger in his eyes scrambled in behind the young cop killer. He'd agreed to water and feed these men, yet he hadn't expected to be involved in a shooting war.

"Why'd you have to shoot, you dumb fool," screamed Haggerty.

"Who the fuck are you calling a dumb fool!" cried Karl Bremer as he levelled his revolver at Haggerty and pulled the trigger.

Bob Knox, ignoring the death throes of Haggerty picked up an Uzi 9mm and slipped off the safety and carefully peered out the window. "By my reckoning, there's five maybe six police outside. If we stay put, there'll be six hundred within an hour." The coolness of Knox chilled Fletcher's bones. The murder of a police officer and an old rancher hadn't fazed him one bit. The man was planning his next move, while Schneider and Bremer looked to his lead.

"No time for a real plan. Surprise, shock and awe!"

Karl Bremer grinned menacingly and reloaded his revolver, which he thrust it into his waistband. Then he grabbed hold of an M16 5.56mm assault rifle. Standing back from the window he opened up the M16 and fired though the window pane. Glass flew in every direction as Bremer's first volley of fire smashed into Crawford's squad car. Laughing as he reloaded, Knox snapped an order.

"Save it!"

Bremer gave a nervous laugh, but did as he was ordered. Fletch had the 9 mm Beretta in hand, ready for God knows what. 'Had Sam Kilbane left him out to dry? Did he think he was already dead?' the thought didn't cheer him none.

Knox paced back and forth, his mind working out a plan.

Schneider grabbed hold of a Browning Auto-5 12 gauge, "I ain't being take alive," he screamed over the sporadic fire from the police outside.

"Hold it," cried Knox. "Karl when I say go, try to hit the gas tank of that squad car you're so fond of. When it goes up, we rush them. The distraction and us charging forward should scare the shit out of them hick cops. Kill as many as you can. Then we grab a patrol car and high-tail it outta here."

"Sounds like a plan!" cried Schneider.

"I'm game," replied Bremer as he patted the M16.

"Fine by me," cried Fletcher. Whatever he thought about Knox, he had to admire his clear head in the face of combat. Dark thoughts raced through his head, 'The son-of-a-bitch just might pull it off.' Fletcher steeled himself for what was to come as he wiped his hands down the front of his jeans and then slipped off the safety catch of his 9mm.

Thoughts of those last moments when Monique had him in her sights flashed through his head. Wade had caused the distraction and Monique had died. Knox was a dangerous man, far more deadly than Bremer or Schneider. If he led them they would kill innocent police men. Fletcher resolved that whatever happens, Knox must not escape.

Knox, Schneider, and Bremer took up positions near the door. They looked back towards Fletcher.

"Go ahead;" said Fletcher to Bremer, "I'll cover your back."

Knox flashed him a look, but readied himself for the assault. He'd seen others during the Gulf War. Tough as nails, but when the fire fight started they froze. He guessed he'd been wrong about Fletcher; the man didn't have the moxie. Fear can grab at a man when you're not looking. Knox steeled himself for battle; there was no time to worry about others. He edged the door open.

"Now!" he screamed.

The staccato sound of the M16 sounded terrifying and then the squad car exploded into flames with an almighty whoosh. Schneider and Bremer at Knox's beckoning took up positions either side of the ex marine.

"Go!" screamed Knox as he squeezed the trigger of the Uzi sending death in a terrible arch of death. Bremer and Schneider raced towards the nearest squad car, firing their weapons at the surprised police officers.

At the same time Fletcher screamed at the ex marine, "Bob, Bob Knox!" Knox stopped in his tracks and turned around, as if in slow motion. Fletcher stood braced in the door frame the

9mm Beretta held firmly in two hands pointing towards Knox's body.

"You son-of . . . ." His words were lost in an explosion of sound as the Beretta barked the ex marine's death knell. As Knox fell to ground Fletcher snapped off two more shots, one of his bullets hitting Schneider in the back, the other flew harmlessly into the sky.

Bullets ricocheted in every direction as Fletcher ducked back inside the ranch house. A fusillade of shots hammered into the door where he'd stood seconds earlier. He heard the familiar sound of Bremer's M16 followed by concerted gunfire from the rifles and shotguns of the police department, and then all went silent.

"We got em, we got em all," cried one of the deputies.

Deputy Emmett Larson shouted, "There's one more, he ducked back inside. This ain't over until it's over."

Each of the deputies understood what Larson was implying. Workmanlike the four remaining officers reloaded their weapons. This was Montana and they were going to administer justice the old fashion way.

Fletcher instantly recognised his plight. No amount of pleading was going to stop these police officers in executing their duties. They wouldn't believe he'd killed one of the terrorist and disabled another, they'd only find that out after the bodies had been forensically examined. By then it would be too late. Sam Kilbane might hoot and holler but after that what could he do? What purpose would the truth hold?

He had a choice, give himself up and be shot down like a dog, or he could hold out until Sam Kilbane arrived to rescue him, but to do that he'd probably have to kill a sheriff's deputy or two. Either way he was as good as dead.

A canister thudded into the cabin. 'Tear gas,' thought Fletcher, 'the bastards are trying to flush me out.' Grabbing the smoking canister he threw it back through the open window. He knew others would follow. Then it struck him. It was his only chance, it was slim, but it was a chance.

"You out there!" he screamed, "I'm with the FBI! I ain't militia and I can prove it." As if in answer a second canister crashed into the room, then a third. Fletcher began to cough, his throat began to burn, his brain felt like it was about to explode. He grabbed a piece of dirty sacking and held it over his eyes, nose and mouth. He had to make them outside hear him. Kicking one of the canisters into another room he slammed the door shut. The other he somehow covered with a bundle of old clothing.

"Jesus fucking Christ!" he screamed at the top of his voice, "I'm working for the federal government. I've a SIM card from a cell-phone. It'll prove I'm innocent! I'll throw it out in a cigarette carton. Put it in a cell-phone punch the no 7. A man called Sam Kilbane will pick it up. He'll tell you who I am."

His last words were barely audible. It was up to the baying mob outside, thought Fletcher. His mind was aflame with anger and frustration. He checked his weapon, if they didn't listen, then guilty or innocent he was going to take some of them with him, *the trigger happy motherfuckers.*

"What the fuck's a SIM card?" enquired one of the deputies.

Fletcher's words registered inside Deputy Emmett Larson's head just as he was about to fire another tear gas canister into the house. He froze. Something about what the man in the house was saying struck a cord, "Okay, throw the damn SIM card outside. Any tricks we burn you alive!"

Deputy Keith Smith, resting on the hood of a squad car looked up at Larson, "When he throws the cigarette carton outside, I can take him," he said patting his sniper rifle.

Deputy Larson thought about it for a second. If it had happen in the heat of battle no one could blame them if they got it wrong. But Larson knew he had to give the man inside the ranch house one chance. Fed or not.

"No! Ease off that trigger!"

Fletcher appeared in the window frame and hurled the cigarette carton as far as he could. Seconds later it was in Larson's hands.

"Okay we got the SIM card, now does anyone know what we do with it."

"Yeah I do," said one of the paramedics. "Give it here."

Larson and Smith both gathered around the paramedic as he took the back of his cell-phone off and took out his SIM card, which he replaced with the SIM card that Larson gave him.

"Now what?" cried the paramedic.

"Punch the no 7."

Chapter 28

Montana

The papers were calling it another Ruby Ridge. The Governor was incensed, the Justice Department called for an enquiry, and the integrity of the Sheriff's department was called into question. The great state of Montana wanted answers. It was left to Sam Kilbane to clear up the mess that was being called The Warlock Ranch Massacre. The papers were having a field day and until they had the full story they weren't letting go.

The first Wade and Alex knew of Fletcher's involvement was when Sam Kilbane appeared on local television.

"Wade come here a second. What was the name of that man from the FBI that paid us a visit?"

Wade stopped what he was doing, crossed the room and gazed at the face of Sam Kilbane. "That's the man," he said as he perched himself on the arm of a leather bound sofa.

They sat spellbound as Sam Kilbane explained away the shootings at the Warlock Ranch.

"There is to be a full enquiry into the shootings at Warlock Ranch, but in the meantime I'd like to read to you a prepared statement. Warlock can not be compared to Ruby Ridge or any other similar incidents in recent history." For the next few minutes Sam Kilbane did his best in a noncommittal way to explain the reasons behind Ruby Ridge. Then he began a full breakdown of events at Warlock Ranch. "Well liked Sheriff Josh Crawford received an anonymous tip off that a cache of arms was being stored at Warlock Ranch. The vagueness of the caller led Sheriff Josh Crawford to suspect it was a hoax call. But his police training would not let him ignore such a threat. Consequently he investigated, and was killed executing his duty. A fine officer and family man, he will be missed by all that knew him. In the fire fight that ensued a deputy Lane Bradley was shot in the arm but is recovering in hospital. FBI agent Harley Truelove was also shot. His wound is classed as serious, but is expected to make a full recovery. Ranch owner Jim Haggerty was found inside the ranch-house dead from gunshot wounds from person or persons unknown at this time. As I stated a full enquiry will be carried out in due course."

"Oh Wade!"

"Quiet Alex," said a very concerned Wade.

"Of the others involved, ex marine sergeant Robert Knox, petty criminal Karl Bremer and ex con Max Schneider were killed by the Sheriff's department deputies in a ferocious shootout. All three are believed to have been involved in the murder of a gun store owner in nearby Polson and a bank robbery in Havre just over a year ago. All of them are implicated in the death of FBI agent Ray Guthrie some months earlier." Sam Kilbane paused for the briefest of moments before continuing, "I can only add at this time my condolences to Sheriff Josh Crawford's family and my congratulations to the deputies that resolved the situation. Thank you."

"No mention of Fletcher," cried Alex.

Wade ignored Alex's outcry as he opened the bureau draw and fished out Sam Kilbane's business card.

Alex recognising Wade's actions stood at his side as he punched in Kilbane's office number.

"I'd like to speak with Sam Kilbane," said Wade abruptly

"And what is this in connection with? Mister?" came the reply.

"Name's Reynolds. Wade Reynolds. And it's in connection with the shootings at Warlock Ranch."

"I'm sorry, but Mr Kilbane is tied up at this moment."

Wade's face grew red with anger, "Listen lady, Mr Kilbane had better be on this phone right now, or I'm getting in touch with the media. Does the name Fletcher Coppersmith ring any bells?"

For a second Wade thought she'd cut him off, but then he realised he'd provoked a reaction. Seconds later Sam Kilbane was on the phone.

"Ah, Mr Reynolds. You're enquiring about your friend Fletcher Coppersmith, I believe."

"Damn right I am. Now stop pussyfooting around and tell me what's happened to him," demanded Wade.

"It's not that simple Mr Reynolds."

"Simple or not, if I don't get any answers within the next minute I'll be straight on to the media."

"Mr Reynolds, I understand your concern, believe me. But there's more to the Warlock shooting than we're making out. Fletcher is safe, but until we've unravelled what really went on with the terrorists we feel it's in Fletcher's best interest to remain in the shadows."

Frustration welled up inside Wade. "I've only your word that Fletcher is okay. I want to see him, and I want to see him now!"

"Fletcher said you were an ornery son-of-a-bitch. He said you wouldn't take no for an answer," Wade detected a trace of humour in Kilbane's voice.

*   *   *

Wade was shocked at Fletcher's appearance; he looked gaunt, tired and undernourished, yet he grinned widely with that trademark smile of his father's.

"Hi Wade, it's good to see you," greeted Fletcher.

"Likewise, but you look like shit," replied Wade.

"Only temporary," countered Fletcher.

With the preliminaries out of the way, Sam Kilbane pushed a document in front of Wade.

"Before we go any further, you need to sign this."

Wade looked quizzical.

"National Security." explained Fletcher.

"Jesus Christ! Is this necessary?" replied Wade. "What ever you tell me remains in this room. You know that."

"He knows it, I don't," interrupted Sam Kilbane. "What you know about the Warlock Ranch situation is only part of it."

Wade picked up the offered pen and scrawled his signature.

"Firstly, I was lucky to get out of the Warlock Ranch with my life. Those boys were hell bent on sending us all to hell." Fletcher recalled the feelings of relief when Deputy Emmett Larson shouted to the house that Sam Kilbane from the FBI had vouched for him, but in the interests of safety, Fletcher was to come out of the ranch house with his hands on his head and to walk forward ten yards before dropping to his knees and lying face down in the dirt. Seconds later he was handcuffed and brought to Larson. Deputy Larson remained stern-faced as he told Fletcher to sit down and remain silent until the FBI arrived.

It was a full twenty minutes before Sam Kilbane's car appeared at the entrance to the driveway.

"Take those damn cuffs off him!" demanded Kilbane as he flashed his ID in Larson's direction. Deputy Larson made to say something but Kilbane cut him dead. "I need a few minutes with my man," then I'll deal with you gentlemen." His tone suggested a dressing down, which Larson and the others weren't about to accept. They stood around talking while Fletcher and Sam Kilbane climbed into the privacy of Kilbane's vehicle.

"Hungry Horse wasn't the target," begun Fletcher. "The real target was Congressman Vince Holbrook." Fletcher continued with what Bob Knox had told him. All the time Sam Kilbane was taking notes. "Bremer on Knox's orders killed the gun store owner in Polson. The Havre bank robbery went off without loss of life largely due to agent Ray Guthrie's intervention. The murder of Guthrie was carried out by Schneider on the orders of Knox." Fletcher paused for a second, his throat still sore from the effects of the tear gas. "Can you get me a glass of water?"

Sam opened the door of his car and demanded water. Within minutes Fletcher was able to go on. "Knox had been approached in Kalispell, by a man calling himself Adam Coulter. He set up the killing of the gun store owner as a test, the same applied to the Havre bank job. Then he warned Knox that an agent was in there midst. He left it to Knox to find him and dispose of the problem. Too many fuck ups led Knox to thinking that nothing really added up. Coulter was treating him like a fool; Hungry Horse would be plain suicide, it was doomed to fail from the start. Which led Knox to believe the third and final test was the real deal. Knox confronted Adam Coulter in a bar in Whitefish, and told him there was a change of plan. The job would get done, but it would cost two hundred thousand dollars. The hit was Vince Holbrook."

"So what you're saying is someone close to Holbrook had set up this apparent series of terrorist attacks to cover up the real reason; Holbrook himself."

"I'm guessing this man has a lot to lose. I think he got cold feet when Knox turned the tables. I figure it was him who called the Sheriff's Department with that anonymous phone-call knowing that particular section of law enforcement was over zealous in carrying out their duties. Which leads me to believe we're dealing with someone high up in Montana's political system?"

Wade sat there enthralled with Fletcher's story.

"That's where I come in," cried Sam Kilbane. "This man must be apprehended at all costs. He might try to assassinate Congressman Holbrook some other way. Fletcher caught a glimpse of the man, not enough to identify him in court, so we have to keep him under wraps until we capture this Adam Coulter."

Wade sat silent for a few minutes. It wasn't in his nature to tell the FBI to suck eggs, but he thought their conspiracy of silence would net them nothing, and it might get Fletcher killed into the bargain.

Rising from his chair Wade looked first at Fletcher, then across the desk to Sam Kilbane.

"Begging your pardon sir, there's five deputies, two paramedics, your two agents and God knows how many others that know about Fletcher's involvement. How long before this Adam Coulter finds out?" Wade ran the brim of his hat through his fingers, 'Damn' it,' he thought. The FBI can suck eggs. "I say you should flush the varmint out. I'm not saying go public with

Fletcher's information, but if you let the corridors of power know that an assassination attempt was thwarted by Fletcher I'm willing to bet that amongst those closest to Holbrook there will be someone losing a lot of sleep."

"You know what you're saying?" snapped Kilbane.

"Sure do!" exclaimed Wade. "Fletcher's a target, whether you like it or not. Let Vince Holbrook know he's a target for assassination, let him know that Fletcher deflected the threat, let Holbrook show his gratitude."

"How do you suggest we go about it?" asked Kilbane, tiring of Wade's ludicrous suggestions.

"My daughter is a good friend of Vince Holbrook's wife," Wade let his words sink in, then turned to Fletcher. "What say we redress the bad name I've given you? Come back to the ranch, if only for Alex to fatten you up. You don't know your enemy, but you do know the best battlefield to fight him on. What do you say?"

Sam Kilbane butted in, "I say no!" The FBI agent didn't like it one bit.

"With all due respect, you sold me a bill of goods. You told me that there was a terrorist cell out there hell bent on death and destruction. We both know that wasn't the case. You used me to try to flush out the man behind the cell. If I'd have known I was putting my life on the line for a lousy politician I'd have told you where to go!" snapped Fletcher.

"Yeah, I hold my hands up; I did what I had to do."

"I understand that, and I guess in your circumstances I'd have done the same. But I'm a free man; I don't have to take orders. Your man who ever he is, ain't likely to be after my hide. But if he was, I can't think of anyone I'd trust more than this man right here"

Kilbane looked imploringly at Wade. "What about your family? If trouble comes a calling, what about them?" It was his last throw of the dice.

"Mr Kilbane, my family are used to trouble, you could say we thrive on trouble."

It was irregular, but that wily old buzzard might have a point, thought Kilbane, and if he's prepared to put his family in the firing line, then who am I to stop him. "Well Wade it looks like you've just bought in. Rest assured we will be keeping an eye."

"Wouldn't have it any other way," replied Wade as he shook Kilbane's hand.

* * *

"Don't think I've changed my mind," said Fletcher as he and Wade headed down the highway back to the Crazy AW.

"Fletch, one thing I learned from your pa, when he said something, there was no going back. Ornery old coot," he said affectionately.

Chapter 29

Montana

"I knew it!" exclaimed Larry to Thadeus Barnes. "It just didn't make any sense. Imagine it, Fletcher working undercover for the FBI."

"Yeah, it don't figure," added Thadeus. "Damn shame about Haggerty. He wasn't such a bad feller, just fell on hard times I guess."

It was the talk in the bunkhouse; in fact it was the talk all over the state. Sam Kilbane had appeared on television a few days after his first broadcast and read out a prepared statement.

"Further to our enquiries, we have an important update. One of our agents had infiltrated the terrorist cell and helped put down the threat these terrorists were causing. He also uncovered a plan to assassinate a leading Montana politician." Quickly Sam Kilbane added, "At this moment in time I'm not at liberty to divulge the name of the intended assassination attempt, only that he has been informed and that a full investigation is being carried out as we speak."

It was short and to the point. Who ever had ordered the hit should be shaking in their boots, that or making plans to eliminate the only person that might be able to connect him to Knox, thought Sam Kilbane. He'd been to the Reynolds Ranch the day after the meeting with Wade and Fletcher and had briefed the family on what to expect.

"If he's got any sense, he'll lay low. I think Fletcher is low risk, but I can't be sure," he added in way of a warning.

*   *   *

Vince Holbrook paced up and down his living room, his head buzzing with all manner of things. The initial shock at learning he was the intended target of an assassin's bullet had stopped him in his tracks, but as the days passed his arrogance returned. His security had doubled, the secret service was working overtime and everything possible was being done to protect him. He felt safer than the President.

"This could work to my advantage," he exclaimed. "The FBI thwarts a plan to assassinate the next governor of Montana. It has a ring to it, don't you think?"

"I'd be more concerned about my own welfare, rather than trying to garland more votes," cried an extremely agitated Carson Burroughs. "You've got your career, your wealth and a beautiful wife, what more do you want?" he added with a barely disguised hint of envy.

"More, Carson! Of course I want more. That's why I'm where I am and you're where you are," he said cruelly. "As for my wife," he said disdainfully, "Dumb fuck bitch, gave me an ultimatum. Clean up my act! I ask you! Clean up my act or she'll file for divorce. She knows very well that a divorce would hurt my political future. If it wasn't for that, I'd divorce the bitch in a second."

Still smarting from Holbrook's vitriolic outburst, Carson added his own advice, "Well then, you've got a choice, comply with the little woman, or kiss your career goodbye." Carson felt the bile rise, for one split second he felt like pulling the trigger himself. It was as if the gods were conspiring against him, first Knox had tried to outflank him, then Ruth had told him the affair was over. It was all becoming too much.

Stunned by the turn of events at the bar in Whitefish, Carson decided to cut all ties with Knox. Knowing the calibre of men that he'd had assembled Carson matched them with an equally dedicated team. An anonymous tip to the right people and he'd got the results he'd hoped for, but it seemed there was a fly in the ointment. Indirectly Knox had saved him from being exposed. From what he'd discovered this agent provocateur didn't know diddly squat. If he had the feds would have been breathing down his neck by now. Carson reasoned that with Knox and his men all dead there was no way that he could now be connected.

It was a day after the Warlock Ranch shootout that Carson learned from inside sources that the FBI informant that had infiltrated Knox's bunch of psychopaths wasn't an agent. The man was a relative or as close as one gets, to the Reynolds family who owned the Crazy AW ranch in the Big Hole Valley. At present he was staying with them at their ranch. Their daughter it seems was Ruth's new friend, the same friend that had been filling Ruth's head with ideas. A fact not wasted on Burroughs.

It wasn't enough that Knox had turned the tables on him, the stupid bitch had to call him up the following day and tell him the affair was over. Didn't she understand, he had far more important things to worry about? His ardour towards her had cooled somewhat since the Warlock ranch killings. The thought of spending the rest of his life in the penitentiary had that affect on him. In Burroughs eyes Ruth had used him just as surely as Holbrook. In his devious mind he swore he'd find a place for her in his plans to destroy Holbrook.

'Starting over wasn't all bad,' thought Carson Burroughs. 'You learn by your mistakes.' He prided himself on his ability to manipulate people, he'd done it with Knox and he'd do it again, only the next time he wouldn't fail.

Holbrook had remained uncharacteristically silent after Carson's unexpected caustic remark. A fact not lost on Carson. His mind was already putting into motion ways to eradicate his problem. Holbrook unwittingly had given him the perfect in.

"I'd suggest you and I pay this Fletcher Coppersmith a visit, offer him your most gracious thanks. Take some publicity shots, do the thing that you're so good at. Milk it for all its worth. The public have short memories, but an assassination attempt, well that sticks in the mind."

"That's not a bad idea Carson, but for how long?"

"For as long as it takes," replied Carson, as a nauseous feeling crept over him. Without wanting it, without trying, hating himself because of it, he was falling back into the familiar role of kingmaker. 'Three more years,' he ruminated, 'three more fucking years of his crap.'

"See to it at once," snapped Vince Holbrook, secretly wondering when Carson Burroughs would ever grow a new set of balls.

*   *   *

"We've a number of guests coming over this Sunday," cried Alex through the open kitchen door.

"What's that?"

"I said we've a number of guests this Sunday for dinner. You've got to get your ears tested."

"Hell, I will. I heard you, just needed it repeating is all," replied Wade. "Now who's coming?"

"Congressman Vince Holbrook, his wife Ruth, you know that new friend of Tara's. I guess there'll be others, drivers, bodyguards and his second in command, a guy called Carson Burroughs. They want to thank Fletcher personally for intervening in the attempt on the Congressman's life."

"Publicity for his campaign more like," cried Wade cynically.

"I've invited Tara, Jack and the kids."

"Good, weather's looking fine; I think a barbeque, seeing as there'll be so many mouths to feed."

"As long as it's you standing over the hot coals?" secretly Alex was looking forward to entertain her important guests.

"Say isn't Jack's brother due this Friday?" cried Wade.

"Yeah, that's right. With all the excitement over the shootings, Fletcher's involvement and his presence here, I'd almost forgotten."

*   *   *

It had been a hectic and unbelievable month. First there was Charlotte's phone-call to Jack telling him he was to become a granddad in the not to distant future, then Ruth's revelation about her marriage to Congressman Holbrook, the dramatic shooting at the Warlock Ranch up in Missoula, *which had kept the good people of Montana watching television as more facts became available* and finally to discover Fletcher was at the heart of it all. What Bob and Sheila would make of it, Tara couldn't begin to speculate.

Jack had taken the day off to drive to Billings to pick them up and left Tara and the girls to ready the house for their arrival. Thankfully Martha Redbird was on hand to ease the burden.

Bob took Jack's advice and flew to Denver where they stayed overnight, had a cooked breakfast and took the short flight to Billings. It was just after one in the afternoon when Bob and Sheila came strolling through to the arrivals area.

Jack hugged his sister-in-law then grabbed Bob's hand, shook it hard and pulled his brother towards him and gave him an affectionate hug.

"Wow it's so good to see you!" he exclaimed.

"You too bruv," replied Bob with that unmistakeable London accent that transported Jack back to another time and place.

It was late afternoon when Jack pulled off the road and entered under the large shingle sign with the words 'Claymore Ranch, Home of Reynolds Horses.'

"Impressive," offered Bob.

*   *   *

Minutes later Tara stepped out onto the porch, followed closely by Kaycee and an unusually shy Merri.

"Believe me, enjoy her shyness while it lasts," remarked Tara. "It's so good to see you again."

Jack offered them a seat on the porch, "There's plenty of time to unpack. What you both need is a drink to unwind."

"You read my mind," exclaimed Bob.

"That's not hard," retorted Jack.

Seconds later Martha Rainbird appeared on the porch clutching a tray full of drinks.

"Now that's what I call service!" exclaimed Bob, as he took the tray from Martha's hands and placed it upon the table. "Name's Bob, pleased to meet you," then he extended his hand. Martha took it and gave it a firm shake, smiled and hurried back into the kitchen.

"Martha's a little shy, like Merri here, but once she get's use to you she's hell on wheels," laughed Tara.

"Well big brother, I hope you're fit. We got some serious work for you."

Bob took a sip of beer from his glass; *he insisted he couldn't drink it just from the bottle,* looked across at Jack and did a double take.

"Only joking," cried Jack, I've taken today off but I've work to get on with tomorrow. Tara will show you around, and then on Sunday we're over to Wade and Alex's ranch for a barbeque. That's Tara's folks. There you'll get to meet some of our friends, a character or two, oh and a couple of local dignitaries."

"You'll meet my friend Ruth," enthused Tara, to Sheila, "You'll like her, I'm sure."

"That would be real nice Tara, I was beginning to think this was going to be an all men affair," remarked Sheila.

"Hell no!" replied Tara, "We bother share the pants around here, but Jack insists the skirts are strictly a woman's garment."

"Following week, we've Dillon's Labor Day Weekend. Biggest rodeo event in Dillon's calendar," added Jack.

"Yeah, I'd say," Tara reflected sadly. Thoughts of her brother Taw and Merri were always more to the fore during that particular weekend.

*   *   *

"All this, as far as the eye can see, is Reynolds land," remarked Jack as he entered under the Crazy AW shingle and drove slowly towards the ranch house.

"Including the mountains?" Bob asked.

"No," answered Jack, "The mountains belong to no man. They're a separate entity, they're your friend one minute, the next they're your cruellest enemy. I have nothing but respect for the mountains."

"That's a bit profound, coming from you Jack," remarked Bob.

"When you've seen them in action as often as I have, you start to believe they're a living thing." For a moment Jack was taken back to that place where they found Monique's body, a forlornly dark and lonely place, places where only evil lurked. Bob noticed the troubled look in his brother's eyes and made a mental note to ask him about it.

Jack smiled as he brought the Ford Explorer to a smooth stop outside the main house. "Nothing gets passed you, does it brother," he said grinning as he switched off the ignition and began to climb out of the vehicle. "Things happened here, you just wouldn't believe."

Chapter 30

Montana

Once Jack had introduced his brother and sister-in-law to Wade and Alex he and Tara left them to become acquainted. Bob felt a true warmth emanate through Jack's father-in-law. The man had put him at ease almost instantaneously. Although they came from two different worlds, Bob could see why his brother had become friendly with this giant of a man. Although not a giant in a physical sense, Wade was a fraction over six foot, strong and muscular, but it wasn't just that, it was his whole persona. He seemed to ooze a natural charm, one that comes with great maturity. Closer to seventy than sixty you'd put his age as mid to late fifties. Bob could sense his zest for life was still as powerful as when he was a young man, a fact that made him envious that Jack had known him for so long.

Alex was all Sheila thought she'd be. It came as no surprise that she was an almost replica of Tara, though older of course, but someone that had lived life to the full, someone that had tasted life's fruits and found them bitter sweet in equal measures. There was a natural honesty about Alex that made her instantly likeable. Small wonder that Jack had fallen for her daughter, thought Sheila. If Tara is half the woman that her mother appeared to be, then Jack was very lucky indeed.

"Right, we've kept you long enough!" announced Wade, "Let's go eat."

It was nothing like the barbeques at home, thought Bob. No small family gathering on the patio, with a few burgers, sausage, chicken drumsticks and copious amounts of alcohol, no this was a grand affair by any standards. There were three long trestle tables covered by several blue gingham table cloths. Each table was adorned with fresh coleslaw, freshly baked bread, colourful salad bowls, baked potatoes and chilli peppers of varying strengths, but the piece de resistance was the barbeque pits, where a side of beef was being gentle smoked and a whole pig was being spit roasted.

Bob and Sheila looked around in amazement; there must have been seventy or more guests at the barbeque. All intent on feeding their faces, thought Bob. As he perused the gathering he couldn't help noticing a number of big guys in suits on the periphery of the party.

"Secret Service, before you ask," volunteered Jack. "See that guy in the leather waistcoat and light blue shirt sitting at the that table over yonder, he's Congressman Vince Holbrook the possible future governor of Montana, next to him that curly haired too good looking for his own good kinda feller in the denim shirt, that's his aide and running mate Carson Burroughs."

"Hah! Not your favourite then?" laughed Bob.

"You could say that, I ain't too sure about Holbrook either."

"Oh yeah, why's that?"

"I'll tell you tomorrow."

"So why'd Wade invite them?"

"Long story, like I said, I'll tell you tomorrow."

"I'm intrigued," said Bob as he took a sip of the excellent Chardonnay he'd picked up from the overstocked bar. "Now who's the blonde?"

"Ah, that's Ruth; she's Holbrook's wife. She's become a good friend of Tara's. We met them a year ago at the Dillon Rodeo."

"I guess you'll tell me more tomorrow," quipped Bob.

"I might at that," laughed Jack.

"She's quite stunning."

"She sure is; now let me introduce you to Fletcher," said Jack as he steered Bob in both conversation and change of direction. If his memory served him well, he recalled Bob wasn't the most tactful of people. "Actually Fletcher is the reason that Congressman Holbrook's here."

"How so?"

"Fletcher's a local hero. He helped foil a plan to assassinate Holbrook."

"You're kidding!" 'It's getting better and better,' thought Bob, 'I'd already thought I'd fallen into a TV movie.'

"Fletch, I'd like you to meet my big brother. Bob meet Fletcher."

Fletcher grinned and extended his hand, "Nice to meet you Bob."

"Likewise," replied Bob.

Both men shook hands and exchanged pleasantries and within the blink of an eye were deep in conversation. No doubt Bob would pump him on the Holbrook incident, thought Jack as he made his excuses and began mingling and chatting with friends and neighbours.

* * *

"Yeah you see, I'd been out of the country for a few years when I get pulled out of the line and find myself being confronted by the FBI. An agent called Sam Kil . . . ."

"Sorry to interrupt Fletch, but I think the congressman is in a round about way heading towards you," warned Wade.

Fletcher looked up just as Congressman Holbrook looked over in his direction and smiled. He smiled back in return and watched as Vince Holbrook accompanied by his wife circulated *as only politicians knew how*, nonchalantly chatting with prospective voters. Expertly he negotiated his path towards Fletcher and Bob.

To the accompaniment of press and official photographers Congressman Holbrook stuck out his hand, "Fletcher Coppersmith I presume?"

"That's me!" he said as the press photographer took a series of pictures of both men shaking hands. "I'd like to thank you personally. From what I've been told I think I owe you quite a lot."

'Damn near got my ass shot off, and this asshole can't bring himself to say thanks for saving his life,' thought Fletcher. "It's appreciated," said Fletcher slightly embarrassed at his own hypocrisy. Congressman Holbrook patted Fletcher on the shoulder, smiled a politicians smile then moving on to mingle once again with his prospective voters.

'Was it worth it,' thought Fletcher angrily, but as Ruth floated by on the arm of her husband she gave him a smile so warm, he suddenly revised his last thought.

"What an arsehole!" Bob quietly remarked..

"My sentiments entirely. Now where were we?" replied Fletcher as he savoured the last of Ruth Holbrook's perfume.

*   *   *

Tara waved across to Ruth, who in turn stopped her husband in his tracks, "It's Tara, she's coming over to meet us. Be nice."

Tara took Sheila by the arm and steered her towards Ruth and Vince.

"Hi Ruth glad you could make it. Congressman," added Tara as an aside. "There are far too many people to introduce you too, but you must meet my sister-in-law Sheila, all the way from England."

"From England! Say you must find this a little different from what you're used too?" said Holbrook in true political form.

"Overwhelming! Bob, that's my husband over there, he and I have been to the States several times, but never to Montana."

"I'm sure you'll enjoy the experience," replied Holbrook.

Ruth smiled at Sheila and extended her hand.

"Hi Sheila, it's really nice to meet you."

"Likewise," replied Sheila and she found she really meant it.

"Isn't this a wonderful setting," exclaimed Ruth as she gazed up into the foothills and above to the purple headed mountains, "I find it quite breathtaking."

"As I was just saying to your husband, I find it overwhelming."

"Well I'm sure you're going to enjoy your stay in our wonderful state. In fact you and Tara should come visit, if you've time."

Sheila looked at Tara, "It'll be fun," said Tara reassuringly.

"I'd like that Ruth, I'd like that a lot. Thank you."

Carson Burroughs butted in to their conversation, a little too zealously for Tara's liking. "I knew it! I knew there was something about your husband," he cried. "I couldn't put my finger on it. I thought I detected an Australian accent, I guess I was wrong."

Sheila smiled awkwardly.

"Hello Carson," said Tara in a cool manner.

"Tara, always good to see you," he said with equal coolness. He'd only met Tara Claymore once before and she'd left a profound impression on him. He didn't like her and now he could see why. Ruth had mentioned her on an occasion and call it intuition, but Carson had felt threatened by her. Now finally the penny had dropped. It was obvious the bitch in front of him had influenced Ruth in her decision to finish there relationship. What was it with this family, he thought angrily, firstly Ruth, and then this family inadvertently foiled my plan to kill Holbrook.

With a politician's smile he excused himself from the group and walked over to one of the secret service men. He was raging inside, but in his coldly calculating mind he was counting his blessings. He'd met his nemesis Fletcher Coppersmith earlier and was relieved that the big man with the flashing smile showed no sign of recognition, a fact that Carson was grateful for, as he recognised Fletcher from the bar in Whitefish. Carson didn't like loose ends, but he had a choice; do nothing and leave sleeping dog lie, or take direct action. Either way was risky. He chose for the moment the former option.

"You don't like him much, do you?" said Sheila after they'd made there excuses to Vince and Ruth and got in line for the pig roast.

"No, not really; in fact I don't care for Holbrook either."

"So tell me," cried Sheila.

"Maybe, sometime . . . Now let's go eat."

"So this is a dude ranch," remarked Bob.

"Hell no!" replied Wade. "Cattle ranching is a tough business, long days and short nights. Hard work summer and winter. If you ain't fighting the cold, the droughts, the government, the cattle that up and die on you, calving, round up time, inoculations, tick fever and a thousand other ailments, you've the bank to fight.

"Wow! I didn't realise. I just assumed with all this land you'd have no problems."

Wade formed a slight grin, "To survive in today's climate you've got to have more than one finger in the pie. Diversification, that's what Alex calls it. That's where she comes in, not only does she do the books, the accounts, the ordering of supplies and such like, she also manages the ranch as an opportunity for city folk to try their hand at being a cowboy."

"Yeah, I can see the appeal. I always fancied having a go myself," remarked Bob.

Wade laughed, "I might just hold you to it. The guest ranch idea was Alex's brainchild; I just insisted we followed the old methods of ranching."

"How's that?" enquired Bob.

"Most dude ranches pamper to their clients, at the Crazy AW, we don't. It's a working ranch."

"I see," remarked Bob.

"I had my reservations at first, but to be fair it's turned out to be a lucrative means of income during the summer months. It doesn't pay all the bills but it sure helps."

"Have you ever thought of selling up? I'd expect you'd get a pretty penny for the ranch and the land."

'Damn blast it, the man's insistent,' thought Wade as he gave him a long hard look which softened around the edges as he remembered meeting Jack that first time. 'Damn tenderfoot!

"I can't expect you to understand, you see, this is my life. It always has been and I guess until the day I die it always will be. I know no other life, nor do I seek it. Tradition is all important to me. I guess you could say I'm a throwback to another age."

"Yeah, I guess you are at that. Forgive me; it's just me putting my own slant on things."

"Forgive you! For what, there's nothing to forgive."

Holbrook and his entourage were the first to leave, to the relief of Wade and most of his guests. A more informal air fell across the entire scene, leaving the rest to enjoy the party.

"Well, I can't say I'm not pleased they're gone," remarked Fletcher.

"Yeah, I share that sentiment," laughed Jack. "Mind you that Ruth is some looker."

"Oh, really, can't say as I noticed."

"Sure you didn't," said Jack wryly.

Later than night as the sky painted another masterpiece of gold and silver Wade stepped onto the porch and joined Jack as he gazed westerly.

"They're quite magnificent aren't they," intoned Jack.

"They surely are," drawled Wade.

"It was a remark my brother made about them that started me thinking. He asked about the land and then he asked if you owned the mountains."

Wade barely stifled his laugher, "He's quite a character, your brother Bob. Says what he thinks, without fear or favour. An honest man, I like him. Make sure you stay close, now you've been given another chance."

"I will, you can count on it. That's why I'm taking him up yonder," he pointed into the distance. "The last time I was up there was when we found Monique's remains. The place smacked of evil and I swore as I turned my back on it, that I'd never return. But Bob's remarks got me to thinking; I need to exorcise my demons. More than that, I need to get to know my brother again."

Wade nodded in understanding.

"I'll let Bob make his own mind up about who owns these mountains."

Wade just chortled.

Chapter 31

Montana

"Well that was some barbeque," remarked Sheila, the following morning. "Politicians, local dignitaries, the secret service, the FBI and our own local hero, nah: that was all a hoax; right!"

"I'm afraid it wasn't," replied Tara. "As for the Congressman and his entourage I'd rather have settled for a nest of rattlesnakes."

"But I thought Ruth was your friend!"

"She is, but that doesn't mean I have to like her husband," stated Tara. "He had us all fooled, me and Jack, well we thought he was the right man for the job. Ma and pa, they thought the same, well maybe Wade did have a few reservations, but on the whole I'd say we bought into his rhetoric."

"What changed your mind?"

"It's not common knowledge, in fact I haven't told ma and pa. Jack knows of course."

"Knows what?" cried Sheila.

"Nothing. I've said enough already," replied Tara.

"Oh come on. I'm not going to say anything. I'm your sister-in-law, we're family."

It struck a cord, 'we're family.' There was something about the way Sheila said I'm your sister-in-law, that made Tara feel accepted. Until that moment Tara had thought of her as Bob's wife. It made her feel warm inside, it brushed away any insecurities she might have felt. "Okay, I'll tell you, only because you'll be gone in a couple of weeks. You've to promise not to tell anyone." For a moment Tara felt like a naughty school girl about to reveal everything. "Not even Bob, especially Bob."

"Oh! You know him too," quipped Sheila. "Okay I promise."

Tara walked towards the door and looked out, "Can't be too careful."

"Get on with it!" exclaimed Sheila, her patience at breaking point.

"Vince Holbrook is as insincere in his political views as one can get. He's totally corrupt."

"Like all politicians," interrupted Sheila.

"Yeah, but more than that; he cheats on Ruth."

"The bastard!"

"It's worse than that, Ruth knows and Holbrook doesn't care. She's his trophy wife, his possession if you like. Smiles sweetly, goes to all the functions, does just about all he tells her."

"Why does she put up with it? I wouldn't."

"It's hard to explain. Ruth came from a small town in Indiana; close knit community, good family, but poor. She meets the man of her dreams; he sweeps her off her feet, next thing you know she's married. Vince gave her all the trappings of wealth, and then he worked on her. Changed her from a small town girl into the sophisticated woman she is now." Tara paused for a moment, not quite sure she should go on.

"So."

Spurred on by Sheila, she continued, "She became dependent on Holbrook, so much so that she turned her back on her family. I'm not sure of the details but basically she burnt her bridges. But it wasn't Ruth, he'd manipulated her, he'd planned things in such a way that she had nowhere to run." Tara could see that Sheila didn't buy it. "Look, I know that doesn't excuse her, but at the time Ruth was desperately in love with him.

"Yeah we've all been there," agreed Sheila reluctantly.

"I've got to know Ruth this last year and she's not as weak willed as you might think.

"Okay I'm still listening."

"Despite everything, Ruth thought things would change between her and Vince once she told him a baby was on the way."

"A baby!" exclaimed Sheila.

"And for a time," continued Tara, "things were better, then she lost the baby. After that things went down hill fast. Unable to forgive Vince's insensitivities Ruth hardened her heart; she decided to make the best of what she had. Then she got involved with another man."

"Good for her! I'm beginning to like her better already."

"The other man . . . . You've got to swear . . . ."

"Carson Burroughs, that creep from yesterday," exclaimed Sheila.

"It's over! Ruth put a stop to it a couple of weeks ago. The man was full on, he's supposed to be Vince Holbrook's best friend, but from what Ruth's told me, he hates him."

"Should I like Burroughs, I'm a little confused."

"No way. She didn't love him. From what little I've seen of Carson Burroughs, he's just another Vince Holbrook waiting in the wings."

"So where does that leave Ruth now!"

"She's ended the affair with Burroughs and told Holbrook that if he doesn't get his act together, she'll start very public divorce proceedings against him which would I'm sure; scupper any chances of getting elected governor."

"Good. I can't wait to meet her again."

"Sheila! You promised not to say a word."

"Relax, Bob's the indiscreet one in our family," she laughed.

* * *

Fletcher was troubled, she'd been just a face in the crowd, but her smile had lit up his world. It felt like betrayal, guilty beyond words, his stomach churned violently, for four long years he'd remained celibate, yet her smile had changed all that. Merri had been the love of his life, a ray of brilliant sunshine in a life full of darkness, but Merri was gone. Why did he feel such guilt, it was just a smile. But it wasn't just a smile; it was much more than a smile.

As he crouched beside Merri's grave he told her about the last few months, how Sam Kilbane had used him, of Knox's double cross and the shoot out at the Warlock ranch, yet despite everything that had happened he felt he was putting his life to good use. He told her of the offer, the bolt from the blue that Sam Kilbane had thrown at him. He told her that his future lay in some faraway place, and finally he told her he loved her, that his love would never die, but he didn't tell her about the smile.

As he rode away, he glanced back at that manicured mound of green and wept. He'd so wanted to tell her about that smile, to ask her advice, to beg forgiveness, to seek her approval. But for what, it was only a smile.

*   *   *

The three women met at an expensive restaurant in Deer Lodge. Tara stole a glance at Sheila and was pleased to see that she was suitably impressed. Ruth had arrived a few minutes earlier and had ordered three glasses of chilled champagne.

"What a fabulous place," exclaimed Sheila as the three women were seated.

"I think so, it's so decadently expensive, but Vince is picking up the tab," replied Ruth with a hint of mirth.

Tara laughed; she could see the irony of Ruth's remark. She only hoped Sheila wouldn't give herself away. She had been so insistent, like a dog with a bone.

As they nibbled away at their Caesar salads, the talk was about how Sheila was enjoying Montana, how it compared to other places she'd been, the latest fashions in London. Then Ruth surprised them both.

"Fletcher Coppersmith!" Two words, which was all it took to bring on a stunned silence. Ruth looked at their blank expressions and laughed. "I'm sure Tara's confided something about my present position." She looked straight at Tara, "I know I would have, in your position. It's only natural."

Tara's face flushed with embarrassment, "I'm so sorry, I . . . ."

"It's not her fault; I backed her into a corner. I'm just a nosy bitch," cried Sheila.

"No!" interrupted Tara, "I shouldn't have betrayed your confidence. I'm so truly sorry."

"There's nothing to be sorry about. If it hadn't have been for you, I wouldn't have been able to face Vince. Life would still have been hell. It still is, but . . . ." She left the sentence half unsaid, aware that her friend was feeling awkward.

"So you're not mad," asked Tara seeking reassurance.

"Of course I'm not mad. Now tell me all there is to know about Fletcher!"

*   *   *

With his morning chores behind him, and a reassurance from Charlie, his foreman, that life on the Claymore ranch could survive another day without him, Jack and Bob climbed into the Ford pickup.

"Today Bob, the mountains beckon."

Bob smiled. "Can't wait."

At the Crazy AW they selected two suitable horses, grabbed a pack lunch each from Alex and took off. Two hours later they were edging their way through the foothills when Jack turned in his saddle. "How goes it?" he enquired after his brother's welfare.

"I'm fine," replied Bob, clearly not as comfortable as he'd have liked.

Jack grinned to himself. His brother could be in the direst of circumstances and he'd never tell you. It was the tell-tale signs, standing up in the stirrups, spreading one's weight around every inch of the saddle that gave it away.

"As long as you're fine, we've still a mite farther to go."

"How far is far?"

"Oh it's far and then some," grinned Jack clearly enjoying his day off.

Half hour later Jack called a halt and watered the horses at a mountain stream. Bob climbed down and stretched his legs. He looked back the way they'd come and made out the ranch in the far distance. He smelt the coolness of the air and marvelled at the clarity of view. Forgotten were the aches and pains, as he gazed at the panoramic vista of the Big Hole Valley. Then as his eyes took in the immensity of his surrounding he gazed with wonder at the majestic high mountains. The tall Ponderosa pines that fringed them were somehow dwarfed by the granite and rock. Too his right on a gentler slope there were groves of Aspen already turning golden against the clear blue sky.

"It's stunningly beautiful!" exclaimed Bob.

As if on cue a bald eagle soared across Bob's line of sight, "It's magnificent," he added as his eyes absorbed all before him.

Half hour later they rode though a copse of silver birch and crossed a clearing before negotiating their way through another stand of birch trees.

"You know Jack, this is spectacular. I can see why you like it here."

"I'm glad the ride is to your liking," replied Jack, pleased at his brother's enthusiasm. "Up ahead is Cougar Pass, where Wade and I found the scats and picked up the trail of the largest mountain lion this side of the Canadian border."

Bob looked quizzical.

"It had been taking Wade's cattle over a period of years," added Jack.

They passed the green mound and small bouquet of flowers on Merri's grave. Bob instinctively stopped himself from asking. He guessed this was close to the place where it all happened. Sombreness descended on the ride as they rode in silence past the old line shack. Then the trees thinned out and the climb became steeper. They negotiated there way slowly until Jack called a halt.

"Step down Bob, we'll tie the horses and walk from here."

Bob looked at his brother, nodded silently, and dismounted. Buttoning up his coat from the icy wind that had got up, he followed his brother as they negotiated the steep incline. Ahead of them Jack pointed to a rocky promontory. "That's where we're heading." As they reached it both men were finding it hard to breathe. The view from that rocky outcrop literally took their breath away.

"Wow!"

"It's quite a sight," said Jack as he pointed in a south easterly direction. "On a clear day, you can see the Tetons. Wyoming and Idaho over there," then he pointed northwards. "And Canada in that direction."

As they climbed back down to the timberline Jack forced himself to look to the stand of rocks and the tiny clump of trees where Monique had breathed her last. A shudder ran through him. He'd intended showing Bob where he'd killed the mountain lion and where they'd discovered the macabre remains of Monique, but something spiritual stopped him.

A few hours later, in the foothills of the Bitterroots they halted their horses and both men turned back for one last look. And Jack could see by the look in Bob's eyes that he had begun to understand his brother's respect for the mountains.

Chapter 32

Montana

With Montana's biggest weekend of the year only days away, the Crazy AW and the Claymore Ranch became hives of activity. Every hand took it upon them-selves to put in double shifts to ease the workload. Even Bob and Sheila lent a hand during those frantic final days. In fact Bob got quite a kick out of mending fences, though the same couldn't be said for Sheila as she mucked out the stables. Lots were drawn amongst the cowhands, the lucky ones got Sunday and Labor Day, while the unlucky ones had to make do with Saturday and an early start back to the ranch come Sunday morning. There were others like Thadeus Barnes that had seen it all before, and opted to work through. And then there was Fletcher.

"I'll stay behind, Thad and I'll look after the place. Let the boys have a few hours to recover from their celebrating."

"It'll be fun, you've got to come," cried Wade.

"Yeah Fletch, you have to come. Tara's entered the barrel racing event, on Jack's insistence. I think he wants us all to put on a show for Bob and Sheila," added Alex.

Fletcher shook his head sadly, "I'm sorry, I don't want to offend anyone, but I just can't, there are too many memories."

Wade made to protest but Alex laid a hand on his arm. "He's got to work these things out by himself," she added in a gentle voice.

Wade turned away, and walked outside. He knew only too well where Fletcher was coming from; it was there not so many years ago that he'd found Merri. There happiness together was immeasurable but so short. 'If only' . . . thought Wade hopelessly.

As Wade stared across the ridges of purple and steel grey mountains and beyond to the fast fading sunset, he thought about the times both good and bad that he had shared with his family in and around the Dillon Rodeo. His first encounter with Alex, the fist fights with Kyle Weaver, Tara's terrible fight with Taw's fiancée; Shelby and the tragic aftermath. The reunion between him and Alex, the bust ups, the attempted seduction by Monique/Courtney, they were all there: ghosts, but ghosts of a life well lived.

*   *   *

"What!" said Tara the following morning?

"Fletcher's not coming to the Labor Day celebrations," repeated Alex.

Tara thought about it for a moment, her mind ticking over. "We'll see about that?" she mused. "Give me a minute," she begged, and left her mother bemused while she trotted off to the room she used as an office. A couple of phone calls later and Tara returned beaming.

"What is it," enquired Alex.

"Wait and see," she said mischievously.

Whilst talking to Sheila at the barbeque, she'd glanced across at Ruth and the Congressman as they were thanking Fletcher for uncovering the plot to assassinate Holbrook. Call it female intuition if you like. It was only a smile, just a moment in time, but somehow it had remained in Tara's consciousness. That smile had radiated through and touched Fletcher like nothing had, since before Merri died. Of course she'd thought nothing of it, just two strangers being polite at a party, nothing more, nothing less, or so she'd thought until Ruth's declaration of interest. That Ruth had stirred something in Fletcher she was quite sure, but to bring them together was another thing entirely.

Ruth was easy, a phone call inviting her to join them all for the celebrations, was greeted with unashamed enthusiasm.

That Tara had asked expressly if Ruth would like to attend the Dillon Rodeo thrilled her with anticipation. He might be there, of course he'll be there, it was all the excuse she needed. With her newly found independence she informed Vince she was going to spend the weekend with her new friend.

"You can come too!" she said lamely.

Vince Holbrook, grunted his reply, saying he had a conference and several meetings to attend in Great Falls.

Tara sought out Sheila and informed her of the dilemma they both shared. "Ruth's coming, and I suspect she's hoping a certain someone will also be there."

"So where's the problem!" exclaimed Sheila.

"Fletcher isn't going."

"But he's got too!" exclaimed Sheila.

"Exactly!

"So," laughed Sheila, clearly enjoying meddling in someone else's love life. "How do we go about getting them together?"

"That's the tricky part," said Tara with a glint in her eye. "We have to enlist Jack and Bob."

Without realising their complicity over the course of a Friday evening at the Crazy AW the conversation got around to the following few days celebrations.

"Sheila and I are really looking forward to it." said an unwitting Bob. "It's a nice way for us to finish our trip."

"Yeah it's a pity you ain't coming Fletch. We could show this brother of mine a rare old time."

"I'd like too, but I sort of said I'd fill in around here," said Fletcher lamely.

"Don't worry Bob, I'm sure we can make your last few days memorable. Sunday night especially, after the rodeo, a couple of beers in the Metlen, dinner at the Lion's Den, then the concert, after that maybe some dancing back at the Metlen."

"Sounds fun," enthused Sheila.

"Oh it will be. By the way I've invited Ruth!" cried Tara.

To Sheila, Tara was so blatantly obvious, but the men didn't seem to notice. "That's great! She's a real nice person; I so much enjoyed meeting her."

Tara's eyes were fixed on Fletcher, hoping for a reaction. Her heart pounded as she searched his face for clues. Was it her imagination? Or did she really see a flicker of interest, she couldn't be sure.

They left the Crazy AW a little after ten, the boys light hearted and looking forward to the coming days' festivities. The girls a little quiet, deflated that their plan seemed dead in the water.

* * *

"You're a devious one, Tara Claymore," chided Alex down the phone the following morning. "I saw though your little plan; almost from the moment you hatched it. Not that I think the men were aware of anything."

"Oh!" replied Tara innocently.

"It worked!"

"What!"

With a slight hint of humour in her voice Alex began, "We were having breakfast, Wade, Kaycee, Merri, and Martha when Fletcher walks in all casual like. "I've been thinking," he says. "I'm suppose to flush out this would be assassin of Holbrook's. I'm hanging around the ranch waiting for something to happen, which it won't. Now Holbrook's wife Ruth, if I'm not mistaken is going to the Labor Day Rodeo. Well if I turn up, it might flush the assassin out."

A grin formed on Tara's face as Alex told her of Fletcher's idea. 'I knew it!' she thought excitedly.

"That damn fool of a father of yours, he nearly spoiled everything by saying, "Well in that case maybe you'd be better off at the ranch." I could have hit him.

"So what did Fletcher say?"

"Oh he made some excuse."

Tara went silent.

"He's coming Sunday!" exclaimed Alex

"Excellent!" cried Tara, the relief clearly noticeable.

Chapter 33

Montana

Ruth's enigmatic smile at the barbeque had caught more than the eye of Fletcher Coppersmith. Carson Burroughs, still smarting from Ruth's rejection, had been watching her like a hawk. Seething with jealousy he caught that smile, he'd seen it before; back in the very early days of her relationship with Vince Holbrook. Her interests it seemed lay with the man that foiled his plans and became a hero overnight. Burrough's thoughts were becoming dark and dangerous.

'Since staying with that Claymore woman, Ruth has changed,' he thought. 'Not only has she put an end to our affair, but she'd somehow or other developed a backbone.'

Carson's mind was working overtime; he'd seen with his own eyes how Holbrook has lost his control over her. Ruth, the woman of his dreams, was fast becoming a loose cannon. A fact that could affect Burroughs future plans as much as the Congressman's. He fought to control his rage, his anger. He'd loved her, he'd loved her far more than any woman could imagine, yet she'd thrown that love in his face. It was something he found hard to take. There was a fine line between love and hate and unwittingly that smile, that mysterious smile had pushed Ruth Holbrook over that line. Murderously Carson Burroughs began devising a plan of action that would to all intent and purpose tie up every loose end.

For that plan to work; Carson Burroughs needed a patsy, someone professional that would carry out his murderous plan; no questions asked. That someone was called Perry Logan.

* * *

Logan had spent seventeen years incarcerated at Deer Lodge, eight on death row, before having his death sentence commuted to life. Now the Gods were smiling on him again. He'd been turned down for parole on two different occasions. He'd mused, why should this hearing be any different? True he was model prisoner, he'd become conditioned to prison life. He attended services at the prison chapel and had begged God's forgiveness, but parole was something he never really expected, to all intent and purpose he was still classed as a dangerous criminal. But parole had been granted. Perry Logan thought he knew the answer. For every favour given, a favour was asked.

* * *

Carson Burroughs knew that Vince Holbrook had an associate that was a member of the Deer Lodge parole board that had turned down both parole applications on Perry Logan. This friend Harvey Kellerman was a family man. A wife that he adored, two little girls and a new puppy, he also had a habit that was very hard to break. When he received a brown envelope which contained several rather humiliating photographs of him his whole world came crashing down.

A week later he received another brown envelope, inside was a single sheet of paper, on it the name Perry Logan, and the date of his parole hearing. It didn't take Harvey Kellerman long to figure out what was being asked of him. What surprised him more was the feint watermark on the single sheet of paper. He'd seen it before, noticed it in fact, it was rather unusual in its design, but more than that he knew it belonged to Congressman Vince Holbrook. Knowing Holbrook the way he did, he knew the congressman was capable of anything. The question was why would Holbrook go to such extreme lengths. Why did he want the release of such a dangerous man? Harvey could only speculate, he shuddered at the thought. His first reaction was to confront Holbrook, but that would drag him farther into why the congressman wanted Perry Logan released. He didn't want to know the details; all he wanted was to get himself off the hook. Perry Logan was released a week later. Stage one of Carson's plans was now complete.

*　*　*

In the days that followed Vince Holbrook told Carson of Ruth's weekend break. It was another fact that Burroughs found hard to bear. He'd seen that smile, he'd felt the bile creep up from his stomach and he'd felt nothing but pure hatred for them both. Whatever else he was, Carson Burroughs was not a foolish man. He'd had a man executed on his say so, he'd masterminded a bank robbery and if it hadn't been for the greed of one man he'd have finished what he'd started. As it was he'd covered his tracks and had evaded detection. His biggest mistake, his only mistake; he'd dallied over his plans, not sure whether to carry out the next stage and time had been his downfall. 'Well not this time,' he thought angrily, 'not this time.

*　*　*

Ruth Holbrook reached the Claymore Ranch with only minutes to spare.

"Oh, thank goodness! I thought you wasn't coming, that you'd had a change of heart," cried Tara, more out of relief than annoyance.

"Don't mind her, she can be a little grouchy when she's a mind," laughed Jack as he took Ruth's overnight bag and put it in the large RV.

"I'm sorry, I got held up. Vince was a little awkward. We had a terrible row. He flew out of the house and drove up to Great Falls. I guess he thought he'd upset me enough that I'd stay at home, but hell no! That was last year's model; this year's model just went back inside and touched up her paintwork."

"Well Ruth Holbrook you look absolutely stunning," cried Tara, "Now hop on board."

Minutes later with the horse box attached and Bucky safely installed, Jack fired up the RV. It was a two hour drive to the fairgrounds in Dillon, enough time to get reacquainted with Tara's family.

"What's with the horse box?" enquired Ruth.

"Oh, that's Jack's idea. Once he knew Bob and Sheila were coming out for a visit, he pulled a few strings. I don't know who he talked to but he got me a late entry in the barrel racing event. Then he told me!" exclaimed Tara.

"That's fantastic!" cried Ruth.

"You might not think so, after the event. I'm thirty five years old. Most of these girls will be in their late teens, early twenties. I haven't got a hope in hell."

"Well I think it's great. I'm sure you'll wipe the field with them," added Sheila encouragingly.

"Yeah, mom's the best. She'll win just you wait and see," chipped in Kaycee.

"The best, the best," chorused little Merri.

Tara coloured up, "Listen to you guys, if I make it to Sunday's final it'll be a miracle."

Secretly she was looking forward to the event. Mary Lou Townsend, a rival from the old days when she and Merri competed on a more professional level had also entered the contest. Tara smiled as she recalled those days of yesteryear, 'racing against Mary Lou will be a lot like old times.'

At the Dillon campground they picked their spot and were pleased to see that Wade and Alex were parked close by.

* * *

Preparations for the evening rodeo were in full swing as the Reynolds and Claymore's mingled amongst their fellow countrymen. All around were food stands, arts and craft stalls, Native American exhibits, beer tents and numerous facilities for kids. Kaycee had already spotted the cotton candy stall.

"See you guys later," cried Alex as Merri pulled her towards the ice cream stand. Tara took that as her cue to depart with Bucky to prepare for the evening.

"Do you need a hand?" cried Ruth. "Those two seem quite a handful." All the time she was wondering when Fletcher would put in an appearance.

"I'm fine, we'll see you guys later," cried Alex as Kaycee tried pulling her in the direction of the cotton candy.

Wade looked over to Jack and Bob and motioned towards the Metlen Hotel.

"I think it's about time we showed Bob a genuine Montana saloon," suggested Wade.

"Great idea," replied Jack.

Bob was ahead of them, walking God knows where.

"He been here before?" enquired Wade.

"No, Bob's just got a nose for it," replied Jack.

"Sounds like my kind of man," cried Larry, as he hurriedly brought up the rear.

"Hey where do you think you're going?" called Sheila, at the fast retreating men. Wade and Larry stopped in their tracks, Bob did his best to ignore it, and Jack laughed as a good humoured Sheila and a rather perplexed Ruth caught up with them.

Sheila hugged Ruth and smiled, "Back home we have a saying, give them enough rope etc. What I say is if you can't beat em, join em."

As they stepped through the doors of the Metlen Hotel and negotiated their way to the bar Bob remarked that he bet this Hotel could tell a story or two.

"There's many a story," grinned Wade as he recalled his youth. "Grab a table; we'll bring the drinks over. Then perhaps I'll tell you a tale or two . . ."

*   *   *

Encouraged by Wade and his promise Bob and Sheila quickly found a table for them all to gather around. Minutes later Larry, Jack and Wade joined them at the table, refreshments at the ready.

Wade took an almighty swig of beer, grinned, then wiped the foam from his moustache. "Dillon was built at the end of the railroad, so naturally it needed a hotel. Course it wasn't nothing as fancy as the Metlen, but it served its purpose until it burnt down, and they built the Metlen in its place. You wouldn't think it now but the Metlen Hotel boasted the utmost in luxury accommodation back in 1898 when it was built. It had hot and cold running water, electricity and exclusive club rooms," said Wade with a cheeky grin. "Don't ask," he added as Sheila started to say something. "The place offered fine dining and dancing up until prohibition."

"Then of course, during the twenties there was Red Mike and her Bits of Muslin," added Larry.

"And those that followed," said Jack encouragingly.

For the next hour Larry and Wade competed with each other with anecdotal stories of the characters that had frequented the Metlen during their younger days.

"Anyway you cut it; the Metlen Hotel became a gathering point for ranchers and cowboys, whether it was to hire on or let your hair down, the hotel catered for all comers. Course it ain't as grand as it once was, but it still eludes an old world charm," said Wade as he continued to remember the good times.

After a couple of beers they rejoined a harassed looking Alex and face painted kids.

"Having fun girls," said Jack gleefully as he picked up young Merri and planted a big kiss on her cheek.

"I guess it's time for us to mosey on over to the arena," drawled Wade. "Get up high on the bleachers overlooking the chutes. Gives you more of a flavour of what rodeo is all about."

Bob nodded his enthusiasm.

The girls shrieked with delight as the rodeo clowns began entertaining the early evening crowd.

It had been a fun day thought Ruth, a truly fun filled day without politics and the tension that went with it, and it wasn't over yet. The rodeo was about to start and she was really looking forward to watching Tara in the barrel racing. It was just a pity that Fletcher wasn't around to distract her.

"Mind if I join you guys?" said the tall imposing blonde haired Jason Connors.

Wade stood up and smiled, "Well if it ain't Mr Rodeo himself." as he grasped the man's hand in a firm handshake.

"I saw you guys from over yonder. They seem friendly, I thought." Jason's smile was as warm as the evening air and his charm emanated through men and womenfolk alike.

"I was just going to grab a handful of hot dogs, mind giving me a hand," said Wade.

"No problem," replied Jason, as both men climbed down from the bleachers.

"Who's he?" cried Sheila.

"He's the star of Rodeo Man. I reckon you don't get that back home," replied Jack. "He used to be a saddle bronc rider, before he became famous."

"We met him last year, when Vince and I were special guests, he was a guest too," said Ruth in whispered tones.

"He bought a few horses from me late last year," added Jack.

"Be fair Jack, more than a few," expanded Alex.

"Seems to get along right well with Wade," added Larry.

"Yeah, that's funny; Wade usually takes a while before he warms to a person. I guess Jason Connors is his kind of guy."

"You could say that," added Alex. "He came from nowhere, just another cowboy riding the circuit. He was reasonably successful from what I heard, but then he got lucky."

"I hadn't seen Rodeo Man when we met last year so I did a bit of checking," chipped in Ruth.

"Oh yeah," cried Sheila with a twinkle in her eye.

Ruth grinned at Sheila, and then continued, "It seems an agent from a television station spotted his potential at the New Mexico State Fair. He'd done well in the saddle bronc event all week and barely missed out on collecting top prize. This agent asked him if he'd ever thought about a change of career. He's supposed to have grinned mischievously and said 'every time I sail through the air."

"It wasn't his rugged charm and strong resemblance to a young Steve McQueen that won him a change of career then?" offered Alex sardonically as she balanced a fidgety Merri on her knee, and then adding, "According to TV Guide, he did a few bit parts in pilots that never made it, then someone produced a script for Rodeo Man. It's into its fourth series as we speak. He hasn't looked back since."

"I guess we won't need Fletcher after all," muttered Sheila under her breath.

Ruth gave her a playful dig with her elbow.

*   *   *

Tara surprised herself, with a sixteen point two seconds score and made it through to the following days final. Mary Lou Townsend also made Sunday's event, with an incredible fourteen point nine seconds, which she found all the sweeter for having beaten Tara. Pleased with making the cut, but secretly smarting at being beaten by her old rival, Tara resolved to reverse that score come Sunday afternoon.

"I'll wipe that smug smile off her face come sundown tomorrow, "she raged.

"That's not like you," gasped Ruth.

"You don't know Tara very well, do you," cried Alex with a smile. "Sweet, kind, and very caring, but when she's in competition she's a real hell cat."

"Oh, don't mind me; I'm just glad I was able to compete with those young un's."

"I thought you were great anyway," added Sheila.

After a full evening of rodeo and a steak dinner at the Lion's Den, the Claymore/Reynolds party drifted back to their respective beds. Alex went first with the kids, Tara followed shortly after, while Wade, Larry, Jack, Bob and Jason retired to the Metlen for a night cap. Sheila and Ruth tagged along a few steps behind.

"Well!" declared Sheila.

Ruth laughed, "Well what."

"Are you going to make a move on him?" she persisted.

"Short answer, no!"

"Why not? He's gorgeous!"

"Look, I'm having fun, I'm meeting nice people. Yeah sure Jason is quite a hunk, but I'd be guessing he's not single. Despite what you've heard, I'm really an old fashioned girl."

"Sorry Ruth, I didn't mean to push; I guess it's the mountain air."

"More like the half dozen glasses of wine."

"Yeah, I guess you're right. Let's go get a night cap."

* * *

Alex couldn't recall the girl's name that came in with a thirteen point three to take first place; she was more interested in the battle of the veterans. Mary Lou Townsend had shot into fourth place with a mind blowing fourteen point seven seconds, shaving two tenths of a second off her fastest time ever.

Tensions were riding high as Tara steeled herself for the ride of her life. She'd already congratulated Mary Lou on her fast ride and doubt was slowly creeping into her mindset. Quickly she banished all thoughts of defeat. Pulling her hat down firmly on her head she braced herself. Bucky stirred nervously beneath her, though fourteen years old he still had the steel and agility in his bones to please his mistress. Tara whispered gently to him as they approached the run up.

"Come on Bucky, one last time. I know you can do it o'l horse."

Bucky whinnied his response.

Ruth, Alex, the girls, Bob and Sheila were frozen in anticipated excitement. Wade and Jason were in deep conversation and were watching from the rails, while Jack and Larry were just hurrying back from the run up.

The starter nodded, and as one Tara and Bucky rode into the arena, shooting past the automatic timer and racing at breakneck speed towards the first barrel. The crowd let out an involuntary cry as Tara spun dangerously close to the oil drum. Bucky responded like a dream as she guided him around the second successive barrel. Sensing her quick time, Tara shouted encouragement to her steed as they spun around the last, making a perfect cloverleaf. She kicked for home, and Bucky flew out of the arena as if on wings.

"That was some ride," cried the announcer, "Tara Claymore, of 'Reynolds Horses' takes fourth place with an incredible thirteen point nine seconds."

A roar of appreciation went up from the crowd, and the Claymore/Reynolds party began to whoop and holler.

"I knew she'd do it," cried Ruth.

"Mummy won!" cried Merri.

"No Merri, mummy came in fourth," corrected Kaycee.

"That was fantastic!" cried Bob and Sheila together.

"I never had any doubt," laughed Alex, "Once Mary Lou came in with that fast time, I just sensed it was the spur that Tara needed."

*　*　*

For the Reynolds and Claymore's the rest of the rodeo was an anti-climax, even the Bull riding. Bob said, he'd like to try his hand and Wade said that could be arranged.

Bob gave him a double take, then laughed, "I think I'll settle for a cold one back at the Lion's Den and an enormous prime rib."

"That sounds like a plan," cried Wade.

Tata couldn't help noticing that Ruth, who was doing her best to appear cheerful looked a little crest fallen. In the rest room of the Lion's Den she asked what was wrong, though she guessed she already knew the answer.

"I thought he'd show, I really thought he'd show," Ruth said sadly to Tara in that quiet moment together.

"Yeah, I thought he would, he definitely seemed interested. I reckon it was the rodeo, you see, that's where they got it together the first time."

"Who got it together?"

"Merri and Fletcher. You know, the girl I told you about."

"I see," muttered Ruth.

Chapter 34

Montana

Alex stirred in the saddle as the familiar smells of leather and horseflesh did battle against the mountain air and Ponderosa pines. Blaze's hot breath joined the affray mingling together on a perfect September morning. Alex detected an icy chill, which she knew would be burned up by the sun's heat before breakfast, and thought it was good to be alive, to be up before the lark, to savour nature at its best. It was a habit she'd got into for more years than she could remember. That early ride was so important a feature in her daily life. Up here on high, gazing down on the valley she loved; was where she planned her days, where her problems were solved, where she could be alone with her thoughts. A warm tear trickled from her eye and ran coolly down her cheek. Here beneath the majestic mountain backdrop she could let it all out, here she could be herself, here she was a woman, complete with all the weakness's that she held in check away from her family. Here is where she wept openly for the loss of her son Taw, gone for more than a decade, but forever in her thoughts. Here where she felt closest to him.

As she wiped the tears away she spied Fletcher riding up to the cabin at Cougar Pass. His continued grief troubled her greatly. She feared he would leave just as grief stricken as before, she above all others understood his loss. How could she not, he was a little older than Taw would have been, but his sorrow was just as deep. She couldn't help Taw but she could help Fletcher. It was time he ended his penance. It was time for him to re-enter the world. Spurring Blaze into a gentle trot she rode down to greet him.

An exchange of pleasantries followed before Alex launched into a load of motherly advice.

"Alex, I know you mean well, and yes I was attracted to Ruth, but the more I thought about turning up at the rodeo, the more I thought it a bad idea. It holds so many wonderful memories for me; it would have felt like blasphemy to Merri's memory if I'd gone there."

"I understand, but I'm sure Merri would have approved. Ruth's a nice girl, she's not the spoilt, assured woman that she makes out she is. Beneath it, she's as warm and tender as any man could ever wish for."

"But she's not Merri," sighed Fletcher.

"Of course she's not Merri, how could she be. She's Ruth, Ruth Holbrook, trapped in a loveless marriage, a small town girl, just like Merri; a small town girl with so much love to share and no one to share it with."

Alex paused; she hadn't meant to say as much. But then she thought how she'd have spoken to her son if only she'd been given the chance. "Go to Merri, sit beside her and tell her how you feel. Tell her about Ruth. You know in your heart that Merri would understand. Stop wasting your life, go out and grab what life has to offer before it's too late."

Minutes later they parted company, one a little wiser and more optimistic about his life, the other a whole lot happier for getting it off her chest.

*   *   *

Fletcher returned mid-afternoon and called on Alex.

"I gave a lot of thought to what you said; it made a whole lot of sense. By the time I reached Merri's graveside I had it all thought out. I knew what to say and how to say it, but the instant I stepped down from that paint horse, well the words just left me. I crouched down and said nothing for maybe five minutes. Then I told her about the smile I'd exchanged with Ruth and how it had made me sick to my stomach. I told her that I felt I'd betrayed her, that I loved her still, that, that love would never die, and then I told her that if possible I would try to find happiness."

Fletcher looked at Alex with tears blurring his eyes; he wiped them away with a gloved hand, cleared his throat and then smiled. "It's been a beautiful day; there hasn't been a cloud in the sky, wouldn't you agree?"

Alex looked perplexed as she nodded her agreement.

"Merri always loved the rain. She once told me it was God showering the land with tiny diamonds."

Alex made to say something, and then stopped.

"It rained Alex, it rained. For five whole minutes it rained as I crouched by her graveside. It was the strangest thing, I looked up and there wasn't a cloud in the sky."

* * *

Minutes later he was heading for Deer Lodge. He didn't know whether Ruth's smile meant anything. All he knew was it meant something to him. From the little Alex was able to tell him, it seemed there was no love lost between Vince Holbrook and Ruth. Nevertheless, he couldn't go driving up to the gates of the ranch and demand to see her. He needed an excuse, a reason, then he swung the car to the side of the road and dialled Sam Kilbane's personal number.

"Sam Kilbane."

"Sam, its Fletcher."

Before he could continue, Sam Kilbane interrupted. "What's up? Why are you calling?"

"Nothing's up. That's the point. I've been stuck at the ranch for nigh on two months and nothings happened. I think we've approached our problem from the wrong direction. If we're to lure this son of a bitch into the open I reckon I need to be close to Congressman Holbrook."

"Out of the question!" bellowed Kilbane.

In truth Fletcher believed the threat was long gone, that whoever had tried to have Holbrook assassinated had gone to ground. It was the best excuse he could come up with at the time.

"I exposed the threat. I nearly got killed into the bargain. I think you owe me."

It was a ten minute phone-call that went backwards and forwards, but eventually Fletcher got the green light.

"If you ain't dead, and nothing's come to light within a month I'm pulling you out, understood!"

An hour later Fletcher pulled up at the gates to the Holbrook Ranch.

"Mr Holbrook is expecting me."

Minutes later he was pulling up to the double doors of Holbrook's ranch house. Vince Holbrook looked agitated as he led Fletcher into his upstairs office.

"Shut the doors behind you," he ordered. Gone was Mr Geniality.

"Your boss called me less than an hour ago and told me to expect you. He said you'd explain. This had better be good."

"Sir, the fact that a plan to assassinate you was uncovered cannot be taken lightly. That no such attack took place doesn't mean a second attempt won't be forthcoming. The FBI have a duty of care. You've bodyguards of your own, I know that, but I did catch a glimpse of the man," lied Fletcher, *he was making it up as he went along.* "Agent Kilbane thought you would be better served if I was close too you."

"No such attack took place, your words. I think it hardly likely that a second attempt to assassinate me will be forthcoming." Holbrook studied Fletcher's facial expression; it betrayed no trace of emotion.

Sam Kilbane had explained to Holbrook that Fletcher though not an official FBI agent had shown himself to be very capable in a crisis. "Basically I'd take it as a great favour if you'd humour me on this one. Between you and me, we're thinking about offering him a permanent position."

To turn down the FBI's offer would appear churlish, even arrogant, considering the Warlock incident. "Very well, but as you've pointed out, I do have my own bodyguards.

"See Williams the housekeeper, she'll fix you up a room, then unless I ask for you, stay in the background, whatever you do don't make yourself obvious."

"I won't; thank you sir," replied Fletcher.

Carson Burroughs looked slightly shocked at seeing the man that had thwarted his plans, when he stepped into the room.

"Carson, you remember Fletcher. Kilbane thought it a good idea to have his presence around for the time being."

Recovering from his shock at seeing Fletcher he said, "Frankly they're right, you can't be too careful." He nodded acknowledgement at Fletcher then walked out of the room.

"Look," cried Holbrook, addressing himself to the rookie agent. "I know your boss means well, so just make yourself at home, help yourself to a drink and get the kitchen staff to fix you a meal." Then the congressman motioned with his hand to leave him.

Fletcher walked out of the office and began making himself acquainted with the lay out of the ranch-house. Ranch-house, "I don't think so," he mused. "This is more like a mansion."

"Hello!"

Fletcher spun around.

Ruth smiled confidently enough, but her heart was pounding, she had so many questions, what was he doing here? Had Tara told him about her feelings? No, that couldn't be, Tara would wait for nature to take its course. Was he here to protect Vince? Or was he here because of me? Her last thought triggered the pigment of her skin to change colour.

"Hi," cried Fletcher. "I've been assigned to keep an eye on Congressman Holbrook," he said lamely.

"Oh! I see," she cried. "Has there been a renewed threat?"

"Not that we're aware of. It's just precautionary."

"Well I mustn't keep you," she added. The awkwardness of their meeting clearly defined.

Minutes later Ruth was on the phone to Tara. "He's here!"

"I know," came the swift reply.

"You know?"

"Yeah ma told me, he'd gone to Deer Lodge."

"W.. why?" cried Ruth, her nerves playing tricks on her vocal chords.

Tara laughed, "You figure it out. He's not officially an FBI agent. Perhaps he's really concerned for Vince and his welfare, or perhaps not."

"Tara, you can be such a bitch," she giggled.

"If you want him, go for it. The worst he can do is turn you down."

*   *   *

Carson Burroughs had seen the meeting between Ruth and Fletcher; it had made him stick to the stomach. He'd loved her, he'd truly loved her, he'd thought that after the barbeque at the Reynolds ranch he'd finally got over her, but seeing them here, together, it twisted the knife. Now more than ever he had murder in his heart, and his new plan began to take shape, a plan that would take him another step closer to the Governorship of Montana. Before he'd thought to just kill his ex lover and her new paramour, but with the new turn of events the plan was becoming crystal clear. Sickening though it was, he needed their relationship to blossom, only then could he implicate Vince Holbrook in their murder. With them dead, Holbrook in custody, the scandal that would surely follow, the men in power would be looking for a new candidate to run at the next election. Who was more qualified? It was a question that Carson Burroughs knew the answer too.

Carson kept a watchful eye on Fletcher during those first few days. They were uneventful accept the change in Ruth's appearance; she looked radiant, much to Carson's chagrin. Nothing had happened between Ruth and Fletcher, but the magic was plain to see. 'They're pathetic,' thought Burroughs, 'the way they spar around with each other. It's like some primitive animal courtship.' His anger was in danger of spilling over, so much so that he had to take in deep breaths to calm himself. As rational thought slowly returned, he remembered he had Perry Logan waiting in the wings. With Fletcher so close to Ruth and the Congressman his plan was evolving far better than he'd first imagined.

*   *   *

Jack buttoned up his coat and settled himself into the rocker on the porch and gazed up into the black velvety skies encrusted with diamonds. His thoughts strayed to the every day life that Bob and Sheila had returned too, a life that without God's divine intervention would still be his, the people, the fast lifestyle, the good living. He smiled to himself as a chill breeze blew across the front of the house causing temperatures to drop. It was a sure sign that winter would be upon them soon with its array of heartaches and problems, another season of fighting the elements where the days became shorter, and the nights longer, darker and colder. Did he miss Marlow? Not in a million years.

Tara walked out onto the porch, "Brrrh, its getting colder," she volunteered. "You're missing Bob, aren't you?" she added.

Jack looked up to Tara, smiled and pulled her close to him, "It was all too short," he said sadly. "But there will be other visits I'm sure. As for me, I'm sitting here counting my blessings. Seeing Bob brought it all back, my old life, my roots if you like, but this is were I belong. I was born for this . . ." He let his words hang in the coolness of the night.

*   *   *

Wade feeling the wind chill pulled the collar up of the old sheepskin coat that Fletcher had sent from Australia. He closed the barn doors, looked up at the night sky and then across to the welcoming glow of light emanating through the windows of the ranch-house and felt a little melancholy. As his boots crunched on the night frost he thought about the ranch, the old Pendleton spread. How with determination and grit, he and Alex had turned it into one of the biggest successful spreads in the Big Hole Valley. He thought about Taw, the heir apparent, the man to take the ranch through into the twenty first century, he thought of Johnny, of his son Fletcher, a natural, born to claim what was rightfully his, but through tragedy had turned his back. He thought of Tara, the one with the most fiery Reynolds blood running through her veins, a woman with the same determination and grit as her parents, but a woman with her own mind, her own vision of what she wanted from life, and the Crazy AW didn't figure in that future. 'Perhaps, he thought, 'if I live long enough maybe, one or both of my grand children will take on the mantle.' The thought cheered him as he knocked the dirt from his boots and entered the house.

* * *

Ruth opened the double doors of the veranda and stepped outside. Immediately the coolness of the night air washed over her, cleansing her of the day's toil. She ran her fingers through her hair subconsciously as she looked into the darkness. She'd hoped with the arrival of Fletcher that things would have moved on. She sensed he wanted her, yet despite the moments shared, there seemed to be a reluctance on his part to take it a step further. Since her heart to heart with Tara, she'd been able to put her life back into perspective. Carson was a mistake. She despised herself for the affair; more than that she felt she'd sunk to Vince's level and it made her feel dirty. And now Fletcher; that she had feeling for a man she'd not had a meaningful conversation with, troubled her deeply. Was it an act of desperation? Was it her chance to break away from Vince's clutches? Or was it more than that? In truth she didn't know the answer.

"It's a beautiful night," remarked Fletcher.

"Oh my God!" cried Ruth, "You scared the living daylights out of me!"

"I'm sorry, that was not my intention." His voice was soothing and comforting, and instantly put her at ease.

"Oh, don't mind me, I scare easily," she answered. "Yes it is; it's a beautiful night."

"Even more so, now you've graced it with your presence."

Ruth blushed uncontrollably as she sought the middle ground. "Thank you, you're most kind, but surely you shouldn't be saying that to me, I'm a married woman."

"An unhappily married woman," countered Fletcher. "You deserve much better."

Ruth felt her hackles rise, "And who are you to tell me how I feel?"

"Pardon me," cried Fletcher, "I meant no offence!" 'Perhaps,' he thought, 'I've read it all wrong,' "I just thought you appeared lost, sorry if I've misread the signs."

His crestfallen appearance sent Ruth's heart racing. 'How stupid of me,' she cried out silently, already his body language was signalling retreat, it was time to unburden herself.

"Is it that obvious?"

Encouraged by her answer Fletcher looked her in the eyes and said, "It is to me. On the surface you seem confident, a little spoiled even, oh and too full on with the Congressman. I don't know what you want out of life, but it sure ain't being a politician's wife."

"What's Tara been saying?"

"What's Tara got to do with it? At the Reynolds barbeque you smiled at me, it might have meant nothing to you, but it meant a whole lot to me."

"And you can tell from a smile?"

"I can."

Chapter 35

Montana

'Its pretty country,' thought Wade as he approached the entrance to Jason Connors ranch at Ennis, 'good grass land from what I can see.' Wade had driven over to Ennis on the request of Jason Connors.

"I don't know what I'm doing wrong; I've hired decent hard working men. Lucas Jacobson my foreman is a mite old in the tooth, but his experience can't be faulted. I just seem to be throwing good money after bad," grumbled Jason to Wade at the Dillon Rodeo. "I know I ain't there much of the time, what with television schedules and now there's talk of a feature film."

"That could be your problem, ranching is a twenty four hour day and then some. I'll tell you what, give me a couple of weeks, phone me, I'll come up and give you my opinion for what its worth."

"I'd appreciate that Wade," replied a grateful Jason Connors.

On first appearances the double slash JC Ranch looked to be in fine fettle. A little over stocked maybe, but otherwise it was running pretty smoothly. Jason showed him around the ranch, taking Wade up into the high country to give him a birds-eye view of the spread.

Wade stretched in the saddle, "Damn leg's giving me gyp," he remarked.

"You okay?" enquired Jason.

"Yeah I'm fine, just an old war wound. Riding accident in my younger days," declared Wade.

"I know just what you mean," replied Jason.

Yeah he missed the rodeo circuit, the adrenaline rush, the girls, the adoration, but the months he'd found himself in traction, the broken bones that took forever to heal, well them he didn't miss.

"This ranch is important to me Wade, it ain't a fad, it's . . . . It's who I am. I was brought up on ranches, my pa he must have worked most spreads from the Canadian border to New Mexico. He was a hired hand, an itinerant worker, who if I'm quite honest never amounted to much. He got killed for his trouble, thrown from his horse at forty seven years old. Hit his head against a tree, died on the spot."

"I'm sorry to hear that," replied Wade.

"That's okay; it was a long time ago. I decided then and there that if I ranched it would be on my terms. That's when I first started in rodeo. I'd ridden all my life, I'd seen lesser riders than me earning money at local rodeos, I thought if they can do it, so can I."

Wade grinned, "Don't I know it. If it hadn't been for the Korean War I might have done much the same. My folks had a small spread up to Big Hole Pass, it wasn't up to much, but it was home."

"Ain't that Jack and Tara's place?"

"You got it." replied Wade. My folks well they died whilst I was away in Korea, so I had me a notion to try running horses on it. Create my own brand, pipe dreams, all I had was my army pay and a few dollars left to me by my ma and pa. I spent it all one night in a drunken horse deal. When I woke up the next morning along with the hangover of a lifetime I was stuck with seventy head of a mixture of horse flesh. I was in Cheyenne, Wyoming, my place was in Montana. That morning as I surveyed my folly I got lucky Paint horse lucky."

Jason gave Wade a quizzical look, "I'll explain later," cried Wade. "Go on with your story."

"Riding the circuit came natural to me. I won more than I lost and began to earn reasonable well, then as the years passed I got to dreaming about owning my own ranch, only to have those dreams dashed when I broke one bone too many. But then I got TV lucky."

"Wade laughed, "Guess I don't need you to explain that one.""

"That's what I'm driving at Wade. In television you're only as good as the ratings. I'm riding high at the minute, but one day some TV producer will come along and I'll be back where I started. That's why I have to make this ranch work."

Wade thought about it for sometime as he leaned on the saddle horn. His horse shifted its position and showed a growing impatience to be moving on. "If that's the end of your land in that direction," he pointed, "and down there in that valley is the other fence line then like I said, you look over stocked. How much open range do you have access too?"

"That I'm not sure of, we'll consult the map when we get back to the ranch-house."

"Yeah good idea, added Wade as he gathered up his reins, "You might like me to take a look at your books while we're at it."

"Fine by me," cried Jason, "We'd better head back if you've seen all you need too."

"Let's do it," cried Wade as he spurred his horse back towards the ranch-house.

A look at Jason's map of the ranch and surrounding areas confirmed what Wade had suspected; there was no open range adjacent to the double slash JC ranch, which would account for the appearance of so many cattle.

"From what I've seen, you're overstocked. The size of the ranch doesn't allow for this many head."

A look over the books later that evening brought to light some uncomfortable facts.

"How often do you do a head count on your stock?"

"I leave that to Lucas. Why?"

"As I've already stated, you appear to be overstocked, but the books tell a different story. I ain't counted but I'd estimate you're fifty head light."

"Are you saying, what I think you're saying?"

"Let's just say, you've been a little too free and easy with that cheque book of yours and someone's taken advantage."

"You mean Lucas?"

"No, I ain't saying who, it could be anyone. Lucas is getting on in years, he could have made a mistake, he could have delegated, he could have like you, had the wool pulled over his eyes, there is any number of possibilities."

"So what should I do?"

Wade tipped his hat to the back of his head, "Firstly, you let Jacobson aware of what you've found out. Don't accuse him outright; just tell him that there are going to be big changes. Sell the surplus cattle and work within your means. You've good men working for you, I can see that, but let them all know who's head honcho."

Chapter 36

Montana

Ruth's life had been turned on its head, ever since that night alone on the veranda with Fletcher where she'd poured her heart out to him. He'd seemed so masterful, so in control, it felt natural to do so. He'd listened as she told him about her life before Vince Holbrook and how he'd come into her life, like a knight on a great white horse. How her dreams, her ambitions, her love had slowly crumbled as he manipulated her, turning her into a glamorous footnote to his political ambitions. She cried when she told him about the miscarriage and he'd instinctively cradled her in his arms. She felt secure, comforted by those strong and powerful arms, she felt safe, yet vulnerable. She'd looked up at him through a glaze of tears, her lips seeking his. He bent his head slowly to the side and his lips gently brushed against hers and then hesitantly and softly they touched. The burning embers in Ruth's body combusted as never before. Her eyes closed and her arms encircled him. The kiss though passionate and full of meaning lasted but a few seconds, but in Ruth's mind she relived it over and over again. He'd seemed awkward as they withdrew from the embrace, like a man on the brink of betrayal.

"I'm sorry, I shouldn't have," he intoned.

"Don't be silly, I wanted you to kiss me," she confessed.

Fletcher smiled awkwardly, "I haven't kissed anyone like that for a very long time."

"I'm glad, I enjoyed it very much," she said brazenly.

Fletcher grinned, "You're too sure of yourself to be real," he laughed.

"I am not," she cried coyly. "I just feel so at ease with you."

*   *   *

A feeling of exhilaration coursed through his body when Fletcher woke up the following morning. He was happier than he had a right to be. For years he'd blamed himself for Merri's death. If he hadn't brought Monique, if he hadn't fallen in love with Merri, if he'd never returned and hid out in the cabin at Cougar Pass. If, if, if .... But now, after that kiss and the quiet talk that lasted until well after midnight he was beginning to put the past to bed.

They'd sat and talked, Ruth had encouraged him to unburden himself. He'd cried in her presence, she'd comforted him, with a soothing stroke and a soft word. She'd coaxed and he'd responded and he felt a great weight slowly beginning to ease. It was a burden that would remain for the rest of his life but Ruth had lightened the load. He wanted her, and she wanted him, but circumstances were difficult. She wanted to escape, to be free of Holbrook's clutches. He'd said he'd stand with her, "and after," she'd said. "After, is up to us," he'd said forcefully.

*   *   *

Carson Burroughs woke with a smile upon his face, by accident he'd walked past the lounge at the very moment that Ruth and Fletcher kissed. Stepping into the shadows he watched as they released themselves from the furtive embrace, oblivious to the malevolent forces that lurked in the darkest corners of the night. It was time to unleash the beast.

Perry Logan was out on license and living in a halfway house a few miles from the state prison. Freedom was supposed to be better than this, he thought ungraciously and then he received a phone call that changed everything.

A metallic voice in monotone told him to look under his mattress at the halfway house. Then it rang off. Perry Logan stunned by the macabre call walked back down the hall to his room, closed the door securely and lifted up the end of his mattress. An envelope containing two photographs, one of a woman, the other of a man, a cell-phone and ten thousand dollars in used twenty dollar bills.

Perry speculated, was it a hit? The phone rang in the communal hallway. Logan sprang to his feet and raced into the corridor and snatched the phone out of another resident's grasp.

In metallic monotone the voice said, "Listen carefully. Ruth Holbrook, Fletcher Coppersmith. Kill them together, I repeat, kill them together. Ten thousand more after the job's done. You've ten days . . ."

Perry Logan looked puzzled, 'Who are these people? With what do I kill them' His mind had already accepted the contract. Getting a gun would be easy; locating the people in the photographs was the real problem. He wasted a day waiting for the phone to ring, and then in desperation he began to trawl through the local papers. It didn't take him long to uncover the identity of Ruth Holbrook.

Staring at the newspaper photo print of Ruth, he began to fantasise. She was a great piece of ass; something special after seventeen years. The temptation to do more than put a bullet between her eyes was overwhelming. The thought bothered him, it had been his downfall in the past, and it was the very reason why he'd done seventeen years in the penitentiary. No, this time he'd be smart, he'd kill them both, without any distractions. No point in putting a signature on his crime. Twenty thousand big ones could buy an awful lot of pussy down Tijuana way. 'But;' he thought lustfully, as he gazed again at the picture, 'she was indeed something special.

Carson Burroughs understood people's weaknesses and more importantly he knew how to exploit them. In his position as attorney at law and aide to Congressman Holbrook he was privy to much private information, the files on category A prisoners was but one example. Over the years he'd kept tabs on the most dangerous prisoners in Montana, especially those on death row. Paradoxically he was an advocate of the death penalty; he'd seen how Perry Logan and others had cheated death. He'd lost count of the sons of bitches that had their death sentence reduced to life. Despite his revulsion at these men, it was a pool of resources at his disposal.

The revulsion he felt for those incarcerated transferred equally to those in higher authority. At an early age Carson had learned that because of their position in society, a number of politicians, local dignitaries and successful business men felt they could get away with anything. It had been the undoing of better men than Harvey Kellerman, but Harvey being on the parole board at Deer Lodge fitted perfectly into Carson Burrough's plans.

Fitting Vince Holbrook up for the death of his wife and her lover would be child's play. Motive was the first thing the police looked for in a crime. Vince Holbrook had a motive; he also had incriminating photos of Kellerman concealed in his safe back at the house. Something he'd confided to Burroughs only months earlier. "It always pays to be one step ahead of the game," he'd boasted. His conceit knew no bounds; he'd even designed an unusual watermark for all his correspondences despite the state's own paper being perfectly adequate. It was a fact that Kellerman when cornered about the release of Logan could and would attest too. But the lynchpin that would seal Holbrook's fate was Perry Logan, the perfect patsy.

Carson Burroughs had read Logan's file and knew he couldn't resist raping Ruth before killing her. That fact alone would ensure he was caught before he could get out of the State. It made little difference to Burroughs whether Logan was killed or caught; everything would eventually point back to Vince Holbrook.

Chapter 37

Montana

It came like a bolt out of the blue. No one was expecting it, least of all Ruth herself. It was a couple of days since the kiss and circumstances had conspired to keep Ruth and Fletcher apart. During those days she'd thought about nothing else other than what they'd talked about, an hour or two of meaningful conversation, a physical attraction, a smile and a kiss that had left Ruth yearning for more. It wasn't enough to build a relationship on, but it was enough for her to tear one down.

Ruth cornered Vince in their lounge area. She was scared, scared that she wouldn't be able to go through with it. He looked up as she walked in the room and his withering gaze turned Ruth's legs to jelly. "We, we need, to to talk" The words trembled on her lips.

"Make it quick, I've work to do!" His tone was condescending and inpatient. It surprised her that until recently she hadn't noticed his superior attitude towards her.

Ruth steadied herself, "Vince it isn't working," she stammered.

"What do you mean, it isn't working?" snarled Holbrook.

Ruth ignored his question, he knew only to well what she was talking about. Second by second her courage rose to the fore, "It hasn't worked in the four years we've been together. I'm leaving you; I'm filing for divorce!" 'There, it was done, she thought, as an immense feeling of relief followed closely upon her words.

Holbrook froze. The look in his eyes told Ruth all she needed to know. Seething with anger he told her he'd see her in the gutter first.

"You might, but I'll be a whole lot happier there than here with you," she shouted back across the room, her confidence growing ever stronger.

Vince Holbrook losing whatever cool he had left, lunged at Ruth catching her a glancing blow with the back of his hand. Caught by surprise she cried out, but too late Holbrook was upon her. She clawed at his face, she lashed out with her legs, but he was too strong as he wrestled her to the ground. She banged her head as the wooden floor made contact and a split second later his heavy body was pinned her down. Viciously he slapped her with his open hand across her face again and again. There was murder in his heart and blood in his eyes. He'd lost all control.

She screamed as he raised his hand and clenched his fist. Was this how it all ends, she found herself thinking? Powerless to stop him, she stared defiantly at the tell tale lines of crimson across his cheek, she stared defiantly at his maniacal eyes as they glowed with madness. She waited defiantly for the blow that would send her into oblivion.

It never came. Fletcher's strong right arm stopped the congressman just as surely as it had held her only two nights earlier. Yanked to his feet, Holbrook turned his anger on his assailant. A glancing blow caught Fletcher's right cheek, and at that moment Vince Holbrook knew he'd made a big mistake. A blow to his solar plexus, another to the side of his head and a final blow to the bridge of his nose sent the congressman flying out of the game.

Carson Burroughs appeared in the doorway, he called for help but neither ventured in to aid Vince or to hinder Ruth and Fletcher as they made their exit.

"Pack a bag Ruth; I'm taking you to Wade's!"

Two burly bodyguards soon had the congressman on his feet, "Go after them," he cried.

Carson barred the door and spoke forcefully, "Listen to me Vince. Your whole future depends on it. Going after the man that allegedly saved your life, look at yourself for God's sake! How do you think it would look?"

"I don't fucking care how it looks!" screamed Holbrook.

Carson held his hands up, "Up to you, it's your political future that's at stake. Just stop for one second. Everything depends on what you do right now!"

Vince Holbrook's political mind slipped back into gear as he signalled for his men to stand down. "You're right Carson. Thank you." The full implications of the little scene were now becoming abundantly clear. "What do I do now?"

"You sit tight, get those wounds dressed. Leave it to me. I can't promise you reconciliation, but with luck I can limit the damage." Carson was in his element, his true talents coming to the fore. He was after all the kingmaker, the power behind the throne.

"Get it done," spat Holbrook his composure returning.

"It'll cost," added Burroughs.

"Whatever it takes," said Holbrook.

He smirked to himself, and left the Congressman to be assisted by his bodyguards. It was working out better than he'd thought possible. He made his way to the quiet of Holbrook's office. Calmly he picked up the phone and dialled the cell-phone number of Perry Logan.

Carson smiled to himself; it was getting better and better. Two bodyguards had witnessed the scene, a couple of cleaners caught the dying venom from Holbrook and he guessed more than one of them would, if need be come forward to testify against their boss. He paused to look at himself in the mirror, adjusted his tie, grinned again, then hurried down the stairs and with seconds to spare stepped out onto the forecourt and confronted Fletcher and Ruth just as they were getting into the car.

"Jesus Christ, Ruth. What happened in there?"

"He attacked me! That's what!" screeched Ruth.

Fletcher put a protective arm around her and looked Carson Burroughs squarely in the eyes. "I don't care if he's the President of the United States; no one treats a woman that way."

Carson nodded his understanding, "Best you take her someplace safe. Leave me to smooth it over," he cried.

"Smooth it over; hell," cried Fletcher. "Just tell him the lady's filing for divorce."

"Listen; don't be too hasty, I'm sure we can come to an arrangement. Where can I reach you?"

"The Reynolds Ranch, but give it a day or two."

"Ruth," said Carson warmly, "You're finally free of the man."

Ruth turned and smiled weakly.

Burroughs watched as the rental car pulled away. He was smirking as he carefully noted down the license plate. A few minutes later he returned to Holbrook's office and relayed everything to Logan.

"I want it done quickly, I want it like yesterday!" His tone though metallic contained anger and hysteria, just enough, thought Carson, for Logan to remember, if he was caught alive.

*   *   *

Perry Logan spotted the rental car on highway 43 just outside the small town of Wisdom. He followed at a safe distance, the hunter stalking his prey. It was like old times. He'd been twenty three, young, cocky and invincible. Clever at his trade, respected in some quarters, but that time he bit off more than he could chew. It was just a routine hit, simple, easy, no problem. A few months later he was on death row awaiting the hangman's noose. It wasn't fair, he wasn't to know they were connected, that they were faces, that they were people of importance. He was a bad man, he freely admitted, but to face years of imprisonment with the threat of death hanging over him, well it did something to a man. He turned to Jesus when his sentence was commuted to life; he thanked God every day for his salvation. He thought about what he'd done and knew that only God could forgive him. But most of all he prayed that one day he'd receive his freedom.

He'd had plenty of time to think whilst in the penitentiary; he'd learned not to take things at face value. He'd been up for parole twice before and both times he'd been refused. Parole wasn't given lightly, and Logan saw no viable reason why he would be considered for release, especially since this time he hadn't applied for it. He could only assume someone wanted him for his particular talents. It was obvious to Perry that someone with major influence in the prison system was working for his release. Who that somebody was would become clearer when they made contact.

His mind had gone into overdrive after that first phone call; the marks were Ruth Holbrook, wife of Congressman Vince Holbrook, the other, Fletcher Coppersmith, itinerant ranch hand and agent provocateur for the FBI. It didn't take him long to figure out that Vince Holbrook, a very wealthy man, a man going places, a man destined for the governorship of the state of Montana was behind the hit, he chuckled at the irony of it.

Twenty thousand dollars was chicken feed. Perry Logan was a lot of things, being greedy yes, but being stupid wasn't one of them. He'd followed them as instructed, even familiarised himself with the intended victims, and then he'd waited for the inevitable phone call. Vince Holbrook would soon find out the price of a hit was a hell of a lot more than a measly twenty thousand dollars.

*   *   *

They pulled up outside Fetty's Bar and Café in Wisdom and got out to stretch their legs.

"Are you hungry," enquire Fletcher.

"No, I just thought it best that we stop, I can't face seeing people right now."

"Let's grab a coffee while we figure out what to do."

Ruth smiled at him and squeezed his arm, "That seems like an idea," she agreed.

The moment she took a sip of coffee and felt it warm her insides she looked sheepishly at Fletcher, "I guess I'm a tad hungry after all."

Fletcher ordered food and they both discovered how ravenous they both were. A feast of simple fare, cheeseburgers, fries, and side salads were quickly despatched. Pushing their empty plates into the centre of the table they both took refills of coffee and relaxed. It was late afternoon when they paid their bill and walked outside to the parking lot.

"We should be at Wade's within half hour," volunteered Fletcher.

"Tomorrow; let's get to Wade's ranch tomorrow," said Ruth, her eyes sparkling with mischief as she looked towards the Nez Perce' Motel.

*   *   *

Perry Logan grinned with satisfaction as the couple made their way to the reception of the motel. Life was getting easier and easier. Now all he had to do was wait it out.

He could almost feel the impatience in the ring tone as his cell burst into life. He laughed to himself as he let the phone ring an extra four times before he answered it.

"Is it done?" asked the familiar monotone metallic voice.

"No! Change of plan. I know who you are and twenty big ones don't buy you a hit Mr Congressman."

Burroughs was stunned into silence, 'Change of plan! He'd heard that line before and it had cost the recipient dearly.

"What do you mean change of plan?" Burroughs replied, now that he'd regained his composure.

"I know who you are, so it's gonna cost you a whole lot more, one hundred thousand to be precise. Furthermore I want it up front before I do the hit. Get it to me in the next few hours and the job will get done before morning, failing that, it gets done soon as I receive the cash."

"I can't get that kind of money quickly enough."

"But you can get it?"

"Yes," came the monotone reply.

"I'm returning to Deer Lodge later this evening, if the money is there, they'll be dead before midnight tomorrow."

"How do I know you won't take the money and run?"

"You don't, just call it professional pride. If I take on a job I always complete it, Mr Holbrook. But if the money ain't there, then I'll be long gone."

"The money will be there."

Carson Burroughs pressed the red disengage button and stared thoughtfully around the room. Holbrook had said, "Whatever it takes," he'd given Burroughs a blank cheque. He began to way up his options; it was going to cost ten times what he'd expected, but it wasn't his money. The delay was the biggest problem, but not insurmountable. On the plus side Perry Logan thought he was dealing with Vince Holbrook. He grinned to himself, soon he would have his revenge on Holbrook and the congressman would be financing the whole deal.

* * *

Fletcher held Ruth in his arms and looked lovingly at her.

"Ruth, this isn't how I wanted it to happen. I've fallen in love with you, yet part of me is fighting to keep the memory of Merri alive."

"I know, I've only known you a few weeks, days really, but I guess I'm smitten too."

"I love you, yet I still love Merri, and I guess I always will," it was said. Fletcher hadn't meant to say it that way, but he couldn't think of any other way.

"Ah!" cried Ruth, "I finally find a good man, only to find I have to share him with another." Her face looked solemn and crestfallen and then she looked up at Fletcher and smiled, "Anyone else, forget it, but you . . . . You I'll make an exception."

"I'm sorry, it's not fair, you deserve better." Fletcher's heart was racing. He wanted this woman, he wanted her more than life itself, but Merri, dear sweet Merri was standing in the way. How could he cast her aside?

"I understand it's too early, maybe . . . ." her words remained unspoken as Fletcher took her in his arms and kissed her.

Tears streamed from Ruth's eyes as she kissed him in return. 'At least,' she thought as he lowered her gently onto the bed, 'we'll have tonight.'

Chapter 38

Montana

Perry Logan gasped as he lifted his mattress, the money, all one hundred thousand dollars was there in neatly bundled used twenty dollar bills. Throwing the neat bundles into a sports duffle, he grinned to himself, now there was nothing to stop him from hightailing it to Mexico. 'Except,' thought Logan, 'the man who had hired him for the job, the man that wanted him to think he was Vince Holbrook.

He'd kept watch on the Nez Perce motel until late. Once he was sure they were spending the night he drove back to Deer Lodge. Leaving the couple free to continue their journey to the Reynolds Ranch was a calculated risk, albeit a small one. In the cabin he could have despatched them without fear or fuss, but now he had to pick up their trail, he hoped that the couple weren't early risers.

He arrived back at the Nez Perce motel around 6am, and was relieved to see the rental car still parked as they'd left it. With time to kill he pulled out the map from the glove box and spread it out across the dashboard. An ability not to panic was one of his attributes, to form a plan and act swiftly and decisively on it had been another. Patience was yet another and forward thinking his greatest attribute. Unhurriedly he studied the map, worked out his calculations and a few minutes later he carefully folded up the map and put it back inside the glove box. As he waited he thought about the woman inside and about the man that had hired him to kill her. An hour and a half later the couple emerged from the motel. Within seconds he was gunning the car towards the 278 highway.

*   *   *

"Damn maniac," cried Fletcher as a second-hand Ford Mustang flew past them like a bat out of hell. "Fool driver's likely to kill himself and others."

Two minutes later they rounded a bend and saw the Mustang half-way into an irrigation ditch with smoke billowing out from the engine.

Fletcher pulled up behind the Mustang and climbed out. He quickened his pace as he saw the driver through the thick acrid smoke slumped over the steering wheel. He learned in to get a grip on the injured man and suddenly Fletcher's world turned black. Ruth who was only a few steps behind him realised too late and her scream died in mid falsetto.

*   *   *

Perry Logan worked quickly; throwing the bodies of Ruth and Fletcher into their rental car he jumped into the driver's seat and stuck the gear shift into drive. He passed the wrecked Mustang, a car he'd hot wired a day earlier and proceeded at an appropriate speed along highway 278, heading south. Two miles down on the right he turned onto an unpaved road and continued west. He'd found on the map that the unpaved road led to Twin Lake an out of the way place.

Arriving at the lake he was relieved to find the place deserted apart from a couple of boat sheds. Pulling up to the side of one, he got out and smashed the padlock off the nearest boat house.

"Wow," he exclaimed, the gods were sure smiling on him. Inside on a ramp leading down to the waters edge was a small thirty foot power boat, the kind that rich people use to pull water skiers. A further look, revealed two Jet Ski's, one in need of repair, the other in pristine condition. Around the boat house walls were racks of neatly kept tools, on the floor oil drums and gasoline cans, several rolls of nylon rope, a few concrete blocks and to Logan's delight a cardboard container with half a dozen unopened bottles of beer. He looked at his watch, then picked up a bottle and twisted the cap off. He reflected on what he'd done, he regretted harming the woman, but she'd fought far harder than he'd imagined. But it was done, there was no going back. It was still early; but he consoled himself while he waited for the phone call by thinking about what he would do with the money, money that would surely change his life.

Darkness fell around Twin Lake and Perry began to relax. The chance of anyone coming down the unpaved road in the dark was minimal to zero. In his line of work it paid to keep the body count down to the barest minimum, innocent people going about there own business could get too messy.

In the limited lighting of the boat shed Perry Logan glanced at his watch and saw in was close to eight o'clock. He judged that Mr Metallic would be getting a little inpatient right now. He stifled a grin; his day was getting better and better.

At a quarter to nine, Logan's cell phone sprang into life. He held it in his hand and let it ring; he wanted the man on the other end to sweat. He answered on the eighth ring.

"Is it done?" came the now familiar metallic tone.

"It's done, but we have a problem."

"What do you mean a problem?" The tininess grated on Logan's ears.

"Firstly, I want another one hundred thousand. Secondly where do you want the bodies dumped, as I've found the perfect hiding place and thirdly I want you to deliver the money to me personally, tonight!"

"You're asking the impossible, where can I lay my hands on one hundred thousand at this time of night, secondly I don't give a damn whether you leave them at the side of the road, and thirdly, why should I risk my neck bringing you the money when you've already done the job."

Through the metallic mono toned voice Perry Logan detected a hint of triumph. He grinned to himself and laughed. "True, why would you risk your neck? Well I'll tell you why. Firstly you ain't Congressman Vince Holbrook, which means you're someone close to him, and I'd judge you have the same connections, secondly I've enough money to disappear, but in doing so I could easily drop the dime on you, after all you've set this up to make it appear that I did it under orders from Holbrook, at the very least the police would come sniffing around. Thirdly I ain't asking for the world, I'm sure you could stump up a hundred grand at any hour."

It was time to play hard ball, thought Carson Burroughs. "No deal!"

"I'm sorry about that Mr Burroughs!"

Apart from a sucking in of breath the phone remained silent. Logan waited knowing that it would take a little time for the last sentence to sink in.

"Now that I have your attention."

"Go on."

"You started this chain of events. Why? I couldn't care less. All I know is I wouldn't be free if you hadn't given me a helping hand."

"So take the money and go, cut your losses," cried Burroughs.

"It don't work like that, it's your turn to get your hands a little dirty. I kinda like my freedom, so as I said, bring the money to me tonight. We dispose of the bodies and with luck I'll be out of the country by the time they're discovered. That way we both get away with it and Holbrook takes the rap."

There was a prolonged silence before Burroughs spoke. "Where can I reach you?"

"There's a boat house on the edge of a lake, I'll be there. I believe it's called Twin Lake. It's at the end of an unpaved road just off highway 278, between Wisdom and Jackson. Check it out on the map. It's nine o'clock; you should be here by one o'clock, just enough time for you to be home in bed before morning."

"Okay, I'll bring the money, but only to the junction of the unpaved road. I'll slow down and drop it off. I ain't risking my ass."

"Gee, and I thought you'd enjoy a boat ride," laughed Perry Logan. "You're not as dumb as I thought. Just bring the money," he added in a threatening tone.

Burroughs pressed the off button, and found his teeth chattering uncontrollably. He'd misjudged the man, it was the second time it had happened, he vowed there wouldn't be a third. With no time to spare he called the Sheriff's department.

Chapter 39

Montana

Sergeant Wayne Randolph checked the loads in his service revolver and motioned to the three officers to fan out as they approached the lake. They'd abandoned their patrol car at a bend in the road not half a mile away. Armed with carbines and two pump action shotguns, the quartet moved stealthily through the undergrowth. There attention drawn to the two boat houses illuminated by the moon as it cast its reflection across the still dark waters of the lake.

Wayne Randolph a veteran of fifteen years in the Beaverhead Sheriff's Department wasn't taking any chances. The call had come in from an anonymous source a little over two hours earlier, about a dangerous killer who it was believed was in the process of disposing of a number of bodies. Wayne had thought the call a hoax, but was obliged to investigate.

With his men in place, covering all four sides, he switched on the portable halogen lighting system and the boat houses were as clear as day, clearer. With the bull horn he announced his presence. It was greeted with a stone cold silence. He repeated his command that the place was surrounded and the occupants of the boat house should come out with their hands above their heads. Again, this was greeted with silence. Sergeant Randolph was beginning to think his first suspicions of it being a hoax were correct, until he ventured close to the first boat house and saw the broken padlock. He froze in his tracks. To enter a building where a dangerous fugitive could be lurching was something Randolph didn't relish. He had a choice to wait it out, then call for back up in the morning, only to find that it was a hoax call after all. The alternative was to storm the boat house. He was nearing retirement but the three officers under his command were early twenties and newly married, well at least two of them were. He chose to wait it out for a further half hour. Then as a cloud crossed in front of the moon he entered the building, shot gun ready to fire at anything that moved. A few minutes later, he gave the all clear.

It was a cool night and the sweat from Randolph's brow was turning icy.

"Okay boys, let's turn this place over, but be gentle, treat it as a crime scene."

One of the first things they noticed was the power boat moored outside the boat house, the engine was still partly warm. Officer Levi Richardson inspected the boat and discovered small traces of blood on the deck area and a cement block with some nylon rope attached to it. Immediately he drew Sergeant Wayne Randolph's attention to his find.

"Jesus! We got here too late."

Minutes later he was phoning in his report. He was supposed to be going fishing with his son-in-law that afternoon, but somehow he knew he was going to be somewhat occupied.

By mid morning the boat house and power boat had been sealed off and designated a crime scene. By noon the discovery of an abandoned rental car just outside Jackson, was suddenly linked to the lake. It was registered to a Fletcher Coppersmith. By mid afternoon a solemn Sam Kilbane was on the scene and the case became the property of the FBI.

Sam phoned the Reynolds Ranch and spoke to Wade, asking if he'd been in touch with Fletcher. Wade detected something in Kilbane's voice.

"What's going on? What is it you're not telling me?"

*   *   *

An hour and a half later Wade was demanding answers from Sam Kilbane.

"I can't tell you much, only that the Beaverhead Sheriff's Department received a call stating that someone was disposing of bodies."

"What's that got to do with Fletcher?"

"Nothing, we hope. His rental car was found abandoned just outside Jackson, we think he may have ran out of gas."

"So where's the connection?" cried Wade his anxiety clearly showing.

"None, except he was on his way to see you. He wasn't alone; he was driving Mrs Ruth Holbrook, Congressman Holbroo . . . ."

"Yes I know who she is!"

"It seems they set out for your ranch two days ago."

"That doesn't make any sense. Jackson is past the ranch, unless they were heading for Tara and Jack's place," Wade said hopefully.

"Then where are they? I called your son-in-law's place just before I called you. They haven't seen hide nor hair of them. They've just dropped off the map."

"But that don't mean squat!" cried Wade, trying desperately to cling onto some hope.

"She's high profile, he's been on the news . . . ." Sam Kilbane left the rest of his sentence unsaid.

Wade turned away and looked towards the lake, the inference unmistakable, then back to Kilbane.

The FBI agent answered the unasked question. "We're making arrangements to drag the lake tomorrow, first thing." Sam hadn't known Wade very long, but seeing this big tough rancher ageing before his eyes was pitiful to watch.

"I'd better get back; Alex will have to be told."

Wade turned away from the Federal agent and walked slowly back towards his vehicle. As he drove along the unpaved road, he clung to the hope that Fletcher was still alive. Alive, he thought, that's funny; Fletcher had died that day up at Cougar Pass. Though teary eyes Wade remembered how they'd stood toe to toe and faced down Monique Delacroix and Jonas Clay. How Fletcher had squeezed the trigger of his nine millimetre and ended the life of the woman he'd loved without reservation until he met the real love of his life Merri only to see her die only minutes after Monique passed.

His thoughts turned to his daughter Tara, how would she feel at the death of her friend and just how hard would she take the loss? He took a deep breath and an involuntary sigh past his lips. He steeled himself for the task ahead; the next few days were going to be tough and he'd have to be strong for his family.

*   *   *

"How does this make me look?" cried Vince Holbrook. "The dumb broad races off, god knows where, and disappears."

'He wouldn't entertain the idea that she'd been killed and dumped in a lake. No, the prospect of that being the truth wasn't something the congressman could accept. Not because of any true feelings he had for Ruth, more because the scandal could harm his future chance at being the new governor of Montana.

'Well Mr Vince Holbrook, I've got news for you, not only is the scandal of a dead wife being fished out of a lake, bad publicity, but being chief suspect in her murder is going to get you life or better still a cell on death row,' thought Carson Burroughs as he listened to Holbrook's rants and ravings.

It had come as a shock that Perry Logan was smarter than Burroughs first thought; that he'd figured out who was really behind his parole had been a blow. Yet on reflection, his decision to call the Sheriff's department in Dillon and tell them about the disposal of bodies in Twin Lake, was a wise move. That the phone call to Logan's cell phone had come directly from Holbrook's office would only implicate the congressman more and more, although Burroughs suspected Logan would have dropped it in the lake, either way, he was in the clear.

"Vince, listen to me. As far as you're concerned, there was no blazing row, you asked that FBI guy to drive her to the Reynolds ranch. What you need to do is be concerned, get involved, get the sympathy vote. Act the concerned doting husband."

"You're right Carson, as always."

'Yeah,' thought Burroughs, 'act the doting husband, with those deep claw marks for the television cameras; perfect.' It hadn't gone according to plan, but the end result would be the same. Perry Logan was long gone, on his way to Tijuana by now. He had been right to call the man's bluff.

It was a solemn evening at the Reynolds ranch, Tara had taken the news badly and Alex had suggested they stayed over.

"It's just not fair, not Ruth and Fletcher!"

"I have to ask myself why, what possible motive could there be for killing them," cried Jack.

"Hold on Jack, they've disappeared, that doesn't mean they're dead," protested Alex hopefully.

"He didn't so much as say, but agent Kilbane implied that he believed they'd locate their bodies tomorrow," said Wade in a very subdued voice.

"I'm sorry to go on about it, but again I have to ask who would possibly gain by their deaths?" insisted Jack.

"Holbrook," suggested Wade, but added, "Too much to lose."

"What about his aide, Burroughs?"

Again Wade shook his head, "Why, what has he to gain?"

"Then we're saying they were murdered by a random killer, hitchhiker maybe?"

"Stop it Jack!" screamed Tara, "I can't accept they're dead."

Alex looked over at Wade and gave a knowing look. "Tara, sweetheart, don't torture yourself."

Tara fled from the room in tears; Jack stared after her, impotent to comfort her. Alex motioned to leave her be and Wade crossed the room and looked knowingly at Jack.

"Give her space. You need to be strong during the next few days."

Chapter 40

Montana

It had been three days since the murders and Carson Burroughs was quietly confident that within the next couple of days the police divers would recover the bodies, what he wasn't expecting was a call to his home number from Perry Logan.

"You thought you were smart, you thought you'd feed me to the wolves, I understand that and I'm not mad. All I want is my money, but the price has gone up," his words were delivered in a cool and calm manner that left Carson chilled to the bone.

Struggling hard to regain some composure Burroughs started to protest, but Logan cut him short.

"I want two hundred thousand; you've got until the day after tomorrow, after that, I drop the dime." His words continued in a calm but menacing manner that left Burroughs in no doubt that he was dealing with a higher calibre criminal than he'd first thought.

"Okay, I won't argue with you. I can see, I've made a serious misjudgement, but it will take me a few days longer to raise that sort of cash."

For one heart stopping moment Carson Burroughs thought Logan had hung up.

"Hello, hello!"

"I'm here; I'm not an unreasonable man. Half today, I know you can get your hands on that amount."

Carson felt an involuntary shiver run down his spine. He was talking to a cold blooded killer and the man was calling all the shots.

"Half today," repeated Logan, "the rest by the middle of next week, Tuesday evening."

"Al'right," stuttered Burroughs. "You'll get your money. Same drop off?"

"No way, this time we meet face to face at the Sportsman's bar in Butte, 9 o'clock tonight with the money. Any more tricks and you my friend are a dead man."

Burroughs started to protest, but the threat left him cold.

"Be there!"

The phone went dead.

Carson stared at the inanimate object in his hand for several seconds before placing it back on its cradle. Taking a few deep breaths he managed to get his nerves under control. Firstly he had to get his hands on another one hundred thousand from Holbrook's safe. Emergency money Holbrook had laughingly called it, squirreled away for any illicit deals that might come along. Burroughs saw the irony of it. What worried him wasn't that Holbrook would notice the money was missing; no he was more concerned about his meeting with Perry Logan. Meeting in a public place was risky, but it sure beat the heck out of meeting in a lonely dark alley.

* * *

The Sportsman's bar was crowded and very noisy when Carson Burroughs entered carrying an old red Kennex sports bag. He wore a baseball cap and dark glasses, he knew he looked ridiculous, but the minuscule disguise, the long duster and the cowboy boots were all that stood between him being recognised; besides it also concealed the 38 police special, stuffed into his waistband. His heart skipped a beat, in the far corner of the bar sitting alone at a small table was the man he'd come to see. A sickly smile played across Logan's lips.

"Who do you think you are, the Unabomber?" remarked Logan.

Carson ignored the remark and sat down opposite. A waitress appeared and Burroughs ordered a beer. The moment she left he placed the Kennex sports duffle at his feet.

"One hundred thousand in used notes," he uttered. The mere fact that he'd been forced to cough up this amount of money and actually meet the man he'd hired went completely against the grain. "The rest, you'll have to bear with me, it's difficult to raise such an amount without raising suspicion."

Perry Logan smiled and it wasn't a nice smile, "If you think I'm letting you off the hook, think again, one hundred thousand by Tuesday evening." Then he smiled again. "You made this difficult for yourself. Arranging my parole and twenty, maybe thirty grand in my hand would have been enough for me to do the job and hightail it to Mexico, but no, you had to have it all sewn up, me included." The anger in his softly spoken words was unmistakeable. "Why?"

Carson Burroughs sweating in the long duster couldn't disguise his fear as tiny droplets of sweat trickled down his face.

"I can see you're scared. In your shoes I'd be too?" Perry Logan was enjoying the other man's discomfort.

Burroughs fingered the unfamiliar butt of the 38, seeking some form of comfort, but none came as he looked at the confident smiling face of the man that had killed for him.

"I spent seventeen years of my life, eight on death row; do you know what that feels like? No off course you don't." The confident smile lifted as he began recalling his time in prison. "You threw me a lifeline, I'm thirty nine years of age and you gave me hope. Why snatch it away." Perry Logan's eyes burned deeply into Burroughs soul and the self styled would be governor of Montana began to quake with fear.

"I'm sorry; I shouldn't have set you up."

"No you shouldn't have. Give me one good reason why I shouldn't kill you right now."

Carson Burroughs lost all control of his bodily functions as he felt a warm sensation slowly creeping across the lower half of his body. Dealing with Bob Knox had been child's play compared to the man in front of him. Ordering a killing, appearing in control, that was something that wouldn't wash with this man.

"Because I can be very important to you in the future," it was the only thing Burroughs could think of at that precise moment. Perry Logan's expression changed, and Carson pushed the advantage. "I can make you very rich, a favour here a favour there."

"Oh yeah!" Greed and avarice welled into Logan's eyes. "You'd better explain yourself."

"Take your parole for instance."

"Yeah, I'd like to hear how you pulled that off." Perry Logan had somehow controlled his anger and was intrigued at just how powerful Carson Burroughs could be.

Warming to his new found confidence Burroughs took a swig of beer and began.

"It was easy," he boasted. When you're in a position such as mine you can find out many things if you're of a mind. I blackmailed a member of the parole board leaving a false clue as to my identity. The man had no choice but to comply with my orders, but he'd believe it was Holbrook that had blackmailed him, or at least suspect. All the phone-calls to you were from Holbrook's office, these would implicate him when the bodies of his wife and lover were eventually found."

"And I guess I was to be the patsy that connected up all the dots."

"In a nut shell," replied Burroughs. He cursed himself for being too flippant, the anger and menace had returned to Logan's face.

"That still doesn't answer my question, why?" The waitress on hearing a raised voice thought twice about asking if they wanted another round of drinks, turned abruptly and made a bee line for another table.

"Easy man, easy . . ." Burroughs swallowed hard, "I had an affair with Holbrook's wife, that's what started it. He treated both of us with disdain. Then she ended the affair. I thought with him implicated for murder I'd be the obvious candidate to stand in his place for the next Governorship of Montana."

Perry Logan looked impressed. "You really are some piece of work, she dumps you and then you decide to have her killed to further your career." He started to laugh, "You really take the biscuit, you're one bad motherfucker! I take my hat off to you." Carson didn't know whether to laugh or cry. "So when the bodies are discovered you were hoping my DNA would link me to the crime and so implicate Holbrook. Perfect, except by me throwing those bodies into the deepest part of the lake. The chances are pretty slim that they'd find my DNA. Which my friend leaves you with diddly squat," a grin formed upon his face. "There is nothing to connect me."

Carson Burroughs grasped at a possible lifeline, "Exactly, you're home free. Take the two hundred grand; live it up in Mexico or wherever. Staying around could implicate you. Take the money and run."

Perry Logan laughed again, "I like you, I really do. You see an opportunity and you go for it, despite having pissed your pants. You should know me well enough by now; I'm not a stupid man. I'm on license, the moment I leave the state I'll be implicated, or at least a suspect, staying put suits me just fine. I've another hundred grand to pick up next week, and I've a friend in the future government of this state. Besides as you said earlier you'll need my services if you're going to run for governor."

"What's that supposed to mean," cried Burroughs, his confidence slowly returning.

"It means, if at first you don't succeed, try, try again. I've read the papers. This wasn't your first attempt at getting rid of Holbrook, you were behind that Warlock ranch fiasco!"

"I don't know what you mean?"

"Liar!" Perry Logan's tone had turned ugly and Carson was thrown off guard yet again. "If we're to become partners, there are no secrets."

"Okay, you wi..win," stuttered Burroughs. "But first, answer me a question that's been bothering me. How did you know that Holbrook wasn't behind your release from prison?"

Logan suppressed a laugh, his eyes twinkling, "That's what's so funny about this whole set up. Holbrook would never in a million years want me to get parole; in fact he'd liked to have seen me hang. I've been a bad boy most all my life; I've been a patsy too."

"What do you mean a patsy?"

Now warming to his subject, Perry Logan had an irresistible urge to get it off his chest. "In 1980 I was handed a contract, I was young, full of spunk, and ready for the big time. I couldn't see the wood for the trees. I was given less than an hour's notice, handed a gun, an address and shown a photograph of some middle aged business man. I was given a thousand bucks down payment. When I arrived the police were on me within minutes. Next thing I know I'm on a murder and rape charge. The rest as you know is history."

"You're telling me you were framed!" cried Burroughs.

"Yeah, by the father of the man you want killing."

"What! You mean Andrew Vincent Holbrook."

"The very same."

"But why?"

"To protect that creature he called a son!"

"Jesus Christ!" exclaimed Carson. His confidence had slowly begun to return. Already his mind had begun scheming about what a hold he'd have over Vince with this new found knowledge.

"Like I'd said before, if you'd only come to me in the first place."

"If I'd had this knowledge," sighed Burroughs.

"But you didn't. You were frightened of getting your fingers burnt. Now go on and tell me what you'd planned, maybe we can really do each other some good," spat Logan.

"Yeah maybe I didn't want to get my fingers burnt, what's so wrong with that? It was an ingenious plan, if I do say so myself." Burroughs warmed to the task. "*Get people fired up enough and they'll do anything. I met this guy called Knox in a bar in Whitefish . . . .*"

Chapter 41

Montana

Sam Kilbane turned into the driveway of the Crazy AW ranch and drove slowly along the half mile track. It was early morning and he'd hoped to catch Wade and Alex together before they went about their daily chores. As he approached the house he could see Wade standing on the porch both hands gripping the hand rail tightly.

Sam turned off the engine and climbed out. Wade stood upright and braced himself. The FBI weren't renown for making house calls unless there was something important to be said. Then Wade's attention was directed to the passenger door of Kilbane's sedan as it opened and a tall swarthy looking man climbed out and grinned, showing a perfectly formed set of teeth.

"Howdy Wade."

Wade did a double take and then stood there open mouthed, transfixed in time.

"Fletcher!"

So overjoyed at seeing Fletcher alive he forgot to curse himself for not believing harder. He'd given the boy up for dead, although he hadn't admitted as much, it was there at the back of his mind.

"Thank God! Alex come quick Fletcher's alive!" he shouted.

Alex flung open the door, and all she could do was stare as tears of joy streamed down her face. Wade grabbed Fletcher in a bear hug and amidst all the excitement Ruth climbed out from the back seat. Alex rushed forward and flung her arms around her.

"We thought you were dead!" cried Alex, "We thought something terrible had happened to you both."

Sam Kilbane stood back and watched with quiet satisfaction as the two couples danced around each other. Hugs and kisses were in abundance, even Sam Kilbane shared in the revelry. As the euphoria died down the inevitable questions were beginning to be thrown around.

"Hold it!" cried Fletcher. "I can't just tell it in little sound bites, you need to be told the whole story, and believe me it's some story. Let's go inside and we'll tell you everything."

"All righty" cried Wade with a smile that could light up a whole town during Christmas.

Once inside the house Alex immediately reached for the phone and called Tara with the news.

"I knew it! I knew it! Let me get the kids together and find Jack and we'll be right over," cried Tara excitedly, "See ma, I knew they weren't dead!"

"Yes dear, you keep saying."

* * *

Sam Kilbane who'd taken a back seat since climbing out of his car stepped forward and gained the centre of the room. He looked straight at Wade, "I'm sorry you've all been kept in the dark, you'll understand why after Fletcher's finished tell you what happened. I must stress that what he has to say must be kept between you all."

Alex remarked, "What about Tara and Jack, I've just phoned them?"

"It's against Bureau policy, but Fletcher insisted you all be told." The FBI man looked directly at Wade, "I must stress, when I met you at the lake I had no idea they were still alive."

Wade nodded his understanding, nothing could spoil this moment. He smiled at Fletcher, then Ruth and finally Alex, before sitting down on the tan leather sofa next to his wife.

Fletcher put his arm around Ruth, "We're seeing each other, if you haven't guessed already."

Alex smiled her understanding. "I think that's obvious. We're pleased for you both."

"Thank you Alex, that means a lot. I don't know if you're aware, but my marriage to Vince was nothing short of a sham," said Ruth. Believe it or not but I loved him and I truly believed he loved me, I was wrong!"

Fletcher hugged her to him, "I ain't that much for words, you all know how I feel about Merri," he paused, thinking through what more he was going to say, "I guess what I'm trying to say, Ruth makes me feel alive again."

For the next fifteen minutes first Ruth, then Fletcher took up the story of the fight at Holbrook's Ranch, followed by the drive to Wisdom and the night spent at the Nez Perce motel.

"We left Wisdom early the following day; we were both unsure of our relationship and what was going to happen next. All we knew for sure was we were coming to the ranch when it happened . . . ."

At that precise moment Tara, Jack and the kids came crashing through the double doors. Tara rushed to Ruth and hugged her tightly; Jack smiled at Fletcher, shook his hand and pulled him into a similar hug. Both kids jumped on grandma.

Tara gave Ruth a knowing look, and grinned. That they'd interrupted Fletcher in mid flow was obvious to all.

"Go on Fletch, go on with the story, sorry we barged in like a herd of buffalo," cried Jack as he let go of Fletcher and grabbed a chair.

"It was the most bizarre few days of my life, unbelievable. We'd just gone a few miles south on highway 278 when some idiot in an old beat up Mustang passed us like a bat out of hell. It must have been at least five minutes later as we drove around that blind spot

up by that big dead tree when we saw the Mustang had spun off the road and crashed into an irrigation ditch.

Fletcher stopped the car and told Ruth to wait while he investigated. Smoke was rising from under the hood and Fletcher suspected the car was going to blow anytime. He could see the driver slumped across the steering wheel. Without a thought for his own safety he opened the door and tried dragging the man clear. Suddenly the prone figure came to life and pressed a Taser against Fletcher's chest and fired a 50,000 volt charge into his body, stunning him long enough to incapacitate him. Within seconds he found himself coupled to the steering wheel with plastic ties. Ruth not realising what was happening was half way to the Mustang when the driver emerged and fired the Taser, he missed and Ruth screamed. They grappled for a few seconds before this guy knocked her unconscious.

Groggy and incapacitated Fletcher and Ruth were bundled into the trunk of their car and were being driven along a dusty unpaved road. Twenty five minutes later the trunk was open and a nine millimetre Beretta was pointing straight at Ruth's head.

The driver addressed himself to Fletcher. "Do as I tell you or I'll kill the girl." His tone was still and calm, there was no reason for Fletcher to doubt his words.

Within minutes the driver had forced the lock on a boat house and motioned for Ruth and Fletcher to enter. "Sit in that corner," he ordered. Then he bound both their hands and feet. Fletcher had tried resisting, he knew that once powerless to defend themselves their lives would be in the lap of the Gods, but the cocking of the Beretta and the look in the man's eyes caused him to desist.

"Now we wait," said the driver of the Mustang.

"My husband is a very influential man. He'll not rest until I'm found. Let us go, we'll forget this ever happened."

The man looked across at Fletcher, "And you, are you an influential man also?"

Fletcher chose to ignore him.

The man mooched around the boat house, picking up things and then discarding them. He grinned as he came across a half carton of beer. Taking one he twisted off the cap and began drinking from the bottle. He twisted off two more caps and handed them to his prisoners. Ruth dashed hers away in defiance, "Feisty one ain't yah!" he exclaimed, "And you, will you turn down a beer, that might be your last."

"Is it money you're after? My husband will pay without question," Ruth lied.

The man laughed, "If it was money you'd both be lying on the highway like road kill." He glanced at his watch, looked at Fletcher, held his bottle out in some bizarre ritual of buddies. "I'm going to tell you a story."

Ruth and Fletcher listened while this man told of an unhappy childhood, of bad company and of the various crimes he'd committed. "I was young and very fit, I hurt people for money, I ain't ashamed, they're have done the same to me if the roles were reversed. By my reckoning if I hadn't been caught I'd probably have killed many times over. That thought and that thought alone shames me!"

He shook his head.

"My name is Perry Logan, I was convicted for the murder of Chad Dempsey and the murder and rape of Erin Ryder. I was tried found guilty and sentenced to hang. Eight years I sat in my cell on death row waiting for death, for a crime I didn't commit. Then a change of policy had my sentence commuted to life imprisonment. Seventeen years I rotted away in that stinking hole at Deer Lodge. I applied for parole twice and both times I was turned down. Imagine my surprised when I found myself up for parole when I hadn't applied. An even bigger surprise awaited me when I found out that my parole had been granted."

Perry Logan smiled to himself as he saw that he had both of his captives' attention. He took a large swallow from the bottle, wiped his mouth with the back of his hand.

"Thirsty work all this talking. One thing you've got in prison is time. During those years on death row I tried going over and over why I was framed. I couldn't figure it out. When my sentence was commuted I did my best to be a model prisoner, working in the library, attending church services and generally keeping my nose clean. I had several run ins with inmates that meant me harm. I was lucky I kept myself fit and my wits sharp. Eventually I found out that someone on the outside had paid to have me killed, after *that I was moved to a different wing and left alone. During that time I befriended the prison chaplain, and through him I was able to get hold of photostatted pages of local newspapers from before, during and after my trial. Imagine my surprise when I came across a photograph of a very rich and powerful businessman, the very same man that had placed the gun in my hand and pointed me in the direction of a murder scene."*

Logan looked at his captive audience, the woman was half listening, but the man was giving him his full attention.

"Another beer?"

Fletcher responded and Logan grabbed two more bottles, "Sure you won't join us?" he cried. Ruth just shook her head.

"I found out over the next two years everything I could about this man and what I discovered gave me the reason why I'd been called out on a freezing cold night in November of 1980. You see he had a son, a son that was the apple of his father's eye. A son that could do no wrong, that was until he coveted his best friend's girl. It all came to a head on Prom night, where the combination of too much liquor, testarone and jealousy resulted in murder. I found the bodies, but I didn't understand that I was being set up until the arresting officer took away the literally smoking gun. The son's name was Vincent Holbrook!"

Now he had Ruth's full attention.

"Buy you a beer now missy?"

Ruth took the offered bottle.

"Now this is where it gets interesting. I was out on parole when I received a phone call. The voice was disguised but it told me it wanted a hit performed on two people. Yes you've guessed. Ten thousand dollars and two photos with the promise of ten grand extra after the deed was done. Now imagine my surprise when I discover the woman in the photograph is the wife of Vince Holbrook. It fair took the wind out of my sails. I'd half expected a call from someone with a favour to be asked, and to be honest after spending seventeen years in prison for something I didn't do, I was prepared to do that little favour. But Mrs Holbrook, you I didn't figure on. It got me thinking. At first I thought it was Holbrook, but that didn't make sense, he would be the last person on my list. Hell he wouldn't have made the list. Are you still with me Mrs Holbrook?"

Ruth looked tired and drawn, but she managed a weak smile.

"I then concentrated my efforts on you Mr Coppersmith. You made quite a splash in the papers a few months back, and funny, Vince Holbrook's name crops up yet again. Now this led me to thinking, someone else was after Holbrook's blood, but who? I received a phone call from this person and was tipped off you were on the way to the Reynolds Ranch, I was given the make and registration of your vehicle. I soon picked you up, and I followed you to the Nez Perce motel. I could have killed you that night. Instead I waited for a call. When it came, I told the man on the end of the phone that I knew who he was and that the price had gone up. I called him by name, Holbrook. Only Holbrook and I know that we would not be having that kind of conversation. He reluctantly agreed my fee and you two spent a very pleasant night together."

Ruth went crimson with embarrassment, while Fletcher began digesting Logan's story.

"I had to ask myself if it ain't Holbrook then who is it?" asked Logan. "To be truthful, my dear friends, I don't know! I was hoping you could shine some light on it."

The realisation came to Fletcher slowly, he could see the shadowy figure in the bar in Whitefish, he was about the same height, the same build, and from what Logan had said was using people indirectly like he manipulated Bob Knox. Fletcher was convinced they were one and the same.

"There was only one person that could have given you the registration of my rental car and he knew we were going to Wade's ranch." Fletcher looked at Ruth and both of them knew.

"Carson Burroughs!" exclaimed Ruth.

"But why?" asked Fletcher.

"Envy, power, disrespect, and I suspect I was part of his motive," cried Ruth.

"You!" cried Fletcher.

"Me. I'm ashamed to admit it, but for a time we had an affair."

"Very enlightening and thanks, but I'm left with a quandary. Do I take this guy Burroughs's money, kill you both and hightail it to Mexico or do I release you and take my chances with the law?" exclaimed Perry Logan.

The phone rang before he could make up his mind. He grinned to himself and let it ring several times before answering. The voice at the other end of the phone demanded to know if the deed was done. Perry Logan looked at first Ruth and then Fletcher, raised the bottle of beer and said the contract had been filled. Then Logan demanded a further one hundred thousand dollars. The metallic voice laughed, until Logan called him by name, the silence at the end of the phone line confirmed to all in the boat house, that the metallic voice belonged to Carson Burroughs. Logan repeated his demand for an extra one hundred thousand dollars and instructed Burroughs to deliver it to the lake later that night. Even giving Burroughs the opportunity to help get rid of the bodies, an offer he declined.

Putting down the cell-phone Perry Logan looked across at Fletcher. "As I was saying, I could kill you both. If I don't the authorities will find out I received parole unlawfully and I'll be sent back to Deer Lodge. Even if it's taken into account that I helped foil Burroughs plot, I'll still end up in the penitentiary. If a carry out Burroughs contract, I'll be hunted down and killed, either way Vince Holbrook might still remain untouchable."

Fletcher stirred as he tried to stand up, causing Perry Logan to back up and point the gun straight at Ruth.

"There is another way. Without proof Carson Burroughs will get away with murder. If he runs true to form he'll be ringing the police or sheriff's department right now. I'm betting from what you've told us that you're not a killer, if you choose the easy option make no mistake they will hunt you down."

Perry Logan mulled over what was said, "I must be a fool, those years in Deer Lodge must have softened my brain, but you're right I'm not a killer." He produced a knife from nowhere and cut their nylon ties. "Miss, I'm sorry I hit you so hard."

Fletcher and Ruth massaged their swollen wrists and ankles while Perry began gathering up concrete blocks and nylon rope. "If what you're saying about Burroughs is true we'd better move fast. The three of us can make like I've disposed of your bodies in the lake. We'll hot wire the power boat and leave it outside, grab *a number of those concrete blocks and attach that nylon rope, throw a number over board and leave one as a gentle reminder to Burroughs of what a luck escape he's just had. Then my friends we get the hell out of Dodge."*

"I received a phone-call from Fletcher late the following afternoon. Just after you left in fact," said Sam Kilbane directly to Wade.

"Yeah that was our fault . . . ."

"After we left the lake we drove towards Jackson only to run out of gas. Luckily it was only walking distance from Jackson Hot Springs Lodge where we were able to book into a cabin under an assumed name. We had breathing space; we had the name of the man responsible for the deaths of several people at the Warlock ranch including a county sheriff, but no proof," said Fletcher.

"Perry was all for running, he couldn't see anyway he was going to get justice," added Ruth.

"You two figure it out, me I'm going to hot wire a car and head for the state line."

"That's not the way. They will hunt you down and if Burroughs or Holbrook for that matter, have anything to do with it you won't make it back to Deer Lodge alive."

For the first time since we'd met Logan seemed unsure. I pressed him further. "I believe you were framed and I'll do all in my power to see you get a fair hearing, at the very least talk to a friend of mine."

"Why?"

"Because you're the key to getting Burroughs indicted. Without you we ain't got diddly squat."

"I received the phone-call and Fletcher explained briefly what had happened," interrupted Sam. "We met up later that night and I took Perry Logan into custody. He'd made serious unsubstantiated allegations against two respected members of state government. We had nothing, we needed proof. Perry Logan agreed to contact Carson Burroughs and arrange a meet. I must admit on the phone Logan was pretty convincing. Burroughs was backed into a corner with nowhere to hide; Perry left him no alternative but to agree to pay a further one hundred thousand dollars. That was the key to his guilt. Needless to say Logan went wired. We got Burroughs dead to rights."

"What about this Perry Logan what's going to happen with him?" cried Tara.

"Good question Tara, at the moment we're keeping him under wraps. Protective custody if you like. We've forensics looking into the case file of the 1980 Dempsey/Ryder murders."

"What about Carson Burroughs, when will he stand trial?" asked Wade.

Fletcher laughed, "His trial won't take place until next spring at the earliest, so that gives me and Ruth plenty of time to get acquainted."

Tara couldn't help noticing that there was a mischievous glint in his eye.

Chapter 42

Montana

Autumn passed quickly in the Big Hole Valley leaving winter once more to take its icy grip. The snows had come early, engulfing the entire valley in a deep blanket of white. Life at the Crazy AW settled into its winter routine and Fletcher found himself very much a part of the daily workings of the ranch.

Ruth too, resided at the Crazy AW, where she helped in the everyday chores of a Montana ranch, surprising everyone with her skill around livestock and with her ability to muck in with the menial and mundane. Alex marvelled at her work ethic, how quickly she'd gone from socialite to ranch hand in one easy move.

Wade too, had noticed how well Ruth had taken to ranch life, more importantly how she'd transformed Fletcher into his old self. As he watched them working alongside each other he allowed himself the indulgence of believing that one day Fletcher would take him up on his offer.

That dream was dashed when Sam Kilbane arrived unannounced at the ranch two days before Christmas. He had things to discuss with Fletcher and Ruth, something to do with the pending trial of Carson Burroughs. Alex invited him to stay for supper which Sam accepted readily. During the last few months he'd been a frequent visitor to the ranch and had become accepted as a good friend. It was over supper that evening when Fletcher dropped the bombshell that would dispel all Wade's dreams and hopes for the future of the Crazy AW.

They'd just finished eating and had kicked back with a glass of wine or two when Fletcher suddenly stood up.

"Folks, I'm glad we're all here," he nodded towards Jack and Tara, to Kaycee and little Merri, then to Alex and Wade and finally he smiled at a slightly fidgety and nervous Ruth. "Two things, firstly, I've asked Ruth to marry me, obviously after she's divorced from Congressman Holbrook. Which I might add is progressing along quite nicely."

"And I've said yes!" exclaimed Ruth.

"That's fantastic," cried Tara, "We're so pleased for you both."

"Can I be a bridesmaid?" cried Kaycee.

"Me too, bridesmaid, bridesmaid, bridesmaid," added little Merri.

Similar cries of affection and congratulations followed before Fletcher was able to resume.

"In the circumstances Holbrook has agreed not to contest the divorce and is making the progress relatively painless. As you're aware, with what's happened all around him he's pulled out of the race for governor and is concentrating his efforts in rebuilding his political career, which . . ." Fletcher paused for a moment and grinned, "If I have my way, won't be worth a plugged nickel."

"How's that progressing?" enquired Jack.

"Yeah when's that son-of a . . . ."

"Wade! We don't want that kind of talk around the dinner table," cried Alex, looking towards her grandchildren. Who to be fair were looking amused at their granddad's outburst. Alex felt sorry for the chastisement, and added with a smile, "save it for later."

Wade smiled over at his wife, no one and nothing was going to stop him from enjoying the festive season. "I just want to know when they're going to charge Holbrook with them murders."

Sam stood up, "I guess I'm the one to shed some light upon that particular problem. We'd hoped to discover DNA evidence, which ordinarily would have been kept, but unfortunately the case file on the 1980 Dempsey/Ryder murder case have miraculously disappeared. It seems that a number of files were lost or destroyed when the storage facility was moved to a more secure and modern unit, which basically means that at this moment we've no evidence against him."

"What's going to happen to Perry Logan? Is he going back to prison?" asked Tara.

"I think I'm best equipped to answer that question," stated Fletcher. "Perry Logan is instrumental in the prosecution of Carson Burroughs and as such he's still being held in protective custody. After the trial, his particular circumstances will be taken into consideration. The fact he was released unlawfully means, strictly speaking he's heading back to the penitentiary. Unfortunately without evidence to the contrary his conviction of the Dempsey and Ryder murders still stands. That he chose to give himself up and help uncover a political assassination plot does go in his favour."

"But that's so unfair," exclaimed Alex.

"My point entirely," added Fletcher, "Which brings me back to the second thing I need to say. Sam, didn't just come here for a free meal, he came here to tell me that my application to become an FBI agent has been approved."

"Yeah, I must say it was touch and go. Being involved with a crime family and the shooting at Cougar Pass, didn't sit well with a number of the board, but when I pointed out that Fletcher had never had a criminal record I was able to convince them otherwise," said Sam.

"That's fantastic!" cried Jack as he stood up and shook Fletcher's hand.

Amidst the back slapping and congratulations Alex stole a glance at her husband. Wade's disappointment was clearly etched across his face. The past few months he'd believed in a dream, a dream he'd thought was slowly coming to fruition. It was his dream, not Fletcher's. Taking a deep breath he put on a brave face and joined in wishing Fletcher good luck in his chosen career.

"Son, your daddy would have been so proud." Wade hugged him and Fletcher responded in kind. Only Alex could see the heartache behind the mask.

"In the boat house when we didn't know whether we were going to live or die, I watched a man that had been given his freedom and enough money to start over, not a good man, but a man that had done terrible things in his past life. I watched as he agonised over taking that opportunity or doing the right thing, knowing that he could face spending the rest of his life behind bars. I like to think he made the right choice. I promised him then that I would do all in my power to see his conviction overturned. Joining the FBI, goes part way to helping that man."

*   *   *

Later that evening when their guests had gone there separate ways, Alex, buttoned up her top coat and joined Wade on the porch. It was a clear and crisp moonless night, allowing the stars that burned brightly to appear like diamonds on a bed of velvet.

"You know I've never grown tired of looking at the night sky, it's just indescribably beautiful."

Alex put an arm around him and cut through the small talk.

"It wasn't as if he'd made any promises," she said gently.

"I know Alex." He smiled down at her and gave her a reassuring hug in return. "It's funny, but to be honest I don't blame him. This isn't the kind of life most people would wish for; you've got to be born to it."

"That's not strictly true, look at Jack."

"Yeah, but he's the exception."

Alex smiled, he was right of course; this wasn't the life most people would choose, it was hard, unforgiving at times, uncomfortable, full of heartbreak, fraught with danger, but the rewards, when they came, made it the best life in the world. And Alex thought she was the luckiest woman alive to be living and sharing that dream alongside this big hunk of a man.

Wade was silent for a time, as he stared off into the darkness of the valley, lost in its mesmerising grip.

"Strange as it may seem, I think Fletcher's finally found what he's been searching for most all his life. It's his destiny. He's experienced far more than many of his contemporise, he's walked on the periphery of crime; he's known heartache and loss. I think the path he's chosen is the right one. His law degree will hold him in great stead, but most of all he's the type of person that wants to make a difference. He's good people Alex."

"And so are you," she said as she leaned up and kissed him.

*　　*　　*

Christmas came and went; New Year celebrations were a mixture of fun, frivolity, and anticipation at the pending birth of Charlotte's baby. It was also tinged with a hint of sadness. Fletcher and Ruth were leaving for Washington DC where he was to begin his training at Quantico.

"We'll be back, before you know it," cried Fletcher. "Carson's trial will be here sooner than you think."

"And don't forget our wedding; we're getting hitched just as soon as my divorce comes through," added Ruth with a smile.

Alex, Wade, Tara and Jack watched as their car disappeared from sight on its way to Billings airport and the start of a new life. Each of them lost in their own thoughts.

*　　*　　*

A week after Fletcher and Ruth's departure came the welcome news of Charlotte's new addition to the family. Harry Bartlett arrived weighing in at a respectable 8lbs 6ozs.

"When are you thinking of going?" said Tara when she and Jack were alone.

Jack noted the concern in Tara's voice and loved her all the more for it. "Sweetheart, we're all going. It's about time my daughter met the rest of her family."

"We can't just leave; we've too much work on."

"Like I've said before, we're a family and families do take vacations from time to time. I've had a word with Wade and he's gonna loan us Lance and Jed to help out while we're gone. Two weeks tomorrow we head for England. I can't promise the weather mind."

In Tara's head, dark clouds were already looming. She knew her fears were unfounded, yet the thought of meeting Debbie so soon still filled her with anxiety.

Chapter 43

Montana. 1998

Over at the Crazy AW plans were afoot. Alex, never one to let grass grow under her feet had been thinking of ways to refresh her working guest ranch. Bookings had died off a bit during last season and Alex felt that she needed something more to offer her clientele. Wade could sense her unrest.

A few days later Alex walked in with a mischievous smile on her face. "I've been thinking about a new concept for the ranch. Okay, we've covered the overnight pack trip, the spring roundup, the drives to spring and winter pastures, the fall colour ride, etc, but we've never thought about a trip though the Bitterroots up over the Continental Divide."

"That's because it's too far away from the ranch. We'd have to have a trail head at one of the furthest reaches of the ranch. Then we'd have to establish a base camp somewhere where we could work out scenic routes over the Divide," said Wade, "the logistics would be immense."

"Not as immense as you might thing," gushed Alex. "Remember last Sunday, we were both looking out at the mountains, they still hold a fascination to us, after all the years we've lived here. Well after listening to what you had to say I began working out a strategy. You want a little adventure; I know you do, I can see it in your eyes; well I'm giving it to you."

Wade wasn't convinced. It was extra work, the logistics would be enormous, and there was no way of knowing if it would catch on.

"I'm not so sure Alex."

"Trust me," she cried.

Wade knew that when Alex latched onto an idea it was hard for her to let go. "Just how many city folks will want to leave the luxury of your cabins?"

"Leave that to me. Most of our clientele have told me they'd return more often if we'd a base camp operation up on the Divide. They see it from afar, they imagine what it would be like, and then they do the Bob Marshall, the Weminuche Wilderness or the Superstitions' or the like. It's the one thing our outfit doesn't cater for; well that's about to change."

The enthusiasm in Alex's voice was undeniable.

"We'd have to make it as safe as possible. What this ranch doesn't need is some litigious asshole suing the pants off us."

Alex laughed, before she broached the subject with Wade she'd made all the necessary enquires.

"Our insurance will go up fractional, and all we need is just an amendment to our existing paperwork. I've been into it all with Charlie Freeman. He seems to think if you use existing hiking paths, maintain them yearly there's likely to be no problem."

Wade thought back to his days in Tucson when he led city slickers into the Saguaros for the Circle R ranch. He thought about old friends and associates, there was Dan Shepler from out of Bayfield, Colorado, his outfit operated in the San Juans and the White Mountains in Arizona, then there was old Vern Wheeler down in Tucson, long gone now, but if memory recalled he also worked the Superstitions and Sonoma. It was a challenge for a man of his advancing years, but Alex had wetted his appetite.

A day later he came around.

"First chance we get after the thaw, I'll get right to it. Bud and Clem can give me a hand. We'll set up the trailhead first thing. Make sure we're in radio contact with the ranch, then we'll make a start on uncovering these hiking trails."

"We'll need a base camp high up. Ten thousand feet or less would be preferable. Then at the beginning of each season we'll erect the tents and the cooking facilities and we're all set," replied Alex. She smiled at her man. She hadn't seen him so all fired up for quite sometime.

Chapter 44

Marlow

Bob and Sheila's smiling faces greeted the Claymore's as they emerged through the double doors into the arrivals lounge. Jack with a little help and hindrance from Merri, managed to push their trolley piled high with suitcases through without them cascading to the floor.

"Welcome to England," cried Bob as he gave Tara a great big hug. Sheila in turn gave Jack a hug then instinctively turned to Tara. After exchanging greetings, she asked Tara to fill in the spaces concerning Ruth and Fletcher.

"Phone-calls can only tell the half of it," said Sheila, "I need filling in on all the details."

Tara laughed, "All in good time."

Merri clung to her mother's hand while Kaycee forced herself between Uncle Bob and her dad.

Although it was late winter, the skies were a clear blue and a hint of spring was just around the corner. Jack couldn't help but remember those days of yesteryear, the feelings of hope and the promise of a warm and balmy summer. But then he remembered how those hopes faded as the days grew longer and the skies greyer. It wasn't always that way, sometimes like now in February the weather could be unnaturally warm, leading people to believe that this year was going to be the best ever, only to have their hopes plummet. The only thing that was predictable was the weather, it was always unpredictable. Whereas in Montana, what you saw was what you got.

Then Jack's thought turned to Debbie, he was wary about his feelings and how he would react? His emotions were something he had no control over. That he loved Tara with all his heart there was no question, in fact since they'd been back at Big Hole Pass he'd found he loved her more than he'd ever thought possible. The thought that he could have lost her, only strengthened his feelings towards her; he hoped seeing Debbie wouldn't spoil it.

As they pulled onto Bob's drive, Charlotte came out to greet them. Jack's heart surged, his little girl had grown up. He couldn't help but notice how she'd a new found maturity and confidence that only childbirth could give her. He smiled down at the little bundle in his daughter's arms as she offered the baby up to him.

"Say hello to your grandson. Say hello to Harry."

Jack took his grandson in his arms and held him gently. Time at that moment seemed to stand still, the heartache, the anger, the confusion, the dramas and tensions of more than a decade just seemed to melt away. That one moment, that solitary moment meant everything.

Kaycee cried, "Let me hold him."

Jack suddenly aware of Kaycee tugging on the corner of his jacket looked at Charlotte for confirmation.

"Go ahead dad; it's about time my little sisters got to know their nephew."

* * *

Over the two weeks of their stay Charlotte became a big hit with her sisters. It was Charlotte this, it was Charlotte that, Charlotte, Charlotte, Charlotte. Even seeing Debbie wasn't the ordeal Tara thought it would be. She invited everyone over for drinks and nibbles one afternoon.

Jack had felt his heartstrings being plucked at seeing Debbie for the first time since he'd said farewell. It was only natural that he'd feel that way given the circumstances, but as he gently squeezed Tara's shoulder he knew he'd made the right choice.

As the afternoon wore on, he chatted briefly with Debbie, then in a private moment he asked if she was truly happy. She smiled then said one word, "immensely."

"I'm pleased for you."

It was an afternoon thwart with an underlying tension. Debbie decided to take the bull by the horns. Catching Tara alone, Debbie sought to breach the gulf between them.

"He's a good man Tara, look after him."

Tara taken unawares felt her hackles rise. But just looking at Debbie was enough for her to realise that Jack's former wife wasn't patronising her, she was just saying what she truly felt. Somehow it strangely relaxed Tara. She smiled back.

"I will, I truly will."

They hugged and both women felt a genuine warmth between themselves. It felt to Tara like an unspoken truce had suddenly become a new beginning.

Jack in turn had seen the half drama unfold smiled across at James and then followed him into the garden for some air. There were things that needed saying.

"The garden's well kept," he said feebly. Small talk, reflected Jack, how so typically English.

"Mostly Debbie's work," said James. "She seems to have a knack when it comes to growing things."

For a few moments there was silence between them, the reserve of the English, thought Jack, it needed breaking down, he smiled self consciously, and held his hand out. 'To hell with small talk.'

"I didn't get to say it when I was here last, but thanks for looking out for Debbie. She didn't deserve what got served up to her."

"You're right she didn't." said James, still a little wary. "But if circumstances had been different I might never have met her." James gripped Jack's offered hand and shook it. "She's quite something."

"She certainly is," cried Jack a little choked. "Look after her." It didn't need saying, but Jack felt he had too.

James nodded his agreement. Uncomfortable as the conversation was, both men like their wives had come to an unspoken understanding. "Let's grab ourselves another beer," said James.

"Now that is a good idea," declared Jack.

*　*　*

During that fortnight in February, Charlotte bonded with her siblings and became an equally good friend to Tara. Being young Charlotte saw things far differently than her parents, her attitude towards her father's wife was far more relaxed than Tara could ever have imagined. Already mature beyond her years, motherhood had taken it one step further. The girls loved her and thought it real neat that they had an older sister with her very own baby. Kaycee informed Charlotte that as soon as the baby stops crying they're to come to the ranch for a holiday. Charlotte laughed at the simplicity of Kaycee's words and said she'd love to. While little Merri seemed to spend most of the two weeks attached to poor Charlotte's legs. Everywhere she went Merri was under her feet, looking up at her with a cheeky smile spread across her face.

For the adults too, the holiday was just as memorable. No longer was there any underlying tension. Debbie and James floated in and out during their stay, remaining long enough yet managing to retain a fine balance. Jack even took Tara to a football match at Upton Park to see his beloved West Ham. They drew 2-2 against Blackburn Rovers in the F.A. Cup, the occasion was both magical and memorable. Never in Jack's wildest dreams had he ever expected to be sitting in the stands at the Boleyn Ground with his beautiful wife Tara.

"Who won?" exclaimed Tara.

"No one, they've got to have a replay," explained Jack.

"Why?"

"Forget it," he laughed, "you wouldn't understand." He'd already tried explaining the off side rule, and received a blank expression for his trouble.

During those two short weeks they managed to pack in Windsor Castle, the Tower of London, Buckingham Palace and the Houses of Parliament. It was a whirlwind of activities and Charlotte had been in the thick of it. Then all too soon their vacation came to an end. Tearful farewells and promises of visits followed before the long arduous flights home.

Chapter 45

Montana

They were hardly off the plane before Kaycee and Merri bombarded Alex with stories of castles, knights of old, the baby and quaint houses, *an unusual observation by Kaycee,* amongst many other exciting topics. It was only later when the kids were in bed that Alex was able to ask the one really important question. One that had been dwelling on here mind since they flew out.

"How did it go with Debbie?"

Tara smiled, she knew her mother had been dying to know. "It went really well actually. I think we've reached an understanding."

Alex delved deeply into every facet of her daughter's encounter with her nemesis until she was sure Tara wasn't papering over any cracks. Satisfied that the trip had been a spectacular success she excitedly told Tara about her new venture.

"It's a bit of an undertaking," said Tara.

"Your pa's all fired up. It's given him a new lease of life."

"That's Wade. Any help we can give just say the word."

"I'm sure he'll call on you," said Alex gratefully. "Now tell me more about your visit to England."

As the days passed Jack reflected on his visit and felt satisfied. This life he'd chosen, this path was one he'd never have gone down if circumstances had been different, but his brief stay with Pam and Phil in Kentucky had stirred his interest in horses. Meeting Wade and embarking on this great adventure had forced it into his blood. It was his life now, and even a few brief weeks away couldn't stem his feelings for this way of life. As the season began to change, fresh challenges had begun to fall upon his shoulders. None insurmountable, but challenging nonetheless. Jack smiled to himself, living here; facing what nature threw at him was what it was all about. It was as if fate had conspired to make it happen.

* * *

There was still a nip in the air as Wade, Bud and Clem Barker drove the horse trailer to the area they'd designated as the trailhead. For a couple of days they cleared the surrounding woodland and erected a fine corral. Then they built a shelter which was to house the radio transmitter, extra food and grain and all manner of supplies that might be needed in an emergency. There at the trailhead they were at the farthest westerly point of the ranch, beyond was uncharted territory and radio transmission would be non existent.

The old hiking trails were overgrown and treacherous in places. Wade found the going slow and meandering as the elevation grew steeper. Then of a sudden it opened up into a clearing and levelled out for a few hundred yards. All around them giant monoliths of granite swept up to meet the cloudless sky. Forests of Ponderosa pine darkened their path, before giving way to clearings of grass strewn with huge boulders and scrub. They crossed a shallow stream and the ascent started to become steeper. On one side an immense wall of granite rose majestically into the now clouding sky, whilst on the other the ground swept down to a fast running river. The path turned at a right angle and Wade needed to urge his horse upwards, the mount's breath rasped with the effort, thankfully it was only momentary as the path soon levelled out.

Wade and the boys brought their horses to a halt to catch their breath. The air was becoming thinner, not enough to hamper their progress, just enough to let them know that sooner rather than later they'd have to find a suitable spot for the base camp. Wade looked around, the scenery was becoming quite spectacular. Down below, maybe several thousand feet was a lake of pure turquoise, fringed by a forest of pine trees and surrounded by immense mountains.

Pushing on Wade wondered whether they'd ever find a suitable place for the base camp when suddenly they rode up through a glade of trees and came across a clearing shielded from the elements on three sides by trees and granite. What made it so impressive was the vista that stretched before them, a vast opening of land, sweeping down towards Idaho. It was stunning; there were no other words to describe it. At approximately ten and a half thousand feet above sea level they'd found the perfect base camp.

Wade glanced at his watch, clearing the path and generally riding carefully they'd taken seven hours to find what they'd been looking for. The big man guessed that with work done on the paths and trails, they'd be able to knock two hours off the journey.

Clem took the horses and attended to them while Wade and Bud erected a couple of tents. Firewood was quickly gathered and within an hour the three men were sitting around a campfire eating a hot meal. As dusk began to settle their eyes turned towards the open vista and they were lost in an abundance of colour as nature put on an electric light show so spectacular that man's ingenuity could never hope to match. They continued to stare until the light faded from the sky. It wasn't long before the effects of the thin air coupled with the extreme efforts of man and beast saw the men slowly climbing into their bedrolls.

The next six weeks saw a hive of activity as provisions, tents, corrals, horse feed and assorted utensils were carried up the mountain. Alex named the base camp, Chief Joseph's Lookout.

As she pointed out, a little stretching of the truth went a long way.

The last things to be erected were the toilet facilities, along with an improvised shower cubicle.

"What the hell! There's a stream over yonder, ain't that good enough for em!" yelled Wade as his men began erecting the facilities. He laughed inwardly; as he remembered he'd said the very same thing to Alex almost word for word many years before.

By the second week in June, the first batch of would be 'Cowboys' were picked up from their hotels in Dillon and were transported to the trailhead for a week 'On the Divide.'

Since Wade had discovered the base camp looking out towards Idaho, Alex had photographs taken of all the spectacular scenery and had a brochure printed, which she mailed to all her old clients. She had a new addition added to her website and placed advertisements in all the relevant glossy magazines, *Western Horseman, American Cowboy, Cowboys and Indians etc.* At first the interest was slow, but as news got around the interest grew. By late July and August, Alex was pulling in an average of six to eight guests a week, on top of her usually full to capacity rooms at the guest ranch. During late August and into the first week of September she had a full capacity of fifteen guests all booked up for the fall colour ride.

* * *

The month of August was eagerly anticipated, not just for the end of season finale at 'Chief Joseph Lookout' but because Fletcher and Ruth would be arriving to give evidence in the trial of Carson Burroughs. But August came and went, Burroughs's trial was put back a couple of months, much to Alex's relief. The first season at the Lookout had gone better than expected and she received rave reviews from her enthusiastic guests.

*   *   *

When the trial did finally happen, it was around Thanksgiving. Fletcher and Ruth arrived at the Crazy AW on the Tuesday before, allowing them time to join in the festive celebrations before the trial on the following Monday. During Thanksgiving dinner Wade asked about the welfare of Perry Logan.

"It appears to me this Logan feller got a bum deal. I know he had to go back to the Pen, but all the same he could have killed you both."

"That's true, and there ain't a day goes by that I don't think about it. If he was the killer that the state thinks he is, then why ain't Ruth and I at the bottom of Twin Lake?" stated Fletcher.

"Well at least he's in the regional prison in Missoula County," added Jack.

"That weren't of the state's doing, if they'd had their way he'd have gone back to Deer Lodge," said Fletcher bitterly.

"Sam Kilbane interceded on his behalf, said he need to be incarcerated somewhere less hostile as he was a key witness in the Carson Burroughs case and as such was in danger of an attempt on his life," added Ruth.

"Yeah, hopefully his testimony in Burroughs case will lead to an appeal for parole," added Fletcher.

"Is that all the state's offering!" exclaimed Alex.

"At the moment that's the best deal on the table. Our first priority is to get a conviction of murder, incitement to kill, and the unlawful kidnapping of yours truly, against Burroughs."

"But surely Logan's claims of innocence in the Dempsey/Ryder murders and his cooperation in the apprehension of Carson Burroughs must be taken into account," said Tara.

"It's not that simple Tara. Perry Logan's allegations are just that, allegations. Sam had a long talk with him and convinced him that due to his involvement in the case against Burroughs that getting another parole hearing was the way to go."

"In the meantime Vince Holbrook goes free," protested Tara.

"In a nut shell," sighed Fletcher. "But I gave Perry my word that I'd do all in my power to get to the truth."

"Fletch has a file this thick on Holbrook," Ruth indicated with her finely manicured fingers a gap of an inch. "Between training courses at Langley and field work, he's spent every waking hour on Perry's case."

"Not all I hope," said Alex, "he has a soon to be bride to look after," this said with a mischievous glint in her eye.

Then the conversation drifted to much lighter things, such as Tara and Jack's holiday in England, the baby, the reaction of Kaycee and Merri and countless other more pleasant topics.

*　*　*

The trial of Carson Burroughs lasted two weeks. Fletcher and Ruth's testimonies along with Perry Logan's account, plus the wire taps were enough to secure a conviction. The prosecution was going all out to secure the death penalty. Weapons used by Bremer and Knox at the gun store in Polson were brought in as evidence, along with accounts from the deputies that were involved in the shootings at the Warlock Ranch. For once, the FBI was painted in a good light, though the excesses of the Sheriff's department's deputies were played down. A bitter irony, thought Sam Kilbane.

The prosecution, incensed by Carson Burroughs abuse of power and influence were pulling out all the stops. Eye witnesses were coming out of the woodwork. Sam Kilbane had his agents working full out, questioning everyone and anyone. A hunter had seen Burroughs cycling away from the town of Whitefish, a bartender in the same town swore that he'd served him around the same time, numerous witnesses from the Sportsman's Bar in Butte, an agent that had unwittingly told Burroughs about the agent Guthrie, these alone should have guaranteed the death penalty, but instead the judge recommended that Carson Burroughs should spend ninety nine years at Deer Lodge maximum security wing. To some it wasn't enough, but Fletcher thought spending twenty three hours a day in solitary confinement was punishment enough.

The only real sour note happened after the trial was over. The judge stated that Perry Logan, though acting in the best interests of justice had violated his parole, breaking curfews, handling firearms and associating with known felons. Sam tried to reason with the judge, explained yet again that strictly speaking Logan had broken no parole rules as he hadn't officially been given parole. That he'd given himself up voluntarily cut no ice with the judge.

"It appears he's been moved to Missoula County on your say so," stated the judge. "I don't know how you pulled it off, and I don't want to know. But in my opinion the man's a murderer and a rapist, even Deer Lodge would be too good for him."

Sam bit his tongue; the less people knew about Perry Logan's accusations the better. Securing a conviction against Burroughs had been the first objective, going after Vince Holbrook would be an entirely different proposition.

Chapter 46

Montana, 1999

It was a little over six months before Fletcher and Ruth returned to the Crazy AW. When they did it was a surprise to them all. Fletcher called from Billings Airport to say they'd hired a car and were coming out to the ranch.

"You should have called and let us know you were coming," cried Alex. "Wade would have driven up to fetch you."

"It was a spur of the moment sort of thing," responded Fletcher. "Yeah we didn't want to put him to any trouble," interrupted Ruth.

"Well, we'll see you both around supper time."

"Sounds good," replied Fletcher.

As Alex put the phone down she began to fret, it wasn't like Fletcher to do anything on the spur of the moment; something was up. Whatever it was, it was perfect timing, Tara and Jack were coming over that evening.

It was a warm summer's evening, the breeze was warm to the touch and the skies had just begun to change colour as Fletcher and Ruth's hire car drove under the Crazy AW shingle. "It's gonna be a beautiful night, see the way the mountains seem to shimmer as the sun's light falls across them," Fletcher casually remarked.

"It could be yours; you've only to say the word," said Ruth.

"And you wouldn't mind."

"If that's what you want."

"It isn't," replied Fletcher.

"It's them," cried Tara excitedly.

Jack and Wade sauntered onto the porch, beer in hand and joined Tara and the kids on the steps. Alex followed seconds later, wiping her hands on some kitchen roll.

The car rolled to a gentle stop and Fletcher grinned from the driver's side.

"They look well tanned," exclaimed Tara.

Alex smiled, she'd detected something in their voices, but until that moment she hadn't figure out what. "You usually do when you're just back from honeymoon."

"What!"

Tara's eyes immediately focused on Ruth's left hand. The conformation sparkled from her third finger.

"We've something to tell you guys," started Fletcher.

"I think we already know, judging from that huge rock and gold band. Oh come here," cried Tara as she excitedly ran towards her best friend.

"Congratulations Fletch," cried Jack.

Wade waited his turn, slowly digesting the scene. Everyone had thought they'd get married at the ranch, but Wade had always thought differently. He'd seen the pain and anguish that emanated from Fletcher's face up there on Cougar Pass and knew this place held to many sad memories for such a happy occasion to take place here.

"Congratulations you two!" he exclaimed as he wrapped his strong arms around them both.

*　　*　　*

Over dinner Ruth told them that Vince had not contested the divorce and had been downright amicable about the whole thing. "I couldn't understand it myself; until I heard he'd got himself a replacement, then it all fell into place. You see Vince might have given up on being governor but he hasn't given up on his political ambitions."

"Yeah, that's where I come in," said Fletcher. "I've been looking into Vince Holbrook's past with a fine tooth comb, but as yet I haven't been able to uncover anything of value."

"What's happening about Logan?" enquired Wade.

"Perry Logan as you're aware has been languishing in Missoula County for the best part of eighteen months. I've tried and Sam sure as hell has tried but the best the state is willing to offer is a parole hearing for next year, it ain't much but it's the best he could do in the circumstances," he looked apologetically at the faces around the table. "Hopefully Perry will get his hearing and be out this time next year."

"Let's hope so," cried Alex.

The mood was a little sombre until Tara sparked up the conversation.

"Right now I want to hear all about the wedding and that fabulous honeymoon in Hawaii," she cried.

"Well!" exclaimed Ruth excitedly, "After my divorce we decided to have a quiet little wedding away from everyone. I know it sounds mean, but after such a hectic year we thought, what the heck, let's go for it. We did visit my parents."

"How did that go?" interrupted Tara.

"As you know I'd plenty of ground to make up. It wasn't so bad actually. I think Vince brainwashed me so badly; I lost all confidence in how my family would react. It took Fletcher to show me the error of my ways."

She glanced across to her new husband and smiled.

"We had a great time with them, both ma and pa shed a tear or two, and to be honest I cried buckets. Pa took Fletcher aside, as fathers are apt to do, and it wasn't more than five minutes before Fletcher had charmed the pants off poor pa. He was absolutely fantastic with the entire family."

"Yeah, he'll do that all right," chipped in Alex. "How did they take you sneaking off to get married?"

"Ma protested a little but when we told them we'd thought it through and that our minds were made up, she came around to it. Pa insisted on giving us a thousand bucks as a wedding present. Fletch refused, but pa wasn't for giving in. Ma and I want you to have it! he said. There wasn't much Fletcher could say after that."

"So I'm guessing the reason why you planned a quiet wedding was because of your folks," stated Tara.

"You got it in one; we thought it a little unfair to throw them into a melting pot of people they'd never met. Both Fletch and I want to become a little better acquainted with them; I've still bridges to mend."

"Okay, you're forgiven. Doing this family out of a family wedding is tantamount to treason in our book. So go on get to the good bits," joked Tara.

Ruth's eyes lit up as she recalled the last week or so, "We decided that the Kahala hotel and resort on Oahu fitted the bill."

"Oh, that sounds so romantic," sighed Tara.

"Oh it was," teased Ruth. With a twinkle in her eye she described the marriage ceremony at sunset on a well manicured lawn in front of a gleaming white gazebo with the ocean as backdrop.

"Okay, stop, stop, stop! This woman should be locked up, for mental cruelty," exclaimed Tara laughingly, "Now go on, bitch!" Tara was there, she was hanging on Ruth's every word.

"It was a simple ceremony and the hotel supplied a few guests so we didn't feel so alone. Then after the sun had gone down Fletcher and I took a stroll along the white sandy beach. There was Hawaiian music softly playing in the background and the gentle lapping of the surf as it kissed our feet made it a night of sheer magic."

"Oh, I can imagine!" said Alex enthused by Ruth's vivid descriptions.

"The Luau was to die for," continued Ruth. "We drank Mia Tia's and Rum punch and dined on roast pig cooked in a traditional imu, *which is a pit dug into the sand*. It's cooked slowly during the day and when it's ready they serve it with poi, lomi salmon, chicken long rice, sweet potatoes, rice and salad. It's real good." Ruth laughed, "Oh, I nearly forgot, you get lei'd too."

The three women chatted well into the evening, Tara making a mental note to tell Jack that one day when the girls were off hand, they should book a trip to Hawaii. Wade and the boys took themselves outside and settled down on the porch where they drank beer, laughed out loud and generally enjoyed the evening hanging out.

* * *

Ruth awoke to find Fletcher already up. She lay there in silence knowing where he'd gone so early in the morning. Part of her felt a slight pang of jealousy but on the whole she'd come to accept that Merri was and always would be a part of Fletcher that would remain private. She knew he was still hurting, and she loved him all the more for it. She was confident in his love for her, something she'd never experience with Vince. He was hers, he always would be, she'd known that from the start when he'd poured out his heart to her. She understood that Merri was a part of him and that she always would be, and bizarre at it seemed, to love Fletcher she found herself loving Merri. Ruth's love for her man was unconditional.

* * *

It was in late September when Tara got the call. Excitedly she phoned Alex, "Ma you'll never guess . . ."

Alex stopped her in her tracks. "You're going to tell me Ruth's expecting a baby!"

"Ho . . . How the hell did you know that?" asked Tara.

"I've known it from the very first. There's something about a woman when she conceives, don't ask me what it is, there's just an aura about them," said Alex in way of an explanation. "It wasn't just the romance of Hawaii that caused that twinkle in her eye."

Tara, now truly believing that her mother was a witch, began excitedly to talk about the pending birth.

Chapter 47

Montana. 2000

Winter held the valley in its icy grip. Temperatures rarely went above 20 below, cattle died on their feet, horses too, it was a heartbreaking time. Even before the first snowfall, a lightning strike had taken out eighty of Jack's neighbour's sheep. It was to Jack at least, the worst winter for a decade. But the man was resilient to nature's setbacks; tough winters were what it was all about. Survival, facing the elements and coming through it all was what made a man stronger.

Wade had faced many a winter, none more so than the hard winter of 1954 where ranch after ranch faced terrible losses and some their homes and livelihood. Since then he and his family had prepared for the worst and had managed to keep their losses to a minimum, he only hoped that Jason Connors had been as fortunate.

Jason's ranch had temporarily picked up since Wade's visit, but as an absentee owner it was inevitable he'd pay the price. His fledgling movie career had kept him away from the ranch for most of the winter. On its own that would have been bad enough but his foreman Lucas Jacobson died in the October, leaving the overseeing of the ranch to others. Lack of experience and direction, coupled with Jason's contractual requirements put the ranch in a perilous position. The freezing temperatures and biting cold winds dealt him a blow that was impossible to recover from and his entire stock was wiped out. With mounting debts Jason was forced to sell up to his neighbour during the spring of 2000 at a knockdown price. His dream of ownership of a working cattle ranch was no more.

He sounded more upbeat when he phoned Wade a few days after the sale and asked if they could meet up.

"It happens, there weren't nuthin' I could have done different," he said, "last winter cleared me out. With the sale of the ranch, and what I got put by from five series of Rodeo Man I just about broke even. If it weren't for this movie deal I don't know where I'd be." Jason went on to say that his movie career was finally taking off. After mixed reviews over his first venture onto the big screen he'd been signed up to appear in a big budget revisionist western movie. In light of such notable films as 'Dances with Wolves' and 'Unforgiven' the studio thought Jason Connors more than capable of carrying the movie and so herald the return of the Western.

"I've a couple of months before shooting starts and I was wondering if I could come down and talk over a business deal?"

"Why sure," said Wade, "Let me check the diary." A brief silence followed before Wade came back on the line. "You're in luck. I'm free next weekend"

"I'll be there."

When Wade put the phone down he was troubled, "There's somethin' he ain't saying. Things ain't right."

"It's just you, you're becoming more cynical as you grow older," commented Alex.

* * *

It wasn't all doom and gloom as a day later testified. Alex rode out to meet Wade on the snowy east pasture. From the way she rode Wade could tell something was eating her.

"Hey, Alex, what's up?"

"Nothing to worry about, unless you think an eight pound bundle of fun called Johan is anything to trouble yourself with."

Wade's face lit up, Fletcher and Ruth had finally become parents. Wade and Alex had been expecting the news for the last couple of weeks, but with Jason's call, it had slipped right out of his mind.

"Well I'll be a son of a gun," he cried. "I'll give them both a call when I get home, that's great news."

Wade returned to distributing the winter feed, his mind racing back to those old days when he and Johnny had ridden tall. Looking skywards, he eased himself in the saddle. "Well Johnny, you've a grandson, who'd have thought it. Guess I'd better take a look at the stock, pick him out a paint horse for when he's able."

* * *

Jason drove down to the Crazy AW that weekend and asked Wade if he could hire on, for board and lodgings.

Wade looked surprised and a little puzzled, until Jason grinned that grin of his.

"I'm due to start filming the movie in a couple of month, so I thought I'd best acclimatises myself to sitting in the saddle twelve hours a day."

Wade sensed there was more too it, Jason was a Westerner, born in the saddle most like, riding was in his blood. But experience had taught him to let people get around to what's on their minds in their own time. "We'd be mighty honoured to have yah," he replied. "Though I got to tell you it won't be a church picnic."

"I wouldn't have it any other way," replied Jason.

* * *

"What's the movie called?" asked Alex over supper later that Saturday night.

"It's working title is 'Soiled Dove,' though I dare say that will probably change for something a little more catchy."

"Soiled Dove!" exclaimed Alex.

329

Jason grinned, "Yeah, it's about a lady of the night, during the 1880's."

"Well that's different," cried Wade.

"Who's playing this lady of the night?" asked Alex.

"That's the exciting part, Keeley O'Hara, she's up and coming; hails from Ireland so I believe."

"She's that dark haired Irish gal," said Wade.

"Wow! And you're her leading man," said Alex excitedly.

"Not exactly, it's about her relationship with two men, one a rancher, the other a gunman."

"Which one are you?" asked Wade.

"Hah! I play the rancher. They're looking at Landon Merritt to play the gunman."

"Landon Merritt, from what I've heard he's so full of himself," added Alex.

"Landon's okay, just a mite full on," said Jason defensively. "But my part, well it's a peach of a role from what I hear. I haven't read all the script yet, but it appears to have the makings of one hell of a movie."

They chatted light-heartedly though dinner, joked about television celebrities and Jason asked about their association with the Congressman Holbrook affair and finally after dessert made plans to visit with Tara and Jack the following day. Then Wade gave Alex a knowing nod to make herself scarce.

"You boys go take in the night air, while I clear away these dishes. It looks a right pretty night, from what I can see."

Jason made to help clear the table but Alex shushed him away.

"Go sit on the porch," she instructed.

Both men grinned, grabbed their glasses and stepped outside. Alex was right, the sun had just descended below the highest peaks and already its light was radiating its fiery colours.

"Who's supplying you with livestock?" said Wade as they settled into the two porch rockers.

Jason grinned, well it was more like a grimace, "That's the other reason I'm here. You once worked with Lennie Moscowitz. He's the director on this picture; he said that either Jack Claymore or Wade Reynolds were the men to see."

"Lennie Moscowitz, that tight fisted cigar smoking Jew from New York!"

"That's the one," exclaimed Jason.

"He's still around?"

"He's big time now, made a few indie's then got snapped up by the big production companies. Lennie said he worked with Jack in the early nineties, seems that son-in-law of yours made quite an impression."

"I'd say it was Tara that made the impression, if my memory recalls, she banned Lennie from smoking that fool cigar in the house, sent him outside in the snow and cold," laughed Wade. "Shouldn't you be talkin' to Jack?"

"Maybe, but I need to talk to you first. This movie is big, locations are a nightmare and we're to shoot in Texas and Montana. Lately a number of movies have been shot in Alberta, scenery there is pretty spectacular and it's cheaper than filming in the states, but Lennie wants this movie to remain faithful to the book, says he wants it to be as authentic as possible."

Wade noted the tension in Jason's voice, "Stop me if I'm wrong, but reading between the lines I'd say Lennie Moscowitz hasn't changed one bit. He's sent you down here to feel me out. He wants the loan of the ranch and he wants it cheap."

Jason's face flushed with embarrassment, and he stood up. "I'm really sorry Wade. I'll get my coat. I knew it was a bad idea."

"Hold it!" cried Wade, "Don't be so hasty! There's something you ain't tellin'."

"Forget it. I shouldn't have allowed myself to be talked into it."

"Sit down boy, at the very least you can tell me everything."

Reluctantly Jason sat back down, his demons slowly cooling until he was able to reach rational thought. Then taking a calculating breath he told Wade everything.

"The truth is without this movie I ain't got shit! Moscowitz knew that when he called me. The ranch, like I said, took all my spare dough. Rodeo Man got cancelled after series five and my other movies didn't make much of a dent. This is my last throw of the dice."

331

"So you're saying that if I don't agree, the movie doesn't get made."

"It gets made all right, but up in Canada, without yours truly! This movie looked to be my last chance at the big time, it's only a supporting role, but I know I could make the part my own."

Wade looked at Jason and smiled, "You still can, tell that penny pinching son-of-a-bitch I've agreed on principle and he should send me his schedule and we'll see what we can do."

"Wade, you don't have too. I'll get by, Lennie Moscowitz can go hang!"

"Sure you'll get by, I've no doubt. I only wish you'd felt confident enough to have confided in me in the first place. We'll make this movie, we'll make it as authentic as Lennie Moscowitz wants and you'll give the performance of your life."

"Why are you doing this for me, I ain't but known you a handful of years?"

"I've been there," said Wade, "I've been on my uppers more than once."

Jason looked surprised. "Really Wade, I'd never have guessed it."

The big man grinned, as he found himself going back in time, to his first horse drive with Johnny J and to the establishment of the ranch at Big Hole Pass. Johnny and he had worked damn hard to make his pa's old ranch into a profitable venture, to see it all but wiped out in that winter of 54. But he'd stuck at it and turned it around. Although times were hard back then, in a way they were easier. Now life was more cut throat, and sentiment, what little there had been, was non existent in the cattle industry of the new century.

"Yeah, more than once," Wade repeated.

* * *

A month and a half later the production company moved in. Wade having some little experience of a movie company's set up had cleared an area for the motor homes, canteen, viewing rooms and toilet facilities. Alex had insisted he make sure the area was as far away from her guests' accommodation as was humanly possible. Wade knew only to well that unless the ground rules were adhered to from day one; a movie company could and mostly would take advantage. To all intents and purpose the main ranching scenes could be filmed in a six week time span. Wade had a clause written into the contract stating that an overrun of more than a two week period would incur a major financial penalty. Knowing Moscowitz of old, Wade felt sure the movie, or at least the part filmed in the Big Hole Valley would be completed on time.

Jason made quite a stir when he showed up five days later with Keeley O'Hara. Guests, ranch hands and film crew alike were mesmerised by her delicate features, her jet black hair that clashed in a startlingly pleasing way with the most stunning cobalt blue eyes they'd ever seen. But it was her easy way around the production crew that caused the biggest stir. She was a star in the making, destined for stardom at the highest level but there was no side to her. She was as relaxed with carpenters, key grips, wranglers and cleaners as she was with the big executives of the film company.

"I tell you Wade, Lennie Moscowitz might be the lowest thing to craw upon the earth, but he sure as hell knows how to get the most out of his actors."

"Yeah, Lennie's like that. He'll squeeze them until there's nothing left," said Wade sarcastically.

"No! I mean . . . I've read the script through and through. I rehearsed my first scene with Keeley's stunt double, over and over. He did the same with Keeley. Then when he was happy with the scene he threw us together, no introduction. It took two takes, but the chemistry it, it really explodes."

"It appears that you're smitten," laughed Wade.

"You could say that, yeah. You've seen photos of her right? Just wait until you meet her in person."

"Bring her over for dinner, Thursday night. I'll ask Jack and Tara to join us," suggested Alex.

"You'll have to invite Lennie Moscowitz," added Wade.

Alex shrugged her shoulders, "Whatever!"

"Add a little spice, Lennie might hightail it out of here quicker than expected if Tara has anything to do with it," laughed Wade.

*   *   *

The dinner was a resounding success. Lennie Moscowitz and Tara found safe ground, the cigar was smoked outside after the meal. His eccentricities left safely at home in his apartment overlooking Central Park. With his success had come a growing maturity and confidence, allowing the warmth of his character to show through his tough New Jersey exterior. Alex was enthralled with Keeley as the young lively colleen regaled her with tales of her childhood in Ireland, and Jack and Wade joined Jason in their joint admiration of Keeley.

"Tell me Jason, if Lennie did such a good job with you and Keeley, what's to stop him doing the same with Landon Merritt?"

Jason looked up, his face clouded over at the possibility. "Nothin'," he uttered.

*   *   *

Six weeks ran into seven, then eight, bad weather halted three more days of filming, one member of the camera crew broke a leg and Landon Merritt arrived two days later than he was expected for a crucial and pivotal screen, but all in all the filming met with wide approval from the Director down. There were scenes still to be shot on the sound stage and a couple of scenes set in West Texas to be filmed, but Lennie Moscowitz was more than pleased with the progress.

Wade and Alex walked out onto their porch one morning just as large snowflakes began to fall. It was the noise of the passing caravan of motor-homes, horseboxes, trailers and cars that alerted them to Lennie's departure. They stood and watched as a slow procession of film crew silently and slowly made their way past the ranch and headed back towards the tall posts with the wooden shingle and inevitably the highway. Lennie waved as he passed them. That he'd overrun his schedule by three weeks incurring a hefty penalty soured him somewhat, but not enough to lose sleep over. He was pleased with how it was all coming together. The daily rushes just blew him away.

Jason Connors was the last to leave; driving up to the house he stepped out of his car and climbed the few steps onto the porch. Wade stepped out to greet him followed momentarily by Alex.

"I'm off now guys. Just thought I'd thank you once again for what you've done for me. Hopefully one day I'll be able to re-pay you."

"It was nothing," replied Alex. "We enjoyed the distraction."

"Nevertheless, it can't have been easy, running a ranch, the guest ranch and a bunch of fool movie people."

Wade looked warmly at the tall laconic ex rodeo man come movie star and held out his hand. "It's been a pleasure, just don't leave it too long before you come visit. Bring along that little Irish gal next time."

"Yeah, I'd like that. She's really somethin' ain't she?"

Keeley O'Hara and Landon Merritt had departed a couple of weeks earlier and were filming in West Texas, much to Jason's chagrin. During the filming Jason had become Keeley's constant companion, but there were key scenes without him that needed tweaking. Jason only hoped that Landon wasn't doing any tweaking of his own.

"Its early days, but I am real fond of her. I'm hoping things will develop some." Jason paused momentarily, "Anyway it's time for me to go. I'll be in touch. Wade, I'd just like to thank you once again for helping me out. You don't know how much it means to me."

"I think I do," replied Wade gently. "Now if I was you, I'd saddle up and go rope that pretty little filly."

Jason grinned that grin of his, tipped his hat and climbed back inside his car, a quick wave and he was gone. Alex threw her arm around her husband and both of them watched as Jason's car disappeared into the fast darkening skies.

Chapter 48

Montana. 2001

There was none of the fanfare of the preceding year as 2001 slipped almost anonymously into being. A relatively mild spell, compared to the previous winter, breezed through the valley. Chinooks were like an oasis in a desert of snow and all the more welcoming. Spring flowers arrived early and burst into life as they pushed though the fast melting snow, a signal for winter to banish itself from the world's stage. It was a time of renewed hope, a new beginning. But already the warning signs were making themselves known. George W Bush against popular opinion defeated Gore and became the 43rd President of the United States.

Jason's movie was released in early spring, to late too be considered for the Academy Awards that March, and probably too early to be remembered for the following year. The film though receiving rave reviews from some quarters jumped into the ten best films at number seven, stayed around for a few weeks before dropping out. It had box office appeal, but mostly among western movie fans. It wasn't Lennie's finest hour, but it did propel Jason into the limelight. His performance rated very highly with the top directors and production companies. So much so that offer followed offer; for Jason the movie had paid off big time.

Washington DC

A stark reminder of the sick minded people that saw death and destruction as a means to an end was highlighted when Timothy McVeigh was executed on the 11th June.

"Good riddance to bad rubbish," cried Fletcher as he read the newspaper that morning in his Washington apartment overlooking the Lincoln Memorial. "What in the world possesses men to act so barbaric and cowardly?"

"I don't know darling," sighed Ruth, "I guess, it's in the way they were brought up, some set back in their lives, a traumatic event. Who knows what drives them? I only know that if you hadn't been involved in the detection of Carson Burroughs, then we'd never have met." She bent down and kissed him gently upon the forehead.

It was typical of Ruth to defuse Fletcher's angry outbursts. She saw neither rhyme nor reason to get upset about things she had no control over.

Fletcher got the point, "Yeah I know, but it just makes me so mad. I just wish that son-of-a-bitch Holbrook was behind bars. I've dug and dug, but I can't put him at the scene.

"Just be grateful Logan's been granted parole. It's a funny thing, but when he held us captive he really scared the hell out of me."

"He should've. The man was a harden criminal, spending seven years on death row could really turn a man. Luckily for us, age had mellowed him. I just wish I could prove him innocent." The frustration was clearly visible. "Holbrook set off a chain of events that could've ended with us at the bottom of that lake."

It was always that way, whenever Fletcher closed a case it took him several days to unwind. It was Fletcher's first day off in eleven weeks, and Ruth intended steering him away from his work. He'd been assigned to a series of bank robberies that in itself was bad enough, but it ended messy. The taking of a couple of hostages towards the end of the pursuit ended tragically. One hostage died in the ensuing gunfight along with all three of the bank robbers. It was the first case Fletcher had been put solely in charge of, and it had taken its toll. Once cornered Fletcher had offered them a way to end it without bloodshed, but one of the robbers, high on crystal meth discharged his weapon killing a bank teller stone dead. Fletcher had no choice as he gave the order to the sniper unit to open fire. It was over in seconds, Fletcher reproached himself for not taking the robbers when he had a chance.

"It happens! There's no telling how people will react in any given circumstance. You followed the book," said his commanding officer.

Later that night he talked it out with Ruth, "I don't know whether I'm cut out for this work. I feel my talents are more in detecting crime and preventing it rather than being at the ass end of it."

"You should have a word with the Bureau, ask for a transfer maybe," Ruth volunteered.

"I could, but for some reason or another they feel I'm more useful to them as an operations officer.

Ruth laid a hand on his, smiled then said, "That's because you're good at it."

Montana

Jack received news that Bob and Sheila were planning a visit in late August, September time.

"We're planning a trip with two other couples through the Western states starting in Denver," said Bob enthusiastically.

"That's great Bob, so where are you headed?" asked Jack.

"Well we haven't quite worked out our itinerary yet, but we figured to be at your place around Labor Day weekend. Show them a real rodeo, you know," laughed Bob.

"Well, you let me know when. We'll plan on something special."

Much as he was pleased that his brother was planning on a visit Jack's mind was pre-occupied with the searing heat that gripped the whole valley. Tempers were frayed and patience was stretched to the max as the ranchers in and around the Big Hole Valley eked out what pasture land they could between their herds. Jack along with Wade had seen the warning signs early on during the spring thaw. Precipitation had been unusually down during April, a fact evidently missed by some of their neighbours due most likely to the wet cycles of past years. Selling off yearlings, using feedlots, culling less productive pairs and utilising different pastures had seen Wade weather the drought, others had done the same but some were struggling.

In Jack's case he'd sold off a good part of his stable stock at reduced prices early in the year. He took a small loss, but nothing compared to the loss he'd have had if he hadn't been prepared to listen to his vastly more experienced father-in-law. Nonetheless the heat was still causing him and Tara problems, having his brother stay for a few days around Labor Day would be a distraction, a welcome distraction, but one that he could well have done without.

Jack figured that by late August, September maybe, the searing heat would begin to break up. Storm clouds would begin to form, bringing with them the inevitable downpours that in turn would bring their own problems. Nonetheless it was the life he had consciously chosen for himself when he worked alongside Wade as itinerant cowhands back in Bayfield during the great whiteout so many years before.

*   *   *

The weather broke during the second week of September, and early snowfall had left the Bitterrroots with a light dusting of snow. Temperatures dropped, hitting the mid to low eighties, a respite long-awaited by farmers and ranchers alike.

Wade appreciated this time of year, the Labor Day's celebrations behind him and winter not to long in coming. It was a window, a beautifully framed window of colour, the reds and gold's of the aspen, the darkly brooding greens of the pines, the clear blue unblemished skies above the majestic hues of purple peaks now half covered in a glittering shade of pure white. As he sat his buckskin atop of a rise he gazed at the wonders of nature. He felt as one with the land and the world's troubles seemed so very far away.

He was awoken from his day dream by a rider heading hell bent for leather towards him. He recognised her at once, it was Alex and she seemed in an almighty hurry. Something was wrong he told himself as he spurred his horse towards the fast approaching Alex. Her face confirmed his fears.

"What is it? Is it the kids? Tara, the girls?"

"No, the kids are fine," replied Alex reassuringly. "All hell's broken loose in New York. You need to see what's going on," she added breathlessly.

As they rode back towards the ranch-house at a fast lope, Alex filled Wade in of what she'd seen on the TV. "It's just awful, I couldn't believe my eyes! A report came in that a plane had crashed into the World Trade Center. Then before my eyes another airliner crashed into the second tower. It's just horrible!"

Throwing their reins over the porch rail Wade and Alex raced into the den, Larry, Bud and Thadeus were there staring spellbound as the news repeatedly broadcasted over and over the planes crashing into the World Trade Center.

"It's a hoax, it must be," cried Wade vainly.

Then there came reports that the Pentagon in Washington had been hit by yet another airliner.

"Oh Jesus," cried Alex, "they're jumping! People are throwing themselves out of windows, I can't look any more."

Wade and the others were transfixed, staring into the screen, bewildered, bemused, and in a state of shock, when another report that an airliner had crashed into a field at Shanksville Pennsylvania.

"What in the blue blazes is happening!" cried Thadeus.

Just then the phone rang. Alex snatched it from its cradle.

"Oh mom it's just awful, what's happening?"

Alex calmed her daughter down, "Where's Jack? You need to be with family right now."

"He's here mom, right beside me. We're coming over right now."

Tara gathered the kids up with Martha Redbird's help and bundled them all into the sedan. Minutes later they were gunning the motor onto the highway.

Utah/Arizona Border

Eight hundred miles south at Monument Valley on the Arizona/Utah border, Bob and Sheila, along with their friends were oblivious to the drama unfolding on the Eastern Shoreline. Sheila and the girls were taking timeout, washing their hair and just chilling, while Bob and the guys were rock climbing, around the cabin they'd stayed in the night before. Bob had woken a little before seven to a glorious orange sunrise. Realising this was a photo opportunity he quickly threw his clothes on and grabbing his camera and van keys, raced out of the cabin and jumped into the white Minivan. Realising the image would quickly fade he gunned the vehicle down the hill to get a better shot of the sunrise with Monument Valley as a dramatic back drop.

"It's just, just . . . spectacular," he mumbled to himself. It was 7.03 in the morning Mountain time. Satisfied he'd got the shot he required, Bob took one last look before returning to the van and a slow drive back to the cabin, oblivious to the drama that was unfolding two thousand miles east.

The boys returned around 9.45. to find the girls refreshed and ready for the drive up to Moab. Before they could start on their day long drive they had to check out of Goulding's Lodge main reception. Bill had elected to drive this section, so as they laughed and joked their way down the slight hill to Goulding's Lodge main reception desk they were still in the dark as to what was going on.

Bob was designated to pay the night's accommodation while the others waited in the van. A few minutes later he reappeared shocked and a little shaken by what he'd just been told.

"I've just heard some news, I can't believe it. It seems terrorists have attacked the World Trade Center!"

"What!" cried the group in unison.

"Terrorists have somehow or another crashed two planes into the World Trade Center."

Immediately Bill turned on the radio. For ten minutes they listen in silence, slowly gathering it all in. Then Bob spoke, "The receptionist asked if we were heading home as most airports have been ordered to shut down. I told her we had the best part of two weeks before we were heading home."

"It can't be as bad as they're making out, can it?" asked Sheila.

"Of course it can, it might even be worse," snapped Bob.

Unbeknown to the group it was a prophesy that they would all become aware of on the journey up to Moab.

"We were there, all of us last year, we stood on the very top!" exclaimed Bill's wife Carol as she digested the news.

"How the hell are they going to rescue those people that were on the floors above the crash sites?" exclaimed Sheila.

"Best not speculate," chipped in Kay.

"I suggest we carry on as usual, there ain't anything any of us can do." said Bill.

"Bill's right, there's nothing we can do, and if they've closed all airports we're stuck here," added Fred.

Bill slammed his door shut, more as a signal for the others to follow suit, then turned on the ignition. With only the car radio to go by everyone speculated that it couldn't be as bad as it seemed.

There comes a time when certain events become frozen in time, for Bob and his friends that moment was only minutes away. They'd driven a short distance along the highway when Bill glanced in his rear view mirror and pulled over.

"Check out the view," he cried suddenly.

The group slid back their sliding doors and filed out, still absorbed in the dreadful news that was emanating from the radio. It was Fred who understood first why Bill had pulled over.

"Yeah, I see it," he declared and pointed back the way they'd come. The girls were puzzled at first until Bob explained that the long straight highway behind them stretching all the way down to Goulding's Lodge and Monument Valley was the iconic cover of the Best of the Eagles CD.

Immediately the group knew the significance of the view and began taking photographs. It was a poignant moment in time, a reference point to one of life's tragic moments. It was underlined by a convoy of Hell's Angels riding two abreast up the highway towards and past the group. A blaring of horns accompanied by arms raised and hands outstretched in the universal sign of peace. The group returned the salute. It was over in a matter of seconds, but the message was loud and clear. The peace of the world had been shattered but already there were signs that the country, no the whole free world were coming together in the nation's darkest hour since Pearl Harbour.

Washington DC

Washington was in chaos. People were waking up to the tragic events in New York and the shattering news that the Pentagon had also been hit. Panic hit the streets as the news media predicted possible further strikes. It was as if World War Three had just started. Ruth desperate for news of Fletcher called his cell-phone.

"I can't talk right now, I'm heading to the crash site at the Pentagon, I've got to do something to help!"

"Be careful!" cried Ruth into the phone, relief and anxiety clearly detectable in her voice.

"I'll do just that, now do me a favour, stay home until I call. I don't want you and Johan running around Washington until we know what we're up against, you understand!"

"Ye..yeah," Ruth muttered, "Be careful, I love you!"

"I love you too honey," then the line went dead.

* * *

In the days that followed, when the sheer size of the attacks were known and the death toll was reported, the nation asked itself how did it happen? Why did it happen? What are we going to do about it? The nation was hurting like never before.

Montana

For Wade, it brought back memories of Korea, for surely the United States would react, drawing America into yet another foreign war. Al Qaeda was a terrorist organisation operating out of Afghanistan, a country run by the Taliban. Bush, he believed would invade Afghanistan, sooner rather than later. Wade only hoped it would be a swift and decisive victory, but he feared for the American people. Even at seventy one Wade still felt the patriotism of his youth, the fire in his belly still burned fiercely, his resolve as hard as steel, but it was tempered by life's experiences.

Alex felt very much the same, but feared that America would be going it alone. Surprisingly she was comforted by her son-in-law's brother Bob, when they visited a week and a half later. They'd opted for a southerly beginning to their trip and had missed out on the Labor Day rodeo. There trip was due to culminate at Denver but due to the circumstances of 9/11 they'd swung a wide loop to take in Dillon and Jack's ranch. During the three days that they stayed the talk inevitably found its way back to 9/11, and what the world's reaction would be.

"Mark my words. At the moment the whole world is outraged, but when the dust settles, you look and see who's still standing at America's side. It'll be us, the British. Never mind the rest; it'll be us that'll be standing toe to toe. You're not alone in this."

It was said on the day before Bob's crowd drove back to Denver for their flight to London. It was bar talk, but nonetheless for Alex it had a comforting ring about it.

344

On the 7th October the United States and their closest ally the United Kingdom invaded Afghanistan. Their objective was to capture or kill Osama Bin Laden, destroy Al-Qaeda, and remove the Taliban regime. Giving safe harbour to terrorists was something that wouldn't be tolerated.

Washington DC

In Washington, the attacks had a profound affect on Fletcher. He'd seen at close hand the death and carnage at the Pentagon and as an investigating officer at Shanksville. For months after, he and fellow agents pieced together the movements of the terrorist cell. The mistakes that were made and the lessons that were learned had a lasting effect on Fletcher.

"We need to guard our borders better! We should be on the alert for any signs of a terrorist attack, before it's had time to be put into action," he told Ruth. On the now infrequent visits to Wade and the rest of his family Fletcher told them how life as they knew it had changed since 9/11. "Our security at home is paramount. They can go fight their wars in far off lands, but its here that the real battle is." No one was surprised when he left the Bureau in 2002 and enlisted in the newly founded Homeland Security Organisation. Fletcher had at last found his vocation. No longer would he be clearing up after a crime, now he would be heading a task force in detecting terrorists' activities before they came to fruition.

Fletcher's change of direction was someone else's gain. In a far corner of their apartment, in a filing cabinet marked under H a thick manila folder began to gather dust.

Chapter 49

Montana. 2002

Vince Holbrook, his aspirations still unfulfilled, divided his time between his commitments to the state of Montana and his family business. His Great Grandfather was one of the original "Copper Kings." His Grandfather continued the tradition and along with copper mining, he heavily invested in coal and petroleum. By the time Holbrook's father took over the reins, the family firm was worth a vast fortune. Vince had wanted for nothing, his playboy looks and his philandering left him with no appetite to learn the family business. That was until the beginning of the eighties, when his father finally brought him under his control. A little while later Vince Holbrook pulled himself together and earned a degree in law and politics; thanks in part to his best friend Carson Burroughs.

Vince had seen Carson's potential and used it to his own advantage. Not stupid by any means Holbrook studied hard but it was Burroughs who had the wherewithal. Partnering up with Carson was the smart thing to do, "Your brains and my money, we'll own this country before we're forty," cried Holbrook often. It was an arrangement that suited both young men. Only Holbrook hadn't taken into account the way he treated people. It was the way he'd been brought up by his doting mother until her death in 1978 and he couldn't see past it, and to his cost Carson Burroughs had turned against him spectacularly.

The scandal of his divorce and the alleged assassination plot led the powers that be to withdraw their support for Holbrook running for governor. For a time Vince found himself out in the wilderness, hanging onto his position by the seat of his pants. Then his luck changed, the purse strings were finally cut when his father eventually died in 2001.

At forty three, head of a multi-million dollar corporation Vince Holbrook was back with a vengeance. Over the years he'd been forced to watch and learn. His father's company was amassing large profits year on year and Holbrook saw no reason to change things. In his own words, "If it ain't broke don't fix it." He let the board know that he was in charge, but unless there was a drastic drop in those profits, they could continue to run the company as they always had. Of course he wasn't that trusting, he employed a private firm of accountants to keep him apprised of any sudden moves in the market that he should know about.

Safe in the knowledge that his fortune was in secure hands he was able to devote his time to the three Ps, Politics, Power and Philandering. One thing his father had taught him was to always know on what side his bread was buttered. Back when he had high hopes of running for governor he'd thrown his weight on the side of the farmers and ranchers. Being put on the spot by the likes of Wade Reynolds he'd responded chameleon-like and given him a sob story about being brought up on a ranch in the Judith Basin. It was part true, but mostly fabrication. He had spent some time on the ranch, but it was one of his father's ideas to toughen him up.

Now the sole beneficiary of his father's vast fortune Vince began to buy his way back into favour, only this time he wasn't going off half cocked. 2002/2003 was going to see the re-emergence of the newly refined Vince Holbrook. First thing on his agenda was to obtain the best public relations firm that money could buy.

"I want the best. I don't want junior personnel; I need the most experienced person available."

"Have no fear, we're sending you the very best."

"I'll have my driver meet him at Billings on the 22nd."

"We'll let you know what flight she's flying in on the day before."

"She!" exclaimed Holbrook.

"Yes sir. Mrs Seagrave. She's the best in the business."

* * *

Vince Holbrook stared out of the large picture window as his driver pulled onto the extensive driveway with his charge. The Congressman was due for re-election and a public relations officer couldn't have come sooner. He guessed she'd be a power dressing dyke of around his own age, very butch, but able to handle any given situation. What he saw as he gazed out of the window was nothing like he'd imagined. Fortyish, he'd got that right. But as she unfurled her elegant frame and flicked her blondish hair from her face he continued to stare. He was mesmerised by her style, her poise. Her face, framed by a shaggy bob of expensive highlights was both attractive and wanton. Fuck public relations, he wanted her.

Vince stepped out of his office and walked into the elaborate high ceilinged lobby and waited with anticipation as she walked in. He noticed her high heeled shoes, Vera Wang, her elegantly styled suit was obviously Gucci, her handbag Louis Vuitton, but rags would have looked just as good on her five feet seven inch frame. She was absolutely stunning and she knew it.

"Mr Vincent Holbrook, I presume," she said as she extended her hand.

"You must be Mrs Seagrave," he replied, "and the name's Vince."

She smiled and he thought the devil was in her eyes.

"If we're going to be working together, best we drop the Mrs Seagrave, call me Shelby."

"Shelby it is, now I guess you need to freshen up before dinner," said Vince Holbrook graciously.

"On the contrary, I'd like to get down to business straight away. Shall we sit down, have an informal chat?"

"Yes, by all means. Would you like some refreshments? A glass of wine perhaps?"

"That would be lovely, just a small glass though. I'm working."

"Robert, two glasses of Sauvignon Blanc." Then as an afterthought he turned towards Shelby. "Is that fine with you?"

"Perfect."

Shelby sat down opposite Holbrook and crossed her legs in a coquettish manner, sending the Congressman's heart racing. She was no angel, of that he was certain, but there was something else about her but for the moment he couldn't quite put his finger on it.

"Right Vince, I'm going to undress you." She was laughing at him as she spoke.

"Pardon," he gulped.

"Figuratively speaking, seriously I need you to be perfectly honest with me. I'm bound by my ethics, like a doctor/patient relationship."

"Why?" he said cautiously.

"Because," she paused for effect, "I'm going to rebuild you from the ground up. I need to know what makes you tick."

"You," he said boldly. "You make me tick."

Shelby laughed, "That's good. Honesty, I like that in a man. But I'm afraid I'm off limits."

The rebuff rankled but Holbrook curbed his disappointment, he had time. "Mr Seagrave?" he questioned.

"Divorced. That's all you're gonna get from me, unless I decide otherwise. Now if you'll excuse me, I'd like to freshen up before dinner."

*   *   *

Over the next three weeks Shelby discussed with the Congressman the forthcoming election and how he was going to tackle his leading opponents.

"Controversially, this being a ranching, and farming state, I'd suggest we go down the opposite road to your opposition. With climate change on the political agenda, the environmentalists are making great strides. Allying yourself with these groups, joining their committees, a donation here, another there. It will get you noticed."

"It could also lose me the election!" cried Holbrook. "This is Montana!" he added for emphasis

"On the contrary, standing up for the environment, the conservationists will love you. Look at these figures, in the state of . . . ."

* * *

By the time he went on the campaign trail, he half believed what she was telling him. Mesmerised by her, Vince Holbrook delighted in having her on his arm at the many social and fund raising events. She was to him like a breath of fresh air, so much so that the entire campaign flew by. Vince had done something he'd never done before, he'd put his trust entirely in Shelby's hands. The man was well and truly smitten. When he was re-elected no one was more surprised than him, especially when Shelby reached up and planted a kiss upon his lips.

"Congratulations Vince, you're a winner!"

As the crowds of well wishes clasped his hand and slapped him on the back, all Vince could think about was the sweet tang of Shelby's kiss and the very fact that his political future was down to her. She'd propelled him back into the spotlights of the political stage once again.

The following morning Vince was surprised to see Shelby's designer luggage in the hallway.

"What's going on?" he cried when she descended the stairs.

"My job here's done. I've other clients to get back too."

"But you never said you were leaving. Well not in so many words." He was desperate for her to stay.

"I'm sorry, you're right of course. I should have given you notice I was leaving." In truth the real reason why Shelby was leaving so abruptly was because she had grown very fond of the congressman during the past few months. It was something she'd not anticipated. She was happy with her life, happier than she'd been in a long while. A romantic liaison with the Congressman though tempting would only complicate that life. Even though the thought of leaving had left her cold, getting the hell outta Dodge had seemed the least painful option.

"Look, stay, have dinner with me tonight. I've a proposition for you. If you don't accept, I'll drive you to the airport myself."

Warning bells rang loudly inside Shelby's head, she didn't need any more complications in her life. 'What the hell!' she thought as she smiled.

"Okay, dinner."

* * *

For three months she'd remained aloof, oblivious to his need for her. She'd gotten under his skin, and he wanted her desperately. She'd been fun, she was good company, she was everything he'd ever wanted in a woman, but she'd kept their relationship at arms length. Well he'd show her. He'd show her he wasn't a two-bit cowboy politician.

"What is that noise?" cried Shelby when she came down for her dinner date.

Vince grinned, "I believe it's our transport."

"Our what!"

Vince took her by the arm and led her out back to an awaiting helicopter.

"Twenty minutes from now we'll be seated at the finest most exclusive restaurant this side of anywhere."

Shelby's smile was one of incredulity.

'The Mother Lode' restaurant was perched atop of a mountain somewhere in the Bitterroot mountain range. Vince pointed it out to a nervous Shelby as they drew closer to the top of the timber line. She smiled sweetly but her white knuckles told a different story. Minutes later she gave a sigh of relief as the helicopter put down on a heli-pad only fifty yards walk from the restaurant. Within seconds the maitre de approached the Congressman and led both of them to an outside table overlooking a magnificent panoramic view over the Idaho side of the Bitterroots.

"It's fantastic!" she exclaimed at the sheer wonder of the view.

"I'm glad you like it," said Vince nervously. What was it with this woman? Why did she have such an effect on him? He was one of the richest men in the state; he was considered good looking, suave, debonair, ruthless even, all the attributes that would appeal to women. Yet something about the woman seated opposite him had turned him to jello.

And then just as the fading light of the sun cast its dreamlike glow across Shelby's exquisite features he knew. It was uncanny, all his life he'd been searching for the one; the true key to his heart. His life had been empty for so long, the women he'd known were as nothing compared to her. A warm glow from the fading light wafted over him as he asked her to stay.

"What about my job, my career?" Deep down she knew what he was eluding too, yet she couldn't help herself as she devilishly forced his hand.

"I want you to be my personal assistant," he cried vainly.

"My work is my life," she continued as she baited him further. "I need more than you're offering."

"If it's money name your price."

Shelby frowned and Vince knew he'd taken a wrong step. "Sorry, I don't mean it the way it sounds."

"I know that, silly," she smiled devilishly.

"This might sound absurd, perverse even, but I can't get you out of my mind."

Shelby looked slightly stunned, "Look Vince, I've grown very fond of you too."

"I'm not just fond of you; I want you to become my wife. I love you, more than you'll ever know." The words were out; he'd played his final hand. "With you behind me, we'll go further than you've ever dreamed," he added desperately.

Shelby laughed, men were such fools, she thought. "You want to marry me, you don't even know me."

"I want to know you; I want to know everything about you. I want you to know everything about me. I want us to be as one."

"I've a history."

"Who hasn't," he replied glibly.

"How do I know you really feel this way? How do I know it's not your way of getting me into bed?"

"I'll prove how much I love you. It'll be difficult, but I won't attempt to make love to you until our wedding night."

Shelby couldn't stop herself from bursting out with uncontrollable laughter. "That has got to be a first, but I'll hold you to it."

"Anything, just say yes."

"Yes," she smiled sweetly, "I'll marry you." They embraced and Shelby couldn't help herself from smiling into the fast sinking sun. At last she'd found a man worthy of her talents, a man that she could share the rest of her life with. Three months later they were married. And as befits a man and a woman of their standing it became the biggest society wedding of the year. It even made the Washington Post.

Washington DC

"I think you'd better take a look see," cried Fletcher.

"See what?" exclaimed Ruth.

"Your ex just got himself hitched!"

For the briefest moment Fletcher thought about the inch thick file gathering dust in a far corner of his office. Then the phone rang, he had to attend a briefing on the latest terrorist alert. Grabbing a slice of toast he lent down kissed Ruth on the cheek, reached across the table and tousled Johan's hair, "Must fly, love you both. See you tonight!"

Ruth looked up at her husband with a warmth she'd never felt for Holbrook, blew him a kiss as he raced out the door. Turning back to the Washington Post, she gave it a cursory look then discarded it in with the rest of the trash.

Montana

Closer to home, Tara flicked through the Billings Gazette before settling on the same press photo of the happy couple. Staring back at her was a face she never expected to see again in her lifetime. "I don't believe it!" she exclaimed.

"What don't you believe," replied Jack absentmindedly.

"Shelby Shannon, that's what! How dare she set foot in Montana!"

"Shelby who?"

"She's calling herself Shelby Seagrove, now she's gone and married that no good bastard Holbrook."

Realisation hit Jack the moment Tara said the name Shelby Shannon. It was before his time, but he knew the history. Tara was glaring at the smiling face of the woman that had broken her brother Taw's heart. Shelby Shannon was back in Montana with a vengeance.

Chapter 50

Montana. 2003

"Don't mess with her," warned Alex when Tara told her Shelby Shannon was back in Montana and was married to the recently re-elected Congressman Holbrook.

"How can you be so calm," screeched Tara. "That bitch caused my brother's, your son's death!"

"Tara, honey, I feel the same way as you, but she ain't broke no laws. Best leave the past in the past. You hear Tara. Them is powerful folks, it don't do to mess with them unless you have too." Alex more than anyone else knew how her daughter was feeling, she also knew that pent up hatred would get Tara nothing but heart ache. "Best you forget she ever existed."

It was good advice and Tara knew it, but it still stuck in her craw. 'Maybe, just maybe', reflected Tara, 'Holbrook and that whore have got what they both deserve.'

Later that evening out on the front porch, Jack gave her the same advice. "I know he was your brother and all, but strictly speaking she wasn't to blame for what he did."

"I know, I know. Ma's told me the same, but it don't make it right. She .... She suckered us all. Now that bitch has the audacity to return to Montana and marry one of the richest men in the state. It just ain't fair."

* * *

All Tara's animosity was quickly forgotten when the long anticipated visit from Matt and Charlotte finally materialised. They'd been promising for years to visit but when Charlotte found herself pregnant with Evie the visit was put on hold. Now with Evie three and Harry six the couple thought now would be the appropriate time to visit.

"We would have come sooner but you know how it is with kids," said Charlotte.

Tara laughed and nodded her agreement, "Men, they haven't a clue."

"You've got that right," agreed Charlotte.

It was a wonderful distraction for the Claymore's of Big Hole Pass. The girls Kaycee, twelve pushing thirteen and Merri now nine, loved their little nephew and absolutely adored their three year old niece Evie.

Jack was as excited as all get out and even took time off work to show Matt and Charlotte around the ranch. There was so much he wanted them to see, but Tara had given him a little friendly advice.

"Don't go at it like a bull in a china shop, show them the ranch by all means but take it slow, I'm sure they'll come visit again."

"You're right Tara, as always. I'll take it slow," cried Jack.

Matt was a little wary of horse-riding at first, but Charlotte, who'd been riding most of her life took to a western saddle like a duck to water. With a little advice and encouragement from Jack, Matt started to build his confidence. And within a couple of days Matt had got the hang of riding and looked to be enjoying himself.

"Thanks for being patient with him," cried Charlotte as she turned her horse towards Jack's.

Jack smiled, the visit was all he could have wished for, then he asked Charlotte a question that all fathers at some time ask their daughters.

"Are you happy?" he said.

Charlotte looked puzzled, "With Matt, do you mean?"

Jack nodded and looked a little awkward.

"I couldn't be happier, Matt's kind and caring, and I love him to bits." She declared.

"I'm glad. From what I've seen of Matt he seems an alright kind of guy."

"He is; he's the best."

"I'm sorry I asked, it's . . . . it's."

"I know. We've missed so much time. I understand how you feel. And I couldn't be happier than I am right now. Two of my favourite men, and I've got you both eating out of my hand," she laughed playfully as she kicked her horse into a fast lope back towards the ranch house.

*   *   *

"I know what we'll do; we'll take a couple of days out, head up to Great Falls for the State Fair. Show you a real live rodeo; eat cotton candy at the Midway." Charlotte, Matt and the kids looked puzzled.

"That's funfair to you guys, Carousels, Ferris wheel, it'll be fun," explained Jack one evening over dinner.

Three days later they found themselves in the thick of it. From the moment the riders rode into the arena brandishing the stars and stripes to the bull riding finale, Matt and Charlotte were enthralled by it all. The look on Harry and Evie's faces said it all, they had loved every minute of it, but especially the fairground.

"Great idea dad, the kids are having a ball!" exclaimed Charlotte.

"Yeah good job honey," cried Tara.

Jack grinned, "Let's go eat."

"Another great idea," joshed Matthew, as they reached the sidewalk.

"Over there," pointed Tara, "If I'm not mistaken they cook the most fantastic steaks."

"Great!" exclaimed Charlotte, "I'm starving."

Jack looked at his extended family and echoed Charlotte's sentiments of a few days ago. He was happy, happier than he'd been in years. He had the life that he was born too, a wife that sent his heart beating nineteen to the dozen, and three kids, one grown, the others fast catching up, and a couple of grandkids to boot. Yeah life couldn't get much better.

Just as Jack was thinking those thoughts a limousine pulled up to the curb and flash bulbs began popping.

"Who's that? Some celebrity or what," cried Charlotte excitedly.

"No one you'd know," laughed Jack. "Celebrities in this neck of the woods tend to be local."

"Oh, and I was hoping it would have been Meryl Streep or Jane Fonda at the very least," laughed Charlotte.

"Don't mock us hayseeds, we're close, big time with Jason Connors," added Tara.

"What, the Jason Connors, he's hot!" exclaimed Charlotte.

"The very same," said Tara with a smug, self satisfying smile across her lips. Suddenly the colour drained from Tara's face. She'd spotted who had just climbed out of the limousine. It was Congressman Vince Holbrook and his wife Shelby.

Charlotte and Matt looked at Tara with alarm. "What's up, did I say something I shouldn't?" pleaded Charlotte.

"Tara!" cried Jack as he saw the cause of his wife's mood change. In a split second Tara was racing towards the limousine.

"Oh shit!" cried Jack before rushing after her.

Matt and Charlotte looked at each other, puzzled by the change of mood they followed with their eyes as Tara pushed her way through the crowd.

"You've got a nerve," screamed Tara as she swung Shelby around to face her. Jack just about managed to throw his arms around Tara stopping her from flooring the Congressman's wife.

Unruffled Shelby smiled back at her attacker and replied, "Hello Tara," with all the poise and class that her training had given her.

"Don't Tara me, you filthy whore. I don't know how you've the nerve to come back to Montana." Tara's eyes blazed angrily.

For the briefest of seconds Shelby's guard dropped. "Believe me; for what its worth, I'm truly sorry for what happened," she said softly.

A member of Holbrook's entourage sensing a possible scene stepped in between the two women and whisked Shelby and the Congressman into a nearby restaurant before Tara could do something she'd regret.

Tara's eyes blazed with hatred as she watched the couple being shepherded into the same swanky restaurant they'd just chosen.

"Come on Tara, there's nothing to be gained, let's gather the kids and head back to the motel," said Jack in an assertive manner.

Tara's heart was racing, her eyes smouldering with hatred, as she fought for control. "Yeah you're right, I've suddenly lost my appetite."

*   *   *

Back at the motel, the anger managed, Tara felt embarrassed. "I shouldn't have gone off on one, least ways not with your family here."

"Don't mind us," said Matt.

"Tara, we haven't known you that long, but enough to know you wouldn't have laid into that woman without a reason," said Charlotte sweetly.

"Thanks, but I think I owe you an explanation."

"No explanation needed, I'm sure she must have had it coming," replied Charlotte.

"No, I think you have a right to know. Many years ago that woman was engaged to be married to my brother Taw . . . ."

By the time Tara had finished explaining the tears were streaming down her face. "You see, if I hadn't have intervened when I did, things could have been a whole lot different."

"You don't know that. If that bitch is anything like you've just described she'd have continued cheating on Taw," said Charlotte. "You can't keep blaming yourself."

"I know, I know . . ."

*   *   *

Political protocol stopped Vince Holbrook from asking his new wife what that woman meant. They were fortunate that Vince's aide was on hand and that Tara Claymore's husband had pulled her away so quickly. A scene was not something that the newly elected congressman needed right now. Nonetheless it stuck in his craw. It wasn't just the averted scene, no, the thing that matter most was that woman had called Shelby a filthy whore; it was the uppermost thought in his mind.

Shelby, like the great P.R. that she was, just laughed it off. "I'll explain later, it was nothing."

The dinner engagement was interminably long, even more so now that he had to wait until they were alone. Holbrook made a curt and precise speech, not the one he'd prepared, but sufficient to satisfy the local dignitaries around the table. Sighting a pressing engagement elsewhere they left as soon as the meal was over.

The limousine ride home was just as unbearable as the dinner and Vince Holbrook stormed into his study. Shelby followed a few steps behind.

"What the hell did that Claymore woman mean, calling you a filthy whore?" he snapped.

"Don't shout at me!" she retaliated. "If you'll calm down I'll explain."

"Sorry honey, it's just that I care."

"I know, and I'll tell you all about it, after you've fixed me a drink." she smiled reassuringly at Holbrook.

Two minutes later, sitting opposite each other in matching Chesterfields, with the ice still crackling in their glasses, Shelby took a sip and crossed her legs.

"I was young, very young as it happens. I'd been in public relations for a little over a year when I was assigned to steer a young up and coming concert pianist in the right direction. He was a year older than me, good looking and charming. Basically he swept me off my feet. We fell in love, became engaged then it all fell apart."

Shelby could see that Vince wasn't buying the fairy tale side of things; he needed all the sordid details.

"There must be more to it than that?" he snapped.

"Okay I'm going to be brutally honest with you, only because I love you and don't want anything to come between us."

Holbrook softened his stance. "Go on."

"As I said I was young, young and very immature. My whole persona was manufactured; I appeared to be confident and sophisticated, which is what I was trained for . . . ." Shelby paused, "That woman was his sister. Do I really have to go on?"

Vince Holbrook gulped, it should have been enough, but he wanted, no, he needed the whole nine yards.

"On a visit to the Reynolds ranch to celebrate our engagement, I became attracted to Tara's boyfriend, a saddle bronc rider called Kyle, something or other. I had too much to drink, I made a pass at Kyle, he reciprocated."

She looked across to gauge Vince's reaction. His anger had been replaced by concern.

"That Tara's a real hell-cat; she came at me like a freight train. We fought, everyone woke up. Taw learned about me and Kyle, a fight broke out between them. It was horrible."

"That's it," cried the congressman.

Shelby shook her head. "There's more. Taw damaged his hand in the brawl; it was so busted up his concert pianist days were over."

"Did you try talking with him?"

"I would have, but his ma was worse than Tara. She told me in no uncertain terms what would happen if I stayed around. What was I suppose to do? I was public enemy number one, so I got the hell outta Dodge the very next morning."

"That's it," repeated a relieved Vince.

Shelby paused, her face screwed up slightly, "Not quite. It was over; I'd screwed up good and proper. It was time to concentrate on my career. I learned months later that he was killed trying to ride a fool horse that nobody could master. I guess I got the blame for that too."

"You should've told me, I'd have understood. Whatever any of them Reynolds or Claymore's think, you've nothing to reproach yourself for."

"Thanks," cried Shelby. "I needed to hear that. I was a bitch, I know that, but it was years ago, I've grown up since then."

"As I just said, you've nothing to reproach yourself for. Now come here, listening to your confession has made me quite hot."

Shelby smiled wantonly, "I suppose you want me to help put out the fire."

"You got that right!"

Vince Holbrook swallowed the last of his scotch and grinned. Shelby was the complete package; she was everything he'd ever wanted.

Chapter 51

Montana 2004

Since Jason Connors career had been given a kick start by his supporting role in the western Soiled Dove, he'd become hot property, completing two or three pictures a year. He wasn't quite A list but it was a busy schedule by anybody's standard. Wade expected him to hit the big time any day now, but then Wade was ever the optimist. So when Jason arrived unannounced in the middle of summer Wade was a little surprised. Jason had taken to visiting at least once a year, but never in the height of Wade's busy season.

Over dinner that night, both Wade and Alex sensed something was amiss, but let it ride. They both knew that Jason would tell them when he was ready. The following morning Jason insisted on working the range.

"After such a great meal, I kinda feel that I need to work for my keep," he joked. With that said he rode over to Larry and got himself assigned to bring in some strays from the north pasture. Wade watched as he threw himself tirelessly into bringing in strays from deep inside the brush. 'Something's up,' thought Wade, 'and by golly I'm going to find out what, come hell or high water.'

It was late in the afternoon before Wade was able to catch up with him. There paths merged somewhere up in the high country.

Wade went too it, "What in damnation's got into you boy!"

Jason sat tall in the saddle, pulled on the reins and wrapped them around the saddle horn. He was slightly taken aback by Wade's outburst. Then he grinned that grin.

"To tell you the truth, I don't feel that at home with those Hollywood types. All froth and no substance. That's why I like it here," said Jason, pointing his gloved finger at the high country and beyond to the towering mountain range, bathed in golden sunlight.

"Yeah, I know what you mean," agreed Wade, slightly distracted by the magnificent vista. "But it can't be all bad surely?"

"You're right, it ain't all bad, and I guess I'm being a little unkind to them folks. Mostly they're nice; I guess it's just me."

The conversation ebbed and flowed, Wade suspected Jason's career had taken a down turn, either that or Keeley had ditched him. Whatever it was he was taking a hell of a time getting to the point. The big rancher hated pussy footing around a subject, so in his emotive style he asked. "In my experience, if there's something to say, best come right out with it."

Jason wasn't surprised, Wade's forth right, no nonsense attitude was legendary. He turned in the saddle, grinned, whilst tipping his hat back.

"There's no fooling you. It's Keeley, as you know we've been seeing a lot of each other in the past few years, worked on two pictures together an all. Well, what I'm trying to say in my clumsy fashion is I'm going to ask her to marry me."

"So, where's yah problem?" cried Wade, relieved that his problem was nothing more than domestic.

"My career's riding high and Keeley's on the verge of becoming a huge box office star. Do I have the right to ask her at this moment in time?"

"How does she feel towards you?" asked Wade.

"I like to think she feels the same. It's just that I don't really buy into this stardom shit. I want to get married, settle down and have kids, lots of them." Jason paused for a moment as he selected his words carefully. "Keeley's on the brink of international fame, she's thirty one, I'm thirty six, we're at the right age to settle down and have kids, but am I right to ask her now? She's worked damn hard to get to where she's at. If she marries me and has kids, all that work will be for nothing."

"Not necessary," said Wade. "What I've seen of Keeley during the times you've come to visit, I'd say she's a level headed girl that more than knows what she wants out of life." Wade stopped and thought about his next words. "I don't know if it's you, I don't know if its international acclaim, but what I do know is if you don't ask her you'll never know."

Jason took his hat off and rubbed the back of his neck, "Yeah, I reckon you're right!"

"Then ask the girl!" snapped Wade, "Ask and be damned!"

*   *   *

On the eve of the biggest premier in Jason's career he proposed to Keeley O'Hara. He never heard the words that tumbled from his mouth as his heart was beating so loudly.

"Yes, I'll marry you," said Keeley, her eyes filling up at the magnitude of his question. "I love you, I've loved you since the first day I met you."

Relief wafted over Jason like a tidal wave. He just couldn't take it in. He sought confirmation. "You're a rising star, aren't you worried that getting married might put a dampener on your career?"

"Are you trying to get out of this proposal already?" cried Keeley in a Southern Irish lilt that he'd come to know and love.

"Hell no," he cried as he pulled her into an embrace and kissed her gently upon her lips. "I want to spend the rest of my life with you."

Any chance that they'd have time to plan their wedding was dispelled by the rave reviews of Jason's latest movie. He played a New York cop in a three hour saga about a family of NYPD cops.

It was directed by Lennie Moscowitz, who purported that this movie would do for the police department what Francis Ford Coppola's 'The Godfather,' did for the Mafia.

Johnny Depp and Leonardo De Caprio had allegedly been considered for the leading role of John Quinn, but Lennie had plumbed for Jason. It was a pivotal role, something that Jason had worked hard on getting right. Keeley loved it, which was all the praise he needed.

Over the next month, "Irish Blue," as the movie was titled, broke all box office records and propelled Jason into super star status. Keeley suggested holding off on announcing their engagement.

"Let's wait a couple of months, see where this takes us," she pleaded.

Warning bells rang loudly inside Jason's head. It was the words he'd feared. "Okay, suppose we do hold off on the engagement, what happens then, your career as a serious actress is going from strength to strength, what excuse will you offer up next time?" Jason hated himself for it. He knew Keeley was serious about her career and he hated for her to choose.

Keeley smiled, "You don't get it do you. Marrying you is the most important thing in my life. I just want you to bask in the spotlight if only for a brief while. I don't want you to wake up five years from now, regretting what could have been."

"I'd never do that," he said.

"Never is a long time," replied Keeley.

"What if I like the spotlight, what then," he teased.

"Then I'll take you in hand. Believe it or not, I'm a level-headed girl, living here in the heart of cuckoo land. I know what's important in life, and I know how to keep my feet on the ground; my parents taught me that at least. Being a top actress is up there on my list of priorities, but marrying you is and always will be top of my list."

Jason pulled her tightly to him, tilted her small delicate chin up towards him and kissed her gently. He knew when he was beaten.

For the next three months they were feted as the celebrity couple of the moment, doing worldwide tours and film festivals. Keeley weaved in and out due to filming commitments, but generally they were never far from each others side Speculation, rumours and gossip were rife around tinsel town and two weeks after they arrived back in Hollywood, they announced their engagement.

A big show business wedding was planned for the 11th September 2004 with the location a closely guarded secret. 100 guests ranging from family members, friends, movie stars, sports personalities and former rodeo performers headed the guest list. Wade and Alex figured prominently on that list.

Jason's true affection for Wade and Alex manifested itself by them receiving their invitation two days before the official announcement, giving 9th September as the real date and the address of the secret location. Both Keeley and Jason wanted a private ceremony without the prying eyes of the paparazzi. It was typical Jason Connors, mused Wade, as he let out a little chuckle.

Even more typical was the snow capped mountains of the San Juans in Southern Colorado which acted as a back drop to Jason and Keeley's wedding. On the sun deck of the spectacular Hamilton Ranch, perched high up on the green slopes of said mountain range they recited their vows. One hundred smiling faces bore testimony to their union, none smiling more than the bride's parents who'd flown over especially.

The ceremony was as spectacular as the dramatic vista that framed the happy couple. The bride looked sensational in a modern understated way, whilst the groom dressed traditionally. *He'd threaten to wear cowboy boots and jeans.* Even Jason wasn't brave enough to suffer Keeley's wrath.

Copious amounts of champagne and canapés followed immediately after Jason had kissed his new bride. Keeley and Jason had done their homework; they'd limited the guest list to a hundred and had got the mix just right as movies stars mingled with family members and sportsmen alike. Both had insisted on only inviting true friends. Lennie Moscowitz was conspicuous by his absence. Wade and Alex mingled for a time, chatting with movie stars and sportsmen then as protocol allows they generated towards old friends they'd known on the rodeo circuit over the years.

"Hell, Alex, I remember Wade and Johnny from way back, Miles City as I recall. Them ol' boys were hell on wheels!" cried Dusty Clanton.

Wade laughed, "If I remember rightly you did your fair share of hell raising!"

Dusty howled, "Sure wish I could raise some dust now. I'll be eighty two next birthday unless the Lord decides otherwise."

"None of us are getting any younger," laughed Wade.

'Where are the movie stars when you need them,' thought Alex. Dusty was okay, but in small doses.

Keeley seeing Alex's discomfort came over and rescued them. "Hey you guys, come over here, I want you to meet my mum and dad."

She whisked them away and seconds later, with another glass of bubbly in their hands they were introduced to Keeley's parents.

"Tis a grand affair, to be sure," said Jimmy O'Hara as he extended his hand.

"It is indeed," replied Wade as he shook Jimmy's hand. "This here's Alex, my wife."

"Pleased to meet you," he said gallantly as he took Alex's hand. "I'll be introducing you to Keeley's mother, Coleen."

"Hi, I'm Alex, nice to meet you both."

Jimmy and Coleen were as unpretentious as Wade and Alex had expected, and before long they were talking like long lost friends.

"To be sure, it's a beautiful day. Look yonder, tis God's creation," cried Jimmy, glass in hand as he pointed towards the distant horizon.

All four of them looked out across the sun deck and marvelled at the clear blue sky and the late afternoon sun as it glittered off the waters of the lake far below. "As beautiful as home, so it is," cried Jimmy.

"We're blessed so we are," responded Wade.

"You'll be having a dram or two, I take it?" asked Jimmy. "I can tell a drinking man when I see one."

"It has been known," replied Wade warming to the little Irishman.

"Get yourself over to Donegal, We'll be showing you a good time." Jimmy's exuberance and Irish charm had a way of disarming most folk and Wade and Alex were no exception.

"Be careful, I might take you up on that, so I might," replied Wade, his use of vernacular only apparent to Alex, who'd noted that he was unable to control that twinkle of mischief in his eyes. "You've a fine daughter," he added, hoping to disguise his little indiscretion.

"Why thank you sir," cried Jimmy.

"Come on now Jimmy, less drinking and more eating. Tis a long night ahead of us," said Coleen as she ushered her husband away, her eyes giving Alex and Wade an apologetic smile.

Alex and Wade smiled back, "Nice couple. I bet he's a lot of fun when the drink takes effect," cried Wade.

"Like you all," responded Alex, as she linked his arm and moved closer to the edge of the sun deck.

The sun was fast sinking behind the Rockies and an orange glow began spreading its fan like farewell.

"Jason sure picked his spot, its beautiful," said Alex softly.

Wade remained silent as he took in the beautiful sunset; a tear began forming in the corner of his eye. "Yes Alex, it's quite something." He paused, considering his words carefully. "I love you Alexandria, as much now as I did those many years ago."

"And I you," she responded, "You're still the most handsome man here. You can keep your movie stars, sportsmen and crippled up rodeo men, I've got the real deal." Her arm slipped around his waist. Wade bent his head down to meet hers and kissed her softly against the now flaming sky awash with oranges, purples, blues and red. It was the perfect setting.

"This here wedding has got me to thinking, well to be honest I've been thinking about it for a while now. Alex I want you to marry me!"

Surprised, Alex looked up at Wade, but words failed her as the magnitude of the question sank in.

"With everything that happened after we got back together it just never happened. We drifted along, but right now, here at Jason and Keeley's wedding I want you to do me the honour of marrying me for the second time."

"Oh Wade!" Finally the words burst from her lips, "Of course I'll marry you."

From the other side of the patio Jason nudged his new bride, "There must be something in the air," he said as they both looked across to the silhouetted figures of Wade and Alex, locked in an embrace against a flaming gold backdrop of sky.

Chapter 52

Montana

"Pa asked you to marry him! I think that's a wonderful idea," exclaimed Tara. "You did say yes?" she added as an afterthought.

"Of course I said yes," replied Alex, her face flushed with happiness. Never in her wildest dreams had she believed she could be so happy. The years just seemed to fall away as she remembered similar feelings she'd experienced in her youth. How was it possible?

"Where are you getting wed?" continued Tara.

"Your pa and I are getting married here at the ranch. We've decided on a low key affair, family and a few friends, nothing elaborate.

"How many bridesmaids?"

"How many guests?"

"But.. I thought you and Gramps were already married?

The questions were endless. Tara, Kaycee and Merri were on her case.

Alex smiled, "As I just said, it's a low key affair, as for bridesmaids, I hadn't really had much time to think about it."

"Honeymoon?" enquired Tara.

"Ah, that one's easy, we're spending a few days in Vegas for the National Finals," said Alex.

*   *   *

It was a bright crisp morning in early December, the perfect day for a winter wedding. Wade and Alex had elected to hold the ceremony in the open air chapel. They'd held several weddings at the ranch over the years. Jack and Tara's wedding being the first, then somehow it snowballed. One of the guests vacationing at the ranch had witnessed the wedding and must have thought it a neat idea. About a year later he phoned Alex and asked if they did conduct weddings other than for family. Alex had been a little taken aback, the idea had never occurred to her. But being the businesswoman that she was, she said, "Sure, let me get back to you with the details." It had proven an extra money earner and even locals had elected to have their nuptials said there underneath a Montana sky. An open air chapel erected hastily for the first wedding had been improved on over the years, though it remained open to all the elements.

Wade had his men erect the wedding arch and adorn it with holly, then they cleared away the snow from the ceremonial area and the seats were all put in place. From the porch steps to the altar a special forty feet of red carpet was unrolled and secured to the partly frozen ground by hammering in metal stakes. All in all it looked a picture with the backdrop of the valley and the towering snow covered peaks in the background.

Wade fidgeted awkwardly in the store bought suit that Alex had insisted he buy for Jason and Keeley's wedding. Neither had figured it would be doubling for his own wedding a few short months later. Tara had insisted on taking her pa into Bozeman to kit him out with suitable accessories, white shirt and grey tie, cuff links and new boots. Wade's steel grey hair and ruggedly tanned features surprisingly didn't look out of place in the dark blue suit, white shirt and tie. In fact they complemented each other. Wade still belied his age, now in his mid seventies; he could easily have been taken for a man ten years younger. In truth he was pleased with his appearance, something that surprised him, until he thought about the woman he was about to marry. Alex could have married anyone she wished, but she'd chosen him.

At his side, doing best man duties was Jack, his dark hair, now graying at the sides, looking equally distinguished. He'd also gone through the Reynolds women's makeover. Tara had insisted he looked his best.

Family and friends, dressed in their finest, filed into the open air chapel, and Wade began to fidget with his collar. He was seventy five, what call did he have to be nervous? Then the music began.

A roar of approval greeted Alex as she emerged from the house; she paused for a moment before she began the slow walk towards the wedding chapel. She wore a long red velvet gown trimmed with white. Her bare shoulders were protected from the crisp mountain air by a white mink stole, a gift from Tara and Jack. "Can't have goosebumps spoiling your special day," cried Tara.

At her side dressed in a black suit stood Fletcher, "Are you ready for this?" he questioned.

"You bet I am!"

A moment's hesitation as she negotiated the porch steps. She clung to Fletcher's arm for support, smiled and then they started the slow walk towards the open air chapel. Heads turned, and watched as Alex smiled radiantly at the crowd of well wishers. "It was," she was to tell Tara and Ruth later that day, "the best feeling in my entire life. I wanted it to go on forever."

Wade turned and smiled at his bride as she drew near. A tiny tear trickled from his eye as she stood next to him. "You look sensational," he whispered in her ear.

"You don't look so bad yourself," she replied.

* * *

The last time they'd visited Montezuma's it was a new concept in casinos. But now as they noted its tired façade, *it resembled an Aztec pyramid*, its stucco walls had seen better days. And although the inside lobby was decorated with carvings and designs from the Yucatan, those that came knew they were visiting for the last time. It was a prime piece of real estate and as such it was worth more being knocked down and rebuilt. Wade reflected how nothing ever seemed permanent anymore.

"If you like, we can cancel, go stay at the MGM, or the Mirage, even the Bellagio," said Wade.

"Here's fine, I like familiarity. We were happy the last time we were here, why not this time," laughed Alex.

"Well if you're sure?"

"I'm sure," she replied.

Once checked in they made their way across the still magnificent twelve story atrium with its vines and foliage draping down from balconies, it brought back evocative memories. Alex reflected on how this time was so different from there last visit. It had seemed so tentative, getting back together after a few years apart, it had seemed so fragile. But this time it seemed so right, so permanent. They'd known each other for close on half a century, yet she hadn't known just how much Wade loved her until he proposed that second time. 'At sixty five I should have been thinking about putting my feet up by the fire, but that handsome hunk of a husband had other plans, and the years just fell away.' Her thoughts were many, varied and pleasant as they took the elevator up to the sixteenth floor.

"It just doesn't get any better than this," she exclaimed after Wade had tipped the bellboy and placed his hand on her shoulder and both of them stared out of the large picture window at a sea of neon.

They arrived at the Thomas and Mack Center for round five of the competition. Tickets for each day's events were hard to come by, but Wade had many contacts, none the least was Jason Connors. When Wade phoned a week after Jason and Keeley's honeymoon and gave him the news, he'd been delighted if a little bemused.

"Darn it Wade, I always thought you were married."

"We were Jason, it's a long story, I'll tell you about it sometime."

"You want tickets, no problem. It'll be my wedding present to you both."

The glittering lights of the area gave way to a pretty cowgirl riding a palomino into the stadium whilst brandishing the stars and stripes. A roar of approval filled the arena as the girl did a full circle. Wade and Alex watched as four times world saddle bronc champion Billy Etbauer riding Snuff Sundance won the round title, his second in that year's finals. The team roping, one of Wade's favorite events saw seven times team roping champs Speed Williams and Rich Skelton win that round, their second in the competition. Molly Powell from Sims, Montana had the fastest run in the barrel racing completing the clover leaf in 13.82 seconds placing her in first place.

By the time the night's events were over Wade and Alex were deep in conversation with others, over who would win the overall events.

"My money's on Trevor Brazile to win his third all-round title," cried Alex, excitedly.

"Maybe, but he'll be in big company if he can pull it off. Ty Murray, Larry Mahan and Jim Shoulders to name three," replied Wade.

Later that evening they played a little Blackjack and Alex won a hundred bucks at poker before Wade pulled her away from the tables. A few glasses of wine later and a very mellow couple rode the elevator up to the sixteenth floor.

By round seven, team ropers Clay Tryan and Michael Jones were taking first spot, Tryan was one of four Montana cowboys to win their rounds that day. Jed Harbinger, now a sprightly eighty five shouted across to Wade and Alex to join him for a drink. The pair duly obliged and soon got re-acquainted with a number of old friends. Billy Maynard, now pushing sixty was there with his third wife Josie, and he was still looking. Wade and Alex stifled a laugh.

"Whatever floats your boat," cried Alex when they were alone later that night.

"Billy was always one for the ladies," laughed Wade. The drink was taking affect, as he found himself walked back down memory lane. "Alex; where have all the years gone?"

Seeing Billy had brought it all back, "Sam Briscoe died of the cancer five years ago, and Jake, poor Jake, I heard he drank himself to death. From what Billy told me, it was more than a week before they found him, dead in a seedy motel in El Paso."

Later that night, when Alex was asleep he poured himself a straight bourbon, threw in some ice and stepped out onto his balcony. He hadn't thought about Jake in a coon's age. The man had literally dropped off the map. Wade reflected how close he had come to doing the very same thing. If it hadn't have been for the shooting at Lucy's cantina in Nogales, the subsequent flight with Jack and the mortally wounded Johnny, and the month spent in the cave hiding out, Wade was sure he'd have drunk himself into an early grave. As it happened that month spent in quiet solitude had focused his mind. Johnny was dead, leaving Wade and Jack to figure out what to do with their lives. They'd talked of dreams, of what might have been, they'd talked of a fresh start, a chance to start all over. It was a tall ambition, but both men saw it as an adventure into the unknown. For them it had paid off. Together they'd helped mend each others lives and for that Wade was eternally grateful.

Seeing Harbinger had reawaken Wade's yearnings for that adventure; he was too old of course, but it didn't cost anything to dream. He tossed his drink down, rose from his chair and walked unsteadily to the corner of the bed. There he looked down at Alex's sleeping form, and knew beyond a shadow of a doubt that he'd lived the life, and that he was the luckiest man in the world.

Final's day at the Thomas and Mack Center saw Speed Williams and Rich Skelton take the title of team ropers for an eighth time. Alex won her bet, Trevor Brazile won the all round for an impressive third time in succession, Billy Etbauer won the saddle bronc for a record fifth time and amongst the first time winners of the National Rodeo Finals, Dustin Elliot won the Bull Riding while Kelly Kaminski of Bellville, Texas won the Barrel Racing.

*   *   *

As the taxi cab drew away from the forecourt of Montezuma's Hotel and Casino, Alex and Wade gave it one last sad look.

"It's been wonderful, I've enjoyed every minute. But mostly being with you is what made it," said Alex softly.

"No honey, it was down to you. I'm shrinking as the years pass, but having you by my side these last few days has made me feel ten feet tall."

"Oh Wade."

As they turned away from the hotel, they could truly say that the Montezuma had during its last days made at least one couple's honeymoon truly memorable.

Chapter 53

Montana. 2005

The New Year came in much as the old one had left. Snow lay thick and deep over the Bitterroots and the valley just glistened with the reflected rays from the wintery sun.

"Another year," cried Wade as he crept up beside Alex and placed his arms around her shoulders. Alex smiled at the comforting warmth of her man's embrace. Together they looked out at the picture postcard view of the mountains.

"We're lucky where we live. I know others feel the same, Keeley's pa for one, but most people don't get a choice where they live. I know winters are tough and our summers are short, but I wouldn't swop it for the world," said Alex. She was, Wade noted, in a very philosophical mood.

"I couldn't agree more," he replied. "Seeing old Jed Harbinger got me to thinkin'."

"That's worrying," quipped Alex.

"I'm getting on in years, but aside from my time with you and the kids, I've never enjoyed myself as much as when I was on the trail. The time I spent with Jack, and before him Johnny, are forever etched in my memory. I just wish I could do it all again."

"I know, I have the same thoughts too, but I realise my capabilities, unlike you. You're nearly seventy five; you still run this ranch like you were only sixty. Most men your age would be content to put their feet up, but not you. Be grateful that you can still do what you do."

"I guess you're right, but I'll be darned if I'll ever put my feet up."

Little did Wade know that before the year was out he'd have seen more than his share of adventure and danger.

An early thaw saw ranch activity increase dramatically, leaving Wade no time to ponder his youth. Spring roundup, calving and moving the herds to fresh pasture took up most of his daylight hours. Alex was right he worked alongside his fellow ranch hands like a man half his age. She also noted that he was never happier than when he had half a ton of horse flesh under him, getting him to slow down was going to be harder than she thought. Because he now thought of her working guest ranch as an integral part of a modern ranch, he'd sometimes volunteer his services. The guests got a real kick out of having Wade around, he was to them during their week cowboying; the real McCoy

Every once in a while he'd take a party up over the Continental Divide to Chief Joseph's Lookout. It made a break with routine and to be honest Wade liked to socialise on occasion with the guests. It was mid July when Alex asked him to take a party of eight up over the Divide. Accompanying him on the trip was Bud Angel, chief wrangler and Blaine Henry who was now head cook and bottle washer for the Crazy AW outfit. Together they made up a three man crew to cater for the needs of a party of eight, five men and three women.

"It should be fun," he said cheerily to Alex as he and Blaine climbed into the pickup for their journey to the trailhead. Bud had taken the sedan to the various pickup points at Dillon's hotels.

"You take care, you hear!" cried Alex.

* * *

Wade and Blaine unpacked the pickup and began saddling up the horses for the ride up to the Lookout. He checked his watch.

"I'd expect them within the hour," he said, more to himself than Blaine.

Forty five minutes later, they saw a trail of dust and guessed that Bud had made good time.

"They were all there waiting, their duffels packed and ready to go, apart from two, I'll fill you in on them later." exclaimed Bud, in way of explaining his prompt arrival.

*   *   *

After Wade had introduced himself and the guests had signed their waiver forms the group were partnered up with their horses. Once saddled, Wade rode in front of the group and explained the rules of good horsemanship. As Bud so eloquently put it, "He scares the shit out of them!"

"I can see some of you appear a mite nervous, well that's a good thing. As you get acclimatised to your horse and he to you, you'll start feeling a sight more confident, and that's a good thing too! Just don't get complacent! You're here to have a fun week and we'll do our best to make that happen. Now let's ride!"

The five hour ride up the mountain, took in some pretty spectacular scenery along the way, but by the time the group reached base camp they were feeling a mite saddle sore and some were a little tuckered out. After unsaddling their horses, Wade encouraged them to give there horses a good rub down.

"They sweat see. Left to their own devices they'd probably roll around in the dirt, but they deserve better than that. It's a treat they'll fully appreciate."

Wade made it his business to explain every time about how caring for your horse benefited its rider. Most people understood and appreciated the knowledge, though some, not many, but some thought that grooming their horse was beneath them. Wade was glad to see that despite this groups' own weariness there was no exceptions, they all began rubbing down their horses.

"Forming a bond with your horse is far more important than you'd think," Wade added as further encouragement.

Wade was thankful the group were worn out and too tired to party as he had to be up early the following morning to meet the two latecomers back at the trailhead. According to Bud, the couple had phoned the ranch and explained that their hire car had broken down and they were going to be a day late in arriving. Alex had said she'd pick them up from their hotel the following morning. "All part of the service," she'd said through gritted teeth.

*   *   *

"What have we got here?" joshed Wade when he arrived at the trail head.

"These two guys are Rick and Sean, they're from England, so go gentle on them, you hear," chided Alex.

"Yeah, Alex, but they're a couple of goddamn Limeys!" joshed Wade in return.

"We're more than that Wade, we're legend!" cried Rick the shorter of the two as he extended his hand in greeting.

Wade's face broke into a wide grin as he took the offered hand and shook it. "You two fellers ride some?"

"Not as much as you, but we've rode a few miles without being thrown," chipped in Sean.

"Well I'm mighty pleased at that boys, because we got a hell of a way to go before chow time. So let's get you two mounted and we'll be on our way."

*   *   *

An hour into the ride and Wade was satisfied he wasn't riding with any novices. "Okay boys, you've shown me you can ride, now we're gonna quicken the pace if you're up for it. Any problems don't be afraid to holler out."

"You got it!" cried Rick.

381

With a quicker pace they made camp around five o'clock. Blaine walked out into the clearing to greet them. "Weren't expecting you before dusk. Coffee's on."

"Well that makes a change, "joked Sean. "Most places usually serve up dish water, slightly warm."

"Oh, ours is the real McCoy, we serve it piping hot," continued Blaine.

* * *

It was an hour before dusk when Bud led the group back into camp. Tired and saddle sore the group dismounted and led their mounts into the corral. The talk was about the day long trip down to turquoise lake, the small herd of deer, the coyote, the flora and fauna. It was one of Wade's favourite rides, and he was sorry to have missed it. It seemed to bring the best out in people. From what he could tell this group seemed to have gelled from the start. There was a lawyer and his nineteen year old son from Phoenix, a couple from Los Angeles, real estate written all over them, a tall willowy Dutchman in his late forties and his rather younger wife, a couple from the East coast and of course the two Englishmen, who'd quickly introduced themselves. It was a mixed bag, but somewhere along the trail they'd all begun to form a common bond.

* * *

It was a couple of days later around the campfire when Rick, one of the Englishmen said, "We've done several horseback trips over the years but the scenery on this trip has surpassed anything else we've seen." Wade who'd taken them to Turquoise lake the second day in, made a mental note. Rick wasn't finished with his praise, "That's not to say the other trips were dull, far from it, but I'd have to say this beats even the San Juans in Colorado."

"Tell that to Alex at the end of the trail, it'll please her no end," said Wade.

There was a chill to the night air and most crept nearer the fire as first Bud, then Blaine began regaling them all with tall tales and downright lies. A couple of bottles were retrieved from several tents and a guitar was brought to the proceedings. Sean the noisier of the two Englishmen took a hold of the guitar and began strumming a few chords before breaking into a couple of songs he'd written and then Bud Angel with the sweetest voice imaginable sung a few cowboy songs, starting with 'I Ride an Old Paint' and finishing with 'Streets of Laredo'.

With creative juices flowing Greg from LA said they ought to write a song about their time up at Chief Joseph's Lookout. The competitive nature in Sean rose to the fore as he suggested they form teams to see who could write the best song. Drinks were passed around and before long two clearly defined groups grabbed pen and paper and began writing. Even Wade and Blaine were drawn into the contest. Greg was the first to finish.

T'was late in September
when we set out for a ride

We were none of us
real cowboys but we all really tried

The day grew longer
and the saddle wore thin

We came upon the camp
and it wondered where we'd been

We were blessed with great weather
and occasionally took a piss

Yup I gotta tell you
it just doesn't get any better than this

The views were thrilling
and the fishing pretty fine

For the next 5 days

fellas, this mountains mine

*It was late the 2nd day
when much to my surprise*

*In rode two more cowboys
both with blood shot eyes*

*We pitched horseshoes
and told all the jokes*

*We sang round the campfire
yep these are true mountain folks*

*We told lies from our youth
and took pictures of deer*

*Only Greg's aching head
telling who drank all the beer*

*Well the trip's almost over
but the memories will last long*

*Yep here in the mountains
you can't never go wrong*

*With these words I'll leave you
because we've done so much*

*Let's not leave these mountains
without staying in touch.*

Then Sean not to be out done gave the group a rendering of his song.

I rode a paint down
The hard mountain trail

Round each corner hopin'
Are guide wouldn't fail

We entered camp
It was such a thrill

It was only surpassed
By a cowboy's will

Oh oh the mountains!

I found myself in an
Unusual place when

I had to reckon my
Time and my place

I enjoyed the finest
Man could provide

But there was still
A burning deep inside

Oh, oh the mountains!

The smell of fresh fire wood
Floats through the air

The men are all gathered
With grease in their hair

Its part of the life that a

Cowboy lives

It's part of the mountain
That we all love so much

It's made even better, by our
Friends, so lets all stay in touch

Oh, oh the mountains!

Wade was asked to judge which was the better, "That's easy, they were both as good as each other. It's an honourable draw." Diplomacy ruled the day until Wade added, "That darm chorus, Oh, oh the mountains, that was pretty catchy."

For the next half hour there was no living with Sean, he was full of it. Wade had to smile to himself, since day one he knew this trip was going to be memorable, he just didn't know just how memorable it was going to become.

* * *

With two days left on the trip, Wade and Bud took the group down the side of the mountain and across a couple of shallow river crossings before descending into a meadow of wild flowers deep into Idaho. Then they rode through a spectacular grove of golden shimmering Aspen before stopping for lunch by a magnificent waterfall. It was the perfect finale to a wonderful trip as the sun shone down from its lofty heights amidst a clear blue sky.

Exhilarated by the day's events the group rode back into camp just as dusk was about to settle. Wade turned in his saddle and looked back the way they'd come and was rewarded by the most majestic of sunsets he'd ever seen. The group in turn, retrieved their cameras from their saddle bags and began snapping pictures of the fast fading spectacular. The gentle clicking of cameras brought Wade back to reality. For almost a week he'd begun to thing of this group as more than just a bunch of tourists. He smiled wryly, Alex's brainchild it might have been, but it was one hell of a legacy to share.

*   *   *

They were unsaddling and grooming their horse when it happened. A member of the group hurriedly pulled his saddle from his horse's back and swung round suddenly, catching the rear of another horse with the saddle horn. The sudden jolt caused the startled horse to kick out, catching the Dutchman a glancing blow against his thigh, knocking him off balance. His young wife screamed and the group scattered to the four winds. A melee of panicking horses crashed and bucked, turning and spinning in all directions. The Dutchman recognising his plight stared into the blinding dust cloud and made a dive for safety. His instinctive reaction saved him from injury or possible death as he found himself outside of the corral.

His young wife was frozen to the spot amongst the excited animals. Bud seeing the danger rushed in and pulled her to safety, then he tried pacifying the crazed horses. He walked in amongst them and before he knew it he was knocked to the ground. Wade on hearing the melee turned towards Blaine, together they raced across the clearing and into the corral area. But it was too late to save Bud from being stomped on several times.

Wade distracted the animals and slowly began to calm them while Blaine dragged the injured Bud clear. At first it looked like Bud had got away with superficial injuries, but he was struggling to breathe, his face contorted into a grimace of extreme pain. Richard Thornton, the quieter of the two Englishmen knelt down beside Wade and the injured Bud. Without asking he took charge, and began examining the injured cowboy.

"Oh fuck! It's not my field of expertise but I'd say Bud's sustained a punctured lung. I'm going to need to ease the pressure."

He looked up from the prone man and seemed to stare into space. His mind racing with what he had to do.

"Wade, we need to carry Bud closer to the fire. We'll need blankets; a sharp sterilised knife and someone grab that shower hose!" he shouted as he pointed to the improvised shower cubicle.

Without questioning his commands Wade and Blaine carried Bud as gently as they could to the warmth of the fire.

"I need light, as much as you can give me," shouted Thornton. "Where's that shower hose, and knife!" he cried.

Bud's face had turned gray and his breathing was becoming very laboured. He was in a bad way and Thornton knew he had to work fast or the wrangler would die a very painful death. Going on instinct, the area of the wound and little else, he judged that it was his left lung that had collapsed.

With the sharp bladed knife now sterilised by 100% proof Yukon Jack, Canadian bourbon, Richard Thornton took a deep breath and made the incision in Bud's left side just behind the rib cage. Seconds later he was slowly threading a section of shower hose into the wound.

All Wade and the others could do was hold their collective breath and pray. Almost immediately a rush of air escaped from the shower hose.

"Right," said a very relieved Thornton, "We need to keep him warm and he needs proper medical attention as soon as possible."

"How long?" questioned Wade, knowing that there was no signal for cell phones this far away.

"I don't know, maybe hours, possibly longer, I just don't know."

"I'll ride for help; we've a radio transmitter at the trailhead, its five hours ride, have we got that long?"

"I don't know, maybe, yes."

Wade raced to the corral and began saddling up his bay mare. Blaine raced after him.

"Wade, its five hours in daylight, it's nigh on impossible in the dark."

"What do you expect me to do? I can't let him die without at least trying."

"Well let me go, no disrespect, but I'm forty years younger than you," said Blaine

"Thanks, I appreciate the sentiment, but I know this trail better than most." He chose not to mention Blaine's gammy leg, a legacy from an accident two years earlier. "You've only been up it three times this season. It's best I go," Wade swung into the saddle. "Take care of everything; give the doc whatever assistance you can."

There was barely enough light for Wade to negotiate his way out of the camp. After that he was relying on his horse to ride by instinct and a few soft commands from his rider. Luck rode with Wade for the first hour and a half, as the full moon cast its eerie light across the great monoliths of granite, casting shadows of demons found only in the minds of man. Then for an hour Wade was enveloped in darkness as the vast density of trees and a giant peak blocked the moon's light.

Wade's horse lost her footing on the shale and scrambled to recover her balance. The old rancher, seasoned by a lifetime in the saddle hung on, trusting to the animal's instinct for survival. It was a close shave as Wade listened to the loosen shale as it cascaded a hundred and fifty feet to the waters below. He made slow going on the steep decline, trusting again to the sure footedness of his mare. Wade's face glistened with sweat as the moon reappeared and cast its blue grey light upon the waters of the stream. Crossing it he began to think he'd make it before daybreak. He half whispered half shouted encouragement to the bay as he pushed her onwards. Her laboured breathing told him she was close to giving up, "Not now ol' gal, just a mite further," he coaxed. Man and horse stumbled on for another agonisingly half hour before Wade eventually caught sight of the trailhead. "Nearly there gal, you can make it."

Wade slipped from the saddle and within a minute he was through to the emergency services. Quickly he explained in as much detail Bud Angel's injuries and the location. Because Chief Joseph's Lookout wasn't on any survey maps he gave his co-ordinates. A helicopter rescue team was readied and within a short time a paramedic crew were on their way to pick him up en-route.

A sudden movement alerted Wade and he turned around to see his horse stumble. He raced to her side as she slid to the ground. Wade coaxed her to get up, but it was in vain. The mare was all in, and nothing he could do would make her stand up. He grabbed a pail and filled it from the water barrel. Soaking his bandana he tried getting the horse to drink, but it was no use. Tearfully Wade watched as the light slowly faded from her eyes. She died as she had lived, heroically. Over the years she'd given him great service, always sure footed, faithful and patient and in her last desperate ride she'd not been found wanting. Wade slowly stood up and wiped at his eyes before slowly walking back to the trailhead.

* * *

Richard Thornton, tired from lack of sleep was the first to hear the rotor blades of the chopper. He glanced down at the body of Bud Angel and for the briefest of seconds thought the man dead, but his eyelids flickered into life.

"It's the rescue team, you're going to be okay," Rick said encouragingly.

At once a flurry of activity hit the camp as bleary eyed guests and Blaine Henry waved at the helicopter as it set down on an improvised landing pad. Two paramedics raced from the chopper and immediately took charge. Half an hour later the helicopter took off and headed for the general hospital at Dillon.

Wade looking more than his age walked slowly across to Richard Thornton. The Englishman stood up from the half crouch he'd been in most of the night.

"What did they say were Bud's chances?" asked Thornton.

Wade half smiled, "They think he's got more than a fifty percent chance. That's all they'd say," he replied. Clasping Richard on the shoulder, he added, "Whatever the outcome, you done one hell of a job, Doc."

It was Richard Thornton's turn to smile, "I'm not a doctor, not in the way you think. I'm a veterinary surgeon!"

* * *

Bud Angel's life hung in the balance over the next seventy two hours. A lesser man might not have made it, but his general health and fitness honed by years of manual labour contributed to his eventual recovery. As to be expected it made the local papers and media, and for the next week or so Richard Thornton the veterinary surgeon from England and the septuagenarian rancher from the Big Hole Valley were fêted as heroes.

* * *

As the year came to a close, Alex reflected on what a very eventful and enjoyable year it had been. Every aspect of the ranch had turned a profit, not a big one, but a profit, nonetheless. Ranching like farming depended on many things falling into place. A little profit here meant the ranch's future was guaranteed for yet another year. Ranching was a full time business and it took blood, sweat and the occasional tears. It wasn't everyone's ideal, but for the like of Wade and Alex; it was what they got up in the morning for.

Alex had never questioned Tara and Jack's decision to remain a small operation, as it allowed time for them to follow other pursuits, and already Kaycee was leaning towards an academic career. Jack had insisted that his children should be open-minded about their future. The horse ranch was a profitable outfit, manageable with fewer overheads than the cattle business, and the prospect of time off on an occasion more likely. Not that Jack took the opportunity that often; for he'd proven to be a shrewd operator with a fine business brain. Knowing that the Claymore Ranch was in good hands, allowed Alex to sleep well at nights.

The only cloud that Alex could see was the one hanging *on an occasion* over Tara. She still smarted over having to share the same State as Shelby Holbrook. Alex had tried talking with Tara, but it fell on deaf ears.

"Just when I think I've got her out of my system, that bitch appears in the papers at this or that charity function."

"Turn yourself off," advised Alex.

"It's not that easy. All I'll say about it is; that bitch had better not catch me within arms length!"

Alex sought comfort in Tara's last words on the subject. She felt the same hurt as her daughter and had wanted to see the woman get her just deserts, but Alex soon realised that a life time of hate wasn't going to bring Taw back. All it did was gnaw at her soul, but as the years passed Alex felt that hatred slipping away, she only hoped Tara would someday feel the same.

Chapter 54

Montana. 2006

As the New Year of 2006 took hold and spring began its yearly transformation, Alex looked back over the old year's events. It wasn't long after Wade's midnight ride that he was asked to appear on several local television channels. His dry sense of humour, his devotion to the American Way and his downright stubbornness about everything new, brought Wade a semi celebrity status, so much so that a local television station requested doing a feature on the ranch, the history and the future.

Wade said he wasn't interested, but Alex always hungry for ways to promote the ranch, saw the potential of the forty minute documentary.

"It'll put us well and truly on the map," she'd said as she cajoled him into accepting the film company's offer.

"When are they figuring on shooting this feature?" he'd replied half-heartedly. He knew he couldn't hold out for long when Alex put her mind to something.

"Spring roundup!" Alex replied and waited for the flak that was sure to follow.

It did, but when the noise and hullabaloo had died down Wade reluctantly agreed, stating that he'd give one interview, lasting no more than five minutes and not a second over.

Alex agreed.

The television crew filmed several interviews, shot film of early morning scenes, cattle being driven to summer pastures, the roundup itself and all that went with it, shots of the ranch, the Bitterroots and the sky, all in all they were there for around two weeks filming all facets of ranch life. At a private viewing of the completed film even Wade was impressed by the beauty of the feature.

"It's just a pity they couldn't film the aches, the pains, the early mornings, the cold, then we'd have something to show," he'd half joked.

"Then it wouldn't have been entertaining," replied Alex.

The documentary had had a profound affect on him, it had brought into sharp focus that one day the ranch would pass into the hands of strangers. To an outsider you'd hardly notice a change, but Alex saw it for what it was. There was no use talking to him about it, it was something he had to work out for himself. As it happens, it was young Merri several weeks later that brought him back to reality. Without realising it she rekindled the flame, not strictly true, that flame was destined to always remain alight, but it did rekindle the quest for knowledge, and the thirst for adventure.

"We've been doing a project at school about wild horses. Something to do with the BLM whatever that is!" said Merri one weekend in late spring, when she was over visiting with her grandparents.

"That's the Bureau of Land Management," replied Wade, pleased that she was talking about something that he knew a little about. "You see the Mustang was introduced to the Americas by the Spanish in the 1500's. Over the centuries they multiplied and in the early 1900's they were estimated to be around two million wild horses roaming the plains."

"Wow! Mrs Fowler never told us that," exclaimed Merri.

Wade thought about whether he should go on. Mrs Fowler, who ever she was, might not touch on the more unsavoury side of managing wild horses. But his grand daughter had brought the subject up and she deserved to know the facts; warts and all.

"However, since 1900 the government saw the Mustang as a resource to be used as they saw fit. Some were used by the military but a great proportion were slaughtered and sold on as horse meat and pet food."

"Gramps, that's gross!"

Wade put his hands up in mock surrender, "Don't shoot the messenger," he protested. "It wasn't until 1959 before a law was passed to protect the mustangs."

"Thank God!"

"Do you want me to go on?" asked Wade a little concerned. Alex had given him a knowing look, and poor Merri looked slightly distraught.

"I brought it up Gramps," she said, appearing far more grown up than her twelve years.

"Okay," said Wade with a look towards Alex for approval. "In 1971 the government brought in the Wild Free-Roaming Horse and Burro Act. The act afforded protection for certain established herds of horses and burros."

"Where does the BLM come in?"

"The Bureau of Land Management is responsible for the protection of these animals under the 1971 act."

"So the horses can multiply like before?"

"Not exactly . . . ." Wade looked to Alex for support, none was forthcoming. "These herds of wild horses have to be managed, they can't be allowed to over populate public rangelands."

"You mean, they're okay unless they trespass onto grassland that you have your cattle roaming over."

Alex smiled wickedly at Wade, knowing the hole he was digging was getting bigger and bigger.

"I don't have a say in it."

"So, if they over populate the government have a cull."

"No," said Wade brightly. "They have what they call a capture program. Every now and then they capture a certain quota of these feral horses and put them up for adoption. Your Pa's bought some that way."

Alex looked disapprovingly as she saw her husband trying desperately to divert Merri's attention towards her own father.

"So what's the 'Burns rider'?"

Just about then Wade would have willingly strangled Mrs Fowler. The woman was an obvious agitator against government policy. "It's an amendment brought in to allow the culling of certain horses, namely horses that are older than ten years and horses that have been offered up for adoption three times without success."

"So it's a bill to legislate for the wilful slaughter of wild horses."

Wade saw no other way to wrap it up. "In a word, yes," he said. "But there has been considerable opposition to the bill."

"How do you feel about it Gramps?"

"I feel as you feel. The mustang is a symbol of our freedom, and as such should be allowed to run wild and free as nature intended. But, and it's a big but. If any creature is allowed to multiply, to do as it pleases, then eventually it will be the author of its own destruction. These capture programs are designed to keep our wild horses running free for centuries to come."

From the comfort of the kitchen, Alex listened, proud that Wade had taken the time and patience to explain in great detail what for a twelve year old was a difficult subject.

During the next few weeks Wade pondered his conversation with Merri. She'd shown great interest and maturity when told about the BLM and the capture program. Which was as it should be, Merri having shown more interest in running the family horse ranch than her older sibling. That was off course if Jack and Tara ever decided to put their feet up. It was with this thought in mind that Wade paid Jack a visit.

"It's Merri, she's been chewing the fat about the capture program."

"You've been getting it too," replied Jack.

"Yeah well it got me to thinking about the old days, in particular my first horse drive with Johnny, and then our drive up from Jed Harbinger's. Do you remember how you felt when you drove those horses down Main in Miles City that morning all those years ago?"

Jack smiled knowingly, that moment was one he'd cherish forever.

"Do I!"

"Well Merri going on about the wild horses got me to thinking. There's somewhere in the region of thirty thousand horses in holding facilities all over the country."

Jack looked warily at his father-in-law; the old man usually had a point to make. It wasn't long in coming.

"The Pryor Mountain Wild Horse Range, with its program of horse management seems a likely place for us to take Merri and Kaycee, if she's a mind. We could go during summer break. I think it's only right for Merri to have a balanced view of how things work."

"If you're thinking what I think you're thinking forget about it," said Jack.

Wade ignored Jack's words, "We'd have to run it passed Tara, but I've a few contacts at the Pryor Mountains. What I figured was, we could take the girls, get someone to show them around, give them a basic knowledge of the program."

"And that's all?" asked Jack.

"Well we could take a look at the stock, maybe purchase one or two."

"Stop right there!" exclaimed Jack.

What Jack hadn't planned on was Merri lingering in the back room. She'd heard every word.

"I think it's a great idea Gramps!"

Wade smiled. Jack knew he was on to a loser.

*　　*　　*

School was out. The summer temperatures were in the high nineties when Wade, Jack, Kaycee and Merri set off for the Pryor Mountains. It had started out as just a day, maybe two, but as the event drew closer, Wade and Merri began working on Jack. When they got Tara and a slightly reluctant Kaycee on board, Jack's defences crumbled.

It started out as one, but developed into ten horses adopted from the Pryor Mountain Horse Reserve. Wade insisted on paying, but he also insisted on having the last word about which horses they were purchasing. It was only after the horses had been vaccinated and were ready for transportation that he suggested driving the horses across country; Jack stepped in and said no.

"I understand where you're coming from, and yeah it would be some drive, and yes I'd get a kick out of it myself. But these ain't the good old days, back then we hadn't a choice and our only responsibility was to ourselves. I know Kaycee and Merri are perfectly capable of handling the drive, but there's no need, we've the transportation at our disposal."

"Yeah, I guess you're right, I wasn't really thinking straight. We're dealing with wild horses and the terrain could be mighty tricky. I guess I forgot myself for a moment; I only thought that Kaycee and Merri would love the experience."

"I'm sure they would, and that's why we ain't telling em."

Wade saw the wisdom in his son-in-law's words. He also took note that in a small insignificant exchange of words a symbolically monumental handing over of the reins of his family had taken place. Jack could so easily have given in to the whimsical ideas of an old man, but he'd stood firm in his protection of his family. Wade smiled to himself, safe in the knowledge that his family would be in safe hands when he eventually rode off into the sunset.

Wade had enjoyed four wonderfully rewarding days with his granddaughters as they rode freely with the herd cutting out the horses. The last words on the four day trip were best left to Merri on the journey home.

"Gee Gramps, this weekend was so memorable in more ways than I can explain, but riding alongside the two men I love most in the world is what made it."

Even Kaycee, who was still fighting with her choice of careers, was moved by the whole weekend.

*　*　*

"Now the work starts little lady," said Wade when the feral horses were safely in the corral at the Claymore Ranch. "You got the rest of the summer to work these horses. I know you've got a way with horses, it ain't conventional, but it works for you. For every one that you tame, I'll pay you a hundred bucks."

"Really Gramps!"

"You're darn tootin' I will. I chose those mares carefully. In your hands I'm sure you'll turn them into right smart cow ponies, maybe some will be saddle broke enough for Grams dude ranch."

"A hundred bucks!" exclaimed Kaycee. "You'll need help," she declared.

Merri smiled, "Sure Kaycee, but you'll have to earn every dollar."

Wade looked over at Jack, "Takes after her mother, that one."

"She sure does," replied Jack.

*   *   *

By the end of summer, Jack and the girls delivered nine saddle broke horses to the Crazy AW.

"That's nine hundred bucks Gramps," cried Merri excitedly.

"Only nine?" questioned Wade as he inspected the horses.

"Yeah, I kept that little Mustang, the dark tanned one. Her name's Flame. She's mine." Her words were final, to the point and businesslike.

"She'll go far," laughed Wade as he counted out a thousand dollars,

Alex and Tara looked on proudly as Merri took the offered money and handed half to Kaycee.

"I wasn't expecting this much!" exclaimed Kaycee.

"You earned it, besides I've Flame too."

*   *   *

No one could have been prouder of their grand kids than Wade. During the summer Kaycee finally decided on law, while Merri was hell bent on carrying on the family business. It was a pity both of his grand children didn't feel the same way about the land. It would have reassured Wade about the future of his own ranch. He guessed his grand kids were very much like his own. One loved the land, the other loved music. All in all, Wade reflected how lucky he and Alex were at having such a fine family.

*   *   *

That summer break in the company of his two grand kids, stuck out as the highlight of the year. Though young in age both Kaycee and Merri showed great maturity, especially Merri. She was born to ride; she was in truth a real chip off the old block. It was around that time that Wade realised his age. When his kids were growing up he was too busy running the ranch to enjoy them as much as he'd have liked. Perhaps if he'd spent more time with Taw he'd have understood his son much better. When he mentioned to Alex his regrets she put him wise.

"Most men, when they're young spend more time working, bringing home the bacon. You shouldn't reproach yourself."

"I get so much enjoyment out of those kids," he said as he looked across the corral at Merri and her horse Flame, as she put him through his paces.

"I'm getting on in years; I've so much more I'd like to impart to them both."

Chapter 55

Montana. 2007

Wade's good intentions took a back seat as winter closed in on the valley. Feeding the herds took priority over most other things. Out before light and back after dark. Hay distribution was heavy work, some of them bales weighed eight hundred pounds, and that's the ones that were thawed out. Another key job during winter was maintenance of all the varied machinery. Cowboying wasn't just about punching cattle, being a fair hand at mechanics was part and parcel of a cowboy's life, along with cleaning the calving sheds and general repairing of barns and outbuilding. Like most things in life preparation was the key. Running a successful ranch needed good management, as Wade knew only to well. With winter on the back foot it wasn't long before calving and eventually the spring roundup would take centre stage.

Around about that time Alex reminded Wade of his pledge to impart more knowledge to his grand kids.

"What did you tell me last year about spending time with Kaycee and Merri?" she said one spring morning.

"Sorry," he said absentmindedly.

"Your good intentions," she prompted.

Finally Wade understood where she was coming from. "Good point, it kinda slipped my mind."

"I thought it had. The Bucking Horse Sale in Miles City is on in a little over a week's time. Maybe we can take them there?" suggested Alex.

"Them?" questioned Wade.

"Yeah, I didn't mean Merri on her own."

"Kaycee! She's actually showing an interest?"

"Don't get your hopes up. She's hell bent on a law degree. Nothing's changed there. She just thought it might be fun," replied Alex.

Wade thought about it for a few moments, the last few months had been full on, not that he minded, he was never happier than when working the ranch. But, he reflected, Alex had a point.

"Yeah maybe we can," he replied with a smile.

Wade figured that the Bucking Horse Sale at Miles City was probably the best place for young Merri to learn more about the horse trade and have some fun into the bargain. Over the years the event had become more family orientated, though the evenings could still cut up a little rough. Wade suspected that after a full day's entertainment both Merri and Kaycee might be a little too tired to indulge.

Wade phoned the Olive Hotel later that day and found to his surprise that the hotel had a couple of cancellations. "Luck is with us," he said to an amazed Alex.

The Bucking Horse Sale was all it was purported to be. They arrived a little after noon and after checking into the hotel, threw themselves into the action. Wade had guessed right about the girls, they were both plumb tuckered out by eight thirty and Alex said she'd sit with them while Wade, Jack and Tara sampled the nightlife in the Montana Bar and Range Riders.

Tara and Jack lost themselves in the crowd, chatting with some old friends from Hamilton one minute, then catching up with the gossip in Darby the next. Well at least Tara was, Jack was more preoccupied with remembering how down in the stockyards he'd first caught sight of Tara, only he didn't know who she was at the time. He smiled to himself as he sneaked a crafty peek at his wife, still deep in conversation. 'Yeah,' he thought quietly to himself, 'she ain't changed one damn bit.'

Wade too, was lost in his thoughts as he sank a Miller Genuine. "Yessiree!" exclaimed Wade to no one in particular. 'Miles City and the Bucking Horse Sale sure as hell generates many memories.' Johnny J and Wade had seen the elephant in the Montana Bar on more than one occasion. 'Hell raising they called it back then, drinking, laughing, gambling, dancing with pretty girls, oh and fighting. "Yessiree," exclaimed Wade one more time. Both, he and Johnny J had found themselves in the odd brawl over the years, been thrown in the city jail to cool off a time or two. It was a great time to be young and alive, reflected Wade sadly, knowing those days were well and truly in the past.

The Montana Bar evoked other memories, the sassy redhead Kate McKenzie and her husband Tom, the hardened gambler and womaniser. They kept bar at the Montana on and off for more years than Wade could remember. His smile faded as he remembered being told of Taw's death by Thad Granger. The disbelief, the sickening feeling when he realised it was true, the ride to the Big Hole, the seeing Alex for the first time since the divorce, it all came flooding back to him.

The sudden realisation that he couldn't change the past caused Wade to shake himself out of his melancholy mood and order another round. Then he sat down to play cards. As he gathered up his cards he realised that wherever he went, there'd be many memories evoked over the course of the evening, some bad but mostly good. He grinned inwardly before fanning out his hand; a royal flush stared back at him. Perhaps it's going to be a good one after all, he thought and like all good poker players he stared blankly at the pot.

By the end of the weekend all the family were ready to head home. It had been a fun weekend, Merri had shown a great interest in everything she'd seen, she'd enjoyed the sale, the bickering and bartering, the rodeo with its wildest horses on show and she'd enjoyed the parade. Even Kaycee had found the Bucking Horse Sale interesting, she being older and more interested in boys had paid particular attention to one of the young saddle bronc riders.

"She'll need watching," laughed Tara.

"And you should know," teased Alex, not too unkindly.

The last word was left to little Merri, "It was really great fun, we must do this more often."

* * *

More often was three months later. Dillon's Labor Day Rodeo 2007 to be precise. Merri, twelve going on thirty had entered the Barrel Racing contest.

"You should have talked it through with me first," exclaimed Tara. "Winning junior events is one thing, competing against girls at least five years older than yourself is another."

"Yeah that's what I told her," cried Kaycee.

"You knew about this!" rounded Tara.

"It's not Kaycee's fault, I asked her to keep quiet about it. I knew you'd get angry and try talking me out of it.

"I'm not angry sweetheart, I just think you'd be better waiting a couple of years."

"Why? I'm as good a rider as most of the girls on the circuit, better in fact."

"She is too!" conceded Kaycee.

Tara smiled, "I guess I can't talk you out of it then?"

"You got that right," laughed Merri.

"So that's it in a nutshell, Merri's entered the barrel racing contest," said Tara.

"And why not!" exclaimed Alex. "She can ride a horse almost as well as you, and aren't you forgetting you and Merri's namesake both competed whilst at High School."

"We were fourteen!"

"Kids learn quicker nowadays!" replied Alex with a wry smile.

Having won many junior events it was only natural Merri would want to compete with the big girls. Kaycee had tried warning her that moving from junior events to the majors was a giant step but Merri had laughed it off and reassured her that she knew all the angles and that she was confident that she'd win it.

"If I didn't know better I'd have sworn that was me arguing with Merri about the outcome of some event or another," cried Tara.

"Well she is a chip off the old block," cried Jack.

"Hey! Not so much of the old!"

No one was surprised when little Merri made it through to the finals the following day. "I'm gonna win it too!" she cried.

Sitting up high on the bleachers a nervous Tara and an equally nervous Alex watched as seconds were shaved off the previous day's fastest time. What worried the women the most was Merri might try something reckless in order to try to win the race. Good horsewoman that she was, the likes of Tammy Hawkins and Brandi Waylands were far more experienced, in fact a couple of girls had already come in with very fast times. Nails were close to being bitten, nerves were frayed, butts twitched as the announcement of Merri Claymore's name bellowed from the loudspeakers.

Merri and Flame flew into the arena like Pegasus. Both rider and horse spun around the first barrel perilously close to sending it flying. The crowd gasped and held their collective breath as if in anticipation of something special. Merri's time was a shade faster than the leading barrel racer. She went wide on the next, losing a fraction of a second, before turning Flame on a dime to race around the last barrel in double quick time. Alex, Tara and Kaycee screamed encouragement from the bleachers. The crowd were on their feet. Merri, kicked for home a second too early and Flame's rear hoof send the third barrel tumbling. A noticeable groan emanated from the crowd. She'd won hearts and minds the previous day, everyone was willing her to win it. The caller registered her time. At least she could draw consolation from the fact that her time without the five second penalty was half a second faster than the leading rider.

Alex, Tara and Kaycee raced from the bleachers.

"She nearly had it!" shrieked Tara.

Alex smiled at her daughter. That competitive spirit was still riding high. "Next time," replied Alex. Both women knew that for the immediate moment a little emotional support was probably needed. As they rounded from the bleachers and walked towards the competitors area, Merri and Flame walked slowly towards them. The look of disappointment was clearly plain to see. Merri was choked and looked on the verge of tears, but as her family gathered around her she managed to drag herself together.

"I had her. We were that close, I made one slight error and it cost me. Next year they won't see my ass for dust!"

"Merri!" cried a shocked Alex and Tara.

Kaycee looked the other way and grinned. Those barrel racing girls had just seen a glimpse into the future. Her sister had just announced herself onto the rodeo stage. It wouldn't be long before Merri Claymore was competing with the best. She reckoned that the likes of Linzie Walker and Kay Blandford had better watch out.

Wade and Jack hurried over, "Mighty fine riding. That was some show you put on. Next time girl, you'll have them eating your dust!" exclaimed Wade as he swept her up into his arms. All thoughts of disappointment evaporated as her granddaddy held her aloft and she stared down at her pa, his face a picture of pure pride. Merri's heart went out to both of them, her two most favourite men in the whole wide world. She already knew that winning wasn't the most important thing in life; having the support of a loving family around her mattered far more, 'Okay,' she conceded, 'winning does run a close second.'

Seconds after Wade lowered her to the ground, Jason and Keeley emerged from behind the bleachers. "Merri Claymore that was worth coming eight hundred miles for" exclaimed Jason.

"Now I feel pretty bad," cried Merri, "all the way from LA just to see me goof up."

"I'll tell you girl that was some ride! It's earned you and that family of yours dinner."

Something was up, thought Wade. What, he just couldn't figure out? Jason and Keeley didn't come all the way from

Southern California just to watch Merri ride; there was more in it than that. It had come as a surprise to all of them when they appeared from behind the bleachers. Normally Jason would have phoned, but turning up out of the blue, that was something else entirely. He guessed that when the younger members of the party drifted away he'd find out.

Wade couldn't have been more wrong, just as Tara announced that she and the girls were going to turn in, Jason shot a furtive glance towards Keeley. She smiled back reassuringly and he rose to his feet.

"Hold your horses Tara, we've got something that needs saying."

Alex grinned, she'd seen it all before. She looked first at Wade, then across at Jack, 'men!' she thought.

"Shucks, I don't rightly know where to begin," exclaimed Jason.

"We're pregnant!" announced Keeley. "We only found out a couple of days ago."

"Yeah, I'm gonna be a dad! I know we ain't family, but you all are the closest I've got, so I wanted you to be the first to know."

A cacophony of congratulations followed before Keeley added, "I did call my mum and dad in Ireland."

"And so you should," cried Tara.

Amidst the celebrations Wade felt a little choked up. The talk of family, of children, reawakened the memories that had come flooding back to him in Miles City. Stepping outside the Lion's Den he breathed deeply of the night air. He'd thought they'd passed, but the regrets were still there haunting him. He'd so wanted Taw to be a man like Jason that he'd been blinded to his son's real passion. Music was Taw's life and Wade hadn't recognised it. Alex had known, she'd read the signs, she encouraged, she nurtured, she supported. But he, he'd not seen the wood for the trees.

He stepped away from the entrance to the Lion's Den and gazed back in the direction of home. The mountains appeared black, silhouetted against the night sky. It was a beautiful night, to nice for recriminations, but they continued to flood out. He'd believed that deep down Taw had wanted to follow in his footsteps. He'd been wrong, he could see that now, instead he'd been pigheaded, stubborn and arrogant even, so much so that it had for a time cost him his wife and his family.

Wade reflected, that he'd been lucky, luckier than he deserved. He'd met Jack, and together they'd found a way back. Jack was like a surrogate son to him, a man that he thought he could mould in his own image. Yet he'd been wrong about that too. Jack along the way became his own person. He'd taken to the life, embraced it, loved it wholeheartedly, but he'd never let it take a hold on his life the way Wade had.

He let out a faint sigh, and then grinned to himself; he'd been such a damn fool. His thoughts turned to Fletcher, the natural heir to the Reynolds dynasty. But he too had chosen a different path. Even Jason, a friend for nearly a decade, a man well versed in the cowboy life had chosen the movie industry over his natural passion. And who could blame them all.

He just wished that he'd been able to tell Taw how much he loved him . . . .

"He's looking down on us," whispered Alex. "He knows; he knows you loved him."

Wade spun around; he hadn't heard the door opening. "What . . . How did you know what I was thinking?"

"Wade Reynolds, I've known you for a lifetime, I know what's in there," she indicated to her chest. "He never blamed you, not once. He was more like you than you'd think. His was a passion equally as strong as the one that's beating inside of you."

"I know that now," he said regretfully.

"He never stopped loving you. Despite everything he worshipped the ground you walked on."

Tears welled up in Alex's eyes. Wade wiped at his own eyes; then reached out for her and held her close. "I just wish . . . ."

"You know Wade; our life has turned out pretty good considering. Jack and Tara are happy, the kids are lively individuals, Fletcher has been a revelation and your latest protégé is about to become a father. More importantly he thinks enough of you to travel eight hundred miles to break the news personally.

Wade smiled, the cloud lifted and he hugged Alex, "I guess you're right, now lets go join the party."

"I'm always right," added Alex with a grin.

Chapter 56

Montana

The fall was Alex's favourite time of year, the sweltering heat of summer gave way to cooler cleaner air. She breathed deeply of it as she pushed her old faithful mare up through the foothills of the mountains. Every year around this time she took Kaycee, now turned sixteen, and Merri a very cheeky twelve year old, up high into the Bitterroots. It was her way of sharing the wonders of nature with her kinfolk. They lived with the mountains as a backdrop all year round, it could have been so easy to take nature in all its wondrous glory for granted, something Alex wasn't prepared to let happen. She remembered the first time she'd visited the Big Hole. Coming from West Texas as she had, the beauty of the valley blew her away. And today was no exception, the skies were clear blue without a trace of cloud to mar the majestic backdrop of the greys and purples of the Bitterroots. The aspens, shimmering golden against the sky always pleased and excited her, as did the Ponderosa pines as they reached high into the clear blueness of the sky; it tugged at her very being.

It was probably the last year that Kaycee would follow her Gram up into the hills, not that she'd indicated otherwise, but Alex knew that one day the lure of hanging out with friends her own age would take preference. Of course she'd come if asked but Alex was not the sort to press anyone into doing things against their will, as she remembered her own rebellious youth. At least there was still Merri, young but older than her years. Alex estimated she'd take this same trip for a few years to come.

Both girls were expert horsewomen, Kaycee had represented Montana State at student rodeos, winning the barrel racing on more than one occasion, but it was little Merri that showed the most promise, she was cool and confident in all the junior competitions, winning most events that she entered. Even the disappointment at the Dillon rodeo hadn't fazed her.

"Gram, lets go further," cried Merri excitedly.

Alex looked at her watch, then up at the sky. It was still bright and looked to stay light for at least another couple of hours.

"Okay, up to that tall peak yonder, then we turn back." Alex couldn't refuse her grandkids anything.

At the peak they could see clearly into three states, to the west Idaho, to the east Wyoming, and below the magnificent state of Montana. Alex laughed to herself as she recalled it wasn't far from here that she confronted Monique Delacroix and showed her what a real country woman was all about. How mad she must have been when she woke up to find herself bound hand and foot and dapped across the saddle.

"Okay girls, it's time we headed back."

"It's beautiful up here, can we stay and see the sunset," cried Merri.

"We'll see it as good from the porch back at the ranch," answered Alex.

"But I want to see it from here, looking across to Idaho."

"Merri, it isn't possible," cried Kaycee. "If we stay here and watch it, it'll be dark before we get back to the ranch."

Alex listened to the pearls of wisdom coming from her oldest grand child and realised her teachings had not been in vain.

Reluctantly Merri conceded, whilst she might be able to twist Gram around her little finger, her big sister was a different proposition altogether.

As they meandered through the trees the light began to fade more quickly than usual. Alex was a little surprised as she looked up at the dark foreboding cloud that had blotted out the sun and transformed the autumnal scene into a bleak picture of the winter before them.

"We need to hurry girls, if it snows we could take hours getting back home."

Alex was not alarmed, the clouds were ominous but no snow had fallen. It was late in the season but all the indicators were for settled weather. It would probably pass over by the time they were out of the wooded area and besides they were only an hour and a half out from the ranch, enough time for Merri to watch the sunset from Gram's porch. Of the girls Merri was more at one with nature and the environment, whereas Kaycee, though a good horsewoman was less apt to follow in her parents or grandparents footsteps.

Then the snows came, slowly at first, but as the snowflakes grew bigger the forest floor was fast turning into a blanket of white. As the snow thickened the horses began a slow plod. Alex kicked her mare into a fast trot and the girls followed her lead. The path they rode was known to them all and during good weather was easy to negotiate, but now the snows were negating their confidence. The winds got up and the intensity of the falling snow increased. Fearful of being caught out Alex spurred her horse to a lope, both girls un-alarmed at the quickening pace did the same. They were making good time when suddenly Alex's mare lost her footing and slipped throwing her rider.

"Gram!" both girls cried at once.

Alex tried to ride the fall, but her momentum slew her into a tangle of broken boughs, snapping her leg below the knee. The pain seared through her body like a red hot poker, the sickening sound only matched by her stomach as the shock caused her to vomit. Thankfully she passed out before her voice could register a scream.

"Gram! Gram!" screamed the girls as they threw themselves from their horses and raced toward the fallen Alex. They stared down anxiously as their grandma opened her eyes. The pain was excruciating but years of country living had taught Alex the meaning of survival. She bit down hard grinding her teeth against the pain, as she reviewed their plight.

"The horses!" cried Alex.

"They're right here," reassured Kaycee.

"Help me up," said Alex, "we can't hang around here all night," she grimaced.

Both girls tried lifting Alex, but the pain was too great. She couldn't stand.

"Get my rifle from my horse; I'll use it as a crutch."

Kaycee raced over to the horses and retrieved the Winchester from its scabbard.

"Good girl," encouraged Alex through the pain. She could tell that both girls were frightened, then as she attempted to stand, a sound not heard in the valley for decades froze the blood in her veins. Wolves! "Quickly, help me up!"

The baying of wolves grew louder, the horses whinnied nervously, their reins dangling in the snow. Alex fought off a sense of panic, and in as calm a voice as she could muster she told the girls to ease her down and bring the horses nearer. Kaycee and Merri understood their predicament but young as they were they were savvy enough to know not to panic the horses. Easing Alex down onto the fast piling up snow the girls slowly walked back to their horses. The animals alert to the sound of wolves eyed their riders with suspicion as they grew nearer, then a blood curdling howl sent all three horses into a panic stricken rush. Kaycee grabbed at the reins.

"Kaycee! Let go!" screamed Alex as her oldest grand child was dragged ten yards further down the track before letting go.

"Kaycee!" cried Alex and Merri in unison. Then the twelve year old began to cry. It was seconds but to them it felt like hours before Kaycee dusted herself off and began walking back towards her Gram and sister. Merri wiped her tears, and Alex breathed a sigh of relief.

Her relief was only momentary as she spotted a greyish brown wolf not more than five feet from Kaycee's left shoulder.

"Stand still!" barked Alex, "don't panic," she added to calm her grand child. Then she jacked a round into the breach of the Winchester and took careful aim as she sighted the rifle on the wolf. She had no love for wolves and shared Wade's misgivings, but shooting one down in cold blood was something she wanted to avoid. With the rifle trained on the chest of the animal Alex spoke calmly to Kaycee. "Walk slowly towards me, no sudden moves and you'll be alright."

Kaycee, reassured by her Grams words started walking towards her.

"That's it, keep coming," the words had only left her lips when Alex noticed the wolf shift his position into an attack stance. "Oh Jesus, no . . ." she muttered under her breath as the wolf lunged forward.

Without a moments hesitation she squeezed the trigger. The wolf yelped in surprise and pain then went down as if pole-axed, and Kaycee ran back towards Alex

Out of nowhere came five or six wolves, Alex jacked another round into the Winchester. The wolves circled the wounded animal, the scent of blood caused a rush of excitement amongst the pack, and then in a crazed and manic fashion they began ripping the wounded wolf to pieces.

Merri had stopped crying and bit her lip, Kaycee looked back at the mêlée then turned her face away. "Maybe they'll be satisfied now," she uttered hopefully.

Alex eased her finger from the trigger of the Winchester. "I'm sure you're right, the horses will alert Wade. He'll come find us, just you wait and see."

As the temperature dropped the three women huddled together. The pain in Alex's leg numbed by shock and cold was the least of her worries as she watched the wolves devour their own. From the little she knew about wolves in the wild, it was extremely rare for an attack on a human, yet she'd seen with her own eyes what they were capable of. She only hoped they'd leave now that their appetite was sated. Her only fear was that the pack mentality could sense the vulnerability of the three women. How long before dark? How long before the horses reached the ranch? How long before Wade would sense something was wrong? How long before they were found? There were too many imponderables for Alex to consider. She concentrated her efforts at keeping watch against the wolves.

* * *

It was Alex's horse that reached the ranch first, lame and feeling sorry for itself. Larry took one look at it and raced into the barn where Wade was working.

"Wade! Come quick!"

Wade sensing the urgency in Larry's voice dropped what he was doing and raced outside to find Larry standing with Alex's saddled horse.

"She just rode in!"

"Jesus H Christ!" cried Wade as he looked up towards the foothills and the snow clouds.

Within minutes Wade and six ranch hands were saddled up and were heading up towards the timberline.

"Larry, you and Bud, take the right fork, we'll head up the left, Clem you take the centre trail. Three shots when you find them.

* * *

Alex and the girls watched in horror as the pack their faces matted with the dried blood of the downed wolf began to circle them. Their menacing eyes glared like hot coals as they waited for signs of weakness. Alex reassured the girls that help was on its way, whilst keeping the Winchester ready just in case the wolves decided to attack. Her only fear was the intense pain and shock would soon render her unconscious. Trying not to spook the girls she instructed Kaycee to take the rifle if she fell asleep. "I won't but just be ready if I do," she said weakly.

Just at that moment one lone wolf ventured a little to close, his blood stained teeth clearly visible as he snarled defiantly. Alex jacked a round into the breech and fired, just before she slipped into unconsciousness.

*   *   *

Wade took the trail most used by Alex when she rode up into the hills, but his visibility was greatly reduced due to the now blizzard like conditions that swarmed across the entire valley. It was agonisingly slow going as the biting wind lashed against their faces, and it was getting worse as the darkness descended prematurely, hampering their efforts. Fear like he'd never known, *not even as a young man in Korea* gripped him as he thought of the possibilities. His wife and grandkids were missing; the wild weather conditions and the rugged terrain left him in no doubt what could have befallen them. He prayed silently, striking bargain after bargain, hoping against hope that they would be found safely.

It was close on two hours when Wade heard three rifle shots as they echoed across the valley.

"Thank God," he mouthed. Then he urged his horse in the direction of the rifle shots.

It was Clem Barker who had found the women huddled together against a large tree. Climbing down from his horse he'd instructed the two riders with him to break out the blankets and attend to the two girls. Alex he noticed was in a bad way and was floating in and out of consciousness. She had a nasty looking gash across her forehead and blood splatter across her left arm, other than that the state of her injuries were unclear. Clem immediately threw off his Carhartt coat and draped it around Alex's shoulders, and then he covered her with a blanket. He didn't know much about first-aid but knew enough to keep the patient warm. The snow continued to beat down mericilessly.

Kaycee, now wrapped in a blanket told him Alex's leg was broken, and they'd tried getting her on her horse when the wolves came. "Gram, killed one yonder," she pointed. "It was awful," she stuttered. Clem thought she was going into shock.

"Jake, we need to get these girls down the mountain and fast, you and Blaine take them, ride double back to the ranch, I'll stay with Mrs Reynolds until help arrives."

Both men reacted at once and picked up their young charges. Blaine helped Merri up onto the front of his horse and quickly swung himself up onto his mount.

"We can't leave her!" cried Kaycee, struggling against Jake.

"You'se got to, yah here," ordered Clem, "The boys' will see you home safe, I'll alert Wade, it'll be fine, I won't let anything happen to your Grandma."

Jake Harmon's strong hands grabbed Kaycee and threw her unceremoniously onto his horse and within seconds he was back in the saddle.

"Take care of them girls," cried Clem, "Now get outta here!"

The two cowboys lost no time and were out of earshot within a few seconds, then miraculously the wind dropped. Clem lost no time as he fired the three shots from his rifle. They echoed across the valley, hopefully thought Clem they'll alert both Wade and Larry of his find.

*　　*　　*

It was an hour later that Wade spotted the small fire that Clem had started. He spurred his horse violently towards the orange flames. Within minutes he was abreast of the fire and jumping down from his horse.

"How is she?" he asked as he stared down at the unconscious Alex

"It's her leg, it looks to be broken in two places," said Clem. "I told Blaine to phone the hospital and to get someone out to the ranch."

"The girls! Where are the girls?"

Jake and Blaine have got them; they should be at the ranch by now."

Wade said a silent thank you, and then gratefully turned towards Clem, "You did real good, all of you."

416

* * *

An hour and a half later they arrived back at the ranch to find an ambulance and two paramedics waiting for them. Alex was transferred to the ambulance and Wade went with her.

"We'll follow you up," cried Tara. Both her and Jack had raced over after Kaycee's hysterical phone-call. Both girls seemed to have recovered remarkably well considering their ordeal.

"You should have seen Gram's, that wolf was closing in on Kaycee," declared Merri. "Gram's was hurt badly, but she took aim and shot it. She saved our lives."

Kaycee, realising how close she'd come to being attacked by the wolf, could only confirm what her little sister had so gleefully told her mom and dad. "It was horrible, Gram's shot it and the rest of the pack turned on it. They ripped it to pieces."

"Tell them about the other wolf . . . ." cried Merri excitedly.

"Right," cried Jack, stopping his daughter in mid flow, "hospital first stop, get you girls checked over, then we'll see how Gram's is?" It had been a terrible ordeal and Jack didn't want his daughters dwelling on it.

* * *

When they arrived at Barrett Memorial they found an ashen faced Wade waiting for them in the foyer area of the hospital.

"How's mom?" cried Tara, urgently.

"They took her straight into ICU, she's lost a lot of blood, they're hoping to stabilise her before going into the operating theatre. Her leg's in a bad way, but they're hopeful."

"Hopeful!" screamed Tara. Jack put a restraining hand on Tara's shoulder.

"It's always this way. Until they can assess the situation, they can't tell us any more. She's in the best place."

"I'm sorry pa, its jus . . . ."

"I know," cried Wade.

*   *   *

It was in the early hours of the following morning when Wade learned the extent of Alex's injuries. The wound on her forehead was superficial and required a few butterfly stitches. Her left arm had several lacerations, possibly from branches when she fell or as suggested by the girls, a mauling from a wolf. The doctors discounted this theory as there were no visible puncture marks, but administered rabies shots as a precaution. It was her lower left leg that caused them the most concern. It had snapped in two separate places and there were numerous shards of bone that needed to be removed. It was a delicate operation and needed all the surgeon's skills to repair the broken leg.

"Your wife is stable, but it's going to be weeks, months before she's going to be able to walk again," said the surgeon. "I must impress on you, she was damn lucky and she isn't out of the woods just yet. Prepare yourself; she might never walk without the aid of a stick. Walking long distances for the foreseeable future are out of the question. Like I said, she was damn lucky. For a time it was touch and go. We thought we might have had to amputate."

His words cut Wade to the quick, he had no doubt that Alex would make a remarkable recovery despite what the doctor said, but the thought of Alex losing her leg was just too much to contemplate.

Chapter 57

Montana

Congressman Vince Holbrook read about Alex and the Claymore girls' lucky escape up in the foothills of the Black Hole Valley with relish.

"It say's here, the woman's a goddamn hero, fending off a pack of hungry wolves. Horse shit!"

"How so?" exclaimed Shelby.

"Damn woman falls off her horse and says a pack of wolves attacked her and her brood. She panicked, that's all. Damn woman has always been trigger happy."

Shelby remembered some years before when Alex shot a man dead in a dispute over land. If she recalled correctly, Alex was exonerated. Self defence they called it. "I seem to remember reading something about it."

"She got away with it." Holbrook grinned to himself. "That time, she got away with it, this time she won't be so damn lucky, that was a collared animal."

Ever since Ruth and the Reynolds family caused him to pull out of the race for Governor, Holbrook had been waiting his chance. Being on several committees for the environment he was best placed to put leverage on certain people to prosecute Alex Reynolds under the Endangered Species Act. A hefty fine or with luck a custodial sentence would cause the Reynolds clan at the very least an inconvenience. Vince Holbrook knew it was wishful thinking to get a custodial sentence, but he could dream.

*   *   *

Alex had only been out of hospital a few days before she received notice that she was going to be taken to court under the Endangered Species Act. Wade immediately got in touch with a friend at the Fish and Wildlife Services.

"Best you come in and see me," cried Elroy Gardener. "I'll look into it right away. Stop by around three this afternoon, hopefully I'll have something for you."

"Thanks Elroy," drawled Wade as he replaced the handset.

Around three Wade pulled up outside the offices of the Fish and Wildlife Services and climbed out of his pickup. Minutes later he was told by Elroy that several environmental committees had gotten together and were already making a strong case against Alex.

"How's that possible? She was fighting for her life and the lives of our grand kids. It'll be thrown out of court, no, it won't even get to court," he said angrily to Elroy Gardener.

"I know how you feel Wade, but I'm afraid this time you're wrong. They found another wolf mortally wounded not far from the body of the wolf that Alex killed. Ballistics show the bullet was fired from the same rifle. These guys have done there homework, they've gone through your entire history in the Big Hole. They've subpoenaed the records of when Alex spent a night in the cells in 1989 for the shooting of that ranch hand."

"That was self defence and he weren't any ranch hand, the Sheriff's Department exonerated her for it, and no charges were brought against her."

"Wade, I'm on your side, I'm just telling you what you're up against. If it was just that shooting, but it's not. There's also the shooting at Cougar Pass."

"Again, how the hell can they bring that up?"

"Seven people died that day. I know it was a tragic loss for you and your family, but the facts remain that none of the people involved were ever charged with those killings. To an outsider it would seem to suggest that your family is a law unto itself."

Wade seething with rage let it all sink in before he asked what the likely outcome would be.

"At best, they've got to prove Alex was the aggressor, at worst I'd say she was looking at a hefty fine, either way this could drag on for months or even years, totting up a very large legal bill. Which leads me to suggest Alex might be better off pleading guilty, take the fine and get on with your lives."

"The hell we will!" cried Wade.

"Best you think it over," advised Elroy cautiously.

It wasn't the news that Wade wanted to hear, it went against the grain. But despite everything he knew that Elroy might be right, it made good sense to at least think over what he'd suggested.

"I'm obliged Elroy," said Wade tipping his hat as he began to walk out of the office. He stopped at the front entrance. It was just a thought. He turned and addressed Elroy with one question. "Tell me, who'd be so small minded and petty as to prefer charges against Alex when she's only just out of hospital? For Christ sake she's still in a bad way, and might remain crippled for the rest of her life." It was a parting shot and Wade didn't expect any answer.

"Wait a second," cried Elroy as he punched a few keys on his computer. Wade turned around and slowly walked back to Gardener. The Fish and Wildlife officer didn't look up, he remained looking at his screen for several minutes, reading and paging down, before looked up at the questioning face of Wade Reynolds.

"Like I said, best take the hit. There are a number of environmental groups that are fighting tooth and nail to protect the wolf population. It's becoming a big political issue with hunters and ranchers like yourself calling for wolves to be delisted from the Endangered Species Act. Making an example of good hard working folks is one way of hitting back, and with people like Congressman Vince Holbrook firmly on the side of the environmentalists Alex could get caught in the middle."

"Holbrook! I should have known that son-of-a-bitch was behind it!" exclaimed Wade angrily. "Thanks for the heads up."

"No problem," replied Elroy.

* * *

Martha Rainbird was at the front porch when Wade drove up. The look on her face was both grave and full of concern. Wade's first thoughts were of Tara or the kids, but then he saw Kaycee and behind her Merri crying. His heart thumped in his chest. Sticking the pickup into park he jumped out and leapt up onto the porch. He was still agile despite his advancing years, years of working the land had seen to that. Then he saw Tara, her face a mirror image of Martha's.

"She's gone pa!" sobbed Tara.

Wade raced past his daughter and flung open the bedroom door. He pulled up as he neared the bed. Alex lay there, peaceful like, as if sleeping. "No, no, don't leave me! Oh Alex, don't leave me."

Tara put a restraining hand on Wade's arm. "It's too late pa, she's gone. The doc came as soon as Martha phoned him. But it was already too late. He reckons she must have died in her sleep. He thinks it was a blood clot, but he can't be sure. Only that it would have been quick, he said she wouldn't have known much about it."

"But she looks so peaceful."

"I know, I know . . . ."

* * *

Alex was buried next to her beloved son Taw a week later. The snows were eight inches deep but the family gravesite had been painstakingly cleared of it. The family had wanted a small affair, but Alex was known and loved far beyond their valley. Fletcher and Ruth came from Washington, Jason and Keeley now six months pregnant with their first child came up from Los

Angeles. Some family from West Texas, folks Wade hadn't seen in decades flocked in from all points of Montana. Even Jack's brother Bob flew over especially for Alex's funeral.

"I only knew her briefly, but she was a lady of the first order," said Bob at her grave side.

Wade was dying inside. The kindness of people was tearing him apart. He wanted them all to go, to leave him to grieve in peace. He'd held it together for the sake of Kaycee and Merri.

Tara held back until most of the mourners had drifted away. She'd sent Jack home with the family saying she was going to spend the night with Wade. Jack nodded his understanding and said he'd call by in the morning. He knew why Tara wanted time alone with her pa.

Wade sat with his head in his hands, a double bourbon sat on the coffee table beside him.

"Why Tara? It should have been me. I'm seventy seven; your ma had so many years left. She was sixty eight, for Christ's sake!"

"I know pa, it seems so unfair. But look on the bright side, Ma was still a good looking woman. And that's how Ma would want to be remembered."

"Yeah, she was, she could still stop men in their tracks," sobbed Wade, crying and laughing at the same time.

"She wouldn't have wanted to be old. She'd want you to remember her as she was, not as a wrinkled up crone."

"You're right there. I just wish I'd been there when she passed. We never got to say goodbye."

Tara started to cry, it was getting too much. "Pa, she left you a letter. She left me one too. Ma knew she was dying, don't ask me how, but she knew."

Tara handed her father a sealed envelope. Wade looked up, his confusion made Tara want to weep. "Here Pa, take it."

Wade held the envelope in both hands and stared at the, oh so familiar handwriting of Alex.

My Darling Wade.

"I'll leave you alone," said Tara.

Wade didn't seem to heed her words he just stared down at the small lilac envelope with those three words. Fear gripped him as he continued to stare. His hands shook, what madness was this. His beautiful wife Alex was speaking to him from the grave. Finding a paperknife he carefully slit the envelope open. Then he unfolded the sheet of paper.

To my beautiful big hunk of man,

Wade, if you're reading this, then my intuition was correct. I haven't felt myself for days, nothing that I could put my finger on, just a sense of foreboding. Strange as it might seem I'm not fearful of the outcome. I suppose I'm being a little selfish in my old age, but I'm at least spared the grief of your passing. Believe me, you're stronger than me in that way, I couldn't live without you by my side, whereas you've got this ranch. Yes, I know your little secret; I've lived with it most all my adult life. Sharing you with her has been one of the joys of my life. You love this land almost as much as you love me.

I'm gone now, but I'll be with you always. When the winds blow, and the trees rustle, when the rains fall and the rivers break their banks, when the thunder cracks and the lighting lights up the sky, it'll be me. I'll never leave you; I'll always be there at your side.

I'm on my journey now, a wondrous new adventure, but I won't be alone. I can hear him now calling my name; he's coming for me, my son, my beautiful handsome boy, my Taw. He's coming to meet me.

Wade my darling, don't grieve, remember me, remember the good times. And we've had plenty. Oh how I loved you when you asked me to marry you at Jason and Keeley's wedding. You couldn't have picked a more memorable spot if you'd tried. Asking me to marry you again, at our age, how soft, how thoughtful, how you. Yes my gentle giant, I've had a good life, no better than good, the greatest life any woman could wish for.

I love you always. Goodbye my love.

Alex xxxx

Chapter 58

Montana

Alex's death had hit him harder than anyone realised. Her letter went some way to cushion his lost, but it couldn't make up for the loneliness in his heart. Tara, Kaycee and Merri stayed on at the Crazy AW for a few days but when Wade insisted that he was fine, and that he had a ranch to run, Tara and the girls reluctantly headed home.

"I'll phone every evening, you hear," she uttered as Wade closed the door of her sedan.

Although Wade put a brave face on it, he was barely hanging on; his only salvation was to throw himself back into work. Alex had been right, Wade had a ranch to run. For the past couple of weeks he'd left all the running to Larry, who was now well into his late sixties, not that Larry wasn't capable; he was ably assisted by Bud Angel, Blaine Henry, Clem Barker and Jake Harmon. There were enough men usually to run a ranch of the Crazy AW size during wintertime when most of the itinerant ranch-hands had been laid off but Wade just knew had to get back in the saddle, either that or die.

*   *   *

One morning about a month after Alex's death, Wade failed to appear at the stables. It was unusual as he'd made a great show of always being the first up. Larry sensing things weren't quite right went looking for him. He found him sleeping off a drunk on the couch. It was clear to Larry that he hadn't been to bed; someone or something had set him off. Strewn across the floor were various correspondences, one in particular caught Larry's eye.

It was from an environmental agency, offering their sympathies on the death of his late wife. Larry read further down the page.

Due to circumstances beyond our control we have decided to withdraw our complaint and all criminal charges have been dropped.

"Due to circumstances beyond our control . . . . The unfeeling bastards," muttered Larry.

The sound of cartridges being loaded into the breech of a Winchester caused Larry to drop the paper and turn around. Wade was on his feet, busily feeding his Winchester.

"Those bureaucrats can kiss my ass!" exclaimed Wade. "Them darn wolves caused Alex's death. Guess I'm gonna rid these here ranges of every damn wolf in the valley."

"You can't be serious!" exclaimed Larry.

"Never more serious in my life!" snarled Wade. "I've put up with these darn environmentalists for the last two decades. Kill a wolf, justify it, or face a fine. Have young calves killed by a pack of wolves, you've got to prove it was a wolf done the killing or you don't get paid out."

"Kill a wolf, pay a fine, how do you thing they'll treat you if you go up into the mountains and start hunting them down," shouted Larry. "They will find out, best believe it."

"They can't hurt me," said Wade in a deliberate manner, which left Larry with no room to argue. He was the boss, a friend yes, but Larry had learned through the years that if Wade set himself a task, there was no stopping him. And whoa betide anyone that tried standing in his way. Late seventies he might have been, slower now than when he was at his prime, but tough, mean and ornery as an old bull.

* * *

Larry rang Tara and told her that Wade had gone up into the mountains to hunt wolves.

"He'd slept off a drunk; but I'd say he was stone cold sober. He was as mean as a wounded grizzly. Set out with enough provisions to last a couple of days, two rifles and enough ammunition to start a small war. He means business Tara; he even took a fatted calf as bait."

"You didn't try to stop him?"

"Miss, I'd say your pa was looking for a fight, I wasn't going to argue with him."

"Yeah I know; I'm sorry, he's a mean son-of-a-bitch, when he gets going." There were no recriminations in her voice, she knew her father. There was nothing that would have stopped him short of a Sherman tank.

Larry took it in his stride, in Tara's position he'd probably have said the same thing. "I'd say that letter tore his heart out."

"What letter?"

Larry picked it up from the desk and read it to her.

"Oh Jesus!" she cried. "I'll be right over."

* * *

Jack arrived around mid-day with the kids in tow. He'd picked them up from school after Tara had relayed what Wade was planning.

"I thought it best they were with us," he said as both girls climbed out of the pickup to a quizzical look from their mother.

"I guess so; the girls can help make pack lunches for the men."

In that moment a fresh snowfall began to cascade down, making pursuit impossible. "I reckon the best course of action is to wait it out. Wade might get tired of looking and come home." Even before he'd finished the sentence he knew that wasn't Wade's style.

*   *   *

Nightfall came on quickly and the valley seemed to take on a deathly hush. The moon fought valiantly against the blackening skies, but finally relinquished its grip. And the valley descended into darkness. The disquieting cry of a wolf echoed across the Big Hole, punctuating the beginning of a battle to the death.

Wade consumed by anger and grief moved up into the timberline, not far from where Alex had her encounter. Deep into the timber he pushed his horse, the calf following a few yards behind. When he found a suitable spot he staked the calf out and then proceeded to make a dry camp. He saw to his horse then retreated into his hide, checked his rifles and then pulled out some jerky to keep the hunger pangs from him.

It was early evening when he heard the first howl of the wolf, followed closely by another. They were close and getting closer by the minute. As he lay in the quiet of the forest he mulled over his foolhardy plan. Nothing else made sense, his beloved Alex was gone; he'd been hounded by wolves for more than twenty years. Indirectly they caused her death. He blamed the environmentalists, the conservationists, Green Peace, Save the fucking Whale, and all the do-gooders in the world. Those liberal bastards cared more about the environment that the people that lived there. He justified himself, he was making a stand, he wasn't on his own and there were plenty of others that thought like him. Better to rid the valley of wolves than to take a loaded shotgun into the offices of those so called bureaucrats.

The shrill cry from the tethered calf alerted him to the wolf. With his night sight firmly attached to his Winchester he scoped the area. He caught a movement, there it was, its cruel eyes seemed to stare right at him, like a rabbit in the head lights. He swung his rifle slowly to the right, another crouching low, its eyes on the potential meal. Another appeared to the right, then another. It had been a hard couple of weeks, the snows had been persistent and the icy wind blew arctic in colour. These wolves were hungry, hungrier than they been for several winters. They'd looked toward his horse but turned their attention on the easier prey.

He knew he couldn't expect to get them all, sweat trickled from his brow, belying the temperature. His heart beat faster, he breathed deeply, calming himself for the kill. Wade caught the first of the wolves in his cross hairs and gently squeezed the trigger. From memory he swiftly swung the rifle to the right and brought down another. Quickly he rose from his kneeling position and fired another three rounds. He heard a squeal but when he got to the calf they had gone, leaving the dead bodies of their comrades. Wade pulled his knife from his belt and quickly sliced off the tails of the dead wolves.

He slept in his hide until the early hours before venturing out. His luck was in, the weather had been kind. No fresh snowfall to cover the blood trail. He found the wolf a few hours later, weak and dying. He raised his rifle to his shoulder and fired point blank at the dying animal.

*　　*　　*

Tara and Jack had heard the shots in the night, and had hoped that Wade's murderous rage had been quelled. On hearing the shot fired just after eleven in the morning, their hopes were dashed.

Three days and nights shots echoed around the valley. Neighbour told neighbour, bartenders from Dillon to Wisdom relayed the story; eventually word reached the Fish and Wildlife Agency. On hearing the news Elroy Gardener wasn't at all surprised. He'd known Wade and Alex for close on thirty years. Wade Reynolds was hurting and he only knew one remedy for it, and that was to hurt back.

* * *

On the morning of the fourth day Wade, bloodied and exhausted from his ordeal in the wilds arrived back at the ranch. Solemn faced he slid down from his horse. Larry took the reins, "You go in the house clean up, I'll attend to the livestock."

Wade nodded his thanks, and turned towards the house.

"Pa, we've been so worried about you," cried Tara. The relief in her voice clear to hear. What you need is a hot bath and food inside your belly."

"Sounds good," said Wade as he shed his big coat and walked towards the bathroom.

Jack tapped Wade on the shoulder, "Good to see you home safe." Then he walked out the door and across to the stables where he joined Larry and Clem Barker.

"Damn old he bear, killed nine of them if I've counted right," cried Larry with a tone of admiration to his voice.

"That maybe so, but if the authorities find out there'll be hell to pay," stated Jack. Hide those damn trophies."

* * *

Back at the house, bathed and fed, Wade smiled at Tara.

"I've been a damn fool, your mother would have given me hell," he said, his voice lighting up at the mention of her mother. "She said in her letter that I'd be okay, because I had my mistress."

Tara looked shocked.

"The land, your mother was referring to the ranch."

"You might not have much of a ranch if the authorities find out what you've done. Do you know what the penalties are for the wantonly killing of wolves in the state of Montana? $100,000 that's what, and or up to a year's imprisonment. That's for the killing of one wolf. How many . . . ." shouted Tara.

"Nine at a rough count," said Jack as he re-entered the house.

"Nine, oh my God!" cried Tara. "We better make sure no one finds out about it."

"Too late," cried Larry. "An official car from the Fish and Wildlife Agency is coming up the drive as we speak."

Chapter 59

Montana

Vince Holbrook came down to breakfast, his face a picture of pure contentment. He was married to the woman of his dreams, his career was back on track, his future plans, now on a more realistic path, what more could a man ask. Revenge, that's what!

Holbrook had just been informed that Wade Reynolds, the patriarch of the Reynolds/Claymore/Coppersmith clan had just been arrested for the slaying of several wolves. "How many?" he asked.

"According to all reports, the Sheriff's department recovered nine tails crudely hidden in one of the barns at the Reynolds ranch."

"Nine!" cried Holbrook gleefully, "That old rancher killed nine," quickly the congressman did the math. "We'll throw the book at him."

"There are extenuating circumstances," said the voice on the other end of the phone line. "His wife just passed only a few weeks ago."

"Do I sound like I care? That whole family have been causing havoc and getting away with it for years!"

"The man's in his late seventies."

"Good, I'll make sure his last years on this earth are as uncomfortable as possible. Get my legal team on it at once. I want every stone turned over. I want his full history. I want that man broken, I want his ranch, hell I want his life."

"Yes sir. I'll get right on it."

* * *

Shelby was already downstairs when Holbrook literally bounced down the stairs.

"You're in a good mood this morning," she enquired.

"And why wouldn't I be, with the most beautiful woman in the world waiting for me at breakfast."

"It's more than that, tell me."

"You are going to love what I have to say, you're just gonna love it."

Shelby smiled; she hadn't seen her husband so worked up about anything before. "Tell me!"

"This should really please you. As you know, we were going to prosecute Alexandria Reynolds for the unlawful killing of a wolf, but the unfortunate woman died before we could take her too court."

"Yes, I remember," cried Shelby, she hadn't seen Alex since that morning after the Dillon rodeo. She remembered the last words Alex had spoken to her as if it was yesterday, "You're lucky, If it had been me, I'd have killed yah! Don't be here when we get back!" Shelby had taken her at her word and high-tailed it out of Montana.

Holbrook laughed, "That dumb fool of a husband, he took himself on a killing spree . . ."

"What!" exclaimed Shelby.

"Wolves, he went up into those mountains of his and killed nine of them. Can you believe it nine! All endangered species! We're gonna have a field day with this one. I reckon we'll break the man financially; not many of these ranchers are cash rich, land maybe, but not cash. And as an added kicker, this son-of-a-bitch will have to do some time."

"Don't get yourself so worked up about it, let the courts decide, we've bigger fish to fry if we're going to turn you into the next governor of Montana."

Shelby had explained that they had a wonderful life together. They had all the riches that they needed. Using the governorship of Montana as a stepping stone to the White House had been unrealistic. "Aiming too high isn't the way to go. Now Governor of Montana; that I agree with. It has a nice ring to it. Running the State takes a lot less energy than running the country. I'd suggest we aim your political ambitions in that direction."

Vince Holbrook had always thought too highly of himself and he found Shelby's advice hard to swallow. But during one of their numerous vacations he'd seen the error of his ways. Shelby was good at her job, no make that great, thought Vince, but there was something that she was expert at, and that was spending money. He didn't begrudge her that, if fact, he understood where she was coming from, life was for living and if you were rich enough then it was your duty to live it.

Vince Holbrook after thirty years of philandering had found the perfect soul mate. He loved her with all his heart and she in return loved him back. "You're right of course my darling, but indulge me on this one. Wade Reynolds deserves all that's coming to him."

Shelby smiled weakly.

Vince Holbrook had the fish on the hook. It was an opportunity he'd never in his wildest dreams expected, there was no way he was going to let go until he'd punished that family for all the humiliation they'd brought down on him. Yes, he thought, his instincts were right, it was a beautiful morning.

* * *

Wade was arrested that morning when the Sheriff's department located the nine wolves tails. He was taken to the Beaverhead County Sheriff's Department at Dillon where he was charged under the Endangered Species Act with nine counts of malicious killing of wolves.

News got out and pretty soon the Sheriff's Department was besieged by ranchers, farmers and hunters all calling for the release of Wade. The protesters kept up their vigil until late in the afternoon when the temperature dropped. Then in ones and twos they drifted back to their cars, there thoughts still with the rancher from the Big Hole but they knew before they'd arrived that their protest would be futile. Wade hadn't blown the brains out of one wolf, he'd killed nine of them and in anyone's book that was overkill. But at the very least they'd shown their support.

Wade was charged with nine misdemeanour counts and was arraigned to appear at Beaverhead County Courthouse in Dillon on the 28th February 2008.

"You done wrong, and for that you've gotta pay. But I don't see any reason why this can't be tried in my courtroom. I must warn you, there will be a hefty fine, but a custodial sentence; I think we can avoid that."

Tara gave a sigh of relief, while Wade stared stone-faced at the wall.

"Thank you, your honour," said Tara, speaking for Wade. Somehow or other being handcuffed and being brought here in a patrol car had really taken the wind out of Wade's sails. The enormity of what he'd done had suddenly been brought home.

The death of her mother had hit Tara harder than she was prepared to let on. If nature had been allowed to take its cause, Alex would still be here, still here and looking after that big hearted, stubborn fool of a husband. But she was gone and now it was Tara's turn to pick up the pieces. Her father's health was her prime concern, until she was sure he could take it, there was no way she could relax. Thanks to the judge, Wade at the very least would be allowed time to mourn the death of Alex. She'd expected some kind of reaction from him, but never in her wildest dreams did she think he'd put his own future in such jeopardy. He'd been lucky; Judge Spicer could have referred Wade's case to a higher authority. Now at least he had time to adjust to his life before preparing for the arraignment.

* * *

Over the next few days Larry was able to coax him back into working the range. The work was hard and the weather bitterly cold but Wade didn't seem to notice. He finally began to get into the swing of this during his second week. Tara looked in on him every other day and as the days became weeks she noticed a small improvement in his demeanour. Then came the first milestone in the bereavement process; Thanksgiving.

The turkey was brought in and Jack stood up and began to carve, when Kaycee said, "Pa." and looked towards Wade.

He smiled back, "I guess I've got to get used to it."

"Hell Wade, I didn't think, go ahead, you carve," cried Jack, "I'd just as soon sit back and wait for it to be handed to me on the plate."

Wade smiled and took the offered carving knife and fork and began carving the turkey. As Thanksgiving dinners went, it just about passed muster. Wade's own words best summed it up.

"Well, I guess I've got that one under my belt," he joked. "Christmas next, then we've the spring to look forward to."

It was a start.

* * *

Two weeks before Christmas Wade received an official letter from the Fish and Wildlife Agency, informing him that due to the seriousness of his actions, the misdemeanours had been upgraded to felonies and he was to be tried in the Federal Court.

"What!" shouted Tara, "You've got to be kidding."

"I wish I was," replied Wade. "According to what I've been able to find out, I'm to be made an example of. The whole kit and caboodle of environmentalists have thrown their collective weight behind getting a conviction."

"Why now, others have got off with much less."

"Why now, well I'll tell you. There are two reasons why they're going ahead with this show trial. Firstly, they know that it's just a matter of time before the wolf is taken off the endangered species list."

"And the other reason?" asked Tara.

Wade gave a resigned laugh, "The other reason is Congressman Vince Holbrook. According to sources of which I'm not prepared to divulge, Holbrook has been pushing for this since day one. He's sited Alex's shooting of the wolf as an example that we ranchers couldn't give a rat's ass for the environment."

"But that's not true," cried Tara.

"I know that and you know it, even Holbrook knows it. That son-of-a-bitch went after Alex, even though she was crippled up. That I can't forgive. But like a fool I compounded it by playing right into his hands. If the bastard wants his pound of flesh, he's damn well gonna have to work for it."

"We've got to get you the best lawyer possible," said an angry Tara.

"Damn right!" replied Wade.

Later that evening when she was relaying their conversation to Jack she smiled. "You know, there's one thing good that's come out of this,"

"And what's that?" asked Jack.

"Pa. He was so fired up; it was like going back in time."

Jack risked a little quip, "That's worrying!"

Chapter 60

Montana

Vince Holbrook had been incensed when he found out what Judge Spicer had done.

"Damn inbred fool, don't these so called judges give a shit about justice," he raved.

"He'll still have to pay a fine," cried Shelby.

"Fine! By the time I'm finished with him a fine will be the least of his problems."

"Is it worth it? He's an old man, his wife just died, surely that's punishment enough?"

"Shelby Holbrook, are you going soft on me?" It was the politician in him that was able to turn the most venomous tirade into a jokey seductive innuendo.

"As if," replied Shelby. "I just thought that there were far more important things to be worrying about than a silly old rancher."

Shelby normally found her husband's ruthlessness a turn on, some how or other just the sound of his voice in anger pushed all the right buttons, but something about his obsession with the Reynolds family hit an unfamiliar cord.

She found it strange how Vince had charmed her. She'd gone back to Montana, knowing that she couldn't change the past. She'd gone back to do a job, but without realising it, she'd dropped her guard and actually fallen for the guy; that he was loaded was just a bonus. She had to admit they were two of a kind, both ruthless in their own way; both very passionate in their love for each other.

Sex with Vince was far more rewarding than she would have believed. She found herself relinquishing any and all lovers in favour of this most passionate of men. She hoped it would always be so.

*   *   *

Vince called in every favour possible to have the charges against Wade Reynolds upgraded to a felony. He argued that just as the ranching and hunting lobby were pushing to have the wolf taken off the endangered species list, they each and everyone of the conservationist groups should make one final hurrah and stand up for the wolf in its darkest hour. His passion for his subject was commended by most parties and a push was demanded to have Wade Reynolds 'Wolf Slayer' arraigned in the Federal Court at Missoula. Holbrook even went as far as getting Judge Clinton Harrison to preside over the case.

Washington D.C.

"If ever Wade needed help, its now," declared Fletcher over dinner in one of Washington's finest eateries.

"I lived with that man; I know what he's capable of. Why oh why did Wade fall into his grasp," said Ruth as she played with her dessert.

"Grief, I reckon. Wade's a passionate man, he'd have wanted to hit out, and I guess he saw the wolf as the main reason for Alex's death."

"Even with the best lawyer that money could buy, he'll never beat the rap. Holbrook will personally nail shut any avenue of escape. I just wish . . . ." Ruth's frustration was Fletcher's.

"If only we'd found something to link Holbrook to the Dempsey/Ryder murders," mused Fletcher.

"There has to be something in that damn file!" said an exasperated Ruth.

"Honey, I've gone over and over every inch of that file, believe me there's nothing to connect Holbrook. God knows I've tried."

"I know sweetheart," said Ruth as she pushed her unfinished dessert towards the centre of the table.

"Two weeks, that's all I'll need to finish up the case I'm working on, then provided you can get time off we'll take a trip out to see Wade. Whatever else we're able to do, at least hopefully it'll take his mind of things, during the festive season."

Montana. 2008

Christmas came and went, New Year was here then gone and Wade's court day drew closer by the hour. Fletcher managed to find a very good Washington lawyer friend of his that agreed to work Pro Bono for Wade, giving out advice and setting out his case for the defence.

"He's one of the best in the business, trust me. The chance of you getting off on all charges is nil, but with Frank Wellman's direction he should be able to get you off a lengthy prison sentence.

Wade nodded; he understood the gravity of his situation.

A week later Fletcher returned to the ranch with Frank Wellman. Pleasantries were exchanged before the three men sat around the table and began to talk business.

"Wade, I'll come straight to the point," began Frank Wellman. "I don't mean to pry, but how are you fixed asset wise?"

"Like most others I guess. I've a small savings account, a couple of investments, the ranch machinery is all paid for, then there's the ranch and land, a couple of pickups, and the sedan off course."

"Can you cash those investments?"

"I reckon, though at today's prices, I'd be lucky to see two hundred thousand dollars, after forfeitures."

"Whoa, let me stop you right there. The charges the government's bringing are going to come to considerably more."

"I reckon I could scrap another one seventy five, maybe two hundred grand, but that's about it."

"I'm going to be brutally honest with you; my first priority is to get you off serving any time in the penitentiary. That on its own is going to be a monumental task, but I think we stand a good chance of swinging it." Wellman looked to Fletcher for support.

"What Frank's trying to say is you killed nine federally listed endangered species, the groups that brought this case want there pound of flesh, especially congressman Holbrook," said Fletcher.

"Basically Wade, four hundred thousand dollars ain't gonna cut it, the fine will be huge, then there's the court costs. If you're to walk free it's gonna cost. From the little I've heard that Holbrook character wants blood," finished Frank.

"Then I'll go to prison."

"Yeah, and what happens to the ranch in your absence. I'll tell you what, it'll go to ruin in less time that it takes to shake a stick," said Jack as he walked through the door to join them.

"Larry and the boys' will take care of it," argued Wade.

"No disrespect to Larry, but he's pushing seventy, and as for the boys', loyalty only goes so far. You know that yourself, without a pay-check they'll only stick it out for so long." Jack found it was hard telling the man that had taught him all he knew how to suck eggs.

"That no good bastard and his cronies have you over a barrel," added Fletcher.

"Tara and I don't want to see you in Deer Lodge Penitentiary," chipped in Jack.

"Okay, I've got the picture. Frank, what's the bottom line?"

"Let me spell out the hard facts, dumb as it may sound, those wolves could cost you a million bucks to just walk free and still have your ranch and home," said Wellman. "But," he added as I note of caution, "it could cost you a whole lot more."

Wade knew he was beaten, though something in his makeup wanted to hit out. The men sitting around the table, Jack his son-in-law, together they'd faced the elements, every possible hazard that God could throw at them and they'd come through, then he looked at the swarthy Fletcher, his best friend's son and remembered how they'd faced down Monique and her murderous band, then across the table to the no nonsense lawyer Frank Wellman, a man that had agreed to go Pro Bono on Wade's behalf, they all had his interest at heart. He owed it to all of them to comply.

"Supposing you can get me off, will the courts allow me time to raise the necessary cash?"

"That is something we'll have to deal with when the time comes," said Frank Wellman as he brought the meeting to a close.

Chapter 61

Montana

"They've brought in a hot shot lawyer from D.C," laughed Holbrook. He read on until he'd finished the article, then he folded the newspaper. "Well, that suits me fine," he smirked.

There was no response from Shelby as she stared absentmindedly at the beige coloured walls of the dining room. "Reynolds has brought in a hot shot lawyer from Washington."

"Sorry, I was miles away!" exclaimed Shelby.

"Let them argue his guilt, in the end Reynolds will still have to pay and the longer the case runs, the more it'll cost."

"I'm sure you're right honey."

She loved him, she'd not expected it, but those first few months when she restarted his campaign her affection for him grew. By the time he proposed at the 'Mother Lode' restaurant she was infatuated by him. He was good, kind, gentle and rich. And yes it was true, he did have a ruthless streak, but didn't every successful businessman possess one. As the weeks, turned to months, then years her love for him had grown even stronger, it surprised even her. His attentiveness towards her hadn't diminished one bit, in fact if anything it had grown stronger. They were like two peas in a pod, soul mates forever. But this obsession with the Reynolds family was unhealthy. Shelby had thought Vince would get over it. Like most things between man and wife she sensed that a woman was behind it, that deep down he'd cared far more about his ex-wife than he was prepared to let on.

But she'd been wrong! It went far deeper.

Vince sensed her disinterest, "I'm sorry, I shouldn't burden you with such things. I'm forgetting you were once close."

"It's not that Vince, you need to step back from it, let the courts sort it out," said Shelby.

"You're right; I've done all I can. I should leave it up to the people that deal with this sort of thing. Leave justice to the judges' of this world to administrate." As an after thought he added, "Let justice prevail."

Shelby smiled sweetly, "I'm sure it will."

*   *   *

Frank Wellman found getting Wade off a custodial sentence was a little harder than he'd first thought. He'd entered a plea of guilty while the balance of Wade's mind was disturbed. It was a calculated risk, they could have gone for a not guilty verdict but the circumstantial evidence was stacked against him. He'd hoped the prosecution would have accepted the plea and then Wade's confession could work for him. But the prosecution attorney George Mitchell was having none of it, he was out to nail Wade's hide. No doubt on a big fat bonus from a certain congressman.

Mitchell's first course of action was to bring up Alex and Wade's dispute over the land deal at Big Hole Pass. This, the prosecution alleged had climaxed in the shooting death of a ranch hand. Luckily Frank was able to show evidence that the ranch-hand in question was little more than a hired thug.

"A thug perhaps, but surely shooting a man dead was a little excessive."

Frank Wellman had done his homework. He smiled at the prosecution attorney and then produced a copy of the inquest into the death of the ranch-hand where he was able to point out that a self defence plea was accepted. It was a small victory. But it had taken almost a full day to go through.

The following day George Mitchell brought up the shooting at Cougar Pass, where seven people died. Judge Clinton Harrison asked again what relevance this had to the case. Mitchell explained that he was building a picture. Judge Harrison accepted the reasoning and allowed Mitchell to proceed. With relish the prosecution took the jury through all the gory details of that fateful afternoon.

In turn the survivors of that day gave their account of what happened. It was particularly painful for Fletcher; Merri was still very much a part of him. Then Tara gave her tearful account, describing the violent deaths of Tyler Henry and Butch Locklin before Fletcher and her father intervened. The prosecution inferred that as none of the opposing parties survived the evidence was only one sided.

"Your honour, the dead can speak," countered Wellman as he brought up the rap sheets for the dead and laid them out for the court to peruse. He was hoping the suggestion from the prosecution that the Reynolds family were a trigger happy gun toting law unto themselves would be defused. And to some extent his timely intervention with the criminal records had worked, although Frank suspected that some of what the prosecution had inferred would stick in their collective minds.

By day three the real trial finally got underway. It was the most damning as the wolf that Alex shot dead was a tagged animal and if that wasn't enough Mitchell brought up the second wolf that had been killed that day.

"Grams didn't kill it, I did," declared Kaycee, when she was put on the witness stand. The courtroom erupted into a roar of shocked conversation.

"Silence!" cried the judge as he banged his gavel furiously.

"Did you indeed," said Mitchell undeterred by this new turn of events, "Might I remind you, that you are under oath."

"You can threaten all you like, but that's the goddamn truth," spat Kaycee.

"We'll have no blaspheming in my court," shouted Judge Harrison.

"That'll be all," said a smug George Mitchell.

Merri was next up; she collaborated her sister's story.

Despite Kaycee and Merri's eye witness account of what happened their evidence was according to the Judge at best inconclusive.

Frank Wellman, seeing the deck was clearly stacked against Wade advised him not to speak in his own defence, and to let the defence rest on the grounds of diminished responsibility due to the recent death of Alex.

Unfortunately the prosecution was on a roll. A ruse by Mitchell forced Wade to give evidence on his own behalf. Wellman begged him to plead the Fifth Amendment but it was too late.

"I accept that I was wrong to hunt them darn wolves, there is no defence for it. I attributed my wife's death indirectly to the wolf and for that reason alone I am truly sorry."

Frank Wellman held his breath, Wade had said just enough. He motioned for him to step down.

"Mr Reynolds, would you say the introduction of wolves into the north western United States is welcome in the Big Hole Valley," said George Mitchell prosecution attorney.

"You don't have to answer," cried Wellman, looking pleadingly towards Judge Harrison.

"I'll allow the question," said the judge.

Wade knew he should keep his mouth shut, but during the last decade he'd seen his calves decimated by wolves, herds of elk that roamed free had been hunted and brought down by vicious packs and were near extinction, then of course there was the loss of four dogs, one of them a family pet.

"In my opinion, the introduction of wolves into the wild is a good thing, provided they're controlled. But you see your honour, the wolf is a wild animal, it ain't gonna take notice of any damn law." Wade's eyes burned brightly as he addressed the whole courthouse. "So it's got to be policed, and these jokers that are doing the policing ain't up to it. If it's left to the ranchers and farmers to sensibly cull these animals we wouldn't have these problems."

A buzz went around the courthouse and Frank Wellman put his head in his hands.

"Let me get this straight Mr Reynolds, are you saying you don't feel any remorse for the senseless killing of nine wolves in the Big Hole Valley?"

"Hell no! My wife died as an indirect result of wolves being left to roam our ranges without due diligence."

"Thank you, you may sit down," cried a satisfied George Mitchell.

Over the course of the next couple of days Frank Wellman outlined the case for the defence, gaining points for the defendant one minute, only for Mitchell to shoot it down in flames. Kaycee's testimony gained a little sympathy, but it wasn't enough. The damage had been done on day three when Wade had been called to give evidence. Wellman knew then that it would be an uphill battle from then on in. At the summing up both defence and prosecution stated their cases for the last time. Then it was over.

An hour an a half later the jury passed a verdict of guilty.

The courtroom broke into a roar of angry accusations and counter claims, until Judge Harrison slammed his gavel down several times to regain order. As the hubbub descended to an almost hushed courthouse the judge cleared his throat, his actions allowing him time to assemble his thoughts.

"This has been an unusual case, not least because of the wanton killing of endangered species, but the truly sad events that led up to the crime. Therefore I shall delay for one week my decision on sentencing while I consider what in my opinion the most suitable punishment is. We'll reconvene on Wednesday at 11.30. on the 28th March. Court adjourned!" With that he slammed down his gavel.

Chapter 62

Montana

Wade felt strangely nervous as he stood in the dock waiting for Judge Clinton Harrison to pass sentence. Ever since the trial Wade had begun weighing up his options. If it meant prison he'd take it on the chin, though the thought of losing his freedom scared him more than he was prepared to admit. A heavy fine, that was another thing, could he find the money? Would the judge allow him time to pay? What would happen to the ranch?

Judge Clinton Harrison entered the courtroom to a deathly hush. He neither looked at the defendant nor the rest of the courtroom. For what appeared five minutes, but could only have been but one, Judge Harrison, adjusted his seat and then proceeded to shuffle some papers. Then he cleared his throat and looked straight at Wade. Both men held each others glare. Was Wade expected to look down, look away, act ashamed, he didn't rightly know? All he knew was if someone looked you in the eye, you look them straight back. It wasn't a good start.

"I've given this case my utmost attention and whilst I appreciate the extenuating circumstances I find no excuse for your actions. Therefore I have decided to send you to prison for a period of one year, plus a fine of nine hundred thousand dollars, and court costs, however the state will suspend this prison sentence provided the fine and costs are paid in full within one calendar month from today's date."

The gavel slammed down on the bench and the judge still locked in a battle of wills, added, "You're free to go."

Wade glared defiantly. He knew Judge Clinton Harrison had passed the harshest sentence possibly on the word of Congressman Vince Holbrook. But he was powerless to act; Holbrook had shown that unlike Monique Delacroix he was a foe that couldn't be beaten.

"He knows I can't find that sort of cash in a month."

"We'll appeal," cried Wellman.

"What good will that do?" cried Wade.

"It'll buy you time," said Wellman feebly. He hadn't known Wade long, but long enough to know that the man standing before him wasn't the type to grovel.

"I'm shy of nearly three quarters of a million dollars; if we fail I'll be shy of a whole lot more."

"We'll chip in pa," cried Tara. Jack nodded his agreement.

"I can't ask you, I got myself into this mess, I'll just have to find a way out."

Wade knew he was caught between the proverbial rock and a hard place. Doing time was bad enough, but losing the ranch. Either or, would have been hard to take, but both, it beggared belief. Finding the money was next to impossible. Selling the ranch wasn't an option, even if he could find a buyer in time. Prison meant the state would take possession of the ranch and sell it at a rock bottom price to recover the debt and Vince Holbrook might just be the new owner. He wouldn't put it past him; the man's vindictiveness knew no bounds. Allowing Wade a month to come up with the money was neither benevolent nor kind; it was a final twisting of the knife. It was the perfect coup de grace.

* * *

Wade wasn't the type to go down without a fight. He was stubborn, pigheaded and opinionated but he wasn't a fool. Prison meant loss of liberty and loss of the ranch. It was a road he had no intention of going down. There was another way. It wouldn't stop the ranch from being sold from under his feet, but taking a trip down to old Mexico was preferable to rotting away in some stinking penitentiary. At least that way he could withdraw his savings and live like a king until the money or time ran out. It wasn't perfect but what choice did he have?

During the next three weeks Wade secretly withdrew his life savings, cashed in his investments, contacted some old friends in Nogales and arranged a place to stay across the border. From there he would work his way south. All that was left was to tell Tara and Jack. At least Jack would see the final irony of his only choice.

*   *   *

"But pa! You just can't!" cried Tara.

"Tell me, what choice do I have?"

"Pa, you're nearly eighty! What makes you think you'd be able to survive down there?"

Wade looked at his daughter, "Honey, I know you mean well, but I might be getting on in years but there's life in the old dog yet!"

"I know pa, I know you're tough as old boots, but there must be another way. We'll get a loan, we'll re-mortgage the ranch, we'll find a way," she said desperately.

"I ain't going until next Sunday. Hopefully by the time Wednesday comes around and that old Judge is a wailing and a hollerin' I'll be drinking tequila in old Mexico."

"Oh Jesus pa, ain't there nothing I can do to get you to stay."

"Short of a miracle, no there ain't. When I get fixed up, maybe you and Jack and the girls can visit."

Tara felt powerless, she knew her pa like the back of her hand. Once he set his mind to do something, there weren't anything that was going to change his mind. Life had dealt the family many blows over the years, but none had caused her more anguish than her pa having to leave his beloved ranch. Why couldn't people leave him alone, he deserved to live out the remainder of his life in peace, with his friends and family all around him. Tara felt sick to her stomach, she could beg him to stay, but for what? It was better that she knew her father was soaking up the sun in Mexico than rotting away behind prison walls.

"Okay you win," she said finally. "But promise me you'll come over Saturday night, we'll have a special meal, the girls will want to say goodbye." Tara felt tears well up as she rushed from the room.

Jack thought back to those days long gone, when he and Wade had hid out in the cave south of the border. He understood Wade's logic and he figured he'd make out fine. It was by far the better alternative. He held out his hand, "It's been a long ride partner, but just make sure you're here come Saturday. Cos if you ain't, there'll be hell to pay. And you know who'll be paying it."

Wade stifled a grin then took Jack's hand and shook it firmly. "At least I know I'm leaving her in safe hands. If she didn't have you Jack, I don't know what I'd do."

"For the record, I think what you're doing is for the best. You're up against a loaded deck here. We'll do all in our power to get the governor to take another look at your case. Fletcher and Wellman are working on it right know. You taking off ain't gonna be looked on kindly, but I reckon when the governor looks into this case it will be favourably."

They were kind words, reassuring in there sincerity, but a long shot all the same. Wade knew Jack meant well. Tipping his hat he bid Jack goodnight. Then just as he opened the door to his pickup he looked back.

"Rest assured I'll be here come Saturday night." Then he was gone into the night.

Chapter 63

Montana

Wade placed an envelope addressed to Larry on the kitchen table. Inside the envelope was a letter and a cheque.

> *Larry,*
> *Somehow or other I don't think you'll be surprised about what I'm fixing to do. By the time you read this I'll be long gone and I'm hoping you'll keep this little charade up for a mite longer. I'm too old to face prison, and I'll be damned if I'll give that low-life Holbrook the satisfaction of seeing me led away in chains. So I'm taking what's mine and hightailing it. The cheque should cover your wages and the wages of the hands for three months, I'm sorry it's not more. You've been a loyal and faithful friend to me for more years than I can remember, for that I will be forever grateful.*
>
> *Your friend*
> *Wade.*

Wade had decided that after dinner at Tara's he was heading south. Driving through the night he could be safely into Utah before dawn. Then after resting up for a few hours he'd continue his trip south. With luck he'd be in Mexico before his court date on the Wednesday.

Throwing his duffel into the flat bed of his pickup he turned back to the house and gave it one last look. The pull was there, the grip of the old place caused him to falter. He felt a tear trickle from his eye as his life flashed before him. He'd been happy here, happier than any man had a right to be, but in truth with Alex gone the house was like an empty shell. It was the land he was going to miss, the valley had been his home and yes Alex had been right, the land had been his mistress.

Wade turned and didn't give the house a backward glance as he climbed inside the pickup and switched on the engine. An hour later he turned into the gates of the Claymore Ranch. It was going to be tough saying goodbye to Tara and the girls, but he knew that in Jack his daughter and grand kids would be well taken care of. He took a deep breath, switched his face to a smile and walked up the porch steps.

"Glad you came," said Jack as he gripped Wade's hand.

"I was always coming," replied Wade with a smile.

"Beer or something stronger?"

"Vodka seven and plenty of ice."

Tara came in from the kitchen, Kaycee and Merri two steps behind. She hugged Wade to her and kissed his cheek. The girls, noisy as ever followed up and Wade laughing and teasing at the same time lifted Merri effortlessly into his arm and body.

"Whoa, this is just like Christmas!" exclaimed Wade, overcome by his family's expressions of affection. Not an overly emotional man, he thought it odd that his family could be so upbeat. He guessed they were putting on an act, a show of family unity, something he could look back upon during the long lonely days ahead of him.

Jack handed him the Vodka and Seven Up, while Tara edged herself forward. She grinned and handed Wade a slip of paper.

"No need to run pa, you're a free man."

Wade looked dumbfounded as he took the slip of paper and looked at it. He didn't understand, it was a joke, how could it be anything else? Staring once again at the slip of paper he reread it. It was a receipt from the federal courthouse of Missoula showing that the fine and court costs had been paid in full. "What! I don't understand!"

"Let's just say you've a friendly benefactor," said Tara with a grin which had spread from ear to ear.

Wade looked over Tara's left shoulder and gazed disbelievingly into the grinning face of Jason Connors. He'd known Wade for nigh on a decade, enough time to know that he was a proud man, a man that wouldn't accept charity very readily.

"There was no way I was going to let you rot in the penitentiary. Once Tara told me of your dilemma there was nothing more to be said."

"I can't accept it!" said Wade stubbornly.

"I knew you'd say that. That's why I paid it just before close of business last night. It's a done deal. There ain't a thing you could do about it. You're a free man!"

"I don't know what to say, except I'll pay you back, every cent."

"I knew you'd say that also, but there's no need. When Tara came to me with your little problem we kinda got to talking. Seems you've got a problem, had it for years from what I've heard."

Wade was puzzled. Jason looked to Tara for support. "Yeah pa, the problem of who'd run the ranch after you're gone. I told Jason that we were quite happy with the horse ranch and that when the time came we'd have to sell it."

"I had no idea that Tara wasn't interested in running the Crazy AW, I naturally presumed. So the answer was simple. I'd buy the ranch," said Jason nervously.

"What if I ain't in a mind to sell?" said Wade.

"We thought of that too," said Tara pleased with herself. "If things stayed the same, you'd be in prison; the state would have taken the ranch and sold it off cheaply to pay the fine and costs. You wouldn't have any say in it. The kicker would have been if Vince Holbrook and that bitch of a wife decided to buy the ranch. That pa; was more than I could swallow." Her eyes blazed wildly.

"Jesus, honey, for a while there I thought it was your ma talkin!"

Tara smiled at the reference to her mother, then she continued, "You want to pay Jason back fine, but it'll take you from now until god knows when. What we figured was in exchange for Jason's timely intervention he gets to build a ranch house next to yours, and buys into the Crazy AW."

"Nice idea, but ain't you and Keeley busy with your careers?" asked Wade.

"Keeley's a full time mom, making a pretty good job of it too, more than that we're fixin' to add to our family in the not to distant future. Do you really think we'd want to bring them up in a big city? I'm a country boy at heart, always was and always will be. Keeley's of the same mind. So as you can see this fits in right well. Like I was telling you a few years back, movie stardom ain't what I'm about. Owning a spread like yours, bringing my kids up to appreciate their surrounding, to care for their neighbour, to understand Christian values is worth more to me than ten Oscars. I figure to learn all I can from you, and then when the time comes, I'd like to become master of the Crazy AW."

"I don't know what to say," said Wade, he was choked. It was too much to take in. One minute he was making a break for the border, the next, he's a free man, but the kicker, the big daddy of them all, was that the Crazy AW had a bright future. Tears formed in his eyes, as he repeated "I don't know what to say?"

"All you got to do is say yes," said Jason.

"I guess you leave me no choice. Yessiree!"

Wade offered his hand and Jason grasped it and pulled him into a bearlike hug.

Chapter 64

Montana

"You what!" roared Congressman Holbrook.

"I'm sorry Vince; there wasn't anything more I could do. From what I was told Jason Connors the movie star, turned up large as life and demanded to pay Reynolds fine and court costs," wheezed Judge Harrison. "He turned up out of the blue and caught us on the hop. Connors even had his own lawyer with him to take a look over the paperwork. Jesus, Vince that son-of-bitch scrutinised everything until he was satisfied, then Connors paid the entire bill."

"There must be something we can do," declared Holbrook.

"Nothing, those lawyers of Connors left nothing to chance. It's over Vince, best forget about it. It's done!"

"Damn, fucking cowboys!" exclaimed Vince Holbrook. His angry look told Harrison it was time to make a hasty retreat. Vince's week had already started badly, now with the added irritation that Reynolds had escaped prison and more importantly managed to save his ranch, it just fuelled his frustration.

A frustration brought about by Shelby. It was nothing. He kept telling himself it was nothing. She was everything he'd ever wanted and more besides, but things had chanced. Only slightly, he kept telling himself, or at least he was beginning to think so. He'd kept his paranoia in check for more years than he could remember; it was the one chink in his armour. He was probably imagining things, but the paranoia wouldn't leave him. Shelby was precious to him, not only was she good looking with a fabulous figure, she was sophisticated, elegant, intelligent and a devil in the bedroom department.

Her wantonness in the bedroom had kept him from straying, yet it was that very wantonness that was torturing him now. She'd often told him that a little uncertainty was good for their marriage and at first he'd believed her. But of late she'd seemed distant, aloof even.

It had all started around the time of the arrest of Wade Reynolds. He'd been so preoccupied with getting a conviction that he'd let his guard slip. An odd phone-call with no one at the other end, he'd put down to a wrong number, but when it happened again, his suspicions grew. When Shelby told him she had a meeting to attend in Great Falls he'd thought nothing of it, but later in the day he checked her desk diary. There was no meeting pencilled in. This wasn't unusual, as Shelby often forgot to right down every detail in the diary. It was nothing; of course it was nothing the man kept telling himself. His paranoia grew and grew. He'd thought to tackle her about the phone-calls and meeting but realised just as they could be the starting of an affair they more than likely were just as innocent.

Vince Holbrook shrugged off the minor disappointment of Wade Reynolds and concentrated on getting his paranoia in check. It was a dangerous affliction, and from the beginning it had been his Achilles heel, culminating in him having to run to his father to fix things. From that moment on until the death of his father his life was not his own.

Andrew Vincent Holbrook had taken his son in hand and tried to guide him into the family business. It was his only failure in life, but his labours were not entirely in vain as Vince began to study the law. From there it was just one small step to politics. Vince Holbrook justified his father's faith in him and Andrew Holbrook became proud of his son's achievements. He'd pulled strings to get his young son out of the worst trouble of his life, and he asked himself one question. Was it worth it? By God it was!

From that turning point in Vince Holbrook's life he'd never truly loved another woman. He wouldn't let any of them come close; he used them, wined and dined, then bedded them before casting them out like yesterdays garbage. But his political ambitions required a young and beautiful wife, the best eye candy that was ready to be swept of its feet, and along came Ruth. She fitted the bill perfectly. He wined, dined and bedded her, much the same as others that had gone before, and somewhere along the line he'd convinced himself that she was the one. He was wrong and his philandering continued and his shot at the governorship of Montana went begging.

Shelby was different, he knew that the moment he clapped eyes on her. She was everything he'd ever wanted and couldn't have, and she'd swept him off his feet. Pretty faces were just that, pretty faces and nothing more. Shelby was special; it was like being given a second chance. At last Vince Holbrook had it all. But now the paranoia was back and it was slowly decaying his brain.

Drastic action was called for if he was to defeat the monster inside his head. He needed time to think, time away with Shelby, far away from the everyday grind, time to renew his relationship with this most wonderous of women.

"Darling, have you got much on during the next couple of weeks?" asked Holbrook.

Shelby smiled, frowned slightly, wiggled her nose and laughed. "Why?" she was intrigued by his question.

"I've been thinking. You're right, I've been getting obsessed with this Reynolds character and I haven't paid enough attention to you. So unless you have other plans I've decide we're taking a trip to Tahiti next week. Sun, sea, surf, oh and that other S word."

"Swimming," giggled Shelby.

Vince laughed, oh how he loved this woman. She hadn't hesitated, made an excuse or batted an eyelid. If she was having an affair he'd have told by her actions. His paranoia was swept away like a bad smell.

"We're taking a cruise, the finest champagne, a deluxe suite, yes baby we're going first class all the way."

*   *   *

The next two weeks were the most idyllic time of Vince and Shelby's lives. They came back rested, relaxed and reinvigorated. Vince was back on top of the world and Shelby had promised him that when she got back she was going to make a concerted effort in Vince's race for the governorship of Montana.

Life was getting better and better . . . .

Chapter 65

Washington DC

"Freezing conditions claim the life of Congressman's wife"
The adverse weather conditions that have befallen the state of Montana have claimed the life of Congressman Vince Holbrook's wife Shelby. At a notorious hairpin bend on highway 12 near MacDonald Pass, Mrs Shelby Holbrook's Mercedes SLR skidded on the ice and crashed through the safety barrier, plummeting over one hundred and thirty feet into a ravine. Pathology reports seem to suggest her neck was broken on impact. Congressman Holbrook was said to be inconsolable. A close friend of the couple said they were very much in love and had only recently returned from a luxury cruise around the romantic islands of Tahiti.

"That son of a bitch!" exclaimed Fletcher as he reread the story on the front page of the Washington Post, "Ruth get down here!"

Ruth hurried into the kitchen of their apartment, "What's all the fuss?" she cried.

"Read it!" he said forcefully as he pushed the paper in Ruth's direction.

"Oh Jesus!" exclaimed Ruth. "He's killed her!" Her hand moved up towards her mouth. "The bastard's killed her!"

"We don't know that for sure," said Fletcher. "It could have been an accident as the paper says."

"How likely is that?"

"About as likely as him murdering her," he countered.

"I wonder how Wade, Jack and Tara are taking the news. I know Tara hates the woman, but she didn't deserve this," added Ruth as she read and reread the front page.

Montana

Tara couldn't take her eyes off the television screen. Shelby was headline news. Her face smiled back at Tara, then the screen switched to her Mercedes being dragged up from the ravine by heavy machinery. The picture changed yet again and showed a recent charity event where Congressman Holbrook and his wife were guests of honour.

Jack walked into the lounge area, he'd heard the news on his car radio three or four minutes before he arrived back home. "Yeah I just heard, it's terrible," he volunteered.

"Well I can't say I'll shed a tear. The woman was a gold plated bitch. I know you shouldn't speak ill of the dead, but in her case I'll make the exception."

* * *

Larry broke the news to Wade and Jason as they were loading up bales of hay onto the trailer.

"I'm sorry to hear that," said Wade softly. "I wasn't here when my Taw died, so I guess I don't have personal knowledge of the lady," added Wade as he addressed himself to Jason.

Jason was looking a little perplexed, until Larry began to fill him in. "Taw was fixing to marry that young filly, things got out of hand, and Tara and her had a set too. Then Taw got into the action, busted his hand, couldn't play the piano no more . . ."

461

"The long and the short of it, Shelby left Taw with a broken heart. Not long after my son was killed in a riding accident. Best damn rider I've seen sitting a horse," interrupted Wade.

"You mean he commi . . . ."

Larry silenced Jason's reply with a withering look.

"Still what ever she was, nobody deserves to go that way," added Wade.

* * *

Vince Holbrook locked himself in his room. For once the papers had got it spot on, he was inconsolable with grief. They had it all. He kept torturing himself. They had it all, but then she had to spoil things. His paranoia had gotten the better of him, it had fooled him into believing Shelby was having an affair, but it wasn't true, the final irony, it wasn't true. His paranoia had taken the one thing he loved the most in this world, his Shelby.

Everything had been great, no better than great, absolutely fantastic. They arrived home from Tahiti and he thought the monster that lived in the darkest recesses of his brain had been locked away forever.

Shelby had thrown herself back into work almost immediately they'd got back.

"Can't let the grass grow under our feet," she'd said, as she began preparing her first salvo in the promotion of Vince Holbrook for Governor, campaign. And for the next two months it was a whirlwind kaleidoscope of committee meetings, campaign dinners, promotional visits, speeches, donations to charity, and about everything else under the sun, all carefully choreographed by Shelby Holbrook.

Then one day Shelby received a phone-call. Vince wouldn't have noticed only it seemed to knock her off her stride. She recovered almost immediately and Vince thought it was just his imagination, until she told him about an urgent meeting she had to attend. Vince remained silent. Unfortunately for Shelby, the monster that had been locked away in the deepest recess of his mind picked the lock.

Consumed by paranoia Vince stole into her office and checked for the meeting that was so urgent. No meeting had been written down. The genie was out of the bottle. His paranoia was winning the battle of wills. One minute it was telling him that she was unfaithful the next it was telling him it was just his imagination. He thought about hiring a private detective, but changed his mind. For a man in his position it was best to keep his cards close to his chest. He couldn't follow her for fear of being seen, so he decided to observe her movements from afar.

It was the nature of her job, she'd known many people in the years she'd been in Public Relations, it could be an old friend, a business acquaintance, an old lover, or perhaps none of the above. For the time being he'd thought he'd just keep an eye.

*   *   *

As he sat in his darkened room sipping a twelve year old malt he cursed his luck. He'd been brought up in a world of privilege, where anything he wanted was his at the snap of his fingers, but twice the things he valued the most were snatched away. Only this time he didn't have his father to bail him out. This time he would have to rely on his own cunning. He knew that if he was to survive he had to harden his heart. He'd get over this loss, start over. He still had his looks, his power and all the money he'd ever need. She was dead, in the end she'd brought it down on herself, she was a fucking bitch just like Erin Ryder.

Chapter 66

Washington D.C.

"If what we think is true, we're partly to blame!" stammered Ruth. "If . . . if I hadn't spotted the resemblance."

"It's not your fault, it's not mine either so stop beating yourself up," said Fletcher. "I'll make some enquires, see what I can find out."

"I only looked in that old dusty file because of what Holbrook was doing to Wade. I felt so impotent to do anything. I'm a legal secretary, nothing more, but I thought if only I could find something."

"And you did. I missed it; we all missed it, but you found the clue that could unravel Holbrook's little empire."

"But she's dead, she didn't deserve to die."

"Stop beating yourself up Ruth. I retrieved the paper from the trash. I cut the article and photograph of the Holbrook's wedding from the paper. I put it into the file. If anyone's to blame it's me."

"But it was me who brought it to your attention," cried Ruth.

"You showed me an old photograph of Erin Ryder and said isn't there an uncanny resemblance between the murdered girl and Shelby. The girl was twenty; Shelby was what forty seven for Christ-sake!"

"Enough of a resemblance for you to fly to Montana."

"True there were similarities and yes, you'd put it into my head, I had to check it out, but you're not to blame for that woman's death. Holbrook is!"

"You've finally admitted it. You think Holbrook murdered Shelby."

Fletcher looked at Ruth with a resigned look. "Well yeah, I guess I have," he said with his hands up in a gesture of mock surrender. "But you putting two and two together was just one part in a very complicated puzzle."

"I still wish I hadn't interfered," said Ruth.

It was just like Ruth, it was one of the things about her that he loved. It was true she'd played a small part in uncovering Shelby's connection to the murdered girl, but it was left to him to rummage through photo album after photo album and even then it was down to luck that amongst the loose photos at the back of one album he found a picture of Shelby and Taw. The resemblance was remarkable; Shelby at a similar age could have been the murdered girl's twin, never mind sister.

Fletcher thought about the moment he decided to contact Shelby and confront her with what he'd discovered. He'd talked it though with Sam Kilbane, who'd told him to go easy, even leave sleeping dogs lie. But Fletcher felt he owed Wade a debt, not to mention Perry Logan, the man that had been on death row for so many years. With hesitation he dialled her house phone. A man answered on a couple of occasions but eventually he got through to Shelby on her cell-phone.

"Good morning, I'm Sam Kilbane special investigator FBI. You are I take it Shelby Holbrook?"

"Yes," came the guarded reply.

"Would I be correct in assuming that Erin Ryder was your sister?"

"Who?" exclaimed Shelby as she fought for time to recover from the shock at hearing her sister's name for the first time in years.

"Let's stop playing games, you are her sister, aren't you?"

She denied it at first, but Fletcher persisted. "I know this must be painful after so many years but we have reason to believe you can help us in our investigation into her murder."

"I thought that was a cold case!" she exclaimed.

Fletcher punched the air. He'd felt it in his water, yet until Shelby confirmed what he suspected he had diddly squat. "We're pursuing a new lead. As you know the alleged killer Perry Logan has always declared his innocence."

"How can I help?"

"You can either come to the FBI offices at Helena or I can meet you at a place of your convenience. Your choice."

"If I meet you somewhere other than FBI offices how will I know you're on the level?"

"Good question. I'll produce my identity card, my driving license, my library ticket, whatever. If you ain't satisfied I'm who I say I am, you can holler the restaurant down. I take it we'll be doing lunch?" Fletcher was hoping his casual manner would help her drop her guard and relax.

Shelby laughed, "Believe me, if I have just an inkling you aren't who you purport to be you'll wish you hadn't made this phone-call."

Fletcher reflected on his ruse, claiming to be Sam Kilbane wasn't the smartest of ideas, but he reflected that Shelby was a smart cookie and could easily check up on Sam Kilbane to see if he was genuine. Giving his own name, due to the circumstances of Holbrook's connection with Wade's case wouldn't have been the smartest move. Meeting face to face in a crowed restaurant might be a calculated risk, but it was one he felt he had to take.

Shelby intrigued by this mysterious phone conversation quickly arranged to meet him at Chez Deveaux a French restaurant in the heart of Deer Lodge. She'd thought to tell Vince but decided against telling him. This was her past, it was something that she'd put behind her. If this came to nothing it was better left unsaid.

*   *   *

Shelby arrived first and was led to a prearranged secluded table, away from the cacophony of an exclusive French restaurant during its busy period. She'd no soon ordered a glass of Château de Pape when Fletcher slipped into the seat opposite.

"I'll have what the lady's having," he informed the waiter. At the same time he threw his Homeland Security ID on the table. "Please don't make a scene. At least here me out before you do," he added in a cheeky manner.

Shelby scanned his ID, in half a second flat, then with the remainder of that second she recovered her composure.

"I don't know what it is you want Mr Coppersmith and I don't particularly like being brought here under false pretences. I know who you are, now you've less than a minute to convince me not to scream rape!"

"Erin Ryder was not murdered by Perry Logan!" Fletcher saw in her eyes that he'd bought at least five minutes.

Shelby's self confidence evaporated, "He served twenty years, of course he's guilty."

"I suspect you don't actually believe that." Fletcher paused as he watched his words sink in. "Before I go on, I'd like to reassure you this is nothing to do with the Reynolds vs Montana Fish and Game court case."

"What is it you want from me?" she asked guardedly.

"From your reaction, I think I've already gleamed part of it. Why don't you tell me a little about yourself and your sister?"

They were interrupted by the waiter as he set down the two glasses of wine, "Would Madam and Monsieur like to order, or do you need a little more time?" he asked in a French accent that bordered somewhere between Boise, Idaho and Billing, Montana.

"We'd like ten minutes," said Fletcher forcefully, "Fifteen maybe." For what he was going to reveal, he guessed Shelby wouldn't be staying for lunch.

"Before I begin, can I have your reassurance that my life before I came to Montana be kept in the past."

Fletcher nodded and gave her his reassurance.

Shelby nervously cleared her throat, "Erin was five years older than I. We came from the Lower East Side of New York City. We were shit poor, without as much as a nickel to our names, our pa left us when we were both little. But with ma's help we both garnered good grades at school and eventually Erin won a scholarship to Montana State."

Shelby took a sip of her wine.

"She'd only just graduated when she was murdered along with her boy friend. They were getting engaged you know."

"Yeah I heard that," encourage Fletcher.

"Like I said we were dirt poor, the dead boy, Chad Dempsey was from a very rich family. The first we heard about their murders was three weeks after the event. My sister was dead and buried and we knew nothing about it. I was sixteen; I couldn't have raised the train fare, if I'd tried. It broke ma's heart, she took it so badly that eventually she became ill; I spent the best part of two years looking after her. Ma died just before my eighteenth birthday."

It wasn't at all what Fletcher expected, "Do you want a breather, I just never realised."

"No, it's good to get it out in the open. With ma gone I was left all alone. I did whatever menial jobs I could and put myself through college. I found I had a natural aptitude for PR work and spent a few years learning the ropes. I saw how the rich conducted their lives and I realised with my looks and brains I would never go hungry again."

Shelby smiled and took another sip of her wine. Fletcher did the same. He'd never met this woman before, but from what he'd heard she was a bitch of the first magnitude, yet the woman sitting opposite was nothing like what he'd been expecting.

Shelby smiled devilishly; she knew men and she could tell she was winning him over. It felt good, to know she still had it. "Fortunately for me I had an insatiable appetite for sex, and soon realised that men were putty in my hands. I moved up through the firm, partly because of this affliction but mostly because of my skills in Public Relations."

Fletcher knew from his training with the FBI that it was the little things that people said, or what they didn't say, that mattered. He'd hoped to learn more about the murder of her sister than he knew already but he sensed that Shelby knew less than he.

"I quite forgot myself, I've been rambling on. Enough about me, you said Perry Logan didn't kill my sister, then who did?"

"I was hoping you'd be able to tell me," answered Fletcher. "Meeting Taw Reynolds and visiting Montana was no coincidence!"

Shelby was silent for close on a minute. Fletcher had struck a nerve. He waited patiently for her to continue.

"I think we'd better order," she said looking down at the menu as she bought the time she needed, "I'll have another glass of wine."

Fletcher called the waiter over, they ordered and then the waiter replenished their glasses.

"You're very perceptive Agent Coppersmith, it was no coincidence. Ever since my sister's death I'd had this feeling that something wasn't right, that things didn't add up. We might have been poor but those rich people in Montana could have made the effort to contact us. When I found out that there was an up and coming concert pianist on our books and that he was from Montana I asked to be assigned to him. The rest I assume you already know."

Fletcher nodded, "Did you find out anything while you were in Montana, concerning Erin's murder?"

"There was nothing that I didn't know already. Perry Logan was on death row and was due to be executed," she stopped in mid sentence.

"Go on, it might be something!" blurted Fletcher.

"The police report said it was a botched robbery that had resulted in a double homicide and rape. But they never found Erin's crucifix and chain."

Fletcher pricked up his ears, there was no mention on any of the reports of a crucifix. Perry Logan had been caught leaving the scene, the gun still in his hand, there was nothing else found on his person. If he'd taken it surely they'd have found it. But then maybe she'd lost it weeks or months before the murder. "She might have lost it anytime," said the agent from Homeland Security.

"No, she wouldn't have. Our mother saved what she could, we went without, just so she could buy the cross, she even had it engraved with Erin's name on the back. Mom said it would keep her safe."

"She could still have lost it," insisted Fletcher.

"If she did, then it was a couple of days before her murder. When she graduated she sent us a photograph. She was smiling out at us and the crucifix was clearly visible."

It took every inch of Fletcher's self control to stop him jumping for joy. "Do you still have the photograph?"

"Yes, it's in a safe place and its staying there!"

Fletcher's euphoria about the crucifix was quickly dispelled as he realised it would be circumstantial at best. The waiter reappeared and began serving them their meal.

"Bon appetite!"

Shelby giggled and caught the amusement in Fletcher's eye, if only the waiter could listen to himself. "You know," said Shelby as she picked at her food, "that's the most I've told anyone about my past."

Fletcher could see the conversation was going nowhere, he'd thought mistakenly that Shelby had latched on to Vince Holbrook to discover the truth. But it was clear unless she was unbelievably good at deception she didn't have a clue that he might be implicated in the death of her sister. It was an appalling coincidence. It had been obvious from the beginning of there lunch-date that she was concerned about something, but as the meeting progressed and Fletcher reassured her that her secret was safe, Shelby began to relax. They began telling each other jokes and sharing amusing anecdotes. Her manner and actions were not consistent with a woman that knew her husband had killed her older sister. Fletcher struggled with his conscience. Was it right to leave her in ignorance or should he put the cat amongst the pigeons. All in all it had been an enlightening and surprising experience. Shelby was far nicer than he'd been led to believe and the thought of upsetting her apple cart did not appeal.

In the car park at the side of her Mercedes SLR coupe, they said their goodbyes.

"I must say, it's been a pleasure to have met you," said Fletcher.

I also," replied Shelby with a cheeky smile.

Fletcher was about to let the lunch date get the better of him, to let her go, to let her walk back into the arms of the man that had more than likely murdered her sister, he fought the urge, she turned towards her car. He knew from the small talk how much she loved her husband, how they were two of a kind. It wasn't up to him to play god. He fought with his emotions. She wasn't as bad as she'd been painted. She didn't deserve to live in ignorance. It wasn't up to him. In the end he went half way.

"Shelby!" he called after her. She turned and smiled. "It's nothing, just a thought, but how well did your husband know Chad Dempsey?"

He could see the shock, the suspicion, the hurt and he hated himself for it. Ruth was wrong; she wasn't to blame for Shelby's death. He was! And it would stay with him forever.

Chapter 67

Montana

Shelby's funeral was a lavish affair; it was something she would have approved of, thought Fletcher, as he blended in with the two hundred or so mourners. He'd felt compelled to attend, to pay his respects and seek absolution. Ruth had told him he was not to blame, no more than she was in discovering Shelby's past.

"It was just a chain of events; no one could have foreseen what was likely to happen."

She was right of course, but `Fletcher couldn't help feeling responsible. Not content with igniting the flame, he'd poured gasoline over the dying embers.

He'd hoped that his chance remark would have born fruit, but as Wade's trial approached, Holbrook's political train kept thundering on. The frustration, anguish and sheer helplessness he felt as Wade stood to lose the ranch was unbearable. Vince Holbrook was a powerful and dangerous enemy and in some ways far more deadly than Monique.

When Fletcher heard how Jason Connors had bailed out Wade, he was delighted and strangely jealous in equal measures. It was an irrational thought, but one that wouldn't go away. He felt he owed Wade a great debt; the big man had given him an identity, a family and a home. It was for this very reason that he decided to contact Shelby again.

"What is it that you want?" snapped Shelby as she gripped the phone tightly.

"We need to talk!" he'd said bluntly. Despite their first meeting Fletcher decided a more businesslike approach was needed.

Shelby had been taken slightly aback by his gruffness and was about to tell Fletcher where to get off, but his parting salvo as they'd left the restaurant had left her uncertain. Months had flown by since that first meeting, yet somehow it was like an itch she couldn't scratch.

"I think we do," she countered brusquely. "Let's cut to the chase. I'll meet you tomorrow morning at ten in the car park opposite Albertsons on Main."

'Not the intimacy of Chez Deveurex; no, not this time,' thought Fletcher. Shelby Holbrook was mad as all hell. The lady meant business.

*   *   *

Fletcher drove into the car park at exactly ten and saw Shelby's Mercedes coupe parked discreetly nine rows back from the front entrance to the supermarket. He drew up alongside, climbed out of the rental, slammed the door too and walked around the back. A quick glance around, then he opened the passenger door of Shelby's Mercedes.

She tilted her head towards Fletcher and motioned for him to climb in. Almost before he was settled she screamed at him, "What the fuck are you after!" Her Lower East Side roots coming to the fore.

"Easy, easy!" replied Fletcher, raising his hands in mock surrender. "I thought we were friends," he added.

A fiery glare stared back at him, "Friends don't try to muddy the waters. What the hell did you mean when you asked how well did Vince know Dempsey?"

"I think you already know the answer to that one," countered Fletcher.

"I don't know what your game is, but Vince isn't a murderer!"

"I never said he was," said Fletcher glibly.

"You.. you . . . . You implied it," cried Shelby.

"It must have struck a cord," fished Fletcher.

"Okay, okay," she backtracked. "I had a few sleepless nights going over what you said, or didn't say. But you're wrong, beneath that ruthless exterior Vince Holbrook is essentially a good man, a decent man!"

Desperate to push home his advantage, he decided to go out on a limb. "Okay Shelby, I'm going to level with you. We have reason to believe that Vince Holbrook might be responsible for Erin Ryder's murder." His heart went out to her as her vulnerability began to show. She so desperately wanted to believe her husband was blameless

"That's just not true," she declared.

Fletcher pushed his point home, "When we discovered that Erin was your sister, I naturally assumed that you'd married Holbrook to get close to him, to find out the truth."

Shelby shook her head in disbelief.

"I'd made an assumption and I was wrong. I know that now," declared Fletcher.

"So why throw that curve. Do you know how much grief it's caused me?"

"I can imagine. I wasn't going to say anything, but then I thought you had a right to know. I'm sorry if I hurt you."

Shelby's defences weakened and she smiled, and her devastating attractiveness shone through. She wasn't Ruth, or Merri come to that, but beneath that businesslike exterior she was just as vulnerable. Twice he'd met her, and each time she'd made an impression. Despite what Tara thought; he liked her.

"Apology accepted. Now I'd like a straight answer to a question."

"Thank you. Ask away."

"Where does your allegation come from, and what proof have you that Vince killed my sister?" Shelby's heart was beating faster than she'd have thought possible.

Fletcher knew his assumptions wouldn't hold water with her, "Perry Logan, the man that spent half his life in prison for the murder of Chad Dempsey and your sister said he was set up by Holbrook's father. He allegedly handed Logan the gun and pointed him in the direction of the murder."

Fletcher watched the worry drain from Shelby's face, her smile reflected her relief. "You're going on the word of a convicted criminal, and that's all?"

Fletcher declined to mention the abduction of Ruth and himself, the consequential release by Perry Logan and his part in the conviction of Carson Burroughs. And in truth, what evidence did they have against Holbrook. "Look maybe I got things wrong."

"There's no maybe about it. Vince wouldn't harm a fly," said Shelby.

"But he did know Chad Dempsey?" fished Fletcher.

"Yes he knew him. They were best friends at Montana State."

"You did check then," added Fletcher triumphantly.

"Goodbye Mr Coppersmith," came the frosty dismissal.

Fletcher knowing he was beaten climbed out of the coupe, then leaned back inside the car's interior. "I'm sorry if I've caused you anguish, that was not my intention."

Shelby laughed, "On the contrary, I'm glad we've had this little chat. I know my husband and I'm sorry I ever doubted him in the slightest."

Fletcher chose to ignore her last remark. It would have been futile to continue down that road. Instead, he handed her his business card, "Do with this as you will, but if ever you feel like talking don't hesitate to get in touch."

Shelby's well manicured hand took the card from his grasp, and coyly brushed it against her lips before placing it in her designer handbag. "I doubt I will, but I'll keep it as a memento of our meetings. Goodbye Fletcher."

Goodbye Shelby," he smiled, closed the coupe door and walked back to the rental.

*   *   *

He watched from the relative cover of the marble tombstones that littered the well manicured cemetery as Shelby's coffin was lowered into the ground. The pathology report had shown that Shelby had died from a broken neck, consistent with the crash. And in truth the grief on Holbrook's face seemed genuine, his eulogy in the church was both heartfelt and warm and strangely as it seemed the Homeland Security man found him self doubting the words of Perry Logan. Perhaps Shelby had been right after all.

Chapter 68

Montana

Shelby's funeral was all the more poignant to Wade, Alex had died almost to the day of Shelby's fatal crash. He couldn't believe that a year could pass so quickly. He guessed it was the events since Alex's death that had made time fly, the incident with the wolves, the subsequent trial and Jason's timely intervention. Then of course there was the building of a new house to Jason and Keeley's specifications. Wade had remarked that it was going to cost an awful lot of money.

Jason had laughed, "Let me tell you Wade, some of these here movie stars earn an obscene amount."

Wade neither knew nor cared how much money movie stars earned, he was just grateful that Jason had decided to put his money to good use. His only fear was that Jason would find ranch life too dull after living the high-life in Hollywood. His fears and reservations were quickly dispelled when the new house was finished and Keeley moved in. He'd observed how the famous Keeley O'Hara took to motherhood like she was born to it, giving birth to their second child, a baby girl two weeks after they arrived. There was something about her presence that Wade took to at once. She was down to earth, and was soon turning the house into a home. And then it dawned on him, just what it was about Keeley that he so admired, she could have been that sassy young girl from Texas that he met in the Metlen bar so many years ago. It was then that Wade could see that Jason had chosen wisely. He was after all a family man in search of a family. Now he had one and Wade was sure they'd make something of their lives in the Big Hole Valley. 'Family,' mused Wade, 'that's what this ranch needed.'

He found himself reminiscing about those early years, bouncing first Taw, and then Tara on his knee. Yes it was good that one day Jason and Keeley would take over the running of the ranch. And then he found himself thinking of Alex, and he smiled.

When Jason and Keeley named their second child Alexandria after Alex, he was both delighted and a little overcome. He was sure Alex was smiling down upon them.

*   *   *

As the year drew to a close Wade counted his blessings. 2008 had indeed been eventful, not the least for the way his family gelled with the Connors. Jack had become firm friends with Jason and helped with designing the new house. He'd painstakingly helped with every stage of construction, doing as much work as the local construction workers that Jason had hired from Wisdom and Dillon. Causing more than one construction worker to remark, "That Englishman sure knows how to put a shift in, and then some!"

Jason was grateful for Jack's help, and although there was around thirteen years' difference in their age, they got along like brothers. Tara too, found both the Connors fun to be with, along with both his grand children who were spending more and more time at the Connors house. Fletcher and Ruth visited from time to time and Wade couldn't help but note, the dynasty he'd helped create. After him, came Jack and Tara, Fletcher and Ruth, a generation down came Jason and Keeley, followed by Kaycee and Merri, then Fletcher's boy Johan and finally James and baby Alex. Again he thought about his Alex, although to be honest she was never far from his thoughts.

It was while he was musing that Ruth crept up on him and put her arm around him in an affectionate hug. She smiled up at him.

"You miss her, don't you," she said gently.

"Every day," he replied. "She loved this land almost as much as I do. I think she fell in love with it before she fell in love with me." He smiled at the thought, remembering . . .

"I really love it here. From my bedroom window I can see the Bitterroots. Every morning since I've been here I've ridden up through the timberline just to breathe the cool clean air," Alex had said passionately.

Yes, he still remembered that first conversation as if it had been yesterday. "And for nearly fifty years she'd taken that same ride up through the timberline to breathe the cool clean air," he said quietly to himself.

"Sorry, what was that Wade," enquired Ruth.

"Nothing, I was just there . . ."

Ruth didn't know if it was the time, but Fletcher's behavior surrounding the death of Shelby needed to be addressed. And Ruth knew the only one he'd listen to was Wade.

"I'm worried about Fletcher," announced Ruth.

"How so?" cried Wade, suddenly now full aware.

"It's a long story. Some of it you know, some you don't."

"So you're saying Shelby Shannon, is the sister of the murdered girl Erin Ryder! That is some strange co-incidence!" exclaimed Wade after Ruth had outlined the story.

"That's what Fletcher thought. That's why he arranged to meet her," cried Ruth.

"He what!"

"He thought he was on to something, but it turned out, it was just that; a strange co-incidence," said Ruth. "He only went to see her because he felt it would help you. He drew a blank."

"The accident . . ." cried Wade, now beginning to understand.

"After your trial, Fletcher felt he owed it one last try. He arranged to meet Shelby for the second time."

"And he thinks, Shelby was murdered because he was poking into Vince Holbrook's affairs."

"That's about the size of it," exhaled Ruth. "He went to her funeral. You really need to talk to him. He believes he's responsible for her death."

"That's ridiculous. Where is Fletcher?"

Ruth pointed up into the distance, "He left before breakfast, said he was going to put fresh flowers on Merri's grave."

Wade pulled on his top coat, looked at Ruth, "I'm obliged," he said as he tipped his hat and made for the stables.

Ruth watched from the porch steps as Wade and his Buckskin horse stepped out through the snow on their journey to Cougar Pass. Fletcher had taken her up there once a few years ago. "I'll understand if you don't want too," he'd said. Ruth had smiled and said she'd go. She had somehow felt it right to visit that one time. An hour later she glanced outside and could just about make out the silhouette of horse and rider as they pushed on through the snow.

*   *   *

Smoke rose from the old line shack as Wade approached. The Appaloosa that Fletcher favored was hitched outside the run down shack munching on some oats.

"Hello the house," cried Wade.

Fletcher came to the door steaming coffee cup warming his hands.

"Could sure use me a cup," said Wade as he swung down from the big Buckskin. Fletcher stepped back inside while Wade tended to his horse, he returned minutes later with a second cup of the steaming liquid.

"What brings you out here?" asked Fletcher.

"You," came the reply. "Ruth's told me what you tried to do. I appreciate it."

"She send you up here to talk?"

"You could say," replied Wade.

Both men sipped on their coffee, and then Fletcher walked outside and across to Merri's grave. Wade followed a few steps behind.

"I ain't fully over her, I guess I never ever will," said Fletcher as he looked down on Merri's grave. "I love Ruth, of course I do, but a part of my heart will always belong up here with her."

"I know that son," said Wade.

"You know, I never really knew my pa, it's something I regret. We had so little time. Yet knowing you; makes me feel close to him somehow."

"That I understand," said Wade, "Now Ruth says you blame yourself for this Shelby woman's death. Hell, Fletcher, the autopsy said it was a freak accident. There's no way of knowing it was anything else."

"But I feel it in my craw!"

"That maybe so, but some things remain unpunished, that's life. There ain't a damned thing you can do about."

Fletcher kicked at the snow beneath his feet. Then slowly he turned toward Wade, "I guess you're right." He smiled and began walking back towards the horses, "It's snowing in Washington right now. You should come for a visit."

"Snow . . . You know I might take you up on that," said Wade smiling.

Chapter 69

Montana

Vince looked out of his picture window at the rolling hills of snow. Christmas was fast approaching, and he reflected that he'd be spending it alone. The thought depressed him; until he thought about the alternatives. He'd got away with murder, not once but twice. He should have been counting his blessings, but Shelby wouldn't go away.

It kept going around and around in his head. Sometimes he thought it was just a dream, that he'd awake and she'd be lying next to him asleep, but he'd seen her broken body, he'd seen the lifeless form that once had been his wife and he knew the reality of what he'd done.

He'd thought she was having an affair, how wrong could one man be. If he'd have known what she was after, things would have been so much different. But blinded by jealousy, the furtive phone calls, the clandestine meetings, they could amount to only one thing.

And even when he'd confronted Shelby with her infidelity, she denied it. She tried turning the tables; she asked why he'd killed her sister. Taken aback by her allegation he responded.

"Your sister!" Even as he uttered those words he knew, the resemblance so uncanny. He should have known.

"Yes my sister, Erin Ryder, you killed her," she screamed. Her eyes filled with a mixture of tears and flame, "Why Vince why?"

Even then, there was a get out clause; he could see in her eyes she wanted him to tell her it wasn't so. It would have been that simple. He was a prominent figure, he had enemies, and anyone of them could have planted lies about him. Shelby's eyes, her whole body was screaming out at him to deny what she was saying. She began to cry as she implored him to tell her it was an outright lie. But it had gone too far, Erin had never left him, he could still see her eyes as she lay there staring defiantly up at him after the rape. "Do it!" she spat up at him as he pointed the revolver at her. "Do it, do it, do . . . ." Her words lost in the violent explosion that followed.

He'd wanted to confess, to atone for his sins, but his father thought otherwise. Rich and powerful, Andrew Holbrook wasn't about to see his future, the whole future of the Holbrook dynasty dangling from the end of a rope. Taking charge, he commanded his son.

"Go home, clean yourself up, and forget this ever happened."

Andrew Holbrook wasn't concerned about the girl; she was a no one, whereas Vince's best friend Chad was a Dempsey. He came from an equally wealthy family and knowing Tom Dempsey as he did, he knew the man wouldn't rest until someone paid for his son's death.

Vince Holbrook frightened, sickened even, began to realise the implications of his actions followed his father's instructions to the letter. But Erin Ryder's words never left him, they were his constant companion. Until the moment he first met Shelby; after that Erin Ryder became invisible.

Vince Holbrook could only see redemption in Shelby's eyes. She loved him; he could see it on her face. He started to cry.

"I'm sorry, so sorry," finally he would find forgiveness.

First shock, then betrayal, then anger as Shelby's face distorted into a murderous rage, and from beyond the grave Erin Ryder lunged at him.

He told himself after it was over that it was either her or him, but as she charged his survival instincts kicked in as he calmly stepped to one side and aimed a Karate type blow to her throat.

He'd been taught by his numerous bodyguards the marital art some years earlier. He'd enjoyed the course and included it in his daily work out. As designed the blow crushed her wind pipe and snapped her neck. She was dead before she hit the floor.

Shelby's confrontation had brought it all back. He was a coward; he'd always been a coward. Telling his father had somehow absolved him of all blame. When the initial shock had worn off, Vince Holbrook had looked at the implications and understood that some one had to pay the price. That an innocent man was going to face the death penalty didn't cause him any sleepless nights. And throughout his career he'd used and abused without fear, hurt all before him without any qualms. But strange as it seemed Shelby had found something in him that had been lost. It had remained dormant until she ignited that one spark of human kindness. But now that spark was truly extinguished along with the lifeless body of Shelby.

Thinking on his feet, Holbrook began working out how to get rid of Shelby's body without implicating himself. Luckily for Vince it was the servants' night off and he and Shelby had been alone in the house at the time. Quickly he picked up her body and took it undetected through the house and into the back door of the garage. Within seconds he'd laid Shelby neatly into the trunk of her Mercedes. He had become ice cool from the moment he stared down at Shelby's body. His mind began working out a plan of disposal. He remembered how only three days earlier he'd hit an icy patch at a hairpin turn out on highway 12. Grabbing a warm top coat he threw it in alongside Shelby and then he donned one of Shelby's favourite coats. It was a tight fit, but the hood and ear muffs that were attached helped disguise his appearance.

Satisfied that he had things under control he opened the garage doors. Then he slammed the door of the coupe shut, a sound that echoed, he hoped up towards the servants' quarters, and then he revved the car violently before racing off at neck break speed. He chuckled to himself as he was sure one or two lights went on.

Half a mile before MacDonald Pass, Vince Holbrook pulled over to the side of the road. A quick look in both directions told him what he wanted to know. He'd seen only four cars, three going in one direction the other pulled off some three miles back. He took Shelby from the trunk, exchanged coats and placed her in the driving seat. He positioned her hands, now in the first signs of rigour, onto the steering wheel. Then he cleverly wedged one of her three inch heel shoes against the gas pedal while the car was in neutral. Reaching across Shelby's lifeless body, he put the automatic into drive. It lunged forward and Vince Holbrook had barely enough time to pull his arm clear from the fast accelerating Mercedes. The car sped forward at an angle, gaining speed as it advanced towards the bend and the inevitable crash barriers. He watched, transfixed as the four hundred yards became two hundred, then one hundred before hitting the barrier.

For one heart stopping moment Vince thought the Mercedes would stall and come to rest at the side of the road, but the devil's luck was with him as the Mercedes sailed over the barrier and began its one hundred and thirty foot drop down into a ravine. Surprised by his good fortune he spotted a number of logs, possibly lost from a logger's truck, lying parallel against the steel barrier. It had acted as a form of natural ramp. His only disappointment was that the car had not burst into flames. That would have been more than he dared for. Her death, the cause of her death was now in the hands of Powell county authorities. Without giving the wreckage another look he turned around and began walking the few miles back to Elliston, from there he hoped to hitch a ride or maybe steal a car to Avon and from there back to Deer Lodge.

As the nightmare unfolded Holbrook was surprised at his outpouring of grief. He shouldn't have been surprised; despite the circumstances of her death he loved that woman with all his heart. But underneath the grieving he was a nervous wreck, he'd done all in his power to make Shelby's death look like an accident. He faced a barrage of questions; his servants bore witness that Mrs Holbrook had driven off at a neck breaking speed. When asked why and where she was going, Vince broke down and confessed they'd had an argument and that she'd stormed out of the house en-route to Helena, where they had an apartment.

"She had work to get on with Monday morning, she'd have phoned and we'd have made up . . . ."

From an outsider's point of view, it seemed like a small domestic that had developed into a tragic accident. After that round of questions all Vince could do was sweat it out and hope the autopsy report confirmed his story.

No one was more relieved than Congressman Holbrook when the autopsy report came in. Shelby it seems had not been wearing her seat belt and when the car came to an abrupt halt near the bottom of the ravine she'd been propelled forward and had made contact with a number of trees. To his relief the report's findings said her injuries were consistent with a violent crash. The coroner's report read much the same.

Looking out at the perfectly even snow, he thought about his few short years with Shelby. They were the happiest days of his life. But now there was emptiness inside of him. Some would say that in a sense, he hadn't gotten away with murder after all. But Congressman Vince Holbrook was nothing if he wasn't resilient. Despite the outpourings of grief, Vince knew he had the power to bounce back.

Chapter 70

Washington DC

Fletcher stared at the letter. Why? It was a question he'd ask himself time and time again, and he'd never been able to give an answer too, but stare he did. It was post marked New York, nothing unusual about that, and it appeared to be from the law firm Buckley, Harrison and Chambers. He'd often received letters from one law firm or another, but this letter stood out above all others. Taking a paper knife from off his desk at his office in the new Homeland Security building, he began to slit open the letter.

The letter was brief and to the point. He was asked to attend a meeting at the Attorneys at Law's address shown on the headed paper. He was to bring proof of who he was, in the form of a driving license and a passport. A phone number was provided for him to arrange said meeting.

Instinctively Fletcher picked up the phone and dialled the number. When he asked what it was all about, the receptionist could tell him nothing.

"We're a busy firm, and I'm afraid you'll have to ask that question in person."

It was curt and to the point. Under normal circumstances Fletcher would have left the letter in his in tray and waited until he received another, after all he was a busy man also. Yet the feelings he'd felt as he stared at that letter wouldn't go away. Frustrated by not getting an answer he arranged an appointment for the following day.

"I'm flying up to New York first thing in the morning, should be back by early evening," said Fletcher. "I just can't figure what these guys want."

"Perhaps someone's left you an inheritance?" suggested Ruth as she prepared dinner that evening.

Fletcher laughed, "The people that knew me in my past life are all dead," he added. And for the first time in over twenty years he thought about his mentor, his benefactor, Roland Delacroix. He felt a sudden shudder run down his spine. His life had been a mishmash of family. Born to a Crow Indian mother and a father of Norwegian and Crow mixed blood, he'd spent his fledgling years on an Indian reservation in Oklahoma, then after the death of his mother, his formative years were spent as part of a French Creole crime family in Roquefort, Louisiana, where he'd been sent to the finest schools money could buy. Inevitably he'd become a party to crime, but because of his education Roland had insisted he walked only on the periphery of crime. His infatuation with Monique and her insane obsession inadvertently brought him to his destiny.

"I reckon I'll find out come tomorrow," he added.

New York

Fletcher found Buckley, Harrison and Chambers on the thirty third floor of the Chrysler building. Stepping out of the elevator he was confronted by an impressive oak panelled double door with a large brass plate with the wording Buckley Harrison and Chambers Attorneys at Law engraved on it. Fletcher pressed the intercom entrance phone at the side of the door and waited.

"Can I help you?"

"Mr Fletcher Coppersmith, to see Ms Chambers."

"Oh yes. Her eleven thirty."

The heavy door clicked and Fletcher pushed the door open and stepped into an outer office. The whole place had an olde worlde feel about it, belying the building it was housed in. Light oak panelling on all four walls, matching desks and plush leather upholstery completed the picture.

"Ms Chambers will be with you in five minutes. Can I get you some refreshment?"

Fletcher declined.

Minutes later a tall willowy red head of around forty, dressed in a black trouser suit emerged from the inner office and held out an outstretched hand. Fletcher took it.

"Sorry to have kept you. Shall we.." she motioned with her outstretched hand towards the door.

Fletcher walked through and was immediately drawn to the two green Chesterfields facing each other across a large coffee table. Ms Chambers invited Fletcher to sit, and then sat down opposite him.

"Can I get you anything?" she asked politely.

Fletcher growing tired of the politeness and the inevitable delay it was causing declined yet again.

"With due respect, I'm a busy man. I'm tired, I took the first flight out this morning and I'd like you to come to the point."

Ms Chambers unflustered by Fletcher's abruptness, "Yes, I can understand. We've asked you to this meeting without giving you any idea of why you're here."

"That's about it," replied Fletcher.

"We're under instructions from our client to make the necessary checks before we can proceed." Ms Chambers shifted her position on the Chesterfield and continued. "Have you brought proof of your identity?"

Fletcher was getting slightly irritated by the clandestine approach and it was beginning to show. He unbuttoned his overcoat and reached inside his inner jacket and produced his driver's license, his homeland security card and his passport. "Okay satisfied!"

Ms Chamber ignored the strained remark, and carefully scrutinised Fletcher's forms of identification. Satisfied that

Fletcher was who he said he was she smiled and handed them back to him.

"Thank you Mr Coppersmith. I'm sorry if I've caused you any distress, but our client insisted that we check you out thoroughly." She reached into a folder that she'd placed on the coffee table minutes earlier and handed Fletcher a white sealed envelope. Then Ms Chamber rose to her feet extended her hand and said, "It was nice meeting you. Take as long as you like, I don't need this room for at least an hour." And with that she turned and walked out of the room.

Fletcher tore open the envelope, and tipped the contents onto the large coffee table. A key clattered onto the polished surface, then a receipt for a safety deposit box and finally a business card. He picked it up and stared at it. It was one of his homeland security cards. Puzzled he turned the card over to its flip side. On that blank rectangular card was written one word.

Shelby x.

*   *   *

Half an hour later he called Ruth from his cell phone inside a yellow cab on the way to JFK airport.

"Don't wait up; I'm taking a flight to Billings."

"Billings! Why?" asked Ruth.

"On account of what I've found out at Buckley, Harrison and Chambers. It's a long story; needless to say I won't be home for at least a couple of days. It seems Shelby left me something. What, I don't know. I'll call you as soon as I get there."

Montana

Fletcher arrived at Billings a little after ten o'clock that evening having flown via Minneapolis. To tired to think straight Fletcher went to the rental desk and then drove to the nearest Motel, where he crashed for the night.

With a hot breakfast inside him, Fletcher pointed the rental towards Helena. It was a good four hours drive but he did it in three and a half. He located the Valley Bank of Montana on North Montana Avenue in record time. Armed with the receipt and key he was soon facing the grey anonymous lock box. His heart thumped faster as he realised the effort Shelby had gone too to keep the contents of the deposit box safe from Holbrook. Would he find what he was looking for or would the Congressman have got there first. His heart held its beat as he inserted the key into the lock and opened the door.

Fletcher reached in and pulled out a slim folder, inside it, was two sealed envelopes, one addressed to Fletcher, the other strangely enough to Tara. Without opening the envelopes he replaced them in the folder and minutes later he was driving out of the bank's parking lot.

In a nearby motel room, Fletcher opened the envelope marked for his attention. Inside he found the photograph of Erin Ryder at her graduation, and a gold crucifix. Fletcher's heart began to race. He gazed at the photograph and there it was plain to see, her mother's talisman, the gold crucifix. But more importantly than both the necklace and photo was the letter written in Shelby's own fair hand.

It began . . . .

Fletcher,

I guess if you're reading this than I'm probably dead. You're a good man, I sensed that the first time we met, and I'm sorry I didn't pay heed to what you were telling me, but what the heck, what's done is done. I didn't believe you because despite what you and everyone else might think, I truly loved Vince. I agonised over the implications you'd put in my head, but they were just that, implications. You hadn't come right out with it and called Vince a cold blooded killer. I guess if you had, I'd have chewed you out and then confronted Vince with you're allegations. He'd deny it of course, and then we'd probably have turned your accusation over to the

*authorities. But you didn't, and it was so easy to forget.
I suppose I thought it slapped of desperation. But things
were different when we met in the parking lot in Deer
Lodge. There you spelled it out. I couldn't believe your
evidence was taken from the words of the convicted
murderer Perry Logan. A feeling of relief wafted over
me. I was so sure Vince was not a killer. But unbeknown
to me you'd sown a seed. Confident that I'd find nothing,
I began looking at social networking sites, Friendster
and MyYearBook in particular. I looked at Vince's old
yearbooks from High School, and assumed the name of
someone from his class. Luckily they hadn't an account
on Friendster, so I began fishing. It was just idle curiosity
I never expected anyone to get back to me. Within two
weeks I'd received seventeen correspondences from
former pupils. Nothing much, just the odd divorce, the
three children, the career, the, we must have a reunion,
sort of thing. But one of Vince and Chad Dempsey's school
friends went to Montana State. From her I learned that
Vince knew Erin, in fact he'd gone out with her for a
couple of months before they broke up. According to this
person, Vince was beside himself with grief, and when
he found out she was seeing Chad Dempsey he flew into
a blinding rage. Vince never spoke to Chad Dempsey
again. He tried on several occasions to win Erin back but
she rebuffed him each time. The last time was two days
before they were murdered. Erin was so angry at him
that she said, "You think money can buy you everything,
but you're wrong, you're pathetic, you're a loser!"*

*I wasn't expecting it; Vince said he knew Chad
Dempsey from school but that they moved in different
circles. There was no mention of Erin, and believe me, I
knew her, she wasn't someone that would go unnoticed.
I felt sick to my stomach, it wasn't proof of Vince's
involvement but I couldn't help myself, I had to keep
digging, if only to prove you wrong. I hated you, I hated
what you were making me do, I hated myself. But I had
to know the truth.*

I got to thinking about our conversation and realised that Erin's crucifix was the key to my peace of mind. If Vince was guilty then he might quite possibly have taken the necklace and kept it for a keepsake. Silly as this may sound, I thought if I searched the house and found nothing then I'd believe in Vince's innocence. He was so kind and gentle with me, we'd never even come close to a bad word. I just couldn't bring myself to believe, despite what I'd learned from that social networking site. You see I loved him.

Every moment I was left alone I devoted to the search. I worked out a system; I combed every room inch by inch, relieved at every negative search. I left the attic to last, dumb I know. I guess I was putting off the inevitable. It was a monumental task and on more than one occasion I nearly called of my search. It took me two days in all, but towards the end of my search I came across an old suitcase, filled with old photographs dating back to the late 1890's. There were letters, old deeds, documents and an array of memorabilia to vast to write down. Then I saw it, hidden underneath the trinkets and old papers, a small box, the sort that cufflinks come in. I prayed that the contents would be just that, but my sixth sense told me it was something altogether far sinister. My heart nearly gave out as I opened the small box and found my sister's crucifix. Even then I tried not to believe it, but as I untangled the crucifix there it was, her name clearly marked on the reverse side.

I was beside myself with what to do. Vince was away that day and wouldn't be getting back until late. My first thought was do I get in touch with the local police, I dismissed this almost immediately, then because I didn't want to believe I thought about confronting Vince. At least listen to his side of the story. I owed him that much, and then I thought of contacting you, which I dismissed almost as quickly as my first thought. Vince loved me, of that I was sure, if I'd done either the former or the latter and it was proven to be false then I'd lose Vince for sure.

Then I decided to write you this letter, just in case I'd misjudged Vince's reactions.

It was then only a matter of taking this letter and storing it along with the necklace and photograph in my safety deposit box in the bank in Helena. Mailing the law firm the key, your business card and a few precise instructions took even less time. I thought I was safeguarding myself, a little insurance so to speak. But I guess if you're reading this then I got Vince all wrong.

I would ask you one little favour, we met only briefly but I like to think I made an impression on you. I may not have given everyone such a favourable impression, but deep down I'm not as black as I've been painted. So I ask that when you feel the time is right will you hand Tara the letter that accompanies this letter.

I shall be forever in your debt,

Shelby x

The letter was dynamite, it might not be enough to convict Holbrook of the murders of Chad Dempsey and Erin Ryder but it would certainly re-open the case. It might not even prove that Holbrook was guilty of killing Shelby but it was a starting point. At the very least it would destroy any hopes of Vince Holbrook ever holding office again.

Chapter 71

Montana

Vince Holbrook had decided to spend Christmas with friends in upstate New York. When the door bell rang he thought it was his cab to take him to the airport. He was slightly taken aback when he opened the door to Sam Kilbane flashing his badge.

"We'd like you to come down to FBI headquarters in Helena, to answer some questions surrounding your wife's death," snapped Kilbane.

"It's Christmas Eve for Christ-sake. Can't this wait until after the holidays?" replied Holbrook.

"It's best we get this over with, then you can be on your way," promised Kilbane.

"Let me call my attorney!"

"That would be wise sir," said Sam Kilbane. There was nothing Sam liked better than watching a big fish as it dangled from his hook.

"What about my flight?" continued Holbrook as the car pulled onto the highway.

"We'll reschedule for a later flight," Sam added glibly.

*   *   *

It had been a week since Fletcher called in Sam Kilbane, a week in which Sam re-examined Shelby's Mercedes coupe, and sent the crucifix to be tested for DNA. It was a slim chance that they'd fine anything but Sam had promised that he wouldn't leave a stone unturned. Short of exhuming Shelby's body, the pathology lab found fibres from Holbrook's overcoat snagged in the window recess of the driver's side window. In addition the driver's side window was down, which belied the fact that the heating controls were at full heat. It was an inconsistency that proved nothing, but it was enough to re-open the accidental death of Shelby Holbrook.

Sam and Fletcher then switched their attention to the crucifix. When the report came in they were shocked and delighted at what the lab had found. A small particle of what they believed to be blood, the size of a pin head, was discovered lodged in a deep crevice of the engraving. Its DNA matched the murdered woman's. On their own these small finds amounted to not very much, but together they made up enough circumstantial evidence to at least send Vince Holbrook for trial. The congressman was formerly charged at FBI headquarters at 1700 hours on the 24th December 2008. He never made it to upstate New York for Christmas.

*   *   *

Fletcher in the meantime was waiting at Billings airport for Ruth. They hadn't seen each other since he took off for New York nearly three weeks earlier. His excitement at discovering the crucifix and Shelby's letter had sent him on a whirlwind of activity culminating in Holbrook being charged. All the time he'd been keeping his findings to himself and Sam, but now he was free to explain everything to Ruth on the drive down to the Big Hole Valley.

It would be Wade's second Christmas since Alex had died and it was times like these when you needed family around you.

Well tonight Fletcher was going to give the entire family the news of Holbrook's arrest, hopefully before it hit the television and newspapers.

"He's not admitting to anything as yet," Fletcher told Ruth. "But the array of evidence we've got against him looks like it'll buy him ninety nine years in Deer Lodge."

"That doesn't remove the guilt we're both feeling," said Ruth as she snuggled up to Fletcher as he pointed the rental car along Highway 41.

"That's where you're wrong. I've a copy of the letter on me, I'll let you read it later, and from what I can glean from Shelby's letter she must have known she was putting herself in harm's way."

They drove the last forty or so miles in silence, both lost in their own thoughts. Those thoughts were only broken as they approached the entrance to the Crazy AW.

A crowd gathered on the porch as Fletcher's rental car pulled onto the forecourt. Jack stepped off the porch and hugged Fletcher like a brother, Tara two paces behind, hugged first Ruth then Fletcher, before motioning for Jack to collect their luggage from the trunk. Larry gave him a helping hand after a nodded greeting to the pair. The girls, Kaycee and Merri hugged Ruth and began chatting excitedly about what they thought they were getting for Christmas. Then Wade stepped though the milling crowd of family, and shook Fletcher's hand firmly, before giving Ruth a hug. Inside there was more greetings as Jason stood up and extended his hand. Keeley remained seated, fully occupied by baby Alex, whilst James oblivious to the revelry played with his trucks, while his doting grandparents, Jimmy and Colleen watched over him.

Fletcher couldn't help noticing how the light in Wade's eyes, which had burned so brightly when Alex was alive was but a twinkling of there old self. He made a note to ask Jack how well Wade was coping. 'With luck, there'll be a twinkle when I tell him about Holbrook,' thought Fletcher.

Then his thoughts quickly switched to Tara as he fingered Shelby's letter in the top inside pocket of his coat. How would she take it? Would she screw it into a ball and throw it into the fire?

Or would she take it in the way Fletcher hoped? He knew Taw was never far from her thoughts, would the letter open wounds, or would it help somehow? From the little he knew of Shelby, those two brief meetings and the tone and friendliness of her letter, he suspected the letter to Tara was a form of atonement from a woman that believed she was going to die.

The house was filled with good cheer; Jimmy started the party off singing old Irish folk songs. And to everyone's surprise, except Colleen and Keeley, his voice was filled with a rich array of golden melodies, mixed with melancholy moods that had Fletcher looking towards Wade, only to find him lost in wonder at the music in the little Irishman.

As the evening lengthened, First Keeley and her kids, then Colleen and a reluctant Jimmy took to their beds, followed not long after by Kaycee and Merri.

Fletcher waited his opportunity, it was getting late in the evening when a lull in the conversation allowed him his chance.

"This might not be the time, nor the place, but you're gonna find out soon enough. Congressman Vince Holbrook has been formally charged with the 1980 double murder of Chad Dempsey and Erin Ryder!"

"What!" cried Jason.

"You finally nailed that son of a bitch," said Wade.

Jack looked across the room at Fletcher, he sensed the man had more to tell, "What is it you ain't saying?"

"Jack's right, there is more to tell, it's a long story, but I'll try to make it short." Fletcher then turned his attention towards Wade and Tara, "He's also being investigated in the murder of his wife Shelby."

A deathly hush fell over the group of family and friends. It was Tara who spoke first, "At least he did something right!"

"Erin Ryder was Shelby Shannon's older sister!" said Fletcher.

"What!" exclaimed Tara?

Jack instinctively put his arms around his wife.

"Over the last few months we learned that Erin Ryder and Shelby were related. I took it upon myself to meet with Mrs Holbrook, where I confronted her with our findings."

"She must have married him knowin . . . ."

Fletcher cut Tara off, "She was not aware that we suspected Vince Holbrook of killing her sister until I told her. It's something I have to live with. If I hadn't opened that particular can of worms I suspect she'd be alive today."

"I'd say you done everyone a favour!" said Tara, her hackles well and truly up.

"There's no call for that girl!" exclaimed Wade. "I lost a son, you a brother, but she didn't stick Taw up on that damn horse. If she's to blame, then so am I! Diablo was my gift to your mother. A damn fool horse, bad to the bone."

"Let's not get into a slanging match," said Jack as he held Tara firmly. "I wasn't here when Taw died, I never knew him. But I've felt Tara's pain every single day. It's easy to point the blame. Wade, blames himself, I know Tara blames herself, and I reckon that poor woman, if she's a heart blames her self. The truth of the matter, it was circumstances, nothing more nor less. Now lets not open old wounds, it's Christmas."

Fletcher had been right to hold off, his news though welcome, did leave a bitter after taste. Subdued by Fletcher's news most folks saw it as their excuse to drift off to bed, some still had to get up early and put a shift in before the celebrations could start. Firstly Wade, then Jason, followed closely by Jack. Tara had gone outside to cool off. Jack knew his wife, she'd stay outside thinking back to those days when she was young, she'd brood on it for a while then when the cold bit home she'd come back inside. Ruth gave Fletcher a knowing look before retiring. She knew that what Fletcher had to do, he had to do alone.

Moments later he joined Tara on the porch. An outside heater kept most of the chill away. Tara turned her head, smiled and said. "I'm sorry; I shouldn't have gone off on one. It wasn't you I was mad at."

"Well," Fletcher forced a sort of laugh, "perhaps it should have been. I'm not an expert, but I think I'm a good judge of character. I actually liked the woman."

"You what!" exclaimed Tara, a little surprised at what Fletcher had to say.

"She told me a little of your history, she knew it was wrong to do what she did, she never realised the devastation it would cause. For what it's worth I believe Shelby never forgave herself for what happened."

Fletcher placed his hand inside his coat pocket, his fingertips gripped the letter. "When I opened the safety deposit box, along with the letter, crucifix and photograph there was another letter. It's addressed to you."

He pulled the letter clear and held it at arms length. "Do with this letter as you will, throw it in the fire if you must, but remember, this letter was written by a woman that believed there was a strong possibility that she would be dead before anyone read it."

Tara held the letter lightly in her hand, the urge to throw it away almost irresistible. Fletcher, his mission done said a quiet goodnight and disappeared inside.

Alone with Shelby's letter in hand, with a fresh dusting of snow falling all around her, Tara wiped a tear from her eye. So much had happened since Taw took that fateful ride; it hurt her to think of what he'd missed.

Chapter 72

Montana

The fire burning in the hearth was but dying embers as Tara pulled up an armchair to capture the fading warmth. The letter weighed heavily in her hand. The temptation to throw it unopened onto the fire and watch it slowly burst into flame was almost too much to bear. Yet part of her thought otherwise. To leave unopened a woman's last words seemed in itself a form of sacrilege. She'd only seen her once in all the years since that fateful night after the Dillon Rodeo, and that meeting on Tara's part at least, had been full of venom, a poison that had been with her from the initial betrayal. Perhaps now was the right time to purge her self of it. She fingered the letter, she turned it in her hands, she began to tear it open.

> *Dear Tara,*
>
> *Like yourself I have known much suffering and heartache, none more so than how I'm feeling right now. I don't expect you to feel sorry for me, I guess you'd probably think I got what I deserved, and you're probably right. I'm not asking for absolution, I dare say that would be the furthest thing from your mind, but I hope you'll bear with me, as I try to explain my actions concerning Taw.*

I was born into a poor but caring family on the Lower East Side of New York or so I thought. Before I was seven my pa had up and left, leaving my ma to care for me and my older sister Erin. We were left alone much of the time due to ma working every hour that God sends. We could have gone off the rails, but ma had instilled in us the value of a good education. Erin was the real brainy one, and eventually won a scholarship to Montana State. Ma was so proud. Erin wrote home often, but it was mostly about her studies, nothing about the people she knew and the places she went. I think she didn't because she was a little ashamed of her background. It was something I suspected from the start, but nothing could prepare us for what was to come. It was three weeks after the murder, Erin was dead and buried and we knew nothing. After the initial shock had worn off we began to ask why. We never received a satisfactory answer, only that a petty criminal intent on robbery had gunned down this rich kid Chad Dempsey and raped Erin before shooting her dead. It finished ma, she died not long after. I was alone, left with a bitterness and total loathing for the rich, yet I could see that if I was to survive I had to play the game their way. I had my education such as it was, and I had my looks. Sex was the natural progression. It wasn't hard; I'd received an extensive education in the facts of life on the Lower East Side. I liked it; I'm not ashamed to say it. Sex was something I was good at, and I intended making it work for me.

Tara felt her hackles rise. The urge to screw up the letter and throw it to the back of the fire was almost irresistible. She wiped at her eyes and continued reading.

I got a job in a public relations firm and never looked back. I found I had a natural ability for it, and within a short period of time I was earning a semi-decent salary. It wasn't long after that I was assigned to work with a young up and coming concert pianist. In truth it wasn't my scene, but when I learned he came from Montana I saw my chance to learn more about my sister's death. All I knew at that time was a guy called Perry Logan was on death row, awaiting execution.

When I met Taw, he was nothing like I'd imagined, he was tall, and ruggedly good looking, not a trait I'd expected in a concert pianist. He was full of charm and wit. His dark eyes swept me off my feet, and his smile . . . I don't have to tell you about his smile. Within two weeks we were in bed together, within a month we were both very much in love. Yes Tara, despite everything that went on, I was very much in love with Taw. When he asked me to marry him, I was over the moon. It was then that I insisted that he take me to Montana to meet his folks. He told me about your ma and pa's breakup and said he didn't want to go down that same road. I told him hell would freeze over before that happened. Oh, the naivety of youth.

I dressed to impress, I wanted your ma to think I was a sophisticated lady from New York, but deep down, like most things I'd done to get me where I was, it was an act. I was terrified of meeting Alex and you, but I needn't have been. You both shared that same warmth and generosity of heart that Taw had. I was won over the very first time we sat down to eat together. Alex, I know would have been a great mother-in-law, and in you I'd found the sister that I'd lost. When I was with Taw, he made me forget the past; all I could see was a beautiful future. I thought the gods were finally smiling on me.

I hadn't reckoned with the darker side of myself. I was young, immature and weak willed, sex was something I hadn't been able to control. When I met Kyle, I thought he was like a young James Dean in the film Giant, a chip on his shoulder the size of the Empire State Building, but sexy as all hell. You above all others should know what I'm talking about, he was your boyfriend. I know I should have resisted, but the weekend had been so exhilarating and when he came onto me, all my inhibitions were down. It was the biggest mistake of my life. After the fight your ma told me I was lucky, if it had been her instead of you, she'd have killed me. I believed every word. She told me not to be there when they got back from the hospital.

I'd caused such pain, I'd ruined what chance Taw and I had, because I couldn't keep my pants on. I felt ashamed, I don't expect you to believe it, but I felt so very deeply ashamed. I was at Billings Airport in time to catch the first plane out. A week later I was sent on a fresh assignment, I vowed then I wouldn't get emotionally involved. I hardened my heart. Taw rang my apartment in New York several times, I didn't answer, I couldn't face him. Until one day. I'd just that minute arrived back in my apartment, the phone rang and it was Taw. We spoke for several minutes, I couldn't do it anymore, I couldn't face you, your ma or Taw, I was ashamed and I realised at that moment I couldn't go back. I put the phone down on him.

Months later I learned of his death, on that devil horse. I knew then that I was responsible for Taw's death. I've never forgotten him, and I'll hate myself for being so cruel to such a wonderful man until my dying day.

Thank you for taking the time to read this, it means more to me than you'll ever know.

Shelby.

Tara wiped away a tear. The letter had brought it all back to her as if it had been yesterday. The woman had described Taw exactly as she herself remembered. His dark brooding eyes and that smile . . . She was right about that.

Tara felt a sudden tiredness wafting over her as she folded the letter. She glanced at the clock, eleven minutes to one in the morning. It was Christmas day and suddenly everything was right with the world.

Chapter 73

Montana

It might have been Christmas morning for most people, but for the Crazy AW it was business as usual. But with extra hands like Fletcher and Jack to help with the chores, Wade, Jason, Larry and the boys managed comfortably and were back at the ranch house in plenty of time. Kaycee and Merri had ridden out to help around ten and Wade felt a surge of pride that his two grand daughters had felt the need to contribute their labour. He glanced over at Jack and grinned. Jack tipped his hat. His daughters were his pride and joy, they'd come through the bad experience with Alex and the wolf pack unscathed and if anything more adept at dealing with emergencies. He reflected that they could at that very moment be loafing around, playing computer games or even helping Tara and Keeley with preparing Christmas dinner, although he doubted the latter. His thoughts, as always included Charlotte. He'd phoned her first thing and wished her and Matt and his grandkids the best of the season. They in turn were, he suspected, dragged kicking and screaming to the phone to thank Grand dad Jack and Nanny Tara for their presents. Charlotte asked after her two siblings and Jack had told her they were still in dreamland, as it was after all five thirty in the morning. Charlotte laughed and added, "Come late spring we're coming for a visit." It was the best Christmas present anyone could have asked for. Jack also spared a thought for Jared Barclay the son he'd never see. He'd be twenty one years old now, a man. But he'd made a promise, and it was a promise he had no intention of breaking.

Christmas was an emotive time and Jack and Wade weren't alone in their thoughts. Fletcher looked west towards Cougar Pass so high up above the timberline and thought of Merri, lying in the cold, cold ground and an involuntary tear trickled down his cheek. He thought of Ruth, so alive and full of fun, then he smiled, she was a woman to spend the rest of his days with. "Yes," he said quietly to himself, he had a lot to be thankful for, not the least was his love for the two women that shared his heart.

Almost on cue, Fletcher spotted Ruth loping towards him through the snow. She laughed as she drew up alongside him.

"I was getting in Keeley and Tara's way, so I thought I'd better make myself scarce."

"Well you arrived too late, we're heading back," laughed Fletcher.

Non perturbed, Ruth grinned, "Guess I timed it just right. I'll keep you company on the ride in"

Jason was the last rider home, as he climbed down and led his horse into the barn, Larry called over to him.

"We'd just about given you up, thought I might have to eat your dinner for you."

"Why'd you think I was taking my time," said Jason merrily, "You ain't tasted Keeley's cooking yet."

"I'll tell her you said that," replied Larry.

"Don't you dare," said Jason feigning fright.

It was the first Christmas in the new house and Jason and Keeley had invited the whole family to Christmas dinner. There was Wade, Jack and Tara and their girls, Fletcher, Ruth and Johan, Jimmy, not even showing a slight trace of a hangover, Colleen sitting next to her two grandkids, Larry and his wife, Bud Angel and Clem Barker. It was an important milestone in Jason and Keeley's life. They'd been at the ranch a full six months, not nearly enough time to make a judgement, but Jason had visions and more importantly Keeley mirrored them.

The table was laid for eighteen; in truth the table was big enough to sit twenty or more around with some comfort. Before dinner, presents were exchanged and glasses were filled. It was a joyous time and Wade looked on approvingly at his family and close friends. He'd shared so much with them over the years. He looked up at the high ceiling of the main room in the house and thought of Alex, up their on high looking down approvingly.

Dinner was a noisy affair, with everyone chatting at once. The Christmas crackers had caused a stir, as Jack had suspected they would.

"It's a tradition from the old country. You can't have Christmas without them."

The girls and Tara knew about them of course, but the strange looks from Larry and Jason, only added to the hilarity of the proceeding. And then before anyone knew it, they were sitting back in their chairs fully stuffed.

"That was a great Turkey," said Larry, "compliments to the chef," he added as he gave Jason a knowing look.

"Three cheers for Keeley," came the response from the revellers.

"It wasn't all my doing," shouted Keeley through the cacophony. "Tara did just as much.

"Three cheers for Keeley and Tara," cried Bud Angel.

As the noise tailed off Jason banged the table with a desert spoon. "Can I have a little quiet; Wade would like a few words."

Wade stood up and looked at everyone in turn, from his ranch hands, to his extended family, to his grand kids and smiled.

"Its days like this that make life worth living. I'm fortunate to have so many close friends and relatives around me on such an important occasion." He smiled at each and everyone sitting around the table. "This year has been particularly hard for me personally. The loss of Alex, still grieves me as much today as on the day she died, then of course there was that wretched trial, something I could have done without. My own stupid fault, I know."

A hushed laughter greeted his last remark.

Wade took a breath, "They were the downs, the ups, well where do I begin. Jason's timely intervention, the building of this fabulous house, the coming together of my family and friends as one, these things have meant so much to me, but as I said it's been hard, therefore I have decided to take a step back."

"What!" came the collective response.

"I'm nearly eighty, I think it's time for me to hang up my saddle and retire."

The shock waves resounded with a stunned silence.

"Therefore I have made arrangements to sell off my share of the ranch and all its assets to Jason and Keeley. I shall continue to live in my house for as long as humanly possible and I shall help Jason in an advisory capacity. He has reassured me, in writing, that all existing pay and conditions remain the same, or better. Larry, your house is safe for life. Clem, you and Bud along with Blaine and Jake the same goes for you all whilst working for the Crazy AW."

Shock became relief as reality set in. It was something they all knew would happen some day, but never expected it so soon.

"Are you all right Pa?" asked Tara, concern etched across her face.

"Never better," replied Wade, "It's just this year has shown me where my priorities lie. I'll have more time to see the kids, I'll be able to go visit this Capitol of ours, and I'll be able to watch over Jason, show him where he's going wrong. No point in putting it off until I'm in my box, because by then it'll be too late."

"Are you happy?" asked Ruth.

"The only thing that would make me happier is to have Alex here with me, other than that, yes I'm happy. The ranch, my mistress as Alex was fond of telling me, is in good hands, the best."

Jason and Keeley smiled.

Chapter 74

Montana.2009

Before they flew back to Washington, Fletcher spoke with Jack about Wade's health.

"I saw it in his eyes, that sparkle; it wasn't much more than a flicker. I'm worried about him."

"I know what you mean, we've been concerned ourselves. We think it's partly the strain of the trial and the fact that Alex is gone. We'll keep an eye," said Jack.

The New Year began like any other. Wade continued to get up at the crack of dawn and was first most mornings to start the day's chores. Nothing much had changed since Wade signed over the Crazy AW. Only difference anyone could make out was Jason had the final say on everything. It was a transitional period in the running of the ranch, and although Jason did things a little differently to Wade the job got done just as well and sometimes better. Wade reflected that even at his age there were still things to be learnt.

Jason was making a sound job of running the ranch. He'd lived life to the full, jet setting around the world, Hollywood premieres, Cannes, the French Riviera, yet at the heart of it all Jason was a Westerner, he loved nothing more than getting down and dirty.

And it wasn't just Jason that had adapted to the life style; Keeley who had her hands full with her two kids was making plans to re-open the guest ranch. Wade reflected how pleased Alex would have been to know her legacy was getting another go round. Little Merri, now fourteen and still keen as mustard, was Keeley's first recruit.

Jack and Tara were amused, "At least we don't have to worry about Summer Break this year," said Tara.

"I'd appreciate any time you could spare too," pleaded Keeley. "I know you're pretty busy, but it would really be a godsend."

"Putting it that way, how can I refuse, although I won't be able to spend more than two maybe three mornings a week. I'm sure I'll be able to persuade Jack that he can spare me."

"That's fantastic! I need someone with your expertise; your experience will be invaluable. Between us we'll have the guest ranch up and running by early July," said Keeley excitedly.

"I'll see whether I can persuade Kaycee, but unlike Merri she seems to have set her goals in a different direction," added Tara.

"Studying law has its advantages too," said Keeley. "Does she know whether she wants to go into corporate or criminal law?"

"I don't know, it's too early to tell, but it'll be nice having a lawyer in the family."

It seemed funny that originally Fletcher had studied law, albeit to find loop holes, but it had held him in good stead in his future careers. Even now he was assisting in the prosecution of Congressman Holbrook.

*　　*　　*

Holbrook had posted bail and had been out since the day after Christmas. The shock allegations against him divided his friends and business associates. Those that were close to him knew he had a volatile temper and began to believe the unbelievable. The committees he supported began to stop returning his calls. He would have become a social pariah if it hadn't have been for the Holbrook businesses. He retained the best lawyers that money could buy and set about preparing his defence.

Fletcher who was key to the prosecution's case was freed temporarily from his affairs at Homeland Security to help in anyway he possibly could in obtaining a conviction.

Perry Logan, the man originally convicted for the murders and out on license was also being prepared as a witness for the prosecution. His testimony concerning Carson Burroughs, though not directly related to the case was being looked at. If the trial found that Holbrook was guilty of murdering Erin Ryder and Chad Dempsey then Logan stood to gain compensation from the Montana authorities. Both Logan and Burroughs motives would be exploited by the defence.

The trial opened with the selection of jurors. A time consuming process, but necessary nonetheless. Then the prosecution stated its case, the letter, the crucifix and Perry Logan's identification of Holbrook's father looked to all intent and purpose a sure fire case winner. Then Holbrook's hotshot team of lawyers got to work. They tore Carson Burroughs and Perry Logan's testimonies to shreds, despite the evidence stacked against Holbrook. They argued that the blood from the crucifix could have been there days or even weeks before the murders of Erin Ryder and Chad Dempsey. The case was beginning to crumble. When asked why the crucifix was found in Holbrook's possession he'd answered that he'd never seen it before. The defence attorney argued that it could have been in Shelby's possession equally as much as in Holbrook's. The evidence was at best circumstantial, at worse wishful thinking.

After three weeks of evidence the judge did his summing up and the jury was asked to retire. An anxious five hours later the jury returned. The foreman of the jury was asked to stand up.

"Have you the jury come to a decision in this case?" asked the judge.

"Yes your honour."

"What then is your verdict?"

"Not guilty!"

The court was in an uproar. The judge slammed his gavel down several times before order was restored.

"Vincent Holbrook, the jury has found you not guilty, you are free to go."

A sickening smile appeared across Holbrook's lips.

Fletcher's heart was pounding, they were already preparing the case against Holbrook for murdering Shelby, if he walked out a free man, his integrity would remain intact. The prosecutor, prompted by Fletcher stood up and addressed the judge directly.

"We ask that Vincent Holbrook be placed in custody for the murder of Shelby Holbrook."

"That trial is scheduled for the 24th June 2009. Mr Holbrook presents no threat to society and it's doubtful he'll abscond, so I see no reason to grant your request. Mr Holbrook has posted bail of five million dollars."

With that said the court descended into a free for all as flashlights and noisy reporters took centre stage.

Fletcher and the entire prosecution team were devastated. The not guilty verdict had in effect blown the prosecution's case in the murder of Shelby Holbrook. Shelby's letter dated the day before she was murdered would not now be admissible. The motive for murdering Shelby, the crucifix, the photograph, and the DNA evidence concerning Erin's death were in fact redundant. All they had was the autopsy report, which stated that there were sufficient discrepancies in the cause of death to warrant a change from accidental death to death by person or persons unknown. The fact that fibres from Holbrook's coat were found imbedded in the driver's side window could have happened days weeks or even months before the murder.

* * *

The 24th June came around almost too quickly for the prosecution. But they had one rabbit yet to pull out of the hat.

Holbrook sat smugly looking across at the prosecutions bench. His lawyers had assured him that the trial would be just a formality and that he would be a free man before the end of the week.

By day three, the prosecutions case was coming to a close. It was the defence admitted a very plausible chain of events, but the little fact that the prosecution couldn't put Holbrook at the scene or time of the accident meant that it was just one of many scenarios.

"Who says we can't put your client at the scene or within the vicinity of the crime," said Charles Danvers, the prosecution attorney. "We have a witness. A witness that can place Vincent Holbrook in the vicinity of the murder at the date and time said murder was committed."

Holbrook's team were stunned into a shocked silence.

Clem Barker the most unlikely of people had inadvertently locked the door on Vince Holbrook's freedom. Whilst drinking in a bar in Wisdom crowded with itinerant cowboys, farmers and trucker's he overheard one trucker remarking about the recent trial of Vince Holbrook.

"I never thought he was guilty. I voted for the man, he's like from around here. He's got our concerns at heart," said the trucker, referring to the first trial.

"I don't know, those rich folks, they don't give a shit about us poor folks scratching a living in the dirt," said an irate farmer.

"He ain't like that, he's a gentleman and he's one of us. I should know. I gave him a lift a few months back."

"Yeah, sure you did," said his friends as they laughed off the ridiculous remark.

Clem had relayed the conversation to Blaine Henry the following morning. Blaine understanding the significance of the conversation turned his horse and headed back to the ranch, where he phoned Jack and relayed the conversation he'd had with Clem. Jack immediately informed Fletcher up in Helena where he was going over the case notes of the pending trial. It was the break they'd been searching for.

Pandemonium broke out whilst Danvers called the witness to the stand. Orville Tompkins stepped into the witness box. He stated his name and occupation as a trucker. The prosecution attorney asked him many questions, questions he was sure the defence would have asked. He was covering as many bases as was possible. Then he asked Orville Tompkins if he remembered picking up a well dressed man on the night of the murder at Elliston.

"Yes," replied Tompkins. "I drove him to Avon, where the man said he lived."

"And is that man in this courtroom today?"

"Yes sir," he then pointed to Vince Holbrook.

The defence tried to argue that Mr Tompkins was mistaken, that he'd been wrong both with the date and with the identification. The witness held firm.

"I know who I gave a lift too. My eyes and my ears didn't deceive me then or now."

"How can you be so sure of the date in question?"

Tompkins grinned, "I know my own birthday."

Not content with Tompkins statement, Danvers hammered it home, by producing a CCTV video tape from the truck stop that showed clearly a well dressed man matching Holbrook's description entering the truck.

Holbrook immediately spoke quietly to his defence team. The defence asked for an adjournment. An hour and a half an hour later, the defence asked to change Holbrook's plea, to guilty of manslaughter.

"Mr Holbrook would like to make a statement."

Holbrook was then instructed to take the stand. He looked shaken and had aged five years since the trucker had given evidence. Reading from a prepared statement he addressed the courtroom.

"Shelby and I had been rowing; you see I believed she'd been having an affair. I know now that, that was not true. She said there was work she needed to get on top of and that she was going to make an early start of it in the morning. She told me she was going to drive up to our apartment in Helena that night. It was all too much, I accused her of having an affair, we argued and she stormed off to the garage. I raced after her and said I was going with her. "If you must," she'd said. She drove off like a maniac. We had never argued; in all the years we'd been together we never had a cross word until that night. It was the most unreal moment of my life. I tried reasoning with her, but she was incensed by my accusation. We'd almost got to MacDonald Pass and I told her to slow down. She took no notice of me. I reached across her in an attempt to take the wheel. She tried pushing me away, I don't know how it happened but I hit her. It was an accident, a terrible accident. The car skidded on the ice and the rest you know. Shelby was dead, I was unscathed, I panicked, I left her there, for that I'll never forgive myself." Then Holbrook broke down.

It was a convincing performance, thought Fletcher. A performance that could see him walk free from yet another murder.

Judge Barnsworthy looked straight at Holbrook. Then he addressed the court. "Due to Congressman Holbrook changing his not guilty plea to one of involuntary manslaughter I have no alternative but to call a mistrial. A date for a new trial on the grounds of involuntary manslaughter will follow in due course. Congressman Holbrook will be granted bail in the sum of $500,000." The gavel sounded like a thunderbolt as the Judge brought the court proceedings to an abrupt halt.

Fletcher was left both shocked and bemused, 'what did it take to make this man pay for his crimes?' he thought as he stormed out of the courtroom. Later in a bar in Helena he speculated as to Vince Holbrook's sentence, once a new trial date was set. Involuntary manslaughter could mean anything from six to twelve years, even longer. But with Holbrook's legal team working around the clock there was the possibility that he'd face very little jail time. Fletcher felt sick to the pit of his stomach.

It had begun so promisingly with the witness, especially after their disappointment at not getting a conviction for the 1980 murders of Chad Dempsey and Erin Ryder. They thought with Orville Tompkins testimony that they'd finally nail Holbrook but they'd misjudged the power of a very competent lawyer.

Fletcher sipped at his drink. He was in a morose mood as he mused on the events at court. A conviction was certain, but then Holbrook and his legal team had outflanked him just as he was closing in on victory. He'd argued with his legal team and the District Attorney but to no avail.

"All we can hope for is that Judge Barnsworthy accepts our recommendation of a maximum sentence," said the chief prosecutor.

*   *   *

Before flying back to Washington, Fletcher paid the Big Hole a visit. Wade broke open a new bottle of bourbon, "I guess you're gonna need a stiff one."

"Damn right I do," replied Fletcher.

"They ain't our kind of people, those folks look after their own. All I'll say is don't beat yourself up over it. You done the best you could."

"I guess you're right," then he gave a wry smile. "You know something, bad as Monique was, she weren't a patch on Holbrook."

Wade grinned, "Yeah I guess you could say that, at least she was an honest killer," he said dryly.

Chapter 75

Montana

Holbrook's re-trial was set for August 17th. As predicted his trial lawyers left not a stone unturned in their search to get their client off with the minimum sentence. Fletcher sat alongside the chief prosecutor throughout the week long trial. He was hoping justice would prevail, but accepting the possibility that the ex congressman would get away lightly.

Judge Barnsworthy summed up.

"I find this a most unfortunate case, a prominent member of society; a man of good character, a pillar of society, should find himself here in my court. I've listened to all the evidence and I've taken into account the deceit the defendant showed during the first trial. However, I've also taken into account the good works Congressman Holbrook has performed when executing his duties to the state of Montana. I therefore sentence Vincent Holbrook to be confined at Deer Lodge correctional facility for a term of three years."

Pandemonium broke out as flash bulbs and reporters took centre stage. There were cheers from one side of the court and a few not so vocal boos from the other. Holbrook managed a half smile in the direction of the prosecution before he was led away. Fletcher chose to ignore it as he stood up and buttoned his jacket. Not a word crossed his lips as he shook hands with the prosecution team and walked silently out of the court room.

* * *

He had one chore left to do before catching his plane back to Washington. It wasn't something he was looking forward too. But Perry Logan deserved to hear it from Fletcher rather than catch it on a late news bulletin. The man had spent twenty odd years in prison for something he hadn't done; Fletcher couldn't begin to understand how the man would feel once he was given the news. Reluctantly he punched Logan's number into his cell-phone.

"I tried, believe me I tried, but that slippery son of a bitch got away from me."

"It ain't your fault Fletcher; you gave it your best shot. I'm just grateful to have my freedom."

"Yeah, how is everything?"

"The job's fine, I've a nice apartment and I'm seeing someone," answered Perry.

"Someone special?"

"Could be. I'm happy; life after missing out for as many years as I have couldn't be sweeter. I'm just glad Vince Holbrook's in the right place."

Fletcher was slightly taken aback at Logan's reaction, he mused about it on the flight back to Washington. There were lessons to be learned, even from the most unlikely of sources. He guessed it was down to the many years of contemplating life that changes a man, at least that's what Fletcher hoped. His own life could have taken such a turn. It was a lesson, he thought, that I could and should learn. Switching off those thoughts he turned to the more enjoyable phone call he'd placed to Ruth minutes after. She'd told him she'd pick him up at the airport and there was a bottle of wine chilling back at the apartment with their name on it. The late evening promised many possibilities.

* * *

Life in the Big Hole carried on like it had for centuries. Wade always an early riser, stood tall in the saddle as he looked out on the empire he'd created. That it was now in Jason's hands didn't cause him any regret. The fact that life would go on much the same after he'd gone was an assurance he'd not been able to contemplate only a few short years before. Jason Connors had proven a top hand, a man that he'd be proud to ride the river with.

Looking back as he frequently did of later, he counted his blessings. In Korea, he'd seen comrades cut down before their prime; he'd survived the carnage, only to find both his parents dead before their time. Green as grass, he'd started on an adventure that was still unfolding.

It was getting late in the season and already the Bitterroots had their first dusting. Pretty soon the whole valley would grow quiet as the snow turned his Technicolor world into one of white. He smiled into the fast fading light of day and turned his horse homeward.

At home there'd be a welcoming fire lit by Martha, on loan from Jack and Tara these few months. Tara had insisted that since his turn in late spring he should have someone with him at all times. 'Angina' the doc had said, "Best come in for a check up." He wouldn't have bothered but Tara insisted. It was nothing, well at least in Wade's world it was nothing. He was getting on in years, what did they expect? Of late he'd been feeling a little off colour, a slight cold, nothing to worry about; he guessed his old bones weren't as resilient as they once were. Time was fast marching on and at seventy nine what did everyone expect. The last thing he wanted was people fussing around him. Tara had insisted that Martha Rainbird, whose husband had passed away two summers ago, stay on as housekeeper at Wade's for the foreseeable future. As a last resort to shut his daughter up, he'd conceded, but if the truth be known, Wade was glad of the company.

`Another of Tara's concerns was Fletcher; they'd seen quite a lot of him, what with Holbrook's trials.

"All this flying across half a continent isn't doing Fletcher any good," remarked Tara, one evening around the fire.

"Well apart from Christmas I dare say we'll see less of Fletcher now them damn trials are over," said Jack.

"I can't get over it. What is it with our legal system? That man should swing for what he did," railed Tara. "Shelby wasn't my favourite person, but she didn't deserve what he did to her."

Jack reflected on his wife's words. There had always been fieriness in Tara, he suspected on the very first day they met. It wasn't visible to the naked eye, but scratch the surface and she could turn into a ball of fire. Yet since Shelby's letter, that spark of conscience the poor woman had conveyed, had affected Tara and she'd lost some of that fire, and as far as Jack was concerned, it suited her.

"I guess you're right, but the best thing we can do is get on with our lives," said Jack. "Anyway, despite the Holbrook affair it's been a pretty good year all round. Charlotte and Matt's visit was just great. I can't tell you how grateful I am that you made them all so welcome."

"It wasn't hard, Charlotte is such a mature woman, you should be very proud of her."

"I am, and the kids they just simply adore their big sister, and as for our two grand kids they're such fun," said Jack. "Fun," he added "but hard work, I was worn out when they left."

"Talking of kids, I can't wait for the holidays, I miss Kaycee so much," said Tara.

"She's only at Montana State, we see her most weekends," stated Jack.

"Yeah, I know. I just wish Merri was more academic," sighed Tara.

"Don't knock it! When we're too old to continue, our Merri will take over. At least that's something we won't have to worry about," said Jack.

"At least that problem's solved," said Tara, recalling her father's old dilemma.

"Yeah, at least that's one worry Wade doesn't have to think about," said Jack.

"Martha says he's taking the medication, but she has to remind him some days. She said he looks as fit as ever, which is encouraging, I guess."

Jack could see the worry lines etched across her face, her Pa was never far from Tara's thoughts. It was a worrying time, they saw Wade at least twice a week and on the surface he seemed fine. But Jack had been there a few weeks back when Wade experienced a bad angina attack. Wade had sworn him to secrecy.

"You know I can't do that Wade, Tara has a right to know."

"That maybe so, but unless I'm bedridden I intend living my life as I see fit. If she knows, she'll try to curtail the little fun I've got left. I want to live my life the way I've always lived it."

It was hard to argue with Wade at the best of times, but Jack sensed that the man was imploring him to stay quiet. "I'll keep it to myself, but first thing tomorrow, you take yourself to the Doc's. Let him take a look at you."

Wade promised. Jack, knowing Wade as well as he did, said, "I'll phone Doc Bonneville, and make that appointment for you, oh and I'll phone up to make sure you keep it. If you don't, I'll tell Tara."

"And to think I brought you all the ways up here from the Mexican border, just so you can mollycoddle me."

Wade kept the appointment; the Doc wired him up to the machine and gave him a fresh supply of tablets and medication. His ECG results were fine, his blood pressure was normal and the bloods he took for evaluation were sent off.

"I'd suggest you book yourself in to see me in the New Year. We'll take a closer look at you," said the doctor. Other than that Doc Bonneville gave him a clean bill of health, Wade's words. He was for a man pushing eighty in pretty good shape. That aside, Jack knew that Wade wasn't the type to take things easy, he was more likely to ignore the warning signs and continue what ever it was he was doing. Wade had always been a stubborn old cuss and no one was going to change him now.

Jack recalled something Wade had said to him during that month of forced incarceration at the hideout in Johnny J's cave.

It was just after Johnny had passed away, and the conversation revolved around where and when they'd meet their maker. Wade looked up at the stars, then down to the burial mound and said, "I'd like to die in the saddle, with the wind in my hair and a storm blowing up."

It was funny, but until that day when Jack made Wade keep that appointment he'd completely forgotten that conversation.

Washington DC

Events a few days after Thanksgiving eclipsed everyone's thoughts. Sam Kilbane phoned Fletcher.

"Some news just came in that might be of interest to you. It seems Holbrook wasn't a very popular inmate at Deer Lodge. He got shanked in the Laundry room and bled out."

Fletcher's blood ran cold. "Thanks for the heads up," he managed to utter, before hanging up. He recalled Perry Logan's final words after being given the news of the verdict, his words echoed loudly, "I'm just glad Vince Holbrook's in the right place." He'd been calm, far calmer than a man had a right to be. Fletcher had thought the man had mellowed, that the man had suddenly gone soft after all the years he'd spent incarcerated. But somehow he'd orchestrated the stabbing to death of the man that had taken three lives and stolen twenty years from another.

'Perhaps it was justice," thought Fletcher, but it still left a bad taste in his mouth.

Chapter 76

Montana, 2010

Wade's health surprised everyone. Early in the New Year he saw Doc Bonneville for his check up and came away with a clean bill of health. He was taking his meds regularly, doing the required exercise, had given up the odd cigar, though he still partook of a drink or two, and seemed to have obtained a new lease on life.

Throughout that spring and summer the sparkle returned to his eyes as he helped out Jack and Tara with new breeding stock, then filling in for Jason when he and Keeley visited her folks in Ireland. And that glint was there when he was telling tall tales around the bunkhouse to the young university kids that worked for Jason during their summer break.

But Wade was never happier than when he took himself up into the High Country. Alex rode with him on these forays into the wilderness and he was glad of her company. She never left his thoughts, she never would.

*   *   *

The conspiracy was obvious, even to a man on the eve of his eightieth birthday. He'd spoken to Tara only yesterday and she hadn't mentioned a word. Jason and Keeley had avoided him like the plague and there was no news of a pending visit from Fletcher and Ruth. They'd maintain a record of not missing his birthday since they were married. Kaycee, he knew was home from Montana State, but even she and Merri had given him a wide berth. They were all planning something special; he could feel it in his water.

It was a bright blue and clear sky, the leaves on the aspen had already turned golden. It was mid September; the weather he feared was on the turn. Another week, perhaps two before the high passes became impassable. He'd awoken with a spring in his step and after showering he went down stairs to breakfast.

"Do you know what day it is tomorrow," is how he addressed Martha that morning.

"Well, I'd say that if today is Friday then it stands to reason that tomorrow is Saturday," replied Martha.

'Smart ass!' thought Wade, 'always there with a clever quip.'

"What's this?" he cleverly changed the subject, "Serial, yoghurt, orange juice. It's the weekend woman, bring me a real breakfast."

"It's on," replied Martha brusquely. She's already anticipated his mood. He was going riding; she'd heard his spurs on the stairs. A hot meal inside him was always the order of the day when he went for a long ride. Martha had placed a healthy alternative on the table to deliberately wind him up.

"Steak and eggs! I could smell it as I came down," he joked.

With a hearty meal inside him, Wade packed his grip, grabbed his top coat and made for the door. "See you later Martha, and lay off that cooking sherry!"

Martha watched him with a smile as he made his way across the yard to the new barn that Jason had, had erected that summer. "Mr Wade," she was to say later that day and the next, "was in unusually high spirits."

Wade's Buckskin whinnied its greeting as its master patted and caressed his mane. Led from the stall, the Buckskin was quickly saddled and the girth tightened, then Wade threw his grip across the back of the saddle and quickly tied it in place. With one hand gripping the saddle horn Wade expertly swung himself into the saddle. Most men usually used two hands, but even with the bulk of age Wade was still able to throw himself across his horse's back.

"Well ol' horse, today we've a treat in store. You and I are going up into the mountains, as high as you'll take me." He patted the Buckskin and encouraged it to move off at a quick trot.

He took a direct course across the valley floor, over a little stream and waved to Bud Angel and Clem as they were bringing in fifty or sixty head from the northern pastures. Pretty soon the ground became undulating as he gave the horse its head and it moved into a graceful lope. The wind blew icy, confirming what he'd already thought. How many times had he took this ride he could scarcely remember, it felt different each and every time he rode it.

Two hours later he moved in and out of the timberline. He could have taken several routes, a figure eight over to the north, looking out towards Wisdom, Hamilton and Darby. He could have gone south east on a circular route heading out towards Dillon and George Fredricksen's place, but instead he found himself letting the horse lead. Through a glade of aspen, so close the Buckskin slowed to a walk as it negotiated its way through them. Then the clearing, and area where he and the Buckskin could catch their breath and have a spot of lunch, while admiring the view the clearing allowed. As far as was possible, the grassy vista opened out and offered a feast for the eyes, culminating with a hodgepodge of buildings.

"Look yonder boy!" he cried enthusiastically to the Buckskin. He was as far as he intended going, but the sudden urge to visit Merri's grave seemed to lure him onward.

"Well maybe we'll pay our respects, then head on back, o'l horse."

The Buckskin whinnied its approval. The sun was shining. And although they were pretty high up the temperature was in the mid seventies. It was the most beautiful of days, and Wade was mesmerised by the beauty of his mistress.

He said a quiet prayer over Merri's grave, flowers, long dead lay testimony to Fletcher's undying love. The place had a magical aura that seem to suck Wade into the peacefulness of the scene. It belied the carnage that had taken place nearly twenty years before. Then for a second he saw it as it was, a brief flashback, then as suddenly he was back with the peace and tranquillity of the place.

The temperature took a sudden drop. Wade untied his top coat and put it on; the wind had got up a bit. After he'd buttoned up his coat he climbed back on the Buckskin. He walked the horse to the old line shack, looked down at the broken door, still hanging from one hinge. He trotted the horse another three hundred yards towards the rocky out crop, close to where they eventually found Monique's body. The wind was getting up and the skies had begun to darken.

The pain came on slowly at first, and then gradually increased in intensity. Wade gripped the saddle horn like a vice and urged the Buckskin homeward. His left arm and chest felt like they were about to explode. Instinctively he knew that he was in the throes of a heart attack, and that the best chance of survival was to get back to the ranch as quickly as he could. Silently he cursed himself for being a damn fool, venturing so high into the Bitterroots on a whim, was just plain nonsensical. 'Yes, you're a damn blasted fool Wade Reynolds, and then some. At nigh on eighty years old it was just plain foolhardy to venture up into the mountains alone. Then the world went black.

*   *   *

Wade looked up through a gap in the roof at the night sky. Desperately he searched for the North Star. Its position in the sky told him it was around three o'clock in the morning. Jason would have organised a search party for first light. Tara and Jack would be there, amongst the search party. Fletcher too, if he'd arrived from Washington as Wade had predicted. There was four more hours until daylight, thought Wade. Another four, two hours at least, if they pick up my trail. Six hours to hold out.

Wade knew he wasn't long for this world, he'd known that since the nights he'd spent hunting those wolves, he'd known it but didn't care. She was gone, his one true love, and if death had claimed him up there with his collection of wolf tails he'd have welcomed it. Yes the ranch and the Big Hole was his mistress, but Alex had always been the love of his life, he'd never known so much pain, not even the death of Taw his beloved yet misunderstood son could come close to how he felt when Alex died. Tara his wild child had been his salvation, she'd helped him through the difficult weeks and months that followed. Her marriage to Jack had been the making of her, and those kids, Kaycee, the serious one and Merri, a true chip off the old block were something to be proud of.

Yes thought Wade, my time on this earth is close to ending, but I'm leaving a future that at one time I never thought I'd see. Despite everything, I've had a good life, some would say better than I deserve, but I've lived my life to my own code and I've never strayed from it. I've had many friends, none more so than Johnny Johanson. A man I never fully understood until after his death, but even then, God had given me a chance to know him better, in the form of his son Fletcher. A gift I didn't truly deserve.

As Wade faded in and out of consciousness, the sky gave up its false dawn then plunged back into darkness. Wade awoke once more and for the briefest of moments he could have sworn that he saw Merri. She was there, standing at the side of the door now open and still attached to its solitary hinge. She was dressed in a faded pink denim shirt and blue jeans, much like the last time he saw her. She gave him a cheeky smile, one he was sure she reserved for only those close to her. She beckoned for him to stand up. 'What kind of madness is this?' he thought. She called to him again to stand up and go with her. Without question or effort Wade cast off the old horse blankets and sacking and began walking towards her as if in a dream. He caught her eye as mischievously she motioned with it towards the side wall. He caught his breath; his son Taw smiled back at him beckoned him to come closer. And then just as he was going to pull Taw into his arms, there she was, in the centre of the doorway framed by darkness. Alex dressed in that red satin blouse with her long dark hair cascading off her shoulders. She smiled at him in the same way she'd smiled at him that first time in the Metlen hotel. Her smile spread to those dark gorgeous brown eyes and he knew he was home . . .

Epilogue

They found Wade early the next morning in the old line shack; he was wrapped in old horse blankets and sacking and looked like he'd died peacefully. On his face he wore a smile. It was his eightieth birthday.

Wade had been right; it was Fletcher and Jack who found him first. Call it sixth sense if you like, but both men seemed to know just where to look. Fletcher walked slowly from the line shack and pulled the rifle from the scabbard attached to his horse. He sighed once before raising the rifle to his shoulder and fired three shots into the pale blue sky. It wasn't long before the sound of hooves alerted them to the arrival of Tara and Jason. Jack walked out of the line shack to greet them, the look on his face told Tara the news she so desperately didn't want to hear. Instinctively she raced forward only for Jason to restrain her, but Jack motioned for him to let her go. He knew deep down that smile on Wade's face would be a comfort to her in the days and weeks to follow.

* * *

Wade was buried in the small cemetery at the top of the hill alongside Taw and Alex. The mourners came from far and wide, many of them with their own private anecdotes about Wade and the life he led; some funny, a few sad, others downright heroic, but it was left to Garcia, the old bartender at 'Kate's Place' in Nogales to sum up the true worth of Wade Reynolds.

"Senor Reynolds, was a grande hombre, with mucho heart."

There wasn't much more to say after that . . . .

* * *

Jack and Tara still run the Claymore ranch, home of Reynolds Horses. They still supply the finest quarter horses in all Montana. Tara's inherent love of the Morgan, her father's favourite, has seen her continue breeding these fabulous creatures. "They have great fire and spirit; I guess that's why Pa loved them so much."

Fletcher still works with Homeland Security, he and Ruth are now presently living in Seattle with their young son. With parenthood, has come a new and rewarding responsibility, giving Fletcher that often sought but never found stability that he'd always yearned for. They visit with Jack and Tara from time to time and more often than not Fletcher finds the time to saddle up a paint horse from Jason's stables and visits Merri's grave up at Cougar Pass.

Jason didn't let Wade down, the ranch has gone from strength to strength, new barns have been erected, a riding school added to the facilities, new modern machinery, kept to a bare minimum by Wade, have increased, and a tiny airstrip has been added for the Cessna that Jason feels he needs in the ever expanding life of a modern Montana rancher. The other more noticeable change is the new shingle that adorns the entrance to the ranch. Whilst Wade was alive Jason and Keeley didn't have the heart to rename the Crazy AW, but six months after his death they consulted with Jack and Tara about a name change.

"I think Pa would have approved," said Tara. "He always was one to put his own brand on things. Yeah, Wade would get a real kick out of it."

'The Irish Blue Ranch,' sign now swings freely at the entrance to the ranch. But if you were to ask a local from Dillon all the way to Missoula about that ranch nestling close to those towering Bitterroot Mountains in the Big Hole Valley, they would say,

"Yeah I know it, the Reynolds spread." And more than one old coot will tell you . . . .

"Legend has it that on a clear moonlit night if you look out towards Cougar Pass and you stare long and hard enough, the ghost of Wade Reynolds riding tall and proud on a magnificent Morgan stallion can be clearly seen . . . . No shit!"

September 23rd 2010

© *Michael Kennard 2010*

Notes on Montana Sunset

Montana Sunset although a sequel, also survives as a stand alone novel, at least that's what I'd hope for, it's left to you the reader to be the judge. Writing a sequel was always a risky business, it can add weight and value, but equally it can diminish. From my point of view I believe Wade and company deserved another go round and in Montana Sunset I have set out to achieve just that. Montana Sunset has allowed me to finish what I started back in August 1995. Originally when I first decided to write Montana Skies I'd always envisioned it being a long sprawling novel of epic proportions. I suppose subconsciously I knew when I'd finished writing Montana Skies that I'd left a number of unresolved plotlines and that one day I'd return to add a few more chapters to Wade, Jack, Tara and Alex's story.

As a kid I'd always been infatuated with the West, in particular the cowboy of legend. It wasn't a surprise when I decided to try my hand at cowboying, *basically riding a horse over some of the most breathtaking scenery in the world.* Along with a work colleague, called Brodie, *how's that for a cowboy name,* we set off on a series of horseback adventures. We rode through the Superstition Mountains in Arizona, *as legend has it, the home of the Lost Dutchman Mine,* rode the high country in Southern Colorado with Clint Cuddes, *actually his real name was Terry* but dressed as he was in a long black duster, black hat and boots to match, what else could we call him. Drove cattle in

Idaho, and became *The Searchers* as we rode all over Monument Valley, not to mention a few side trips in California, Mexico and Montana. During these times we met a great many characters, some gregarious, others less so, and some downright ornery. During one of our trips we stayed at the Strater Hotel in Durango, Colorado. Unbeknown to me at the time Louis L'Amour had often stayed at that particular hotel and written a number of his novels there. As a young man in my late teens and early twenties I was a great fan of his books. Little did I know that many years later I'd be riding along the same trails that he wrote about. I suppose it isn't surprising that my vivid imagination coupled with all things western would one day see me writing my own novels.

Snag was, what the hell did I know about writing a novel, I can tell you, precious little. I had a title, Montana Skies, a basic idea for a plot but little else. I sent off for a home study course and then I enrolled at a creative writing class. I had a computer; *I take my hat off to all the writers that use pen and paper,* without which I'd never have started. Using my vivid imagination, the knowledge I'd gleaned from my writing class, the self help books that were readily available, I started on the long journey of novel writing.

My first port of call was to check out my locations, first off, Marlow. To be perfectly honest, I'd pencilled in Henley upon Thames as my first location. I'd even written the first chapter with Henley in mind. I hadn't been to Henley for quite some time, but it didn't take me long to realise Henley didn't cut it. Then the strangest thing, we happened upon Marlow, the narrow high street, the pub next to the church, the suspension bridge and of course the Compleat Angler hotel, right next to the fast flowing Thames. We parked in the hotel car park, then with camera in hand we walked back across the suspension bridge towards the town. It was then that I knew Marlow had always been destined to take pride of place between the pages of Montana Skies. In the church grounds were five luminous yellow signposts, one had the words HERE SOON in bold black lettering, the other four yellow signposts each carried one large black letter, J, A, C, K. Here soon Jack, how bizarre I thought. Serendipity or what!

Strange as it might seem I'd never been to Montana when I started to write Montana Skies. I suppose I was making it up as I went along, *actually I was getting my knowledge from books and from my various visits to other States.* A trip to Montana was my wakeup call. Elaine and I flew into Billings in September 1996, where we stayed for a few days at the Northern Hotel. My first impressions of Montana were the vast distances between the major towns and cities and of course the Big Sky. A lot has been written about Montana's wide open skies and I could see why. Sunsets were an array of colours too numerous to count, add a number of spectacular lightning storms and I think you get the picture. During our stay in Billings we visited the Custer Battlefield and drove down into Wyoming, from there we drove up to Miles City, home of the Bucking Horse Sale. We booked into the Olive Hotel across the street from the Montana Bar, where we sat and drank beer with the locals. Some of the stories they told would make your hair curly.

We left Miles City and headed west to Bozeman and then turned north to Missoula. By the time we left Missoula I was panicking. Miles City had ticked all the right boxes but after that other locations didn't quite fit the bill. We decided to head south to Dillon, I'd been reliably informed that Dillon was still an authentic cow-town. We drove through the beautiful Bitterroot Valley and I was tempted, but as far as I could see there were no cattle to be seen, then we hit the Big Hole Valley, land of 10,000 haystacks. Cattle seemed to stretch as far as the eye could see, another box ticked.

Dillon was exactly what I'd been looking for; surrounded by fertile valleys dotted with vast ranches, flowing streams, and historic architecture, it stood at the crossroads of time, a combination of old and new, living comfortably side by side. Steeped in history, you can almost feel the presence of Lewis and Clark, Chief Joseph and the infamous Henry Plummer as you cast your eyes towards the distant mountains. Whether it was luck or just plain fate but we'd found to our great delight that we'd arrived over a rodeo weekend. Pulling into the dusty parking lot, we bought tickets and made like the locals as we headed for the bleachers. Sitting up high we watched in awe as these young men and women showed their skill and bravery as they competed in the day's events. In the distance fork lightning lit up the surrounding skies. At the end of the day's events we headed down the road to the Lion's Den, and sampled the house speciality, prime rib. So fresh I'd swear it was still breathing. Pretty soon the place was alive and buzzing as hungry cowboys and girls began filling the place up.

Hotel Metlen was our next stop. It stood majestically across the railroad tracks from the main part of town. Neon signs glared brightly from the windows and doors. Everything I'd seen so far had ticked the right boxes, the Metlen exceeded all expectations. Once through the doors we found the place knee deep in clientele. Taking a deep breath we negotiated our way through the crowd and walked the entire length of the long bar and then just as we reached the end of the room we found the dance floor. A band was busily setting up for the evening's entertainment, I sighed with relief, we'd found the perfect location. Grabbing a table we ordered drinks and kicked back. During the course of the evening we chatted with ranchers, saddle bronc riders, rodeo organisers, barrel racers, a couple of policemen, a bull rider and even a sleazy lounge lizard, *yes they do exist.* Two days later we drove down to Big Sky and then took in Yellowstone before heading back to Billings. It had taken some looking but I'd finally found my Montana Skies . . . .

About the author

Michael Kennard now lives with his wife in the Oxfordshire countryside where he is currently working on another two future novels.

Lightning Source UK Ltd.
Milton Keynes UK

9 781462 024056